WHITE WATER BAR & GRILL

WHITE WATER BAR & GRILL

a novel of emancipation

Shirley Linkhart

Shirley Linkhart

iUniverse, Inc.

New York Lincoln Shanghai

WHITE WATER BAR & GRILL
a novel of emancipation

iUniverse books may be ordered through booksellers or by contacting:

iUniverse
2021 Pine Lake Road, Suite 100
Lincoln, NE 68512
www.iuniverse.com
1-800-Authors (1-800-288-4677)

This novel is a work of fiction. Barkerville and all its characters and incidents are fictitious, and any resemblance to actual persons is entirely coincidental, although some of its character types are easily found in America's small towns.

ISBN-13: 978-0-595-37235-5 (pbk)
ISBN-13: 978-0-595-81633-0 (ebk)
ISBN-10: 0-595-37235-X (pbk)
ISBN-10: 0-595-81633-9 (ebk)

Printed in the United States of America

Acknowledgement

First Bill and Tee, then Pilar, encouraged and supported me in crafting Suzanne's early story. Then the Barn Owls Critique Group, Alan, Jean, Sherry, B.J, and Sharon, all great writers, helped me shape and polish. Finally, my son, Gary Ellis, created my outstanding cover. Thank you all.

CHAPTER 1

▼

That cold February night in 1962, I perched on my favorite stool at the White Water Bar and Grill. I asked myself for the hundredth time why I bothered to wear out my elbows on the bar when I couldn't even drink a beer for another month. What was in it for me?

For one thing it made me feel grown up. My entire life in tiny Barkerville was like so many others' in our backwater logging town: go to school twelve years, maybe get to be cheerleader or Prom Queen, marry, and likely have a mess of kids.

I liked the darkness of the White Water. The way the revolving beer signs bounced kaleidoscopic light wall to wall and off the line of sparkling glasses behind the bar.

I liked the way shadows played on my face in the smoky, gold-veined mirrors. I felt pretty. My husband, Jimmy, hadn't said I was pretty since ninth grade.

I liked the rhythm of Jimmy's honky-tonk band and his sweet ballads—though he never sang them to me, only to the women that crowded in front of his bandstand.

The main reason I sat there those long winter nights was that I didn't trust him and he'd given me reasons. Being under age, I couldn't drink, but Oregon law permitted me to be in the bar—watching him.

Old Mr. Wilke, the bar's owner, sometimes spiked my Cokes. Most nights he'd lean close, give me a big wink. "There's sweet'ner in there, punkin." He'd repeat the same question, "When you gonna come back here and be my bartender? Men get tired of my old puss." Mr. Wilke bragged of being eighty-nine.

He looked it—a paunchy man with puffy skin, all lumpy and pasty white like an albino toad.

Around midnight, I stared into the backbar mirror and watched interplay between the people I'd known all my life. Behind me familiar couples flowed in circles around the tiny dance floor. I was half into a lonely daydream when wide shoulders in a brilliant white shirt caught my eye. He stood out in the shadows as he wove his way through the shifting crowd. When he moved closer, I saw the flashy grin on his dark-skinned face. The shiny dress shirt, its top two buttons open, stretched tight across his flat stomach.

He smiled at me in the glass and, in a maple syrup voice, said, "Mind if I sit here?"

This gorgeous thing can't possibly be a logger. And he's sure not from this one-horse town.

When I glanced over my shoulder at him, ghostly fingers prickled the back of my neck. "Sure. Be my guest."

Half sitting on his stool with his back to the bar, he bumped my arm as he looked around the room. "Great little place, huh? My name's Mark, what's yours?"

"Suzanne."

Though he faced me, I barely heard him for the applause at the end of Jimmy's song. "I'm from Los Angeles…sold my business. I paint."

I searched my brain for an intelligent reply. "Houses?"

There's no work painting around here in winter—or summer. Fletcher's had that tied up for years.

"Indians. I paint Indians."

I glanced at him and giggled. "War paint?" His hearty laugh surprised me, and I looked him full in the face.

His bold, dark eyes caught mine and held them a second too long—probed deeper than that surface glance we give a stranger. "I want to make love to you," he whispered.

"What?" burst from my lips and my mouth dropped open. I searched his eyes for a split second, then turned away.

What nerve! Did he say what I thought he said?

Looking straight ahead, I grabbed my cigarettes from the bar. Heat rose in my face and sweat popped out on my scalp as I took out a cigarette, then stuffed it back, realizing he'd likely offer a light. My eyes fixed on a blinking Hamms sign, but I kept him in sight in the mirror. My nylon blouse clung to my armpits while I busied my shaky fingers stripping condensation from my Coke glass.

He focused his attention on the bartender and reached for his wallet to pay for the Rainier beer she'd set in front of him. He told her to keep the change, then turned back to me.

"Not war paint!" He chuckled, staring into his beer glass while carefully filling it. "I paint old Indian chiefs…from photographs. It's relaxing, and I'm pretty good at it."

I must have misheard him. What was I thinking?

"That's nice." I gave him a little smile, then shifted toward the bandstand to hide my blush, nodding in time with the music, pretending great interest in Jimmy's song. My ears burned and a pulse throbbed in my palm where I squeezed my glass.

He tugged the back of my hair where it fell below my waist, and spoke quietly, "Don't be upset."

Like cold fingers on naked skin, his touch sent ripples down my spine.

He must have said it!

I stared blindly at the bandstand, intensely aware of his body behind me, the musky smell of his aftershave.

Breathe, Suzanne. He won't bite you.

While I watched the dancers and listened to Jimmy sing "Walking After Midnight" my breathing calmed. Finally, my hands steadied. When I turned back toward the bar, I sneaked another look at his profile when he spoke to the barmaid. Her eyes glistened as she handed him another beer.

"Nice band." He returned to the voice of a curious newcomer. "They play here all the time?"

"Every weekend. It's my husband's band."

"Oh damn!" He snapped his fingers. "I still mean what I said."

Damn, he did say it!

"That wasn't a real cool thing to say to a married woman."

"If I insulted you, I apologize. Guess I lost my manners when I saw your big brown eyes. Apology accepted?"

I shrugged.

We went on to make conversation about life in Barkerville, and I was careful not to make that bottomless eye contact—just quick sideways glances. Mostly I watched him in the backbar mirror, too dark and far away to meet those eyes.

After he'd finished his second beer and got up to leave, he brushed my hair again and spoke low. "See you soon."

My stomach flinched.

Maybe Saturday nights won't be so boring after all.

A few minutes later, Jimmy took an intermission. He spoke to friends along the bar as he ambled toward me, but his eyes never left my face. His mouth smiled, but the angle of his jaw said something different. He stepped to my side, slid his hand under my hair, then clamped his strong fingers around the back of my neck—more like a vise than his usual loving squeeze.

"Who's Pretty Boy?"

"Ouch, you're hurting me." I squirmed loose from his grip. "His name's Mark. He's here visiting people."

His mouth twisted. "You sure got to know him…real cozy." His voice was sharp-edged with sarcasm, as usual when he drank hard liquor. "I'm working. You're over here laughing with that spic. Having a good time?"

Flabbergasted, I tried to explain the bit about painting Indians, but it wasn't funny in the telling. I hated it when Jimmy used that word "spic." He always said it was just a word, and I shouldn't get my bowels in an uproar.

"Are you trying out your new song tonight?"

"Don't change the subject!"

"There's no more to—I told you everything. Besides, he's not Mexican." I stared at him, not quite believing his jealousy, expecting him to tell me he was kidding. As dark as it was, could he have seen me blush? After three years of marriage, I didn't think Jimmy paid that much attention to me anymore.

Without warning, he grabbed my neck again. Hard. He forced me off the stool, pushed me through the crowd and out the front door. With his fingers dug in, he steered me, stumbling through the dirt toward our car.

"Ouch! Jimmy. Stop! What the hell's…?" I tried to pull away, but his grip tightened.

He shoved me into the seat, jabbed his finger into my chest, and shouted, "Damn you, stay right there!"

Too shocked to move, I gripped the cold leather of the armrest as he jumped in the driver's side. "Jimmy—"

"Don't say a goddamn word!" Gravel peppered cars as he spun out of the parking lot and hit the pavement with a squall of tires. The engine of his hopped-up Mercury sounded like it would explode as he raced full-throttle toward our house two miles away.

"Jimmy, please…" I pleaded, touching him on the leg.

"Shut up!" He jerked his leg away.

Afraid to see how fast we were going, I closed my eyes, but popped them open when he let off the accelerator. I nearly pushed my feet through the floorboards when I saw we'd reached the turn into our driveway. Jimmy tapped the brakes, slowed enough to make the sharp turn, cross the bridge, and slide sideways up to the front door.

"Get out!" His whiskey breath blasted me. "I have to get back to work."

In the yellow light from the dashboard I could see the cords stand out on his neck like I'd seen my father's and my mother's voice rang in my head. *Get out. Don't push him. You can't argue with a drunk.*

While he roared from sight, I stood shivering in the February cold. Hot tears of anger ran down my face. I was mortified at being dragged out of the bar, but I also felt a twinge of guilt at how my body had reacted to the stranger.

As a child I'd seen too much of jealousy and drunken rage and had vowed that no man would ever lay his hand on me. Jimmy knew that as well as he knew my body. If he chose that path, I might soon have to act on my vow.

Lying in our bed that night, I thought about our marriage. Through all the years I'd known Jimmy McTavish, he'd never shown jealousy. I'd felt plenty, but didn't show mine either. Since seventh grade, when he first came to Barkerville with his guitar and Jimmie Rodgers songs, I'd loved him.

We'd dated off and on throughout high school, then married the day after graduation. I adored him, and like most foolish girls, I thought marriage would stop his roving eye. It seemed to for a time. He'd been a good husband, and hard-working provider, but Jimmy loved beer.

In October, when he turned twenty-one and took his little band to the White Water, his lust for alcohol moved into the big leagues. Our happy life began to unravel.

Jimmy's hometown fans adored him, especially the girls. Was that why he'd made the scene? To let them know he wasn't firmly attached to his "ball and chain?"

No answer came, but I finally slept. Sometime after dawn he crept into our bed.

Sunday morning, disgusted by his sour breath that filled the room, I watched him sleep. For an instant, I couldn't figure out what I'd loved about him.

Why do things always have to change?

In my heart, I just wanted things like they were before he started at the White Water. Even though the beer had always been there, he'd never been mean. That morning I knew trouble lay ahead because I would not be mistreated.

I dressed and crossed the street to talk to my best friend, Karen—Jimmy's sister. My friendship with her started in the seventh grade, first as a way to spend time around her brother. During my last year of high school, when my unemployed father followed the logging boom to northern California, I'd lived with Jimmy and Karen's family. Karen and I squabbled and grew as close as sisters.

"God, I don't know what to do. Now that he can go in the bar, he drinks all the time. Hard stuff. He gets mean."

I told her about my wild ride home, and then how the stranger named Mark looked like an Aztec god, and what he'd said.

"Sounds like this guy gave you the hots!"

"Not true. Sure, I blushed. I always blush. That's no reason for Jimmy to manhandle me."

"Fess up. You liked it. Handsome stranger rides into town."

"Liked it? Jimmy scared the crap out of me." I rubbed the back of my neck where he'd pinched it. "He's spending so much on booze I can't keep up with the bills...bouncing checks. What can I do?"

"Easy. Take the check-book away."

"They let him run a tab. Mr. Big-Shot buys rounds for the house." Sitting at her breakfast bar sipping coffee, I couldn't see an easy solution. "I think I'll go to work there next month after my birthday. I can't depend on Jimmy."

Karen threw her head back, covered her mouth and snorted. "You? A bartender? I can't imagine."

"I can learn. What else can I do around here? Somebody'd have to die before I could get a job in the bank. Besides, they don't pay anything. What else is there? Sling hash for ninety cents an hour?"

"What happens when Jimmy wakes up?" She wagged her finger in my face. "You got to give him holy hell! Or, he'll just do it again."

"Would that do any good? It's one thing for him to be a jerk, but he hurt—"

Karen shouted, "Get tough! Don't let him walk all over you! Divorce him, damn it. You've got options."

She'd preached to me for years to stand up to him, but that wasn't the way I was raised. Women in my family kept their mouths shut and did as their husbands said. That would have to change though. I didn't know how yet, but I knew that my family's way of life was not for me.

CHAPTER 2

▼

Next morning, as I stood brushing my teeth, Jimmy placed his hand in that same spot on my neck—his usual caress. "What's to eat around here?" He pulled me toward him and kissed my cheek, then felt my stiffness and dropped his hand. "Well, *excuse* me."

I busied myself fixing his breakfast. I only fought in my head—replayed words I'd like to say, but lacked the courage. I had to have a plan before I started World War III.

Go to hell, Jimmy. You can't treat me like crap.

He called my silence pouting.

"I'll tell you one damn thing right now." He jabbed the air with his fork. "You're not going to hang around the bar every weekend. That's that!"

"Mr. Wilke wants me to work for him on day shift. We could use the money."

"No fuckin' way. If you want a job, go to the Dairy Queen. I won't have a wife of mine tending bar. Besides, you don't have the guts. First time somebody looked at you crosswise, you'd be bawling." Jimmy stubbed his cigarette in his plate and moved to the couch. Sunday meant ball games on television.

When March came, Karen planned a party for my twenty-first birthday, an indoor Sunday picnic with her parents and a few of our friends. Jimmy would provide the music. I couldn't wait to be twenty-one.

The Saturday night before the party, he refused to let me go with him to the bar, said I should go over to Karen's and help her get ready for Sunday. After dinner he dressed and carried out some of his equipment.

"Why are you going in at seven?" I picked up six beer cans and the overflowing ashtray from beside the couch. "The music doesn't start until nine. We can't afford to buy drinks for two hours."

"Damn it! Get off my back! Man can't relax awhile?"

I turned away to hide my anger. I didn't want to challenge him with all that beer in his belly.

After he left, I scrubbed the kitchen, slammed things, and talked to myself. Cleaning helped me think.

Twenty minutes later, with my head deep in the problem, the phone jarred me.

The voice belonged to Penny, my nosiest friend. "Hi, what y'all doin'?"

Penny calling me at 7:30 had to be something juicy. "What's up?"

"Well, because I'm your friend, you know, I think I have to tell you. I don't want to hurt you, Suzanne. But, I don't like him making no fool of you."

My stomach fluttered. "What?"

"You know those two old cabins behind the bar? You know, the little dumps Mr. Ross rents out? The one next to the bar?"

Damn it, Penny. Get to the point.

"I think that bleached blonde lives there. You should've seen that bimbo last night at Jenny's party. She danced on the table...no underpants."

My mind pushed away the picture. Something bad was coming.

"The guys was drooling all over themselves, you know. Well, Jimmy comes in after the bar closes...she's sittin' on his lap when I leave."

"It figures. He didn't get in until after daylight." Sick feelings grew in my stomach, burned my throat.

She hesitated. "Honey, there's more."

Shit, Penny, I don't want to hear this.

"Suzanne, you there?"

"Let me have it, Penny. I'm a big girl."

She spoke fast, like that would soften the blow. "I just saw Jimmy go in there with a six pack. Suz, honey, I'm sorry."

"You sure it was him? It's dark out."

"It's light as day back there. You know, that yard light's right behind the bar."

"Jesus, Penny, where'd *she* come from?"

"I think she's Jenny's cousin...up from LA. Guess she's lookin' for work here. Maybe she's a hooker."

"Jimmy would never pay a hooker. They'll screw him for free." I wanted to sound like I didn't care. My mother claimed she didn't care, as long as she was number one.

Penny prattled on for several minutes, but her words didn't register. When she finally hung up, I sat by the phone, angry, humiliated and sick.

Now what? I can't do anything tonight and ruin Karen's party. She's planned for weeks, cooked all day.

I knew exactly what I had to do. Nothing.

The phone rang again. My hand shook as I reached for it.

Karen's voice raised my spirits a notch. "Hey, chess board's all set up. You coming?"

In the most cheerful voice I could muster, I said I'd be right there.

Bored with playing Monopoly, Karen and I had learned chess to pass the long evenings that winter of 1959 when I'd lived with her family. They couldn't afford television, and there were only a couple of snowy channels available anyway. After dinner dishes, we'd close ourselves up in our cubbyhole bedroom with the chessboard on the double bed between us. Before long we'd tune in the dreamy music station from San Francisco and talk about boys.

"God, is Jimmy all you can talk about?" she'd always say. Truth was, I'd longed to be out in the living room where Jimmy sat with his parents practicing his guitar.

I grabbed my coat, glanced in the entry mirror at my red cheeks then ran across the street to Karen's. Without knocking, I walked in with a big smile and said, "Let the games begin."

Hiding my emotions was something I did well. I'd practiced all my life to be the good daughter, the good student, and the good wife. Karen was the one person I could be myself with—but not until after her party.

While we spent the evening hours on our game, I kept the conversation away from Jimmy and by the time we finished I was calm enough to sleep. I tucked my problem away in a far corner of my mind, refusing to look at it for the time being. I was grateful I didn't awaken when Jimmy came in.

At Karen's the next morning, we scrubbed and waxed the floors, then hung balloons and crepe paper streamers. We set up card tables, covered them with her mom's linen tablecloths and hauled borrowed folding chairs in the trunk of her Lincoln.

Her refrigerator was stuffed with potato salad, baked beans, hot dogs, ice cream and lots of beer. Karen had baked a triple-layer cake, which she hid in her bedroom. While we opened cans of olives and jars of pickles and searched for suitable bowls, we played loud music, sang and laughed a lot at each other—like we always did. Then we stood back and admired our handiwork.

Near noon, I went home to change and wake Jimmy. Waking him usually took at least thirty minutes and the party was scheduled for two.

I wiggled his foot. "Come on, sleepy head."

"Go 'way," he mumbled into the pillow.

The old familiar routine began. On weekdays, when he worked at the mill, I started the process at 6:30, rousing him over and over as I cooked his breakfast.

"I'm going to shower. When I get through, you've got to get up."

Why do I do this? I get so sick of it. He'll be mad at me by the time it's over.

I showered quickly, then went back into the bedroom to dress.

"Come on, it's time." For a second, his sweet face caught at my heart. My hand moved to smooth his tousled hair. I jerked it back.

Why is it so hard for me to be mad at him?

"Uh huh," he mumbled, never opening his eyes. "What time is it?"

"One-thirty," I lied.

I pulled on my pantyhose and finally my dress. Ten more minutes passed while I put on make-up and pulled my hair into a ponytail. I leaned over, close to his ear. "Jimmy, please get up, I don't want to be late."

"Jesus Christ!" he roared, and sprang out of bed.

When he stepped out of the shower, I started for the door. "I'm heading over to Karen's. Your white shirt's on the bed. See you pretty soon?" I didn't dare spend time with him or he'd read my face.

A little before two he came in carrying his guitar, looking refreshed and handsome. He cupped my face, gently kissed me. "Happy birthday, hon. You're all grown up now, huh?"

As he hugged his mother and his sister, my heart filled with love. Tears stung my eyes. I turned away.

How can he be such a lying cheat?

As the day wore on and the liquor flowed, he sang the songs his family loved. First, he sang the one he'd sung in my ear at school dances, "Melody of Love." His dad beamed with pride at "Hobo Bill's Last Ride" then cried when he sang "These Hands." His mother begged for her favorite, the wedding vows song. "Do you take this man for the rest of your life…?" Thank God, he looked into *her* face as he sang.

Sick feelings sent me pushing through the crowd to the bathroom. I splashed cold water on my face, then leaned my forehead against the cool mirror and tried to overcome my sadness.

Don't give in to this. Go back out there and be the birthday girl.

By the time we cut Karen's heavenly chocolate, raspberry-filled cake, Jimmy got loud. He loved to argue when he drank, and he cherished a worthy opponent—history, politics, engines, jazz or whatever. He could never engage me in his debates because it felt too violent. I didn't understand arguing for the fun of it. In my family arguments weren't allowed.

Jimmy and a buddy stood in the kitchen splitting hairs over an old football game they'd played in high school. Out of the blue, Jimmy punched a half-empty six-pack sitting on the kitchen counter and sent it crashing through the window.

Already tense, I went off like a bomb. I grabbed him by the shoulders, pushed him backward through Karen's bedroom into the bathroom and into the shower. I reached for the cold water faucet and yelled, "Damn you! You son-of-a-bitch. You will *not* ruin my birthday party."

He recovered from the shock and grabbed my wrists before I could turn on the water. "Wait a minute. Hold it!" He laughed and pressed against my body. "I didn't do that on purpose. It was an accident."

"You *broke* the window," I sobbed. My fire was out. All that was left was surprise at what I had done.

His laughter died in a heartbeat, replaced by an iron-jawed glare and words saturated with sarcasm. "So, I'm a son-of-a-bitch, huh?" He still held my wrists above my head. "Well, far be it from me to ruin your little party." He slammed my arms downward and dashed out the door.

I stayed in the bathroom, looking at myself in the mirror, mascara smeared, nose red. I'd made a fool of myself over nothing—then I had to face everyone. Standing with a cold washcloth pressed to my eyes, I could hear the party break up. People were saying goodbye. Braced, I came out smiling. As usual, everyone acted as if nothing had happened. Jimmy was gone. His dad was taping cardboard over the window.

After the last one left, Karen vibrated with delight. "Holy shit! You tied into him. I didn't know you had it in you." She clapped and jumped up and down. "I love it! Love it!"

"I don't know what came over me. When that glass broke, something snapped. Once my dad broke all the windows out of our house and tipped over the stove. Made me clean it up." I remembered the impotent rage I'd felt then—rage I never dared show.

Karen put her arm around me. "Where'd he go?"

"He probably went to see that whore behind the bar." I opened a beer, my first for the day, and paced while I repeated what Penny had told me.

"No. That asshole. You think she's an honest-to-God whore?"

"I doubt it. A whore would starve to death in this town."

"Want to go down and see?"

Dizzy, I slouched on the couch. "God, Karen. I've got to think about this mess. Get my beer muscles up."

"What's to think about? You need to catch him in the act." Karen, who'd always had to fight for everything, never seemed afraid. "You won't believe it 'til you see it."

"Okay, let me sit here awhile. When I finish this beer, you can take me." I sounded stronger than I felt, but I knew it was a step I had to take.

"What you going to do if he's there?"

Tears welled. "Hell, I don't know."

I stretched that beer out for half an hour while Karen recited all the shitty things Jimmy had done—to her and to me. How, from her earliest memory, he'd been the center of attention in their home. When I lived there, I'd seen their mother dote on him, bask in his popularity, and push him to perform.

"Suzanne, don't forget. When you got Valedictorian, he said it didn't mean shit."

"Compared to his singing, football…I guess it didn't."

I opened another beer and revisited the time he'd hidden his lipstick-stained shirt behind the bed. He gave a hysterical teenager a ride home, he'd said. Jimmy always had an explanation, and I always chose to believe him. Stirring these old memories helped me gather strength.

I stalled, waiting for nightfall so no one would see me check on my husband.

After a few silent minutes, Karen picked up her car keys and rattled them in my face. "Come on. Let's go catch the bastard."

The two beers had in no way prepared me for what I would see.

CHAPTER 3

▼

"Stop here in front. Let me walk." We parked beside Jimmy's Mercury. On shaky legs, I hurried to the back of the White Water. The dumpy cabins stood stark in their gravel landscape, their faded gray faces bathed in cold light. I ducked into the darkness between them.

From the shadows, I saw the dim glow through the filmy curtain in the side window. On an orange-crate coffee table in front of the couch, three fat candles stood anchored in wax puddles. Beside them, two long-stemmed glasses and the half-full champagne bottle. Candlelight flickered over the hourglass of her naked back as she knelt on the floor in front of Jimmy. Her head bobbed slowly, her mass of blonde hair spilled like a golden waterfall across his lap and naked thighs.

Jimmy's head lay back on the couch, his mouth open in a familiar oh. Arms wide, his fingers clutched the cushions as his back arched in obvious ecstasy.

The blood drained from my head and I drew back from the window. My eyes closed against painful tears, I pressed the wall for support. Saliva welled up in my mouth and made a slurping sound as I sucked in cold air.

It was a stag show—and my husband played the stud. The picture scalded my brain.

Oh Jimmy, how can you? How can you hurt me like this? What shall I do? What shall I say? I can't just slink away. Straighten up, damn it Suzanne. Don't be a baby.

When I had calmed some and regained my strength, I peered in the window again. She relaxed on the couch like a playful cat, back curved, porcelain breasts raised. Seated at her feet, Jimmy caught her legs as she pawed at his arms with her toes. Then she smiled in a dreamy way and stroked her blond mound as he kissed the soles of her feet.

Mesmerized, I watched Jimmy pick up a champagne glass and pour a glistening pool into the hollow of her stomach. She giggled and squirmed while he leaned between her legs and slurped the golden liquid with long strokes of his tongue.

My heart screamed. Jimmy and I had never shared such a moment. In the stillness I heard him sing as he rose to mount her.

I drew back again, unable to watch. My heart battered at my chest. Rage finally pushed past my heartbreak. I yanked open the door and faced them. She didn't move. Jimmy pulled off her, sat at her feet and stared at me. The bordello smell in the tiny room slammed me in the face—candle wax, cheap perfume, and their lovemaking hung heavy in the warm air.

After a long moment, I was able to speak, although my voice was little more than a raspy whisper. "Why Jimmy. Why?"

Jimmy's dull look passed and his eyes narrowed. "What the hell are you doing here?"

"Jesus Christ, Jimmy!" I shouted. "Why are you doing this to us?"

His face contorted with anger, he waved his hand at me. "Get the hell out! This is private property."

Choked with sobs, I backed out and pulled the door closed. I leaned my forehead against it while I tried to regain control and think. Gasping for air, I wiped tears from my face and squared my shoulders.

Why should I leave? He's my husband. He owes me an answer.

I kicked the door open, and yelled, "Damn you! Damn you, Jimmy McTavish." My screams were deafening in the tiny room. "You screwed this piece of trash! I saw you!"

His red eyes focused somewhere between us, he spoke without emotion, "What you plan to do about it?"

She stroked her belly, slowly turned her head and looked at me with dead eyes, as if she were glancing at someone unworthy of her focus.

His hand never moved from her thigh. Still his gaze didn't reach mine. Time seemed to move in slow motion.

I spouted the first thing that came into my mind. "I'll shit-can your ass. Once and for all!"

He answered with a drunken smile. "Uh huh." Picking up his glass, he saluted me, then took a long drink.

He doesn't care. I can see it in his face.

Unfazed by my presence, she raised on one elbow, and making no effort to hide her nakedness, reached for her drink. She copied his salute with her raised glass—and that damn impudent smile.

My voice came out weak, filled with defeat. "Are you coming home with me...or staying with this slut?" I knew the answer before the last word left my mouth.

Silence, long and heavy, filled the room as the question repeated in my head.

Our eyes finally locked. Three expressions crossed his face. The drunken empty look changed to one of sadness, like a man who'd made a terrible mistake. Instantly, that was gone, replaced by the familiar look of the defiant boy.

Finally, he turned away and looked down at her. "I'm staying here." He smiled at her. "So, why don't you just leave...and don't let the door hit you in the ass!"

Those words hit like a kick in the stomach. Bile burned my throat. I grasped the doorframe. His words bounced in my head. For a moment, I wanted to beg—plead for him to choose me. Instead, I grabbed the orange crate, raised it over my head and crashed it down on them. Candles, wine bottle, full ashtray and all. As they scrambled and yelled, I backed out the door and silently closed it behind me.

My legs were sticks of wood, unbending and heavy, as I stumbled back to Karen's car. The March wind burned my wet face.

"Well?" she asked, when I collapsed into her car.

Words describing what I'd seen tumbled from my mouth between sobs. "She's bare-ass naked...giving him a blow job. Oh, Karen, it kills me."

"The little son-of-a-bitch!" She consoled me quietly, patted my shoulder as I babbled, then pulled out her cigarettes and offered me one.

"You know how he is when he drinks wine." I was hiccupping. "Jesus, I made him choose." My hands trembled trying to light the cigarette.

"Here." Karen took it from me, lit it and handed it back. "I can't believe he's gone this far. In the morning he'll come crawling back."

"No way. Not this time. When he gets there, I'll be gone. I don't care if I have to pick shit with the chickens. This is it." I took deep breaths and wiped the tears from my chin and neck. "Can I stay with you tonight?"

"Sure, but he'll probably come over looking for you."

"He won't come home until he sobers up. Besides, I'm taking his precious Merc, if the keys are in it."

"Good for you."

"I'll take it out to Penny's. I should drive the damn thing over a cliff."

"Oh, you'll get over this in a few days. Nothing's changed. You've let him get away with crap since eighth grade."

"Not this time, Karen. I saw it. This is the last time."

She followed me when I took Jimmy's dream car and parked it behind Penny's barn, waited while I spoke briefly to Penny. On the drive to my house I told her about dumping the table on them, and she said how proud she was of me for fighting back. I was too.

"Come help me pack." I grabbed two boxes from the garage. "I want all my clothes. No telling what he'll do when he finds his beloved car gone."

"You got a plan?"

I'd worked some of it out on the drive to Penny's. "I'm going to work at the bar as soon as I can get my license. I'm pretty sure Mr. Wilke will hire me. He always asks me when I'm coming to work. There's about thirty bucks in checking, I'll clean that out in the morning. I'll have to borrow from you until I get a payday."

"What if he won't? What if he just says that to all the girls that come in there?"

"Don't scare me. I've got to have that job. Otherwise, I'll have to try something else. If I can't make enough money...just work two jobs."

As I went through the dresser, pulling out clothes, my gaze fell on the wedding picture Jimmy's mother took of us in Virginia City. We looked so happy standing by their new Buick in our graduation clothes. I put the picture in the box with my underwear and sweaters.

"God, Karen, we haven't even been married three years. This is so scary. I've never been on my own...even a day."

"You can do it. You're smart, good looking." She slammed his football picture face down. "You don't need him."

I carried my clothes on hangers out to Karen's car, then finished emptying my dresser drawers. Tears welled up as I looked around the living room at the things we'd bought together—the stereo and TV set we'd made payments on, and the cheap furniture we were so proud of.

"These book-ends were a wedding present." I hugged them to my chest. "The only one we got."

"Then take them. I'm sure they don't mean anything to him. Stay with me awhile, Ron won't be home for six more months."

When Jimmy and I married, Karen wanted to be married too. She got her chance that summer when Ron Daugherty, the neighbor's son came home on leave from the Navy. A career man, seven years older than Karen, he was ripe for the picking. He said he didn't care if she hadn't "filled out yet." Before his thirty-day pass ended, her parents gave consent for them to marry if she'd finish school.

"I don't want to put you in a bad spot with Jimmy."

"Doesn't bother me. We're friends first. I've been fighting my brother all my life."

"I'm pretty helpless right now, huh?"

We unloaded my stuff at her house, made my bed on the couch and watched *Sunday Night at the Movies*. I fought to keep my thoughts away from Jimmy and the Bimbo.

"Seven-thirty. There's the mill whistle," Karen said the next morning as she handing me a steaming cup of coffee in bed. "Bet Jimmy's not at work."

"He won't have me to lie to Brucek." I sat up and took the cup. "I always hated that. Maybe the Bimbo will call."

At ten, Karen and I headed for the bank and the White Water. As we pulled onto the highway, I could see far enough down our driveway to spot a red car. My stomach flipped. "That must be hers."

"Would she have the guts to come to your house?"

"If you'd seen her last night…you'd better believe it."

When I'd withdrawn all but a dollar of our thirty-four dollars from the bank, we went into the White Water on the Grill side and sat at the lunch counter. Karen ordered a Coke while I went into the bar side to talk to Mr. Wilke.

I felt strange walking through that doorway by myself for the first time. There were only two customers and Mr. Wilke stood behind the bar.

He looked puzzled to see me there alone. "Morning."

"I'm here about the job you offered me. I turned twenty-one yesterday."

"Well, how about that! Let me buy your first drink."

"Thanks. I'll take a rain-check…too early."

He hesitated, looked down at the bar and scratched his ear, while I held my breath. "All I have right now is Tuesday and Wednesday—day shift. It pays buck and a half an hour. Night shift pays two."

"I really need full time." But quickly added, "Jimmy and I are separated. I want the job."

He leaned closer, spoke like he knew a secret. "I been seeing how he likes the girlies. You're too pretty to put up with that. Here fill this out and we'll get you licensed…just takes a few days. You can come to work next week."

When I finished the form and passed it to him, he took my hand in both his soft, clammy ones and squeezed. "I'm real glad to help you, honey."

When I returned to Karen, she said, "Well?"

"I got the job. It's only two days right now…day shift pays less." I lowered my voice. "God, he's creepy."

She whispered, "Why?"

"The way he touched me. Maybe it's my imagination. I hope."

The red car was gone when we returned to Karen's, but a note from Jimmy lay on her table: WHERE THE HELL'S MY CAR? HAVE IT HERE BY FIVE! He'd underlined enough to tear the paper.

"I shouldn't have taken it."

"Bull shit! It's your car, too."

"Sure, my name's on it, but it's not really mine. It wouldn't be fair for me to keep it. I'll just make trouble for myself."

"Don't chicken out on this. How will you get around?"

"I'll get a room uptown…walk. He needs it more that I do."

"Well, make him get it himself."

"I'm not ready to fight him now. Please. Let's get it before he comes."

She grabbed her coat and held the door. "Okay, come on my little chicken heart."

We spent an uncomfortable time at Penny's. She loved a good story and probed for all the details. "Men need us so much, you know. He'll come home with his tail between his legs."

I chose to make light of it. "She's way sexier than me…a real honest-to-God blonde."

"Like hell!" Karen shook me, then turned me toward Penny. "Guys will gobble her up, huh?"

Penny's fat jowls bobbed in agreement. "That figure…and those brown calf-eyes. You know." She gave me a smothering hug. "You'll knock 'em silly, honey."

When we left, I asked Karen to follow me into our driveway in case Jimmy was home, although the note made me think he was at work. The red car was parked where I couldn't see it from the highway, so I was committed by the time it came into sight.

I jumped into Karen's car, pounded the dashboard. "Damn, they're here! Go!"

As she gunned the car away, Jimmy came out the door, shook his fist and yelled something.

Once we were inside Karen's house, I settled down.

She got out her trusty chessboard. "Come on Suz, thinking about it won't help."

I agreed.

We concentrated on our game and the day passed quickly. When the five o'clock whistle blew at the mill, I looked at the clock, for a second thinking I had to run home and start Jimmy's dinner.

Karen spoke quietly, staring at my Queen. "No supper to cook tonight." She made her move, then went to the refrigerator. "Let's have some beer."

Before we quit it was dark and eight empty beer bottles stood on the table.

Karen gave a devilish chuckle as she packed away the chess pieces. "Let's sneak over there and see what's going on."

We were both tipsy, and that gave me courage. "Let's do it! It couldn't be any worse than last night."

We crossed the highway, giggling as we crept up the long driveway that bridged a three-foot deep irrigation ditch. "Shhh." We held onto each other in the moonless darkness, trying not to crunch the gravel. The more we shushed each other, the more we tee-heed.

When we approached the house, the border of light at the bottom of the living room drapes told us they were up. My favorite, Ray Charles singing Georgia, flowed from our stereo.

Karen whispered, "They'll never hear us."

We moved silently from one side to the other of the two front windows, but the drapes fit too well. Karen moved around the house to the kitchen side. A block of light shone through the lace curtains.

"Come on. We can see," Karen said, pulling on my arm.

Due to the slope of the ground, the window ledge was over six feet high.

"Let's give it up," I pleaded, sobered by the cold air and afraid to look.

"No way! I want to see her. I'll find something to climb on." She slipped behind the garage and returned carrying a tire. "You steady it." She leaned it against the house, and then climbed up, holding the ledge.

"What's happening?"

"Jeez, you should see them." She spoke too loud in the still night. "Jimmy's back's to me, they're dancing…buck naked. Can't see her face. Wait, they're stopping. Jimmy's got—yuck! I can't look!" When she turned away, the tire slipped and she collapsed on me. My elbow hit the house with a loud thump.

"Shit! Run for it!"

Pell-mell, we charged away from the lights, into the blackness—headlong into the irrigation ditch. When we hit the cold water, screams erupted. We clambered up the opposite bank and lay on the grass, breathless, choking and snorting with laughter.

The porch light came on and Jimmy's naked torso appeared in the window.

"Yeeoorowe!" Karen let loose a blood-curdling female cat's call.

Safely beyond the light, half-frozen, we clutched our stomachs and rolled on the grass.

"That should bring about a hundred tomcats," I whispered, between laughter and hiccups. "Let's get the hell out of here."

CHAPTER 4

▼

In a few days, when Mr. Wilke called me to work day shift, I was down to my last dollars.

The bar was clean and modern, built on the spot where a crazed wife burned down the ancient Big Timber. White Water Bar was nothing like that old dungeon which had smelled of mop water and urine when I'd gone in as a teen to beg nickels from my dad.

The bar's back door stood open and the air smelled fresh. April sunlight shone through the glass-brick front and bounced off the long L-shaped walnut bar.

It was eerie inside the big empty room—strangely quiet and hollow sounding. Mr. Wilke invited me behind the bar and stayed close, showing me where everything was located while he explained procedures. He demonstrated how to sanitize the glasses, operate the spigots for mixes, and prepare the lemons and limes.

"This is your shot-glass." He held up a tiny, thick glass that stood upside down on a white towel in the bar's gutter. "Don't over pour. Just fill it up to the line. Beer's in the case behind you."

As he moved around pointing out the many facets of my job, I tagged along and tried to remember all he said. He tapped a brown book beside the cash register. "This one's for cocktails. People don't order too many around here. Mostly just highballs."

Cocktails? Highballs?

I kept nodding and smiling.

About hip level, he pointed out a metal rod attached below the bar. "Here's where you break your bottles." In a bin below lay a single whiskey bottle. He picked it up, jammed its already-chipped neck onto the rod, wrenched downward and finished off the neck. He dropped it and spoke in a stern voice. "Break it the minute it's empty."

I stared at the bin.

"It's the law. Breaks the seals so they can't be refilled. Oregon don't want us refilling them with California booze. Taxes."

"All this looks lots easier from the other side."

Don't say that, stupid! You want this job don't you?

He glanced at me often as I repeated things to myself, looking bewildered, I'm sure. "You'll soon get it. You know how to make change, don't you, honey?"

"That I know. I worked at Hamburger Heaven in high school."

"Honey, I've got something to do in the kitchen." He patted my shoulder as he moved past me. "You just look things over, I'll be back before we open."

The quiet hum of cooler fans and the clicks of a revolving Hamms sign were the only sounds, as I stood alone behind the massive bar.

Walking the length of the thirty-five foot bar, trailing my hand along the track that held the ashtrays and bar towels, I imagined the bar full of after-work loggers, all swigging beers. Simple, easily opened beers. I memorized what brands were behind each of the three glass-front cooler doors.

Beginning to feel more comfortable, I stopped at the shelves of glasses and wondered how I'd know which one to use for what. I leafed through the bartender's book. Pictures of the proper glasses were next to each recipe. Just as I looked up Margarita, which I knew was a fancy drink, Mr. Wilke returned.

"It's time to open." He settled onto a stool at the curved end of the bar near the back door. "I'm right here if you need help."

Feeling a little sick, I stood looking toward the front door, gripping a clean ashtray. Mr. Wilke's eyes were on me, so I picked up a wet towel and wiped the full length of the bar. I felt so small, standing on my tiptoes to reach the far edge.

In less than five minutes, Arthur Bench and Bill Gerly came in.

"Well, well, what have we here?" Bill said. "You can't be old enough to be back there. Art, I used to buy this little gal a pop out in front of the Big Timber when she was knee high to a grasshopper."

"Yep, me too," Art said, "I knew her daddy when he was knee high to a grasshopper. Give us an Oly, honey, and I'm buyin'."

I knew exactly where to find the Oly, but where was the bottle opener? I stood there with a beer in each hand looking helplessly at my new boss. He pointed to where it was mounted under the bar. I set the beers and glasses in front of the men.

Bill waved them away. "Nope, no glasses. No need to dirty 'em on us."

I took Art's money, returned the glasses to the shelf and stood near Mr. Wilke. He smiled and nodded. "Now you go on down and talk to them, honey."

Brother, what am I going to say to these old geezers?

Just then a couple who'd also known me forever came in. "Well, hi there, Suzanne. How long you been working here?"

"About ten minutes."

"We'll just take a couple Bloody Marys."

I reached for the book, looking toward Mr. Wilke. He shook his head. "Here, I'll show you. You won't find it in that damn book." He got up and mixed their drinks. "They don't want no celery." He motioned for me to deliver the drinks, then sat back down. "That's a buck-fifty."

I took their ten-dollar bill and counted back their change as he watched.

The wife pushed a quarter toward me. "Shake you for the music."

Though I'd seen the game played, I'd never done it myself. I handed her the dice cup. She clamped her hand over it, rattled the dice, and then with a flip of the wrist and a whap of the leather cup, rolled them across the bar.

"I've got three fives," she said.

I upended the cup and piled the dice on top of each other.

"No, sweetie. Stacked dice. Try again." She beat my two pair, so I handed her a quarter and marked it down on the sheet by the register.

As the time dragged past, I became more relaxed. That is, until Mr. Wilke said, "Go down there and cut Bench off, he's sleeping on the bar."

I knew what "cut off" meant, but it hadn't yet occurred to me that I'd have to do it. "But he's only had three beers." I cringed at questioning Mr. Wilke.

"No, honey, he ain't drunk. Sleeping on the bar's against the law. When he gets a couple beers in him, he just nods off."

I stood before old Arthur and watched him for a second. Sure enough, he was sound asleep with his head on his arms and one hand clutched his empty bottle. I tapped him gently on the elbow, but he didn't respond. I tapped harder, still no response. I was about as effective as a mosquito on a rhino.

Looking over at Mr. Wilke, I knew I'd better get the job done. I took hold of both his arms and shook him. "Wake up, Arthur, you'll have to leave now." He partly lifted his head then settled back down. I rattled him again, speaking louder.

He mumbled, then raised his head to see who'd disturbed him. "Huh, huh, huh?"

Expecting the worst, I repeated, "You'll have to leave now."

He rubbed his eyes, looked as if he didn't know where he was, then scratched his gray stubble. He squinted at me. "Sure, sure, little one, I'll be going now." He waved over his shoulder as he lumbered out the door. "See you folks tomorrow."

"That wasn't so bad," I told Mr. Wilke.

"Good practice for you. You'll have to do that every day. If the liquor inspector catches him sleeping, you and I'll both be in trouble."

By six-thirty I was exhausted from tension. And my feet were killing me.

Karen picked me up outside. "How was it?"

"Not too bad. Being Tuesday, it was mostly old farts drinking beer. Nothing too hard. Hope I get lots better before Friday afternoon though." I looked across at my driveway as we turned into Karen's house. "What went on over there today?"

"Didn't see anything of them but when I went out to the mailbox at noon, both cars were there. He probably comes home for a nooner."

"I suppose she's fixing him a nice hot lunch? Drives me crazy to think of her in my house. Sleeping in my bed. But, that's what I get for leaving."

"I'd kick your butt if you didn't leave. Besides, she won't be there long. My brother's used to someone with brains, he'll never stay with her."

"All I hope is he sticks with her awhile. Long enough for me to get him out of my system." I slipped off my shoes and rubbed my burning feet. "Through all these years…seems like when I'm just about up to here with him, he knows it…starts sweet-talking me. Of course, this is his worst yet."

"That's why you've got to make it stick."

"I want to, but I can't just turn it off like a spigot."

During my third week on the job, Mr. Wilke changed me to the night shift, full time. I was sick of the same old codgers every day—going on with their clucking. "Why when she was a little tyke, she looked just like Shirley Temple…with those curls." The pay raise thrilled me. I'd be earning enough to get my own place.

Karen set her alarm to pick me up after work that first night and sat out in front in her bathrobe with the motor running while I learned the night-shift side work.

"You can't come for me every night. As soon as I get my next paycheck, I'm going to move uptown to one of those cabins behind the bar."

"Yuck! Not where the Bimbo lived?"

"No way! The other one's empty and bigger. I looked in the window a couple days ago. There's three rooms. It's dirty and the furniture's junky, but I'll paint as soon as I get the money."

"Suz, you don't have to do this. You can stay right here, take my car to work."

"I need my own place, Karen. You know what I mean? Then I'll really be free." I chose my words carefully. "I love you, but as long as I stay here, I'm still not on my own. See?" She had to know the move was for the best.

"Can you manage the rent? Need a loan?"

"No, I'll be fine. They rent it by the week. Fifteen dollars. No first and no deposit. I've got to get some stuff from our house." I needed things from the kitchen, and my new bedspread—to cover the couch in the cabin. "I'll talk to the owner today, try to tie it up until Friday."

Karen went into her bedroom and came back with a twenty-dollar bill. "Here, go ahead and pay the rent tonight. We can move your stuff tomorrow, then make a raid on Jimmy's while he's working.

"I damn sure don't want to run into the Bimbo."

Karen said she'd been watching, and the curtains were never opened until almost noon. Then, after Jimmy had lunch, the Bimbo high-tailed it out and didn't come back until just before the five o'clock whistle. "You're not scared of that little sexpot!"

"Not exactly. I just can't stand battles."

She laughed. "You're in a hell of a job then."

"I feel different behind that bar, stronger sort of. I can't explain it. When I'm back there, I'm in charge. For the first time in my life."

"Good for you, Suzanny!" She gave me a crushing hug. "Let's plan on going over right after she leaves tomorrow."

Before work that evening, I paid my new landlord the first week's rent and was given the keys. In my haste to move in, I'd forgotten the electricity deposit, but the light coming in through the window was bright enough to see the layout. I'd raise the deposit from my tips by Friday.

My last morning at Karen's, she fixed omelets for our breakfast and we talked while we waited for Jimmy's lunch hour to pass. When the one o'clock whistle blew, she walked to a spot in the trees where she could see across the street to the driveway. Two minutes later, she yelled that the coast was clear.

"I feel creepy doing this," I said, as we walked into the quiet house with our cardboard boxes. "Three weeks ago this was my house, now I feel like a burglar."

Karen held her nose. "Smells like a goddamn garbage dump in here." She flipped on the kitchen light. "Look at this! The sink's full of scummy dishwater. Christ, what a pig."

Dirty dishes, pots, and pans covered the counter. I opened the refrigerator. A packaged lunchmeat and a pint of Best Foods mayonnaise sat on the top shelf. A plastic bowl of leftover spaghetti I'd cooked last month and two six-packs of Budweiser stood on the lower shelf.

"Guess she knows how to slap together baloney sandwiches." I picked up a plate with a cigarette butt sticking out of a dry, half-eaten sandwich. "Crap, I'll have to wash these dishes so I can take some."

"Bull! Just put what you want in this box, we'll wash them at my house." Karen picked through the mess, gathering silverware. I scraped food from two plates into an overflowing garbage sack. Moldy coffee grounds and cigarette butts tumbled to the floor.

When I'd finished in the kitchen, I pushed open the bedroom door. The stuffy room smelled of tobacco and stale beer. The drapes were pulled, but there was enough light to see stacks of clothes everywhere. The nightstands were covered with empty beer bottles and the ashtrays overflowed with butts and crumpled cigarette packs.

I threw back the drapes and pushed open the window. When I turned back to the sunlit room, my eyes fell on a pair of her lacy black panties hanging from the lampshade. Memories flooded over me—other nights, my panties. I bit my lip as a sob welled up in me. Emotions I'd been holding back overwhelmed me and I dropped to my knees beside the bed and buried my face in the bedspread.

"Pee-yew!" Karen came through the door. "Oh, Suz, don't." She put her hands under my arms and lifted me. "Let's get you out of here. What else do you want?"

"I wanted my blue sheets." I pointed to the messy bed. "But forget it. I still want my bedspread for that shitty couch."

"Do you want these pillows?"

"Not those. Some in the closet."

The bathroom was also draped with dirty clothes and the bathtub looked like someone had bathed a Cocker Spaniel—blond hairs dried in soap scum on the bottom of the tub. I splashed cold water on my face and blew my nose. As I pulled the last two clean towels from the linen closet, I heard voices.

Loud voices.

My stomach turned over when I realized who was there. I stood still, listening. There was no mistaking Karen's voice. "Just get your sorry ass back out to your car and keep it there 'til we're ready to leave."

"Who the hell are you?" the higher-pitched voice demanded.

"I'm the one who's going to kick your can if you don't get out." Karen yelled, "Now!"

I wanted to hide in the bathroom, but even more I wanted to make her as uncomfortable as possible. I took a deep breath and strode into the living room.

"And, I'm going to help her!" I declared loudly.

I dropped the towels on a chair when I spotted Jimmy's football trophy on the bookcase. I grabbed it and moved toward her with its hefty base raised.

She stepped back, hands up in front of her face. "You bitches are nuts. Lay a hand on me I'll have you arrested. I'm a minor, you know." In spite of the brassy talk, her bulging eyes darted back and forth between Karen and me as she backed out the door.

Karen moved toward her. "You're minor, all right, pretty near a zero. Should have your humping little ass beat to a—"

"She's not worth dirtying your fingernails." I stepped in front of Karen. "All the hell she's got going for her is that fly blown slit between her legs. I feel sorry for the ugly little thing."

"Fuck you!" she yelled as she slammed the door.

We watched out the window as she jumped in her car and roared out the driveway making a rain of gravel.

"Well, well, my little chicken, you put the wind in her sail." Karen grabbed my hand and held it high. "Score one for Suzanny."

Back at Karen's, tears flowed as I washed dishes and she talked to me about how much better off I was going to be. I started toward her car with the clean dishes.

"You can't move in there 'til you get the power turned on."

"I appreciate you letting me stay here, but I really need to be alone. If you give me a little fire wood, I'll be fine."

By the time we'd unloaded everything at my cabin, she had to leave. Her husband would be calling from Germany at five o'clock.

She hugged me. "Don't waste any more tears tonight. Go to work and knock 'em dead."

"Don't worry. I'm done crying for awhile."

I built a fire in the tiny wood stove, then hung my clothes in the so-called closet—a metal pipe hanging from heavy wires attached to the ceiling with bent nails. A lumpy, pee-stained mattress lay on the steel bed frame. Beside it, a peeling veneer nightstand with a dime-store lamp.

When I moved the bed so the morning sun could hit my face, the mountain of dust bunnies reminded me I had no broom. The ugly, flowered, maroon and gray linoleum had at least been swept—everywhere but under the bed. I moved it back until I could afford a broom.

In the kitchen, the cupboards and drainboard looked clean enough in the dim light, but closer inspection showed decades of accumulated filth. I lined the only drawer with newspapers left over from building the fire and put away my two-piece set of silverware. When I turned on the faucet only drops of rusty water came out. I'd forgotten about city water.

Another deposit. Only one flush until tomorrow.

I stoked the fire, put the bedspread on the couch then sat down and looked around. The smell of the dust came up through the cover, but I didn't care.

Tingling with excitement and fear, I leaned back and imagined painting the dirty walls, hanging new curtains, buying a better couch—as soon as I got a few paychecks.

As the sun went down, the trepidation of living alone for the first time in my life became more vivid. I made up my bed with a clean mattress pad, changed clothes and went to work at six-thirty.

The evening was busy, but peaceful. At three in the morning, when I returned to my cabin, the thrill of being on my own came again. Inside was warm from the fire. The rooms were bathed in the glow from the mercury vapor light shining through my front window—my very own perpetual full moon.

CHAPTER 5

▼

At work Friday night, I prepared myself, constantly watched the door for Jimmy. We hadn't been face to face for nearly a month, and I worried he'd be furious about our raid on his house—and on his Bimbo. As the clock crawled toward nine, the members of his band arrived. The place was hopping so I didn't notice him come in, but when I looked up from the sink and saw him, my legs went weak.

He came to the bar, but didn't speak.

"What would you like?" I hated my voice sounding high and scared.

"Shot of Seagram's and a beer."

I set his Budweiser and whiskey in front of him. He slapped down two dollars and strolled to the bandstand.

The evening passed in a busy blur. Because it was my first Friday night behind the bar, I was slightly out of control, and painfully aware of Jimmy staring down at me from the bandstand. Every time I glanced his way, he smiled toward the crowd, but his eyes followed me.

The music ended at two o'clock. He unhooked the amplifiers and rolled up cords while his fellow band members packed their instruments outside. When he started out with his last piece of equipment, he motioned with his head for me to meet him at the end of the bar.

Here it comes.

"You did a great job tonight." Before I could answer, he grabbed my hand, pulled me toward him and kissed me on the forehead. "Good night, babe." He turned and strode out the door.

Damn you, Jimmy. Don't sweet-talk me.

Saturday night was even busier than Friday, but I was more comfortable with his presence. When he didn't approach me after the band quit, I was a little disappointed. But, I had something new to worry about. I'd suspected something creepy about Mr. Wilke from the beginning.

Earlier, I'd been in the back room bent over getting ice when he'd come up behind me and pressed his pelvis against my butt. I turned around in time to see a glazed look in his faded old eyes, just before he sputtered, "Oh, oh, sorry. I need a case of Hamms."

I was pretty sure I knew the difference between a simple bump and a pelvic thrust.

The next time Marie, the other bartender, and I came together at the sink I brought it up. "I think old man Wilke just nudged me with his you-know-what in the back room."

"Damn! I thought he'd lay off you…being you're so young. The old bastard's nearly ninety. Wonder he can even get it up."

"I'm not sure it was up, but the spirit was willing. He ever done anything like that to you?"

"Once last year."

"What happened?"

She gestured with her fist. "Grabbed a handful. Told him 'touch me again like that, I'll yank 'em off.' Scared him." She nodded toward his wife who sat a table. "He just likes to dream. His old lady would clean his plow if she caught him."

"God, I couldn't handle him. Not like that."

"Don't worry, he won't hurt you. Just stay out of the back room when he's behind the bar."

"Don't ever leave me here with him at closing time, okay?"

"Sure, kid, I'll watch out for you."

Through no fault of her own, Marie let me down the following Tuesday night. It was unusually slow, so he told her she could go home at midnight. Needing money so desperately, I was pleased he didn't send me, and flattered he thought I was able to handle things alone—never thinking ahead to closing time.

Later, as we got busy again, he came behind the bar. "You go on home," he told his wife. "I'll help Suzanne close up."

My heart sank.

I steered clear of him that last hour, carefully timed my visits to the back room as I restocked and prepared to close. After the doors were locked, he mixed two drinks while I washed glasses and ashtrays. The house usually bought bartenders a drink after work, and I liked to rest a few minutes and have one before going home.

Rather than insult him by refusing, I sat down at the end of the bar. He'd started to count the money, and I thought he'd be occupied long enough for me to down the drink and be gone.

The instant I sat down, he picked up his drink and sat beside me. "Getting a divorce?"

"I don't know." I hadn't yet faced the idea of divorce.

"Girly like you could go a long ways…played your cards right." He spoke low, almost a whisper. "You could have *lots* of nice things…*lots* more money than your wages. We could get along *real* good."

"What do you mean?" I knew by his caressing tone that I didn't want to hear the answer, but what else could I say?

Staring straight ahead, I could feel his watery gaze bore into the side of my face. I hunkered down over the Johnny Walker he'd poured me and gripped it with both hands. I hated the smoky taste of Scotch, and I didn't want his favors, but I'd do as much as I could to keep my job.

"You could let me touch those fine titties of yours sometimes." His voice was syrupy. "Maybe let me see them."

An image formed in my mind. My stomach tightened and a shiver ran down the back of my arms.

"You could find something extra in your paycheck. Just don't hurry home after work." I felt his breath on my ear and winced as a drop of spittle hit me. "We could get along real good. I'd make it worth your while."

Still staring straight ahead, my voice nearly failed me, coming out in a breathy croak. "I couldn't…do something like that Mr. Wilke."

"You just think on it, little darlin'." He ran the back of his shaky finger down my cheek. "You better get out back to that little cabin of yours, get some sleep."

Fear, like thunder, rolled through my body at the mention of where I lived. When I got home, I locked the door for the first time—and left the old skeleton key on the inside. No one locked doors in Barkerville.

I lay in the dark and stared at the stars out my back window.

God, what am I going to do? What if I turn him down? I have three dollars in the bank. What if I have no job?

He hadn't fired Marie, I reasoned. But had he even propositioned her? Why did he have to ruin everything? Mine was the best paying job in town—probably the only one. I had big plans. I could save enough to get a car, maybe even go back to school. I loved school and had the grades, but my folks had no money for the foolishness of college. To them girls should marry at eighteen and start families. Thank God, I'd been able to prevent the babies.

Filled with a whirlpool of thoughts, my head ached. I'd been so happy the past three weeks—making my own way, comfortable in my little cabin. I couldn't bear to give it up. There had to be a solution. Determined not to go back to Jimmy, I tried to imagine what it would be like to do what Mr. Wilke asked. My imagination didn't want to go there.

How hard can it be to let the old fool touch me? No one but Jimmy ever has, but what if I do it? I need this job if I'm going to make it on my own. His wife is always close by. He'll never be able to do much. I wonder what kind of extra money he means? Maybe I can do it.

Talking seriously to myself until the dawn erased the stars, I must have changed my mind a dozen times, and never quite reached a firm decision.

The next night at work, I avoided Mr. Wilke's eyes, still unsure if I could go through with it. He sat at the end of the bar as usual and watched me work. I'd learned the job so fast he'd cut the other bartender back to just weekends.

Mid-evening, he came behind the bar and puttered around, leaned across talking to people, buying drinks. All the while, he watched me like a cat watches a hummingbird. When I had to go into the storeroom for disinfectant for the sink, I waited until he was occupied and dashed back quickly. He'd started toward the doorway when I came out.

An hour later while he rested on his stool at the end of the bar, I used the opportunity to go after clean bar towels. As I reached for them on the high shelf, he came up behind me and clutched my breasts. My moment of truth had arrived. I stood still, barely breathing. My skin burst into goose bumps.

He moaned.

Good God, what am I doing? What if he tells?

Cheeks burning, I sidestepped and left the room. He stayed back there awhile, then came out and sat by his wife. As the evening passed, he stayed beside her. Lucky for me, she didn't go home before closing time.

Thursday night started the same except that his wife went home around ten. As soon as she left, he came behind the bar, visiting with people, watching and waiting. Around midnight, he motioned to me. "Come in here a minute, I want to show you something about this ice machine."

Reluctantly, I followed.

The moment we cleared the doorway, he lunged at me. He kneaded my breasts with both hands. Facing him was much harder. I closed my eyes and thrust forward my chest, turning my head away from his hot, foul breath. The minute or two that passed seemed an eternity. Finally I pulled away. "I've got to get out there."

He didn't come out for a while. When he did, he staggered slightly and shuffled to his seat at the end of the bar.

Closing time came much too quickly. When he locked both doors and turned off the main lights, fear moved up my thighs to my solar plexus. I cleaned up while he poured us each a Johnny Walker. I'd sneaked a double shot of Black Velvet into my coffee cup a half-hour before closing—for courage. Its warmth had already spread through my body and calmed the dragonflies in my stomach. I drained the Scotch he handed me.

He poured another one. "This will make you feel good." He gathered the dirty ashtrays, then turned to where I stood tidying the backbar. "Are you ready to show me those perfect titties?"

I looked at us in the mirror. The bottle display lights, shining upward in the darkness, cast strange shadows. He was a white-haired monster lifting my sweater with pudgy, gnarled hands. Chills ran up my ribs and I stifled a gasp.

I pulled away, turned from the mirror and unbuttoned my sweater then let my bra drop to the floor. Barely breathing, I locked my gaze on a spot of gray and white stubble on his chin. His shaking fingers circled my breasts. He breathed hard through his mouth, working his tongue at one corner of his lips.

His fingers, icy snakes crawling on me, caused my nipples to harden. He moaned and lowered his slobbering mouth to one, then the other.

Oh God, help me stand this.

His Scotch breath slithered up my nose. Nerves trilled from the back of my neck and across my scalp as I fought to breathe and to calm my stomach.

He slid his hands down to my hips. "Let me see this," he pleaded.

I jumped back. "No, sir! You know what our deal was. That's as far as it goes." My strong, steady voice made me proud.

He dropped his hands to his sides. "Okay, okay."

"What if your wife comes back in here?"

"She won't. She takes her pills, sleeps 'til morning.

"Well, I have to go now." The liquor and nerves had me reeling.

"Okay, okay. One more minute, then you can go."

I put on my sweater, stuffed my bra in my purse and slipped out the back door. Once home, I locked the door, put a chair under the knob then dropped my clothes on the floor and went straight into the shower. The long, hot soak, the alcohol, and the tears I shed helped me shut down my guilty mind and sleep.

Friday morning, payday, I hurried to the bar for my check. Mr. Wilke handed it to me with a proud smile.

"My wife and I are going away for the weekend. Marie will take care of the money and all. I'll see you Tuesday."

A three-day reprieve—what a relief. I hurried out the back door and peeked in the envelope. Behind my sixty-eight dollar paycheck sat a crisp fifty-dollar bill— the equivalent of twenty-five hours' wages, enough to repay Karen and cover my utilities for two months. I stuffed it back in the envelope and pressed it to my chest.

Whoever breaks this bill will know I did something terrible for it.

I was dying to confess to Karen, the only person in the world who wouldn't judge me. I ran back inside and called her to come take me to breakfast.

She picked me up and drove us to the other end of our six-block town—to the all-night diner we called Ptomaine Tony's. Although Anthony left town sometime while I was still in grade school, the faded sign above the flattop brick building still read Anthony's Fine Dining. A long succession of owners and leaseholders had passed through, each one caring a little less about the old building's appearance, until it came into the hands of the current owners. The middle-aged couple kept its well-scuffed floors spotless and hung starched gingham curtains on its clean windows.

"What's with you?" Karen half-smiled as she slid into the sagging Naugahyde seat of the booth. "You look weird."

"I've got something to tell you. Don't know how you'll take it."

Her smile faded and her forehead creased. "What? You're not back with Jimmy? Tell me."

"Promise me you won't tell anyone." I crossed the front of my blouse. "Cross your heart, hope to die. This is serious."

"Yeah, yeah. What?"

"No! You've got to say it."

"Okay, I promise." She crossed herself.

I took out the fifty-dollar bill and spread it on the table.

"What's this?" Her eyes narrowed and her mouth hung open. "You didn't steal it!"

"You know I'd never *steal*. Old man Wilke gave it to me."

She smiled, looked pleased at my enormous bonus.

Just then the waitress brought us each coffee and a menu. I scooped up the fifty and gave Karen a "be quiet" look.

We exchanged with the waitress, and Karen, no doubt puzzled by my actions, kept smiling until the woman walked away. Then she dropped the friendly smile, straightened her back and spoke like a mother. "What's going on?" Her fingers drummed the table.

For a moment I was afraid to tell her. I'd never done anything so terrible and didn't want to lose Karen's respect. I took a deep breath and whispered across the table. "I let him touch my boobs."

"WHAT?" Her outburst nearly rattled the windows. "You did what?"

Customers, two booths away turned to look.

I grabbed her hand. "Shhh!"

Smiling sweetly at the nosy people, I continued to squeeze Karen's hand until I decided she had the message. Our waitress, on hearing the outburst, took her order book from her pocket and came our way.

Karen asked for a Denver omelet, and since I hadn't given a thought to what I wanted, said I'd have the same. While I waited for the waitress to get out of hearing distance, I sipped my coffee, and studied Karen's incredulous look.

Before she could make another outburst, I leaned toward her and whispered, "He asked me. I didn't know what to do. Said he'd pay a lot. Damn it. I just *did* it."

"Jeezus. I can't believe you'd let that old coot touch you." Her eyebrows shot up to her hairline. "The Virgin Queen of Barkerville High. God, how could you stand it?"

To shock Karen was not easy, but it was plain to see she was stunned.

"I got half-crocked. Just pretended I was a high-class call girl. Remember how we did when we were kids? Then I stripped off and let him go. You should've seen him. Thought he'd have a stroke."

Karen sat, arms folded, looking at me. I couldn't read her expression. Was it disbelief? Disdain? Uncertainty about that look scared me. Did my best friend think less of me for what I'd done? Didn't she understand that I had no choice?

"Don't look at me like that, what's the big deal?"

"It's definitely not a big deal…just not like you. Like something I'd do maybe, but not you. Now what?"

"It can't be as hard the second time. Fifty bucks is a lot of money. If you've got change, I'll pay you what I owe."

While we ate breakfast, she kept shaking her head, a sly smile on her lips. "You're something, you know that?" After a few minutes, she said, "God, I hope you didn't do this just to pay me."

"It's not just you. I've got to make the rent and utilities, try to pay some of the bills I left behind. Hell, I still owe the Avon lady." I pushed my plate away and lit a cigarette. "I've got to buy a car. If I don't keep up our credit at the bank, I won't be able to buy one. That's some joke, huh? Me getting groped to pay the bills."

"I'm really scared for you, Suzanny. What if the old pervert—?"

"I'm telling you, this is not a big deal. First of all, he's too old. I'm sure I could handle him." Though I pretended not to care, discussing it made my stomach queasy. "What's with Jimmy?"

"Red car was gone this morning. Maybe they had a fight. Bet she's tired sitting home weekends while he plays. Poor little baby can't go in the bar…keep her eye on him."

"You think she sits home?"

"No way. I walked over there last Friday night before I went to bed. Her car was gone half an hour after Jimmy left."

That gave me some satisfaction.

When the Wilkes got back, he could hardly contain himself. Like a faithful dog, his eyes followed me everywhere. I was afraid he'd give himself away to his wife if he didn't stop staring at me. He said he was tired from their trip and went home early with her, giving me peace for another night.

Near ten Wednesday evening, Mark the Indian-painter walked through the door. When our eyes met, his smile spread from dimple to dimple. "I heard they had a sexy new bartender down here. Never dreamt it would be you."

I got his beer and waited while he fished money from his wallet. The memory of what he'd said to me that night in February brought heat to my cheeks. After all the trouble that night started, I was uncomfortable seeing him again.

He touched my fingers as he handed me the dollar bill. "I knew we'd meet again. How long have you been here?"

"Just since the first of April." Blushing and tongue-tied, I smiled and tried to make small talk. "Shake for the music?"

He won and grabbed my hand as I held out the quarter. "Come over here and help me pick some tunes."

Since I had few customers, I followed him to the jukebox. My body hummed as we stood close together and looked at selections. Although I stared at the titles, I couldn't make sense of them.

He tugged the end of my ponytail. "Sorry. I can't keep my hands off this hair."

What is it about long hair that drives men so silly?

He put his lips close to my ear. "I'd love to see that spread out on a satin pillow."

My stomach muscles rippled.

Mark stayed for a couple of hours. Each time I came near we exchanged pieces of information.

"I've been painting since I graduated high school in 1952. Spent three years in college to stay out of Korea."

I did the math. *Holy cow! I was in fifth grade.* "I was born and raised here. I graduated in '59."

"I was almost married once. She took off with a football coach just before the wedding."

"Sorry."

"It was for the best."

Between our mini-conversations, I caught Mr. Wilke watching me. He came behind the bar, straightened things and waited for his chance. In a short time, the Seven-Up dispenser went dry, so I had to go into the back room to change the tank. I had to control my face completely—Mark was watching me.

"Who's that Mex?" Mr. Wilke asked, reaching for me.

"He's visiting friends."

"Just don't forget our deal tonight."

"Don't worry."

"Did you like what I put in your paycheck?"

"Sure. But I've got to get back out there."

I decided not to tell Mark about my separation. Life was too complicated. I wanted to see more of him though, so when he got up to leave, I said, "Be sure and come back now."

"My lady, you can depend on it."

Mr. and Mrs. Wilke went home around midnight, but an hour later he came back. Business slowed and the last customer left at one-thirty. The policy was never to close early, so for the next hour I cleaned everything in sight to avoid him. As closing time came closer, I slipped whiskey in my coffee cup for the second time.

When I began refilling beer cases from the back room, there he was, waiting while I went back for one case after another. Each time he reached for me. Finally I had no more business back there so he moved to the dance floor where he picked up ashtrays from the tables.

Standing by the front door, he watched the clock hand move to half-past the hour, then locked the door, shut off the lights, and came back to the well to make our drinks. I couldn't stand the thought of another scotch, so I asked for a peach brandy.

"Why, that's a perfect drink for a little punkin' like you." He poured me a double on the rocks.

As I sipped, the sweet liquor warmed my stomach, spread a glow to my arms and legs. I sat on the end stool and steeled myself.

Across from me, he leaned in on the bar and pulled a tiny jewelry box from his pocket. "I've got a present for you."

I gulped my brandy. Accepting a gift was awkward for me under normal circumstances, and accepting one from him was far from normal. Scenes from movies came to mind. *It's just a part. Play it!* Like the femme fatale in a B-movie, I said, "Oh, you shouldn't have."

"Go ahead, open it."

Since I'd turned my imagination loose, I visualized a brilliant diamond ring as I slowly turned the ring box in my hands. I even got into the role enough to smile up at him as I sprung open the lid. When I looked down, fully expecting jewelry, the gold nugget he'd stuffed in the ring slot disappointed me.

"You could drill it…wear it on a chain." He demonstrated by holding the nugget—bigger than a fifty-cent piece—near the middle of my chest. "But don't wear it in here."

Careful not to touch him, I took it from his hand, put it in the box, and sweetly thanked him. Still in character, I rose and slid my Angora sweater over my head.

"I like the feel of your sweater."

"Want me to leave it on?"

"No, no." He stepped closer with his arms outstretched. "Let me."

I turned my back to him. His hands shook as he fumbled with the hooks on my bra. Just as I was about to reach back and do it myself, it came loose. He reached around me, caressed each breast and was breathing heavily on my back when someone banged on the back door.

"Jesus, who's that?" I twisted away, grabbed my sweater and held it to my chest.

CHAPTER 6

▼

"Who's there?" Mr. Wilke said.

"Jimmy McTavish."

"Shit!" I grabbed my clothes and ran for the back room.

"Be there in a minute," I heard Mr. Wilke say.

What the hell's he doing here?

All fingers, I got into my bra and pulled on my sweater. I ran my hands through my hair, and then hurried from the back room with a handful of bottles. It was a weeknight and Jimmy should have been home in bed. But there he was, and he looked sober.

While he exchanged pleasantries with Mr. Wilke, I saw the ring box sitting in the bar's ashtray track and casually dropped a towel over it.

Though sure that my hot face gave away my guilt, I tried to sound nonchalant. "What you doing up so late?"

"I've been to bed." He ducked his head in his little-boy way. "Couldn't sleep so I came to take you to breakfast. How about it, babe?"

I wanted to go with him but dreaded the conversation we still hadn't had. In the month since my birthday party I'd rehearsed what I'd say to him when the time came, so I agreed.

As we left together, he was the perfect gentleman, opening the doors, gently steering me by the back of the neck as if nothing had changed between us. Ptomaine Tony's was empty, except for the cook and waitress sitting at the counter. We sat in a booth in the back.

Jimmy took out two cigarettes, lit them both and handed me one. "How do you like your job?"

"It's okay."

"You know, I never got to give you your birthday present. I been thinking I'd give it to you some Saturday night…didn't want to do it in there." He shoved a small gift-wrapped package and a card toward me.

I took the card in my hand but made no move to open it.

"Come on, please open it."

I truly doubted he'd purchased it back in March. He didn't ever buy me presents. He always said, "You have the checkbook, get what you want."

I slowly opened the envelope and a lump rose in my throat. My mind flooded with heartbreaking images.

Stop it! Don't cry for him.

The card was a beautiful tribute to a much-loved wife, someone I didn't feel anything like. Words like "love of my life" and "forever" touched me—as he'd planned. Try as I might, I couldn't stop the tears that welled up. I kept my head down, blinked them away as I studied the blurred image of the card. It didn't work. A tear escaped and fell to the front of my sweater.

He reached across and tipped my head up. "I didn't want to make you cry, babe. I wanted to make you happy."

When did you want to make me happy? On my birthday? You made me happy all right. Screwing that Bimbo. That's the way, Suzanne, get mad.

I stared at him, trying so hard to hate him. All the things I'd planned to say to him flew out of my mind. His image, swimming before my eyes, was one I'd loved for a long, long time. Love was a hard habit to break.

"Open your present. Please." His brow wrinkled in a practiced sad look.

I picked at the tape, and slowly removed the wrapping, carefully smoothed and folded it. My eyes wouldn't focus and I felt woozy. I put down the unopened box and called the waitress for a glass of milk, then ordered breakfast.

"Milk? What's this?" Jimmy leaned forward and pressed the back of his hand against my cheek. "Are you okay?"

"Guess I'm a little high…had a stiff drink after work."

His voice oozed with nice. "I hope you're not going to take up drinking."

That's a hoot, coming from you.

I looked him straight in the eye. "You needn't worry. The last thing I'll ever be is a *drunk*." He looked away first, maybe taking that last word to heart. I remembered my first beer. Although he'd been drinking since I met him in grade school, it had taken years to persuade me to join him. Unfortunately I found myself using liquor for my courage, but I considered it temporary. Mostly, I didn't enjoy the taste of it—or the way it made me feel. Growing up, I'd seen too much of the damage done by alcohol, including my own marriage.

Joke's on me. I've surrounded myself with the stuff.

Jimmy lowered his face to the table, trying to look into my downcast eyes. "Come on, open it." He cradled the small white box in both hands and offered it to me.

I let out a sigh of resignation, took it and removed the lid. A round gold locket lay on white cotton. I popped it open. "Damn it, Jimmy...why now?" He'd put in a high-school snapshot of himself on one side, mine on the other. I snapped it shut and pushed it toward him. "When it's too late...you come up with this."

He covered my hands, stroked my wrists with his guitar-callused fingers. "It's not too late, Suzanne, we can work this out."

"How the hell can we work anything out...you're shacked up with that Bimbo. You made your choice, remember?"

"She's gone. I told her to get her ass out of my house." His eyes darted back and forth between my eyes and my mouth. He squeezed my hands until they hurt. "I'm so sorry. To tell you the truth, I don't remember much about that night."

"Well, tell me the truth about one thing." I jerked my hands away. "Were you drunk for the past month? Did you just sober up at three o'clock this morning?" Playing the bitch was all that kept me from breaking down.

He gave me his saddest look. "Do you like the locket?"

"Who wouldn't?" I felt familiar pangs of guilt, brought on by his whipped-dog look. The alcohol in my brain confused me and I didn't know what I was feeling from minute to minute. As I ate my eggs, I tried to sort it out.

After we finished, he pleaded, "Let me come home with you. I won't do anything you don't want me to." His voice was soft and convincing. "Just let me hold you while we sleep."

Tired, lonely and confused, I let old desires take charge. "Just for tonight, that's all."

When we got to my house, I went in without turning on any lights. I wanted to satisfy my need for the comfort of his arms—without looking into his face. The mercury-vapor moonlight trailed across the living room, through the bedroom door and across the bed. In the close space, I could smell his after-shave—the Olde Spice I'd bought him for Christmas.

I dropped my skirt, then stripped off my Angora sweater for the second time in less than an hour. As I did, I firmly dismissed thoughts of Mr. Wilke. Jimmy's hands, much more practiced than the old man's, easily unhooked my bra and slipped off my panties. There was no need for me to be coy. I'd decided at the restaurant to make love to him. I let the alcohol and the passion sweep me along under his skilled hands, with no thought of yesterday or tomorrow.

When the morning sun on my eyelids woke me, Jimmy was gone. Lying in bed, watching the dust particles float in the sunlight, my mind went back to what I'd done. I thought of the gold nugget hiding in my purse, along with the locket and Jimmy's birthday card. My life was filled with complications. I wished I could go back and start over. I loved being on my own, but so far I didn't like the decisions I'd made. Thoughts of Mark crowded into the picture. I was attracted to him, and my night with Jimmy hadn't changed anything. I looked forward to seeing Mark again at the bar. But that meant Mr. Wilke, too.

This is so hard.

That evening, just as I'd hoped, Mark came in around eleven and stayed a couple of hours. And, just as I'd hoped, Mr. Wilke went home early. I went home alone at three.

Friday morning Karen knocked at my door. "Come on, let's go have breakfast. I can't wait to hear what's happened in the latest episode of the Virgin Queen's sex life."

"You don't know the half of it." I got my purse and coat. "I need to stop in the bar and get my pay check."

The bar was empty. Mr. Wilke handed over my pay envelope with a lecherous smile "You'll really like what's in there. How about letting me fix you a nice hot toddy?"

"No thanks, I'm with someone." I pulled my hand from his soft, clammy grip, then stuffed the envelope in my purse even though I was sure he wanted to watch me open it.

When Karen and I settled into a booth at Tony's, I took it out and laid it in the middle of the table. "God, this is giving me the willies...you open it."

"No problem for me." She ripped open the envelope. "Jeezus, a hundred this time. What'd you do?"

"Nothing more than I did last week—in fact, less. Wednesday night Jimmy showed up right in the middle of it, then Thursday night they went home early."

Karen turned the bill over and over, reading it, rubbing round-faced Franklin. "You know this is the first hundred dollar bill I ever had in my hands."

"Me, too. It's probably the only one in town." I set the ring box on the table. "Get a load of this."

"Oh no! From him?" She grabbed the box and opened it. "Wow! That baby must be worth a bundle."

"I don't know, but he told me not to show it around."

"Suzanne, this is getting scary. He's going to start thinking he owns you. What about Jimmy showing up?"

"He knocks on the back door at quarter to three. When I heard Jimmy's voice, I nearly crapped. I was half-crocked and half-naked."

"Did he suspect?"

"God, no. He'd never dream…wanted to go to breakfast." I pulled out the locket box and put it in the center of the table beside the ring box.

"Now what?"

"You'll see."

She lifted out the locket and opened it. "That phony shit, he's trying to get you back. Bet his girlfriend went bye-bye."

"Said he ran her off. Who knows?"

"And?" She looked me straight in the eye with her knowing look.

"Don't ask me why. The booze, I think. He *is* my husband after all. So if I'm going to screw someone, I might as well keep it in the family."

"What did he say? You two aren't going back together are you?"

"We didn't say much of anything. Just did it…haven't seen him since. I don't want him back. I like being on my own. That Mark I told you about keeps coming in every night. He seems like an intelligent, refined guy."

"I wonder what Jimmy will do if you go out with him?"

"We'll see. 'Cause I got a feeling it won't be long."

That night Jimmy came in an hour before time to start the music. He looked handsome and confident as he strode toward me. "Hi, babe. How are you tonight?"

"I'm okay. Want your usual?"

"No. Just a Bud. I'm taking it slow tonight. You havin' breakfast with me later?"

"I don't know. We'll see how tired I am." I didn't want to be with him again—not like he expected anyway.

The next hour I was too busy to talk to him except a few words at a time. We shook dice for the music, and he played some heartbreak songs—to get to me like he always did. "Hello walls…"

Mark came in around eleven, smiling that smile I looked forward to. Jimmy watched from the bandstand as I flirted, and when time permitted, leaned on the bar in front of Mark.

Around midnight, during one of his breaks, Jimmy sat down at a table with six young women. Strangers, they were obviously out on the town. Local men, some of them married, buzzed their table all evening. Jimmy ordered them a round of drinks and danced to the jukebox with a big-busted redhead. Jealousy tickled at my heart for a moment. Mark looked puzzled as he watched me watching Jimmy.

During the evening, Mr. Wilke caught me in the back room. "Did you and Jimmy get back together?"

"No."

"We've got some time to make up." He reached for me. "I been missing out lately."

"I'm too busy. Marie might come back here any second. I've got to go."

When the music stopped at two, the redhead helped Jimmy carry out his instruments and they didn't come back.

A questioning frown creased Mark's face. "Was that what it looked like?"

"Yes, it probably was. We've been separated over a month."

His eyebrows shot up. "Are you dating?"

"I haven't yet."

"How about going to get something to eat when you get off?"

"Maybe we could do something in the daytime. I'm off on Sundays and Mondays."

"Great. How would you like to go to the movies Sunday afternoon? About one o'clock? We could have lunch and drive to Eugene."

"Sounds good. I live in number two, out back of here."

Mr. Wilke hustled around picking up glasses, staying close enough to overhear our conversation. He told Marie she could go home at two and we'd finish up.

After everyone had gone and the doors were locked, he asked me what I wanted to drink. He poured his usual Johnny Walker and poured me a double Black Velvet on the rocks. The whiskey tasted smooth and went straight to my legs. I hadn't eaten since my late breakfast with Karen and I knew the liquor would do its job fast.

He put his arm around me as I sat on the end barstool. "You goin' out with that guy?"

"Yes, I am." I turned away from his old-man smell—that awful combination of mothballs, body odor and bad breath.

"Did you like your paycheck, honey?" His dentures clacked in his half-open mouth. His lips were full and wet; barely holding back the pool of saliva dammed up behind his lower plate.

Slipping into my role, I forced myself to keep looking at him and smile. "Yes, it really helps me out. Can I have a refill?" While he went to get the refill, I unbuttoned my blouse. I'd worn my black lace bra.

When he saw the black lace and cleavage, he sucked in his wet breath and spilled part of my drink. He stared at my chest, his tongue darting from side to side like a schoolboy.

I shrugged out of my blouse and stood up to face him. His shaking fingers traced the lace edge down to the front fastener, which he easily unhooked. He did his tit-worship ceremony, rubbed and kissed as I stood passively trying to think of anything else.

Bringing me back with a jolt, he pinched my nipple. "I don't like that guy. Better not let him touch these."

"Ouch!" I pulled back and slapped his hand. "You're hurting me. Don't do that!"

His voice hardened. "Do you understand me?"

My long-time habit of appeasing kicked in. "Yes. Yes. Yes. I don't plan to."

"Good." He smiled again, his voice going all sweetness. "Then, I'll give you your present."

He pulled another ring box from his pocket. Done in deep red velvet, it looked antique. He'd scared me enough that my hands shook while I lifted its lid. It was a ring—a huge ring. The filigreed setting held several diamonds on each side of its large red stone. It flopped on my finger—too big around and too big across.

"You can get it sized some day. Don't ever wear it here."

"Thank you. You're very generous." I nearly gagged on my words.

"You are the one who's generous. You make me happy and you deserve nice things.

At home, I kneeled beside the bed in the dark and slid the ring as far back under the mattress as I could reach—next to the gold nugget. On my knees there, my hand touching both gifts, a familiar sick feeling roiled my stomach. I slumped to the floor and tears stung my eyes. Against my will, I replayed the slimy scene with Mr. Wilke.

How much longer can I stand this?

As usual, I refused to allow my conscience to be heard. "It's not my fault," I shouted.

I jumped up, turned on all the lights and grabbed a paperback book I'd been reading. Curled up on the couch, holding the book before my face, I read the same words over and over.

No use. I flung the book across the room.

I had to allow myself to think about the situation I'd created with Mr. Wilke.

Looking back at my decision, I realized how foolish I'd been. If I'd refused him in the beginning, he probably wouldn't have fired me. I'd panicked.

I reasoned that, being a gentle, generous man, he would likely keep me on even if I backed out of our deal. I was an asset to his business, a fast, reliable bartender. Even as I made the decision to end it, I knew in my heart that to tell him would take all the courage I could ever muster.

When morning came, I had something new to worry about. After my shower, I noticed several tiny red spots at the edge of my pubic hair. *What the hell?* Closer inspection was called for as the explanation began to dawn on me. I pulled off one of the spots and examined it closely. It moved and it had legs.

Damn him! How could I be so stupid?

As soon as I was dressed, I called Karen. She couldn't stop laughing. Said she didn't know what to do, and she was "sure as shit not going to the drugstore." The rest of the day, aware that little creatures were crawling around in my most private place, I could hardly sit still.

The minute Jimmy came to work that night I hustled him into a corner and pounded his arms that reached for me. "You SOB, you gave me crabs."

"Calm down, babe. I didn't know it 'til this morning. I was going to tell you tonight."

"You better tell that red-head you slept with last night, too, asshole."

"I didn't sleep with her, Suzanne. In spite of what you think, I don't sleep with every woman I see."

"Well, what are you going to do about it? I'm not going to a doctor."

"Use camphor, it kills the little critters. But be careful, it can burn like hell."

"Mr. Wise Guy, how do you know so much about it? You've been here before?"

He gave me a disgusted look. "I talked to the guys at work."

"I guess your Bimbo gave you a little going away present, didn't she? She must have chippied on you, huh? It doesn't take three weeks to get crabs."

"She was a slut. Does it make you happy to hear me say it?"

"Yes!"

He reached out to stroke me. "I'm really sorry I did this to you, babe. Really sorry." When he felt me stiffen, he stepped back. "What's going on with you and Pedro?"

I gave him a go-to-hell look, turned and walked away. Sleeping with him was another mistake I'd never make again.

CHAPTER 7

▼

Mark strolled in at his usual time, winked, then sat down in front of my mixing station. My cheeks warmed as he smiled at me, his white teeth glowing in the dim light. There was little time for me to do more than smile back and pass a few words as I worked the bar. The way Mr. Wilke had reacted I chose to be careful with my attention.

Jimmy watched intently from the bandstand, as did Mr. Wilke from his seat at the end of the bar. The room seemed to grow smaller with the three of them in it. How could Mark miss the other two staring at me?

As the long, tense evening drew to a close, I was relieved that the Mr. and Mrs. Wilke said good night. The next time we were alone, I intended to tell him, but I still didn't know what I would say.

Jimmy packed up his equipment and left at two without a backward glance. He was probably too embarrassed about the crabs to pester me.

Mark stayed until I said "last call" at two-thirty, then got up and left with the rest of the crowd. "See you at one tomorrow," he said. "Sleep well."

I did.

Sunday morning I awoke early, groaned at the gray and drizzly sky. First I thought of my date with Mark, then I remembered my unwanted pubic guests. *Yikes.* I jumped into my clothes and dashed across the street to the grocery store. Although my face flushed, I told myself that the clerk would have no idea of the camphor's intended purpose.

I spread the medicine all around, careful of the delicate parts—but it didn't matter. I'd have walked through fire to get rid of the loathsome creatures.

Who knows where the nasty critters are hiding?

In just three hours, Mark would arrive, so I stripped the bed and the spread off the couch. I poured the oil on my hands, and smeared it around on the mattress. It might not kill them, but maybe it would run them into the next county. Next I lugged the bedding down the street to the Laundromat and poured in enough bleach to poison the buggers.

While the washer ran, I rushed back home to built a fire in my little stove, then left two windows and the front door open to air the house. After everything dried, I put the bed back together, hoping to lock in any odor.

Since I had no manual for the killing of crabs, I decided they should be dead by noon. I showered, planning to give them another dose later. When I came out of the bathroom, the damp air and the wood heat had cleansed the house of all traces of the camphor.

Mark arrived promptly at one o'clock. In daylight, he looked even more handsome. Dressed in sharply creased slacks and a silky ivory shirt, he looked like he'd stepped out of a movie magazine. My pulse raced with nervousness. Inviting a man I hardly knew into my home was quite different from seeing him in the bar. I picked up my coat and edged toward the door.

"We better get going," he said. "It's a half hour to Springfield. Red Falcon has a great brunch until two. Are you hungry?"

"Starved. I forgot breakfast."

He hurried to the passenger side and opened the door to his red convertible, which sparkled with beaded drops of rain.

"Your car's gorgeous. You just polished it?"

"I keep it paste waxed. My '56 Caddy's destined to be a classic, you know."

While we ate, we talked about our lives. He'd grown up in California, enjoying its warm weather and beaches. Since I'd spent my entire life in Barkerville, I didn't have much to tell. But he drew me out on my marriage, and what had happened to Jimmy and me.

In the movie, I was extremely aware of the place where our shoulders touched. After a few minutes, he reached for my hand and held it loosely. I felt like a high-school girl, far removed from Mr. Wilke and crabs and my failed marriage—so ordinary and comfortable there in the dark, laughing at Jerry Lewis. When Mark squeezed my hand, Jimmy's ring pressed into my fingers and brought me back to reality.

Driving toward Barkerville after dark, I asked him how long he was going to be staying in town.

He glanced at me, his eyes bright in the dashboard's green light. "That depends."

I wasn't sure what he was getting at, so I just smiled.

When we pulled up to my door, my earlier nervousness returned. He'd made no moves on me. Should I ask him to come in? Dating was all so new to me. Did I dare?

He made no effort to get out of the car, so I followed his lead and leaned my head back against the seat, then closed my eyes. He reached across and turned my face with his soft hand. "Why the heavy sigh?"

"No reason."

"I'll bet you're worried about me wanting to come in…get tangled in that hair of yours," he whispered, as he nibbled at the corner of my eyebrow.

I didn't answer.

His lips found their way to my mouth and covered it with a long kiss that I felt deep in the center of my body. Several years had passed since a kiss had caused that kind of electricity to shoot through me. I was shaken. When the kiss ended, I pressed my feet to the floor to stop my knees from shaking and tried to slow and quiet my breathing. I hoped he didn't realize the chaos he'd created in me.

He seemed in complete control of himself—unlike I'd expected. He pulled away, leaned back on his seat, took out cigarettes and offered me one. I declined. I couldn't steady my hands. He hummed a ditty from the movie as he smoked.

I soon recovered and relaxed.

"I'm afraid I'm going to have to leave your lovely company in a few minutes." He fingered a strand of my hair. "I have to play at O'Dougals over in Springfield tonight."

"Play?"

"I play the piano. Usually, I'm on the piano-bar from eight to ten."

"You never told me you were a musician."

"Well, it never came up." He frowned. "You're not down on musicians, are you?"

"No. It's just…music has caused me a lot of problems." I was disappointed. He probably had a girl in every port. "Thanks for lunch and the movie."

He opened my car door and walked me up on the porch. In the doorway, he pulled me to him, held me close for several seconds. His muscular arms around me felt good.

I put my face up for his kiss and he gave me a quick peck. "Bye for now. I'll see you soon." He hurried to his car and I went inside.

The sexual fire he'd started still burned. I sat down on the couch and hugged myself.

What am I doing? Don't I have enough problems without getting involved with another musician?

Restless and disturbed by thoughts of whether I really wanted to start a new relationship—and its inevitable outcome—I tried to imagine having sex with someone other than Jimmy. Fear of that kind of intimacy, with a man so much older and undoubtedly more experienced, made it impossible to contemplate so soon.

Rain pounded and wind whipped around the eaves of my little house, invading my thoughts. I hated windy nights, and I didn't want to be alone with all my thoughts, so I decided to go next door to the bar for dinner.

On Sunday evenings, local wannabe musicians came to the White Water with their instruments and held a sing-along—Mitch Miller style. The country folk of our town loved the oldies, requesting the same songs over and over. A surprising number delighted in climbing up on the bandstand to sing on microphone. One schoolteacher I'd known all my life dominated the stage until our ears ached. Someone would say, "Come on Jen, give somebody else a chance." She'd go away hurt and refuse to even tap her foot the rest of the night.

"Well, look who's here," one of the regulars said as I stepped in through the back door. "Can I buy my favorite bartender a drink?"

"Sure, I'll have a Bud."

"You gonna get up there and sing for us tonight?"

I shook my head emphatically. "Oh, no! I don't sing."

"You do, too. I hear you singing behind the bar all the time. You're good."

"Thanks a lot, but I don't sing up there." Except with Karen, I sang only under cover of the jukebox, never around home in front of my husband—or any other musician. I quit the choir when grandma told me I couldn't carry a tune in a bushel basket.

I ordered a burger and fries from the kitchen, then sat at the bar with my beer and hummed along with the crowd. It was a good crowd—everyone laughed and sang together on the stormy spring evening. Spending my first night on the opposite side of the bar since I started work, I felt secure and happy with my community of friends. When the sing-along ended at ten, I slipped out the back door.

In my cabin, lying in bed, I relived Mark's kiss. Thoughts of us sitting in the red car under the yard light with the rainwater snaking down the windshield, making its strange patterns on his handsome face, played in my mind. How my body reacted. What harm was there in a kiss? None. While the Oregon rain drummed on the roof, I fell asleep with that answer in my mind.

Monday morning, when I rolled over in bed, sunshine hit my face—blazing through my bedroom doorway as it first rose above the eastern hills. Karen arrived before I'd dressed. We'd planned a trip to Eugene to shop for paint, a bedspread and curtains for my bedroom.

"Whatcha been doin'?" She watched as I rummaged for something to wear. "You haven't called since Saturday. What about the crabs?"

"God, that was creepy." I told her what I'd done about them Sunday morning.

"What's happening with old man Wilke?"

I handed her the ring. "Could be a ruby for all I know. It's so big."

"Suzanne, this has got to be worth a damn fortune. Shit, I bet he *is* giving away his wife's jewelry."

"I feel bad. But, damn it, I need it more than she does. If it weren't me it'd be someone else. Just so she doesn't find out it's me. Not a peep to anyone. I'm telling him I'm done."

"How's he going to take that?"

"That's what I'm worried about. Saturday night he got ornery about Mark. He heard us making a date."

"You've got a date with Heart-Throb? When?"

"Already had it. We went to a movie Sunday."

"And?"

"And he kissed me. I shook for ten minutes."

"Is that all? Did he try anything?"

"No, he didn't. He's a perfect gentleman…almost too perfect."

"What'd you want? To farm out your little visitors?" She roared at her joke.

"You know I wouldn't sleep with him. But, a couple more of those kisses wouldn't hurt. He's a musician."

"Oh no! That's all you need."

"Piano-bar. I bet babes hang all over him, just like Jimmy…he always comes in late.

"You going out again?"

"Maybe. He's the best looking…most interesting guy in this town. Do you think it's too soon for me to go out?"

"Hell no! What do you think Jimmy's doing? You deserve some fun."

We had a good time shopping, eating and talking the rest of the day. After dinner, Karen dropped me off at home around eight. There was a note on my door: "Came by to see how you and your little friends were doing. Love, Jimmy."

No use chumming it up to me, mister. I'll never sleep with you again.

CHAPTER 8

▼

The rhythm of my life stayed good for a few days and I rehearsed what I'd say to Mr. Wilke the next time that we were alone. Friday morning when I went into the bar for my paycheck, he and Mrs. Wilke sat at a table with two women. He excused himself, moved to the bar and gave me my pay envelope.

When he started back to the table, he motioned me along. "Come on, I want to introduce you," he said. "These ladies over here are the new owners."

Stunned, my heart flipped at thoughts of unemployment. My legs felt weak as I followed him to the table.

"I'd like you to meet Marge and Lindy Milligan. They'll be taking over on Monday."

"Glad to meet you, Suzanne. I hear good things about you," the younger one, Lindy, said.

"I hear you're a hell of a bartender," Marge said. "We'll darn sure be keeping you on. Neither of us plans to spend much time behind that bar."

Relieved, I stood at their table smiling foolishly with the pay envelope in my shaking hand. It quickly dawned on me then that my situation with Mr. Wilke would end without my needing to tell him.

Eager to see what my envelope held, I excused myself to go back home. Just outside the back door, I ripped it open. Two crisp one hundred-dollar bills were tucked behind my $68 check. This would be the last of it. Thank God. *And, thank you, Mr. Wilke.* He probably knew all along that he'd soon be gone—that's why he'd been so generous. Whether he knew or not, I was damn glad it was nearly over.

That night and the next, he hovered like a hungry buzzard, then extracted his full measure at the end of both shifts. Saturday night, the last night I'd have to perform for him, he somehow got his wife out of the way early. His attention in front of the Milligan sisters made me nervous, but if I could keep them from noticing anything, I'd be home free. Better yet, if they'd linger after closing time, I might escape altogether.

Escape was not to be—they filed out at two.

As he locked the doors and turned out lights, Mr. Wilke's shoulders slumped and his feet shuffled. He looked sad and dejected. I felt sorry for the old man. I tried to believe it was sadness at giving up the business he'd run for so long, but I didn't think so. I thought he was sad because he was old and lonely.

"The van will be here tomorrow. We're moving to Portland. This will be our last drink together." He leaned against the bar in front of me, forcing me to look at him. "What can I get for you, sweet punkin'?" He patted my hand. "How about a nice Christian Brothers? You've worked very hard."

"Perfect. In a snifter, please." Sometimes the old man made me feel special in a way I'd never experienced. Who else in the world cared if I worked hard? Not Jimmy, for sure. In the time I'd worked for Mr. Wilke, he'd found many ways to be considerate of me, beyond the money and gifts.

Entering my role as his plaything, I had a glimpse of why young girls might become the wives of old men. His adoration filled my need to feel special. At that moment, I could imagine myself the child-bride of some rich old gentleman, escaping Barkerville forever. Having no money worries. Living in a big house. Driving a new car. When the trail of my imagination reached the point of consummating such a marriage, I shuddered.

Swirling the brandy, breathing in its fragrance, I stayed in my fantasy. I owed Mr. Wilke the best final act I could muster. "You were good to give me this job and the gifts. You've more than kept your side of the bargain. Thank you."

"No, no. I thank you." He patted my hand again. "You have given me the last pleasure I'll have in this lifetime…a lovely gift to a lonely old man. My wife hasn't let me touch her for twenty years." He lowered his head, his voice low and sad. "And…that's a long, long time." He sat quietly beside me, drinking his Johnny Walker, his usual eagerness temporarily replaced by melancholy.

After finishing his drink, he turned to me. "I have one more gift for you."

He pulled another jewelry box from his pocket and flipped it open. Inside, on an intricate gold chain, a diamond pendant sparkled in the dim light of the back-bar. He looked up at my sudden intake of breath. "Oh, you like this one?" He smiled proudly. "I bought this for my wife when we first met, but she has never worn it in the thirty years of our marriage. She was your age when I gave it to her." He held it, spinning, in front of me. "It's a flawless diamond. Two carats…so take good care of it. Let me put it on."

Watching the pitiful man saddened me. Tears stung my eyes. He'd married a woman thirty-seven years his junior. Had she been a gold-digger like me? I chose to think so. It helped salve my conscience about taking her diamond.

Get off the sentimental jag and get this over with.

I stood and slowly unbuttoned my blouse, revealing the black lace I knew he liked. His arthritic fingers fumbled in my cleavage where the fastener nestled then he released the hooks. He raised the long gold chain over my head and let the diamond drop between my bare breasts.

"Look here." He turned me toward the smoky mirror. As I turned, the pendant caught the light, shooting brilliant sparks. "It belongs there between those perfect titties."

With a moan, he lowered his face to my chest. When he'd satisfied his need, he raised his head. Cradling my face in his clammy hands, he pleaded, "Please, let me see all of you. I won't touch. Just this once."

Still in a sympathetic mood, I picked up my brandy snifter and drained it while I thought this over. *What the hell? What can it hurt?*

He poured more brandy. I took another drink, starting to feel that familiar tingle in my legs as the glow spread from my stomach. Without a word, I unzipped my slacks and stepped out of them. I stood tall, shoulders back, in my black lace panties. As his gaze moved up and down my body, his breathing changed to a huffing sound, his glazed, watery eyes were wide.

"Oh, my." He spoke more to himself than to me. "Oh, my." A long minute passed. I stood like a statue as he made quiet sounds. Finally, reality crowded back—reality that what I was doing was not an act in some play, but the real thing—something disgusting.

I stepped back into my slacks.

"Thank you." Light glinted off a tear coursing down his wrinkled, white face. "Thank you, so much."

I looked away, deeply embarrassed. More than anything, I wanted it to end—to be out of there as quickly as possible. I couldn't shake the guilt about taking the diamond.

I picked up my brandy glass and held it toward him. "Here's to your retirement."

He tipped his glass to mine, then wiped his face and sniffled. "Here's to your future. You'll make something of yourself, I'm sure."

"Thank you."

When I'd finished my brandy, I put on the rest of my clothes, said good night and left by the back door.

In my cabin, I pulled the curtains in my bedroom and took the other gifts from under the mattress. I sat looking at them, thinking about what I'd done to get them. I felt more shame at the magnitude of the gifts than what I'd done to earn them. Had I taken unfair advantage of an old man? Of his wife? I knew nothing more about her than what he'd told me. Was I no better than a whore? Should I return his gifts? Every ounce of my being answered, *absolutely not*, and I ordered my conscience to be still. After what I'd done to get them? It was unthinkable. I needed the jewelry—my ticket out of Barkerville.

Eventually, I convinced myself that my actions were justified, and that I had given fair trade.

Sunday morning when Karen and I got together for breakfast, I told her about the new owners and about my last night with Mr. Wilke. I handed her the necklace. "It belonged to his wife. She'd put it in their safe deposit box…left it for years."

"Wow! She's going to crap when she finds that gone." Karen dropped it in her lap and clamed up when the waitress came, then pulled it out again when she left. "That's one hell of a diamond. How big do you think?"

"He said she never gets in the lock-box…she'll find out when he dies. Two carat."

"Jesus, this is big bucks."

"I know one thing, I'll never do anything like this again." I held up my right hand. "So help me God."

"It turned out okay. You got the best end of the deal." She polished the diamond on her shirt. "What's going on with you and Mark?

"Saw him in the middle of the week, but not Friday or Saturday. Maybe he's playing somewhere." When the waitress started toward us with our food, I motioned for Karen to hide the pendant. "Jimmy's little redhead waited for him both nights. He told me last weekend he wasn't sleeping with her, but I bet he is by now. You seen anything of him?"

"Dinner at mom and dad's Thursday night. Mom asked him if you two were getting back together. He said 'doesn't look too promising. She's hot for some spic.' How did he know?"

"Jesus. I hate that word. Because I flirted my head off right in front of him."

Karen and I spent the rest of Sunday in her lawn chairs working on our tans in the May sunshine, and then we drove to Eugene to a movie.

Monday morning I began the job of painting white over the dirty sky-blue in my living room. With the door open to let out the fumes, I saw Mark's car cut across the White Water's parking lot. When he stopped in front of my porch, I stepped outside, roller in hand.

"Well, Mr. Painter, you're just in time." I gestured for him to come inside. "Show me your stuff."

He got out of his car and looked me up and down. "You're mighty fetching in those baggy jeans...that scarf on your hair."

I curtsied. "You're too kind."

Mark, in tan slacks topped with a butter-yellow sweater, definitely looked like someone who didn't belong in Barkerville. From the top of his carefully barbered head to his suede loafers, the look said style. And money.

Following me inside, he picked up the small trim-brush that lay in the paint tray, dipped it and with quick, bold strokes, began to draw on an unpainted section of the wall.

"What the—?"

He put his finger to his lips. "Shhh. Turn sideways."

Watching him glance back and forth from me to the wall, I soon realized the figure he was drawing was my profile, not an Indian. But with my high cheekbones and long hair it could have been. I smiled, remembering the first night I met him when I'd asked if he painted war paint.

"I love it. I want to keep it."

"Do you have string and a pencil?"

He tied a length of yarn to the pencil and used it to draw a circle around his picture, then I picked up the roller and quickly painted up to the line that framed the white lady in the blue circle.

"In a couple of weeks, when it's dried, you can wash the wall." He grabbed the roller and filled it with paint. "Let's get this job done and go for a ride."

I took it from his hand. "You can't do that in those fancy clothes. They'll look like mine."

We laughed and threatened each other with paint, then compromised—I finished the wall while he brushed fluffy clouds onto the blue ceiling.

After we'd cleaned up, he said, "Ready?"

"I'll change." I partially closed the bedroom door but we talked while I dressed. I felt completely at ease with a semi-stranger in my house as I undressed, pulled on shorts and a light sweater and quickly pulled my hair into its usual ponytail.

He whistled his approval when I came out of the bedroom. "How about showing me around the valley? We'll put the top down. Better get a jacket."

The early spring temperature was in the high seventies—nearly perfect. Wildflowers filled the roadsides and fields. I directed him west toward the bottomland.

We approached what remained of my family's land. "Stop here." I pointed out a grove of oaks at the edge of a meadow where the remnants of a log cabin with a stone fireplace stood. "My great, great grandfather, Ebenezer Holly homesteaded this over a hundred years ago."

As we sat in the sun, looking across the field to the river, he gently ran his fingers up and down the back of my neck. "Where did your grandparents hail from?"

"He came here from northern Texas by way of the California gold fields in his late twenties. Up 'til then, he had quite a life. As a boy, he lived with the Comanche for two years."

"No! My mother was White Mountain Apache, raised up in northern Arizona. She moved to California, too…Los Angeles. Before I was born. My father left when I was in college. I quit then and started my insurance business."

"When I was young and foolish, I planned on college. But it wasn't in the cards."

"Why? You seem smart."

"No money. So, I married instead. Want to walk to the river?"

As we walked toward the stream, he held my elbow, guided me through the tall grass—all the time caressing my arm.

"When Ebenezer was five, he and his older sister were playing in a meadow like this. Indians crept up and grabbed him. His sister got away…or maybe they didn't want her, I'm not sure. They rode for weeks to the Indians' camp."

As we continued toward the river, I told him of the search party his father formed and how they gave up after two months.

While we walked, Mark picked Bachelor's Buttons. Seeing a man pick wildflowers was a first for me. It made me ever more fascinated with him.

We sat on a log, and he worked with the flowers while I continued the story. "His father, a Captain of the Rangers, got Sam Houston to treaty with the Indians. Finally, after two years, they brought him back. His mother barely recognized him…except for his mess of curly red hair. He had a fit when they pulled him from the arms of the old woman that cared for him. She was heartbroken, too."

"He probably couldn't speak English. What did they do then?"

"Sent him up to Oklahoma to boarding school to be sure she didn't come back for him."

Mark looked up from the garland he was weaving from the flowers. "What a story."

"Don't know a lot more, except his love for the Indians changed a few years later. A small band that crossed the Red River to steal their prize stallion killed his father. Ebenezer stayed in Texas long enough to fight with the Texas Cavalry. Then he and his brother got the gold bug."

Mark stood, pulled me up and placed the blue flower wreath on my head. "There. You look just like a princess."

There by the river, warmed by the sun, I felt like a princess.

While we made our way back toward the car, I told him that my grandfather, who lived just over the rise, still had the little beaded buckskin suit of clothes. "Would you like to see them sometime?"

"I'd love to take a picture...to paint from."

We drove on and I pointed out another ranch. "This is the land Ebb's brother homesteaded. They both had big families. Half the people in this valley are related to me, so careful what you say!"

Mark's hand rested on my bare leg as we rolled along—probably a casual gesture on his part, but distracting to me. All my awareness centered on that smooth hand, the brown fingers with their close-cropped nails against my white thigh. That spot on my leg grew hotter.

"Pull in this road...I'll show you where I was raised."

We drove down the long lane and stopped at a gate.

Mark put his arm around my shoulders and played with my hair. "I can see you in that barn, milking the cow...giving the cat a squirt."

"Never! I hated that barnyard stuff. I took care of the house and the yard."

"Oh yes, now I'm getting it." He made a camera-like frame with his fingers. "There you are baking bread, churning butter."

"No, that's me ironing with the flat-irons, washing on the washboard. I hated that place."

He lifted my hands and looked at my palms. "Perfect, no scars or calluses here." He nibbled my fingertips, sending ripples of excitement up my arms. "Do your folks still live here?"

"Nope. The IRS took this place four years ago. My dad was a logger who didn't keep up his payroll taxes. They moved to Eureka after that."

Our next stop, the old swimming hole, was deserted on that spring Monday. He fetched a blanket from his car's trunk and spread it on the warm sand, and then we stretched out beside the green water. I lay on my back, looking at drifting clouds, listening to the rushing water and buzzing insects. The sweet smell of nearby azaleas floated on the air. After the chilly ride in the convertible, the sun's heat made me drowsy.

Mark found my hand on the blanket and squeezed it then sighed. "Perfect."

Minutes passed without words. Crickets chirped, birds sang, a far away duck called.

After awhile, Mark rolled to his side, raised on his elbow and looked down at me. "I notice you've taken off your wedding band, but you still wear the diamond."

"Keeps people guessing."

"I like a mystery woman." Dark eyes smiling into mine, he leaned down and kissed me—not the deep kiss of our last date, but a very friendly kiss. Though gentle and sweet, I felt it in the same place I'd felt the first one. His hand rested on my waist and I knew he recognized the reaction as my stomach tightened. He pulled back and looked at me with a quizzical smile, as if asking how far to go.

"Let's stay here and enjoy the sun. And go slow," I said.

He sat up and looked out over the McKenzie. "Perfect."

I lay with my eyes closed as he pitched stones into the river and talked about his childhood in El Monte. He'd been raised in a strict Catholic family but no longer attended church. He mentioned he'd tithed $6,000 to his church when he sold his business. I was astounded that he'd give so much to a church he no longer seemed to care about. All in all, he seemed like a decent guy—not arrogant, as he might be with his Valentino good looks.

From his fist, he sprinkled a tiny stream of sand across my arm. "Let's go out to Sophie's and have a beer."

The tiny tavern, twelve miles upriver, was owned and operated by Sophie Tortelli, whose real name was Ruth. She'd gone a little crazy when her husband died. For twenty years, they'd operated a small sporting goods store in Barkerville. As a close friend of her youngest daughter, I'd spent time in her home and store over the years, watching the husband control his wife and six daughters with gentle, but old-world ways.

As soon as she put him in the ground, she began to make up for lost time. She sold the store and bought the tavern, changed her hair color from nearly white to golden blonde, and changed her name and the tavern's to Sophie. Her drab housedresses were traded for skin-tight jeans with boots or skin-tight lamé with golden slippers. Her five-foot tall, Jane Mansfield figure spilled from whatever she wore. I'd heard last winter that she danced the bunny hop in the nude after a night of strip poker at her tavern. I loved her, but sometimes I felt embarrassed for her when she went to extremes.

"Do you know Sophie?" I said.

"No. But I've heard about her."

"Prepare yourself."

When we walked in, Sophie yelped. "Eeyow! Suzanne, how the hell are you, sweetie? I haven't seen you in a coon's age. I heard you shit-canned that chippy old man of yours. Who's this beautiful hunk of meat?"

"Now, behave yourself, Sophie. This is my friend, Mark."

"He's got a scrumptious ass, honey. Does he know what to do with it?" My face flushed and so did his. "Looky at those red faces. Folks, these two been doin' the nasty."

"Sophie! You're impossible. Give us a beer. I want a Bud and I think Mark wants a Rainier. You've made him speechless."

He nodded, laughing. "Sophie, you're everything I've heard."

"And more, honey. You come see old Sophie anytime."

We drank our beers and watched her. I loved the sound of her soft Missouri accent. Her tiny tavern was full, as always. Everyone hung around to see what outlandish thing she'd do next. Sophie's incredible energy amazed me. She never seemed to slow down.

She came from behind the bar and did a quick bump and grind then dropped into the lap of a surprised truck driver seated at the table next to the jukebox. After pulling off his hat, she ran her hands over his balding head and nuzzled his cheek.

"Wanta dance, big boy?"

He ducked his head, whispered something and wrapped his arms around her butt.

"You naughty boy." She laughed, pretending to slap his face. "I said dance, not make a pass. When I want you to feel my ass, honey, I'll let you know."

She jumped up, swung her hips to the beat, and danced back behind the bar.

"Now, I gave that fella' the chance to rub bellies with me, didn't I?" she announced to the laughing crowd at the bar. "There ain't a damn truck driver comes in here with any guts. Suzanne, I been hearin' for years what lovin' machines they are. Ain't a single one'll prove it." She grabbed Mark's hand with both of hers. "You a truck driver, kid?"

"Sure wish I was, Sophie."

His brazen answer surprised me.

"Hot damn, I like this one." She kissed his hand with a loud smack and winked at me.

As she moved on down the bar, teasing a trio of fishermen about their fishy smells, Mark said, "I love her. She's priceless. Does she really live up to that talk?"

"Sometimes."

When we got up to leave, Sophie rushed from behind the bar. "I just gotta give this beautiful thing a hug before he leaves."

She wrapped her arms around Mark, straddled his leg and squirmed in his arms. He looked helpless and sweaty-faced as he patted her on the back and looked over her shoulder at me.

I tugged his arm, laughing in mock anger. "Come on, Sophie, give me back my man."

"Oh, all right." She released him, her eyes twinkling at her audience. "Now, if she don't treat you right, honey, you just come see old Sophie." She threw us a kiss. "Bye, bye, kiddies."

It was nearly dark when we left Sophie's, too cool for top-down driving. As we neared my house, Mark said, "Sorry to leave, but I have a gig at nine. I've had the best time today I've had in ages. Are your days off the same with the new owners?"

"As far as I know. Sunday and Monday."

"Good, then how about us going to the coast next Sunday. I'll pick you up as early as you want to get up."

"I haven't been there for over a year. I'll be ready at nine."

He shut off the engine when we got to my house and I boldly leaned across him and tilted my face for a kiss. He wrapped his arms around me and kissed me long and hard. The kiss sent wave after wave from my lips downward through my body. When he groaned softly and squirmed in his seat as he released me, I knew it had the same effect on him.

"As Sophie would say, you sure make my blood boil." He gave me one last peck. "You'll excuse me if I don't get out."

CHAPTER 9

▼

Tuesday, my first night under the new bosses, didn't seem very different. Instead of Mr. Wilke, the Milligan sisters watched me. They sat at the end of the bar, like owners always did. I studied them, too.

Lindy Milligan, who looked fifteen years younger than Marge, was the pretty one: shapely, lean and muscular with an exotic face. Her olive complexion, dark-brown hair without a strand of gray and raven-black eyes made her look Mexican or Italian.

Unlike Lindy, Marge was pale and washed out—ash blond hair, turning white, and milky blue eyes. She'd dressed in an unbecoming tee shirt that emphasized her large breasts and huge belly. With a flat butt and bird legs, she probably didn't weigh any more than Lindy, but she was anything but exotic.

In spite of these differences, something in their faces told of their sisterhood, a similarity too vague to label. They had to be half-sisters. Since the women both bore the same last name, I assumed they might be spinsters.

They seemed good-natured most of the evening but started to bicker toward the end of my shift. Because business was slow, I had time to stand and talk with them.

"I've owned bars for thirty years," Marge said, her voice loud and coarse. "Mostly beer bars. My first one...I was only twenty-five. Up in Washington. Metaline Falls, on the Canadian border. That was before I married Milligan."

Milligan's her married name? There went my theory about spinsters.

She continued her story, drew air pictures with her highball. "I figured out where the money was damn early. Not husbands. No, siree. Bars. That's where the money is. Bars." She downed her seventh vodka and Squirt, then motioned for another. They were affecting her speech, and the lid of her slightly crossed left eye drooped. "Never should've married that son-of-a-bitch. Always had his sights on my bar." She jerked her head toward Lindy. "Among other things."

"Damn it! Don't start on that again." Lindy, who'd matched her drink for drink, turned on her stool to face Marge. "That was a long time ago."

Marge slapped the bar and raised her voice. "Not damn long enough for me to forget what he did to us."

I jumped in to sidetrack their argument. "Where was the last bar you had before this one?"

Marge gave me an unfocused smile. "Up in John Day. Ever been there?"

"No, I guess I don't know John Day." *How could I, I've never been out of Lane County.* "Washington?"

"No. No. Oregon. Over east of the mountains. Little town on the John Day River."

Lindy's voice went soft. "Was a working-man's bar, like this one…only ranchers, too." She chuckled, looked up at the ceiling and smiled. "Those gypo loggers are such damn fools…alls they know is fightin', fishin', and fuckin'. Kept us going…trying to keep the peace. Wore me out. That's why I don't go behind the bar any—"

"Wasn't *all* that wore you out," Marge interrupted. "Was all them loggers chasin' you." She hee-hawed and slapped Lindy's arm. "One of these days one of them'll catch you, too."

"Don't bet on it!" Lindy fluffed her hair. "I just love 'em and leave 'em. One bad husband's enough for anybody."

Finally, after one more round, the sisters stumbled out back to their home. The Wilke's mobile, part of the deal, made it easy for them to get home when they drank too much. Many bar owners who drank found this the best arrangement. If an owner drove and got a 502, she'd almost surely lose her bar license, if not her driving license. It was illegal to drink any alcoholic beverages in their own bar, but neither the Wilkes nor the Milligans seemed to pay attention to that law.

As I closed that night, I puzzled over what I'd learned about the sisters. Marge had married a Milligan, and Lindy's name was Milligan, too. Married to brothers? Not really sisters at all, but sisters-in-law? Not likely.

As the week passed, I saw Jimmy and Mark sometime every day. Jimmy came in after work for a few beers. He'd sit at the end of the bar where I usually stood smoking during slow periods. I assumed he hoped to talk to me, but that time of the evening I was much too busy to chat. I decided his current redhead must be just a weekend date, because weeknights he seemed at loose ends.

One night, he grabbed my fingers when I wiped the bar in front of him. "Hey, babe, why don't you come home and keep me warm tonight?" He winked. "We won't tell your boyfriend."

"No, thanks. I know what's on your mind." I found it fun to flirt with him— a familiar old habit. But, when he had too much to drink, he was sarcastic and I wanted nothing to do with him.

He stayed past ten on Thursday, and Mark came in. My stomach lurched when he sat down beside Jimmy at the end of the bar.

"Howdy," I heard Jimmy say.

"How you doing?" Mark glanced at him, then turned to me. "Suzanne, my usual, please."

Too busy to stand and monitor their conversation, I still heard enough to make me nervous. Things like, "My *wife* will shake you for the music."

As they talked, I could see Jimmy's jaw muscles tighten, but Mark continued to look cheerful. After a tense fifteen minutes, Jimmy abruptly left.

Mark chuckled. "He doesn't seem like a bad sort of guy, but he sure wanted me to know you were his wife."

CHAPTER 10

▼

Right on time, Mark picked me up Sunday morning. Dressed in jeans and a sweatshirt, his hair still wet from the shower, he looked more like he belonged in Barkerville. We headed west to the coast, and in two hours were eating breakfast in Florence, a quaint coastal town at the mouth of the Siuslaw River. After finishing, we drove slowly up the coastline under cloud-spattered skies. We stopped at a beach near Otter Rock. He opened the trunk and handed me a folded blanket that lay beside a wicker picnic basket.

Very fancy.

He carried the basket and led the way down the beach and around the headlands. In a private spot, out of sight of the highway, he set the basket down and I dropped the blanket on top.

We explored the tide pools, and then climbed rock cliffs along the water enjoying the tangy salt breeze. After two hours, I was exhausted. "Enough! I'm pooped. Can we stop?"

"I didn't mean to tire you. Let's go back."

He took my hand and led me back to where we'd left the basket. He spread the blanket and we plopped down. There between two huge drift logs, we were protected from blowing sand.

He opened the basket and I watched in amazement while he unfolded a beautiful, pansy-print tablecloth, two wineglasses, and a bottle of Chianti. After pouring my wine, he pulled a huge switchblade from his pocket. I couldn't take my eyes off that wicked-looking knife while he cored and sliced the apples, then cut slices of bread and cheese. It seemed so out of character. He wiped the blade on his cloth napkin and put it back in his pocket.

Blushing, tongue-tied by the romantic setting he'd prepared, I blurted the first thing that came to mind. "Such royal treatment."

He brought an apple slice to my mouth. "The forbidden fruit."

"And when you have me under the spell?" *Brilliant, Suzanne. You need lots more practice at this game.*

"You will have to wait and see. It takes time…and wine to weave my spell." He poured his glass and refilled mine.

Because I saw Mark as a man of the world and myself as the country bumpkin, all I seemed to come up with was stupid, inane remarks, even though I was desperate to make a good impression.

He put his arms around me, removed the rubber band holding my hair, and then held me arm's length away. "There. I've waited a long time to do that." The wind blew my hair in a wild swirl that covered my face. He laughed, parted it like tent flaps and looked into my eyes. "Guess that won't work out here."

With the scarf from around my neck, I captured my flying hair and tied it back from my face, then took off my shoes and socks and sat sipping wine with my toes dug into the sand.

Resting in the sun, we did not speak, just ate and drank and stared across the breakers. The cadence of the crashing waves seemed to hypnotize me. After awhile, I stood up to stretch and looked over the drift log. The tide had come in. To my horror, I saw that the beach we'd walked in on had disappeared.

"Mark! Look!" Panic rippled in my stomach. "We need to run. Water's up to the rocks."

He jumped up. "You're right, let's go."

I picked up the blanket and Mark threw everything else into the basket. He followed as I ran down the beach with my shoes and socks in hand.

Over a hundred yards away, the rocky cliffs came down to what a couple of hours earlier had been hard sand, but had turned into lapping waves and white foam.

When we reached the cliffs, we stood catching our breath.

Mark, looking hesitant, grabbed my shoulder and shouted into my ear, "What if we wait it out? Climb over?"

Shaking my head, I mouthed a no.

I studied the sea, gathering courage to dash into the icy water. "Watch for the biggest wave." I yelled louder, my voice nearly swept away by the wind and crashing sea. "After it comes, run! There'll be small ones."

Mark's face had reddened. He looked unsure, glanced down at his feet, then pulled off his shoes. Poised to run, he held the shoes in one hand and the basket in his other.

I scanned the sea, watching its rhythm, gauging its depth as each wave rolled back. Filled with anxiety, I shouted, "Watch out for a sneaker!"

As soon as the next big wave hit and rolled back, I screamed, "Come on," and dashed into knee-deep water without looking back. I felt the sand suck from under my feet. Water rushed up to my thighs, and all I could see before me was water.

Just then Mark went by, grabbed my arm and pulled me along. A few more steps and I could see the beach sand on the other side. Another big wave slammed us. The shocking icy water on my chest tore my breath away and wrenched the blanket from my hand. I held tight to my shoes as I lurched forward, stumbling over rocks in the receding water.

Finally, my feet hit solid sand.

Mark, out of breath, dropped his shoes and bent over with his hands on his knees. I heard him utter a prayer. "Thank you, Father."

We both gasped for air, while we watched Mark's picnic basket bob in the surf. His crimson wool blanket fanned out on the sea like a bloodstain.

As was my usual reaction to an accident, I felt responsible in some way. "I'm so sorry about your stuff."

He stroked my wet hair. "It's not your fault."

I gave one last glance at the red splotch and turned toward the parking lot. "I'm freezing, let's go. At least we saved our shoes."

My teeth chattered as we squeezed what water we could out of our soaked jeans and sweatshirts. We put on our wet shoes over wet socks, then climbed into the car. Mark's lips were blue and his hands shook while he fumbled with the ignition.

"We can't drive for three hours in these wet clothes. This heater's not worth a damn."

Deep in my misery, I didn't answer.

"We'll get a room in Newport...so we can dry out."

Still, I said nothing, just sat hugging my wet sleeves. My tangled hair soaked his car seat.

Neither of us spoke in the ten miles back to Newport.

Near the middle of town he turned off at a sign pointing to the Mermaid Motel. When he went into the office, I sat in the car like a soggy lump. I'd never been to a motel. Jimmy and I had spent our wedding night on his aunt's couch.

Would he say I was his wife? I turned my engagement ring on my finger. Reality pushed its way through my cold-numbed brain. In a few moments I'd enter a motel room with a man I'd only gone to a movie with.

Mark opened my door and stood aside for me to enter. "Let's go." He was in charge of the situation and I let him be. "Get inside where it's warm."

Head bowed, I went to the rear of the room and looked out the sliding glass door toward the sea. He rushed to the heater, then to the electric range in the kitchenette next to me. I leaned my head on the glass and shivered, too numb to think what to do next.

Mark pressed a towel to my chest. "Here, wrap your hair. Take off those wet clothes."

I stared at him. *How the hell am I going to do that?*

"You've got to get out of them. You'll get a chill."

Standing there like a six year-old the first day of school, I stammered, "I th-th-think I already have one."

"Here." He grabbed the bottom of my sweatshirt, lifted it over my head. My arms automatically crossed over my bra. "You can leave that on, okay? Now, let's get those jeans off." He unbuttoned, then unzipped and tugged on them. Head down, I pulled them the rest of the way. "Go get in the shower," he ordered, "the hot water will warm you."

Eager to be out of his sight, I obeyed. When the water was as hot as bearable, I got in, then with my eyes closed turned from side to side letting it pour down my frozen arms for several minutes. Warm at last, I stopped shivering.

I felt the cool air as he pulled aside the curtain and stepped into the tub behind me. He whispered in my ear. "Move over." His hand moved up under my hair. "Are you getting warm?"

"Much better."

I felt silly standing in a shower in my underwear, and started to think ahead. Here I was in a motel room with all my clothes wet and a man behind me, probably naked. I couldn't stay there all day with my eyes closed.

"I'm warm now, you can get under here and I'll get out," I said.

Putting his cheek next to my ear and his hands on my shoulders, he pressed his upper body against my back. "Please don't."

My heartbeat quickened and sexual feelings, trying for a moment to win over timidity, stirred in my body. Quickly though, my timidity took the upper hand and I stepped out of the shower.

He laughed. "Coward!"

While he showered, I quickly pulled off my panties and bra, dried myself and made a sarong from the towel. His silk underwear lay on the oven door. I put them and mine on the oven's rack, turned the oven off and closed the door. After wringing them, he'd draped our jeans and sweatshirts on the two kitchen chairs and set them near the baseboard heater.

When the shower stopped, I turned my back and looked out the slider at the surf. I heard the bedsprings squeak. He spoke gently. "Come on in here. You can't stand there by the window all night."

In the near-darkness, I could see my own reflection and him sitting up in the bed behind me. There I was, in another of those spots I kept getting into, spots where my choices were limited.

Grow up, damn it. Quit acting like a teenager.

Embarrassed, I wanted to tell him not to look, but instead said nothing, just backed over to the bed and slid between the sheets, towel and all. I lay hardly breathing, covers to my chin.

Mark threw back his side of the blanket and jumped out of bed "We might as well watch some television." I caught a glimpse of his bare butt before I squeezed my eyes shut. "Want to watch this?"

"I don't care," I mumbled.

He found something that satisfied him, and then I felt his weight back on the bed. I opened my eyes then, staring at the screen while he sat up in bed beside me.

"We're sure having a hell of a day, aren't we?"

I nodded, glancing at his body. The muscles in his arms and chest rippled in the flickering light of the television. His tousled black hair fell into his eyes, Elvis Presley style.

As we watched Ed Sullivan, my mind was in overdrive. His naked body next to me made it impossible to comprehend what I was seeing on the screen.

Oh my God, I can't believe I'm here. What if Jimmy followed us? He could burst through the door. What if Mark makes a pass at me? What if he doesn't? Karen will never believe this.

After Ed Sullivan's last act, Mark scooted down into the bed, rose on his elbow and turned toward me. I forced myself to look at him and we made our first eye contact since we'd entered the room. "You've never done anything like this, have you?"

I looked at the ceiling. "You think I've been in a motel with a stranger before?"

"I'm not exactly a stranger. We've known each other a couple of months now." He put his hand on my cheek, turned my face toward him and kissed me tenderly and long, then pulled back and gave me a sincere look. "I won't do anything you don't want me to."

You won't do anything. That's just what Jimmy said.

We kissed again. My conscience railed. My body wanted to meld into his. As the kiss continued, it changed from tender to passionate. His hand circled my waist, squeezed harder. My desire grew and in spite of my best effort not to reveal it, my breathing quickened. A moan rose from my throat. My pelvis pressed toward him. I wanted the full embrace.

God! I need courage. I want this. What I need is a drink.

I moved toward him, more and more wanting to let it happen.

His hands moved to my hips and urged me closer. My hands, with a will of their own, found his smooth butt and pulled him closer. We stayed that way, kissing, grinding into each other. Finally, I rolled to my back and spread my legs, inviting him into my wetness with a tug on his shoulder. He lowered himself with a gentleness that made me groan in frustration. I pulled him to me harder. My eagerness stimulated him to long, sure strokes that took him quickly to the peak.

Momentarily, his body relaxed on mine, and then he pulled away, rolled to the side and let out a long "Aaahh."

While the unfulfilled passion slowly drained from my body, the realization of what I'd just done hammered in my mind. What did I know about the man I'd just fucked—yes, fucked—I couldn't call what we just did "making love." What happened to the promise I'd made since childhood never to have sex outside of marriage? I felt disgusted with myself—shamed by the wetness between my legs and by the sound of his soft snoring.

Get over it, Suzanne. This is life as it really is, not as you'd like it to be.

In the flashing lights of the television, I watched him sleeping and the disgust faded. He looked as handsome as ever, not like some ugly stranger who'd seduced me. I tried to recapture what I'd felt when he first reached for me, then fantasized how I might have played the shower scene differently—without the underwear, turning to look at his body instead of fleeing like a scared rabbit. Sleep overtook me somewhere during my shower fantasy.

In the morning light, shame washed over me again.

Just forget it, Suzanne, it's done.

I got my dry underwear from the oven and scurried into the shower, hoping to finish and dress before he woke up. Even though we'd made love, I was not ready to parade myself naked in front of him—or to see him parade in front of me.

As I wet my hair, Mark stepped into the shower and nuzzled the back of my neck. "Let me wash it."

I handed him the shampoo packet. He gently combed tangles with his fingers.

"This is unbelievable. How long since you've cut it?"

"Ten years."

"Don't ever cut it. It's so sexy." He turned me toward him, arranging it over my breasts. "I love your hair."

I pulled back from him. "Please stay in here while I dress, I'm not comfortable like this."

"That will not be easy." He held back the shower curtain while I stepped out.

I quickly dried and put on my still-damp clothes, then moved outside through the sliding doors and stood watching a young boy running in the surf with his big shaggy dog while his parents strolled arm in arm. I heard the door open behind me, but didn't turn around.

He slipped his arm around my waist and growled into my neck. "Want to go on a picnic, little girl?"

"Pretty good trick, Slick. Much better than running out of gas on a country road. You 'bout starved me to death though. Let's go find breakfast."

After we'd eaten, we started home. Somewhere near Florence, he stopped at an old weather-grayed shack with blankets hanging over the windows.

Gently pushing on the top of my head, he said, "You stay here…keep down. I've got some business and I don't want to involve you. Trust me, don't worry about it."

He took a black leather briefcase from the trunk into the house. In less than five minutes he returned.

I was curious, but decided it was none of my business.

When we reached my house, there was a note from Jimmy. Large, angry-looking words demanding to know where I'd been all night. I felt a little sick and a little scared. After all, I was still a married woman.

"Are you all right?"

I nodded.

"I have to go now. I missed my gig last night…but it was worth it." He kissed the tip of my nose. "I'll see you tomorrow night."

CHAPTER 11

▼

Several nights came and went with no sign of Mark—or Jimmy.

I've made such a fool of myself, sleeping with a stranger. I waited four years to be Jimmy's virgin bride. Now look at me.

As the days passed, humiliation turned to anger.

By Friday night, I'd picked up the Milligan sisters' pattern. They drank every day, and then quarreled every night. Bits and pieces of their story came out.

"Milligan cheated on every woman he ever met," Marge said.

"You *knew* that, Marge. He was married when he messed with you."

"Damn him, he was married when he messed with *you.*"

"Let's not go into it again tonight." Lindy turned toward where I stood at the end of the bar trying to look like I wasn't listening. "We quit speaking for ten years over this, for God sake."

Near midnight Mark appeared. With a goofy smile on his face, he caught my eye, threw up his hands and shrugged. "Been out of town," he said, as he sat down. "How are you doing?"

"Perfectly well, thank you. Your usual?"

"You mad at me?"

"Why should I be?" I turned away to get his Rainier. When I set it down I didn't look at him, just took his money and went to work.

What right do I have to be mad? I don't own this guy. But, I'm not going to be a handy lay for him either.

Later, when I saw him empty his bottle, I went back and asked if he wanted another.

"Only if you'll let me buy you breakfast."

I didn't want to end the relationship and have no one, but I didn't want a repeat of Sunday either. "Maybe…if that's *all* you have in mind."

"Fair enough. Give me another beer."

Jimmy, who'd never followed-up on his angry note, came to work escorting Alice. A perky brunette with long, suntanned legs, Alice had been around the block a few times. She dressed in shorts and halter-tops from March to November, titillating men like Jimmy. She'd waited tables down at the Steak House for at least ten years, and had five kids with five different fathers. I'd noticed the way she looked at whatever man she was with—as if he were the only one in the universe. It seemed, although she got around, she was loyal to the guy that brought her to the party. I respected her for that. But it sickened me to see that look directed at my husband.

Saturday would be our third anniversary, but Jimmy probably wouldn't remember.

When closing time finally came, Mark and I went to Tony's for breakfast. Jimmy and Alice were there, just finishing their meal. We were all cordial, and I introduced Mark to Alice, and then went to the table farthest away.

"That's very strange. You two act like you're not married." He looked from me to Jimmy and his eyes flashed. "I would never stand for seeing my wife with someone else."

"He doesn't care."

Thinking of our anniversary made me sad, but I kept up a good front, chattering, putting on a show to let Jimmy know how happy I was without him.

After we'd eaten, sitting in the car in front of my cabin, Mark cleared his throat and spoke fast. "I want to make love to you, but since I gave my word, I won't even ask."

"Good. I like a man who keeps his word." I reached over and kissed him. "Good night, Mark."

Later, in my bed, listening to soft music on my radio, I couldn't stop thinking about Jimmy. Soon I cried for myself and then I cried for him. We'd been so much in love. Two kids who thought we had the world by the tail. Why did it have to end? Why couldn't a man be happy with one woman?

Saturday night, Jimmy and Alice were together again. As the evening wore on, I felt more and more sorry for myself. Although no one in the place knew it was our anniversary, I was humiliated by the attention he paid Alice. He ordered more booze to the bandstand than usual and sent martinis to her table each time.

They were both high before midnight and Jimmy's performance showed it. During the breaks, she sat on his lap and kissed him.

Five minutes to twelve, he tapped the mike and made his announcement. "Before this day ends, I want to send an anniversary message to my lovely wife." He nodded to his drummer who rendered a quick drum roll. Jimmy stared down at me, strumming as he spit out each word. "She...can...kiss...my...ass."

Those who'd heard it turned to each other with shocked looks and raised eyebrows, then looked to see my reaction. I gave none. The smile froze on my face as I continued to pour drinks.

"What a prick," someone said. "No wonder you left him."

My cheeks burned and my eyes stung, but I won. I didn't shed the tears that choked my throat.

After we closed, Marge said, "I like you, kid. We don't need a jerk like that. We'll find someone else to play our music."

"Oh, he was just drunk." *There you go, Suzanne, defending him.*

"That's no excuse in my book. I'm giving him notice."

I felt a familiar flip in my stomach as she said that. I didn't want him hurt, but it would be nice not to have him watching me every weekend.

A few nights later, Marge and Lindy took up their personal problem again.

"Damn it, Marge, I was only fifteen. You shouldn't have left me alone with him so much."

"Didn't I have to go to work to support all of us?" Marge voice was getting louder. "You didn't have to go and marry the son-of-a-bitch after I dumped him."

"What was I supposed to do?" Lindy threw up her hands like a stop sign to Marge's words. "I was *sixteen*, and *pregnant*. I needed him to support his baby."

"Well, he *didn't*. He's been married six times since then."

When they started on the subject, one of them often stomped out mad. It was Lindy's turn. "Maybe someday one of them will shoot the son-of-a-bitch."

After the door closed, Marge spoke matter-of-factly. "Let her go off in a snit, won't change nothing. She came on to my husband." She smacked her hand on the bar. "They got caught."

Do all drunks replay their old problems?

CHAPTER 12

▼

When Sunday finally rolled around, I'd arranged to meet Karen at Tony's for breakfast. I walked, got there first, and selected a booth away from everyone.

She came through the door busting to know about my trip to the coast with Mark. "You've made me wait a whole week."

"I couldn't tell you on the phone." Our telephone exchange was owned and operated from the home of the man who'd built it pole by pole. Anyone who dared use a phone after ten o'clock had better meet his standard of urgency, or he'd cuss the caller out or simply cut off the connection. When I used a public phone, I assumed he was listening. "You know how old Paisley is. He knows my voice. He'd tell half the town."

Eyes sparkling, she grabbed my hands and shook them. "Well? Did you sleep with him?"

While I told my story, she hung on every word. She knew I'd never slept with anyone but Jimmy and she wanted all the details.

"Was he good?"

"God, Karen, I don't know. I was so nervous." I glanced around to see if anyone was overly interested in our conversation. "Not to change the subject...he did something weird on the way home." I told her about the stop at the old shack. "Said it was nothing to worry about."

"Then don't." She looked up from pushing a piece of ham around on her plate. "Hey, wasn't yesterday your anniversary?"

"Jimmy made a fool of himself. Told me to kiss his ass...on stage. Over the microphone. With fan-fare."

"Shit! Why does he have to act like that? What'd you do?"

"Nothing. For once, I didn't cry. The tables turned on him for a change. He's fired. Marge won't put up with his crap."

"No kidding? All that stuff about her and her sister, she sounds like a tough old bird."

After we'd talked awhile, Karen dug into her purse and flashed a driver's license. "I almost forgot. Look what I got."

I studied it. "Where'd you get this?"

"Over in Eugene. This guy sells them for twenty bucks."

"Karen, I can't serve you with this. Everyone knows you're younger than Jimmy."

"I don't expect *you* to serve me, but now we can go other places together."

"What if you get caught?" I looked her in the eyes and pleaded. "Can't you just wait four more months."

"Suzanne, damn it, you're such a scaredy-cat." She frowned and stuck out her lower lip. "I'm tired of sitting home." She took the license back and tucked it away with a happy little pat. "Let's go to Springfield tonight and try this out."

In truth, I was a scaredy-cat. But, I was hungry for some fun, too. "Okay, but only if you let me drive." I'd taught Karen to drive when she was fifteen. She was good, but scared hell out of me when she drank.

She drew a cross on her chest. "You can drive home, promise."

We started early, splurged on shrimp dinners at Captain Mike's, and then went to a small neighborhood tavern. We'd heard the place catered to the young crowd, and that they bent over backwards to have attractive young women hang around.

The handsome bartender didn't even look at the IDs we flashed. "Where you girls from?"

"Roseburg," Karen lied. "I'm Sharon. This is my friend, Barb. We're up here to play." Her wink and smile said we'd come to play with the boys—and the boys got the message.

The hard-bodied, young men, dressed like millworkers, looked us over big time. All except the two playing pool. They didn't strike me as millworkers—or even regulars of the bar. The tall, skinny one with the cigarette pack rolled up in his tee shirt's sleeve had a god-awful, amateur tattoo on his right arm, and scabs on his left, which he picked and squeezed between shots. His greasy, black hair fell in his pimply face as he bent over the table. He squinted against the smoke from the cigarette dangling between his slack lips. He glanced at Karen's butt as she walked to the jukebox. His lip curled in obvious contempt. The guy looked like he'd just stepped out of a bad movie, and had *mean* down pat.

His pool partner, crew cut and pale skinned, stood no more than five feet tall with his round stretch-marked belly hanging below his too-small tee shirt. His jeans drooped low, showing his butt-crack when he bent for a shot. While he waited his turn, he'd scratch his peach-fuzz beard with one hand and rub his Buddha-belly with the other. Quite a mental feat for him, I thought. His eyes roamed the room constantly to see if everyone was noticing what really, really bad news they were.

I watched these characters, careful not to make eye contact with either one. I also noticed the collection of baseball caps and trophies lining the walls of the little tavern—records of its patrons' pride. The Sunday evening crowd put us at ease as we joined the fun and games, comfortable as part of the clan.

Karen sauntered up to the pool table and smacked down her quarter, challenging the winner of the game in progress. She was a natural pool player. She'd practically worn out the old beat-out table in her parents' garage since she was about twelve. Standing there, thumbs in her jeans' pockets, she watched their game.

"My name's Sharon, what's yours?"

The ugly one didn't raise his eyes from the table. His tubby friend looked up at her five-foot-eight with a goofy grin, "I'm Chet. He's Roady."

"Well, boys, I'm here to kick some ass," she drawled, giving them a big smile.

I grimaced at the bartender. He raised his eyebrows, shrugged and made a friendly face back.

Roady sunk the eight ball, then rested his skimpy goatee on his pool cue and squinted at her. "You must think you're pretty damn hot." He pulled a scrunched-up bill from his pocket. "Wanta' put your money where your big mouth is?"

She'd affected a southern drawl. "Damn tootin'! How much y'all talkin' about?"

"How 'bout twenty bucks?"

She took a long pull on her beer and looked him up and down. "Sure, fine with me. Your break."

He only got two shots while she cleaned the table.

Karen worked on her fourth beer, while I drank my second. She showed no effects from the beer and beat everyone who stepped up to the table. By then every guy in the place watched her game, many eager to take her on.

The little tub put up his quarter, then just giggled while she whipped him. I think his job in life was to be a good loser, but not his partner who leaned against the wall, stroked his thin mustache and glowered.

As she sunk the eight ball, Roady slapped down another quarter. "Wanta' make another bet?"

"Sure. You want your ass whipped twice, fine with me. Twenty bucks?"

"We'll see." He dug another rumpled twenty from his crusty jeans and tossed it on the table.

She smoothed it, covered it with a crisp bill from her hip pocket, then set her beer bottle on them. Roady made me nervous, and I half hoped she'd lose, but I was pretty sure she wouldn't. The crowd grew louder, cheering her on while the balls were racked.

Three fresh Budweisers stood in front of me. "Please, no more," I told the bartender. "I can't, I'm driving. Put these back in the cooler."

"You girls aren't driving back to Roseburg tonight, are you?" a fellow standing nearby asked Karen.

"We might...and we might not." She looked back over her shoulder as she bent to make her first shot. "Me and Barb might come over and stay at your house tonight, sweetie."

Damn it, Karen, don't start with that crap.

She stood tall and gave him a good look at her figure. "Or, we might take this money I'm winning off old Roady here and get us a room."

Just then, a well-dressed man about thirty, who'd been standing at the end of the bar, slid in beside me. "Your friend always like this?" He smiled as he watched her. "Sure attracts a lot of attention, doesn't she?"

"That's one thing Karen loves."

He looked at me and grinned. "I thought her name was Sharon?"

"Oops! Didn't I say Sharon?" I batted my eyes in mock chagrin.

"I get it! You two must be stepping out. I see you have on an engagement ring."

"Not exactly. I've been separated for a couple months."

The room grew deadly quiet, except for the clicking of the balls. I turned around to watch Karen and Roady's game. Roady never had a chance. She ran the table.

"Wahoo!" she yelled, as the eight ball fell into its pocket. "Give this poor ass-hole a drink." She picked up the two twenties and stuck them in her bra. "He might as well get drunk, he can't play pool."

"Fuck you, bitch!" Glancing around the circle of onlookers, he dry-spit on the floor. "Take your beer and shove it."

A murmur came from the crowd.

"Watch your mouth, punk," someone said quietly.

"Well, pardon me," Karen said, sugar-sweet, bowing from the waist. "Who's next?"

Another pool player stepped up—not for money.

Karen shouldered her way through the crowd to my side while he racked. "You doin' okay?"

"Let's not stay here all night, that guy gives me the creeps. I think he's a sore loser. After this game, okay?"

"Sure, fine with me."

Very closely matched in her last game, and starting to show her beers, she barely won. When at last the eight ball sank, Roady reached across the table and slammed down another quarter.

She raised her hands in surrender. "Sorry, I'm done."

"What you mean, you're done?" He stepped close. "I'm challenging you."

"Tough shit. I said I'm through."

"Yeah, quit while you're ahead, bitch. You took forty bucks off me. You gotta give me a chance to get even." His shifty eyes looked around for support.

"Give it up!" someone yelled. "She already gave you your chance."

My stomach tightened as he held his ground, both hands on his pool stick. "Come on, Roady," Chet said, putting his hand on his arm. "Let's blow this hole."

Roady jerked away, hissing at him, "Fuck off, Chet."

I looked at the bartender. He stood at attention near the opening in the bar, smacking his palm with a baseball bat.

Damn it, Karen, that's enough. Back off.

Mr. Well-Dressed stood up, too. "Hope your friend knows what she's doing." I felt his muscles tighten where his arm touched mine. "She's liable to get a punch in the face if she doesn't back up."

As several millworkers pressed forward, Roady's eyes darted toward the door. I could see his wheels turning when he looked at the muscle power lining up against him.

Karen stood spraddle-legged, chin high, her pool cue butt end up. I don't know what she thought she'd do with it, but she looked tough.

After a few minutes and more rumbling from the crowd, Roady slammed down his cue stick. He grabbed his leather jacket off the peg by the door. "Come on, Chet, let's get the fuck out of here."

Looking back over his shoulder, Chet laughed nervously as he held the door for Roady. "See ya' all."

I heard their Harleys thunder to life outside, and then a peppering of gravel hit the side of the building as they roared away.

"You're one hell of a pool player, lady," the bartender said. "But, if you're going to start trouble in here, I'd as soon you didn't come back."

My face flushed.

Karen gave him her sweetest smile, tipped him five bucks and said, "I'm really sorry for the trouble. Guys like him bring out the worst in me. Let's go, Barb."

From there, we headed for a quiet cocktail bar, a cozy businessman's spot in the downtown area. When we'd parked, I tried to talk to Karen. "Please be nice. You know I don't like scenes. That biker really scared me. He could have clouted you with his pool stick."

"What did you think of that cute guy sitting by you? I think he liked you."

"He was nice…didn't make a pass. Besides, he's too old."

"I know. You're scared of older guys…always have been."

"What about Mark? He's older."

Just then, I heard the rumble of motorcycles round the corner and echo off the buildings. "Duck!" I pushed Karen down in the seat. We stayed down while the bikes slowly cruised past.

"Is it them?"

We popped up just in time to see Chet's round shape go under a distant street-light.

"Quick!" Karen jumped out and ran for the bar's swinging door.

Giggling, we burst through the door and climbed on a couple of barstools. My heart leapt a moment later when the squeaky door opened again behind me.

It was Mr. Well-Dressed. "I followed you girls 'cause I thought those bikers might be hanging around. They cruised by. Mind if I sit with you?"

"Sure." I glanced at Karen. She gave me the high sign as he settled beside me.

"May I buy you ladies a drink?"

The three of us drank, talked and laughed for a couple of hours. Karen carried the conversational ball most of the time, and our new friend bought the drinks. My slight buzz eased my shyness as the evening wore on. My new friend and I danced a few times, and I learned he was a salesman for a toy company, and had never been married.

By closing time, Karen definitely was in no shape to drive. We'd all agreed to meet for breakfast, including the bartender who was coming on to Karen. Outside, I held out my hand for the car keys.

"No dice! It's my car. I'm drivin'."

"Karen, you're too drunk. Damn it, you promised."

"I'm just a little tipsy. I can sure as hell drive."

Belligerent like her brother, she climbed behind the wheel, leaving me standing on the sidewalk. "Are you coming, or staying here. I'm driving this son-of-a-bitch."

The salesman, sitting across the street in his car, asked if I wanted to ride with him. I felt I had to go with Karen—to protect her—from what and how I didn't know. When we were sober, she protected me, but when she was drunk—far from home and out of control—I couldn't abandon her.

We screeched away from the curb and she ran the stop sign onto the boulevard. Fortunately at two-thirty on a Monday morning, the street was empty. She liked the yelp she got from me by running the stop sign, so she ran the red lights, one after another.

When we pulled into the all-night diner's parking lot, she jumped out of her old Lincoln and dashed inside. I followed. As I started through the door, I glanced back and saw her car begin to slowly roll backwards on the slight incline.

"Karen, the car!"

She looked out, but only collapsed in laughter at the nearest booth. "You wanted to drive so bad, go get it."

For a second, I wanted to just let it go. Teach her a lesson. All the reasons not to flashed through my brain. I dashed after it, jerked open its heavy door and jumped in. Pressing the power brakes did nothing. The car kept rolling, picked up speed and barely missed two parked cars. As it reached the street, I frantically tried to steer, at the same time fumbling for the emergency brake. Finally, in desperation, I pulled the shifter into "park." It lurched to a stop, rocking back and forth on its shocks.

The restaurant window filled with gaping people as I sat humiliated, in the middle of the highway with no keys. Karen staggered toward me, head back, piercing the night with her cackling. "You looked like the Road Runner…Jeezus! Chasing a car through the parking lot."

"Give me the goddamn key so I can get the hell out of the road."

"Now, Suzanny, don't be mad, we're just having fun. Nobody's hurt."

I drove to the far side of the building, away from the onlookers. She followed, finally coaxing me back inside. Karen could be such a pain in the butt, but I could never stay mad at her—any more than I could her brother. I loved them both, something like the way a mother loves her children.

My rescue of the car at least got the keys into my hands for the drive home. Any ideas of romance the salesman and I might have had were lost in the shuffle.

Karen snored all the way up the river. I stopped at her house and steered her inside. "I'll bring the car back tomorrow."

By the time I hit my bed, dawn had brushed away the night.

CHAPTER 13

▼

Seven hours later, near noon, I heard a brisk knock on my door. I grabbed my kimono, gave a swipe at my hair and looked out the window. Its top down, Mark's Cadillac sat next to Karen's old Lincoln.

When I opened the door, he said good morning, walked in and plopped on the couch. Head down, he picked up lint, hair or something from the couch cover and dropped it on the floor. "Came by last night. I thought we might go out to Sophie's."

"Karen and I went to Eugene. We didn't get home until daylight."

He looked up and frowned. "Oh?" His voice went cold. "Thought she was only twenty."

"She has fake ID."

He folded his arms behind his head and stared at the ceiling for a long moment. Finally, he looked at me with a smile that didn't quite reach his eyes. "Want to go for a ride?" The ice in his voice was gone. "I have some business over in Florence." He laughed and pulled me down beside him on the couch. "Promise I'll get you back today."

I poked him in the ribs. "Oh, darn!"

"Wouldn't you like to get soaked again?" He nuzzled my neck.

"No way!"

He put his hand on my bare thigh, slid his fingers between my legs and squeezed my knee. "That won't be necessary," he whispered.

Although it didn't feel right for him to take such a liberty, his cool hand excited me. The familiar sensation arose between my legs and his hand came higher. My body moved toward him as he urgently pressed his tongue between my lips. Too soon, he moved his hands to my back and pulled me on top of him. I could feel his readiness as he crushed my breasts and pelvis against him.

In one clumsy, embarrassing move he half-carried me to the bedroom where he bent me backward over the side of the bed. He dropped his trousers, and then fell on me in a frenzy which lasted mere seconds. As he climaxed, he grabbed my hair and pulled my head back. Finished, he rolled on his side and lay there breathing hard.

I felt humiliated and sick inside. What happened to the gentle lover of last weekend? *Why does he think he can treat me this way? Does he think I'm that easy?*

He ran his finger down my cheek. "Sorry."

I didn't answer, or look at him. My mind scrambled. Should I feel cheap? I did. Did I ask for bad treatment by sleeping with him in the first place?

"You never said if you'd like to go for that ride." He stood and straightened his pants.

I pulled my robe over me, and lay staring at the ceiling. *Well, slam, bang, thank you ma'am.* It seemed as if my storybook man-of-the-world might be something more than I'd bargained for—or something less.

Snap out of it! He's no worse than Jimmy was half the time. It's just the way men are.

He walked into the living room, running his hands through his hair.

I was still not ready to look at him. "I'm taking a shower." Was I going with him after what he'd just done? Had I asked for it, being so brazen in the beginning? Was I being too sensitive? Since I got out so seldom, I wanted to go, but I didn't want to be humiliated.

After dressing, I went into the living room to comb my hair. He stood with his back to me, looking at my books.

"You believe in this Bridey Murphy crap?"

"Reincarnation makes sense to me. Have you read it?"

"No, I doubt I ever will."

I flinched at his attitude, which attacked my core belief, and didn't stack up with his Indian ancestry. I told myself it was no skin off my nose if he didn't believe, then put it out of my mind.

The sunny day was perfect for top-down driving, and I hated to spend it cooped up in my little house, or sitting in the bar, so I said, "Let's get going."

After I delivered Karen's car, we headed west. Along the way he discussed literature and recited poems. I tried to explain my feeling on the concept of karma, but he totally rejected the notion, and I dropped it fast. I didn't want to hear anything that would give me a more negative opinion of him than I already had. If I didn't have respect for him, how could I have any for myself?

When we reached Florence, he drove by the old house he'd stopped at before. After circling the area twice, he parked fifty yards from the house. "I'll be right back." He once again took his briefcase from the trunk. "Trust me, this is nothing to be concerned about."

He'd said it before, but I was beginning to worry.

When he returned in ten minutes, he smiled devilishly, chucked me under the chin, and suggested we find a beach. "I've got a brand new blanket."

We stopped for snacks and beer, and then lay on the blanket soaking in the sun. We each stared at the sky, watched gulls and listened to the crashing of the sea. I was doing a lot of thinking, and we seemed to have run out of much to say. By five o'clock, when the sun's energy waned and the sea breezes chilled me, I asked him to take me home.

Near dusk, when we reached my house, he invited himself in. "I'd like a chance to make up to you for this morning."

My cheeks flushed and my ears felt hot.

"Let me come in and we'll talk about it."

Talking about sex was the last thing I wanted to do. I didn't even talk to Jimmy about sex. "Come on in…but there's nothing to talk about."

He led me to the bedroom where he sat on the edge of the bed, put his arms around my waist and pulled me toward him. I stood between his legs with my hands at my sides. The twilight semi-darkness made it easier because I couldn't see his eyes.

He held my chin and looked up at me. "I know you're very shy…this is probably your first sex besides your husband. Sometimes your naiveté excites me too much. I lose control. I'm sorry. Please let me make up for this morning."

"I…don't think we need to talk—"

"No. Shhh." He put his finger to my lips. "Don't say anything."

He gently caressed my face, circling my eyes and my ears, and the sides of my throat. Reaching behind my head, he took the band from my ponytail, spreading my hair across my back and front like a cloak. He smoothly unbuttoned my blouse, shucking it from my shoulders. My bra dropped to the floor in one move and I stood before him, bare to the waist under my cloak of hair.

"There." With his hands holding my waist, he held me away and looked into my face. "Now." He unzipped my jeans and kissed my belly button. After turning on the bedside lamp, he steered me to the cracked mirror of my ratty dresser.

He pulled off his shirt and stood tall beside me. "See how sexy you look. How can you blame me for losing control."

Standing half-naked beside him, looking in the mirror wasn't comfortable, but I wanted to behave maturely, and play it out.

He pulled my hair behind my back. "You have such beautiful breasts."

I watched his face in the dimly lit mirror as he stepped behind me, cupping them in his hands. I felt my nipples harden as I looked at those dark hands covering them. He lowered his mouth, ran his tongue along my neck.

"Squeeze them harder," I whispered.

His fingers tightened, his hardened sex pressed against my behind. As he stared into my eyes in the mirror, he slid both hands down into the front of my open jeans. There he stroked until I was half crazy. At last, he turned me to face him, and kissed me until I was weak in the knees. I turned off the lamp and pulled him to the bed. We made love for a long time, and then lay in the dark smoking, saying nothing.

After awhile, he rolled over, turned on the light and looked at the clock. "Damn, I've got to go. I'm working tonight…if I have the strength."

He dressed and kissed me good-bye.

CHAPTER 14

▼

Wednesday night the bar nearly emptied by eight o'clock when the after-work locals cleared out. I took a phone call from Mrs. Mallory, a prominent matron of the community. "Is Timmy John there?"

"No." I answered truthfully. I hated lying for men when they got calls—usually from their wives. I'd often call out, with an open receiver, "Are you here?" giving them the choice.

"Are you certain he's not there?" she demanded, in a cranky voice.

"He's not here, I swear. He hasn't been here this evening."

"Well, if he comes in there, you'd better not give him anything to drink. He's on medication...he's been out drinking all day." She went on for a couple of minutes about how his broken leg wasn't healing and how "you people just don't know how I worry."

"Okay. If I see him, I'll send him home."

She called again in a half-hour, even more insistent and demanding. Everyone knew her forty-year-old son, the baby of her large family, was still tightly under his mother's thumb.

About an hour later, he hobbled in, obviously not drunk and easily handling his crutches. I told him about his mother's call. He groaned. The poor man often sat in the bar, and at places like Sophie's, nursing a beer, enjoying freedom and companionship away from his nagging mother.

"I can see you're not drunk, so I'm just going to serve you one. Will you promise to go home when you finish?"

He offered his hand for a shake. "It's a deal."

For the next hour, he sipped on one highball, trading logging stories with a couple of men he knew. I leaned against the rail and put in my two-cent's worth a few times.

"If she calls, tell her I'm not here."

"No can do, friend, I got burned on that once. Someone's wife called from that phone booth across the street. Sixty seconds later she ripped through that door...after my butt."

About eleven he stumped out the door and the incident was forgotten.

The following evening, I arrived at work fifteen minutes early as usual and sat at the bar drinking a cup of coffee. I liked to size up the crowd before I had to jump into the fray. Barkerville's only law enforcement officer came through the door. Sid Delaney, Chief of Police, made up our entire police department. Gray-haired and fat, he'd been cruising town since long before I started to drive. Made even heavier by the squeaky leather holster that held up his belly, Sid always walked as if his feet were killing him.

The customers turned on their stools and kidded him.

"Look out...here comes the law!"

"Better let me buy you a cool one, Sid."

Anyone who knew him would know he was an Elder in the Community Church and a teetotaler.

It was unusual for him to be in the bar, and as I watched him, he searched the crowd and caught my eye. Heading straight toward me, he unfolded his note-book and reached for the pencil in his shirt pocket. My heart fluttered as my mind searched for possible reasons why he'd want to talk to me.

"Tell me about last night, Suzanne," he said, all wrinkle-browed and cranky sounding.

"What?"

He stared at me. "Timmy John."

"What?" My first thought was an accident. "Did something happen to him?"

Ignoring my question, looking sterner than I'd ever seen him, he pressed on. "Did you serve him last night?"

Oh God, something must have happened to him. "Yes."

"Was he drunk?"

I took a deep breath, trying to sound convincing. "No, Sid, I only served him one drink...not because he was drunk." My voice sounded weak and not very believable. I explained Mrs. Mallory's calls. "He stayed about an hour drinking that one drink, then left. Is he okay?"

He lowered his head, writing in his little notebook with a stub of a pencil he kept wetting with his tongue. Without moving his head, he raised his eyelids several times to look sideways at me, then back to the notebook—like he was drawing my picture in that damn book.

"He's okay," he finally answered—as if it would kill him to give me any information. "Are you sure you only served him one?"

"Yes!" I wanted to look away from his intense gaze, but it was important to convince him. "The guys kidded him about it. He made a deal with me...he'd only have one, then go home."

"What time was it?"

"Early. Probably about nine."

Finally, his face softened. He stopped treating me like a criminal and became the friendly cop I'd known forever. "When did he leave, honey?"

God! Why don't you put me under the lights and beat it out of me!

"As I said, he stayed about an hour."

"Must'a been after ten then, huh?" He made a final note and closed his book. Smiling, he patted me on the shoulder. "Mrs. Mallory worries about him."

With that, he left me, speaking to customers as he waddled toward the door. My curiosity about his visit continued to plague me into the evening but I was sure Mrs. Mallory was behind it. By the end of the night I'd forgotten it.

Late Friday morning Karen and I went to Ptomaine Tony's to eat, and to catch up on the gossip.

"Jimmy's shacked up with Alice, you know," Karen said, first thing. "I don't know what he sees in her. She must be ten years older than him...all those kids."

"Well, she's good looking. Experienced. You've seen how she looks at a man."

"She calls him her Teddy Bear. Yuck! I went out to Sophie's with them the other night. Made me sick. She talked baby talk to him all night."

Hearing about stuff made me a little sick, too—but I wouldn't miss it for the world. At times I felt more like Jimmy's sister than his wife. Growing up together had given me a damn sisterly concern for his welfare.

"This cute friend of Jimmy's went with us...we danced our socks off. His name's Joe. He's new in town. Works at the mill. Six foot two...eyes of blue. Just right for me."

"What do you mean, just right? Jimmy's age?"

Hand to her forehead, rolling eyes, she imitated a swoon. "He's sooo sexy. Maybe twenty-five or so."

"I hope you're not planning to sleep with him."

She clawed at her arms, shaking her head. "That is *all* I've thought about. We kissed all the way back from Sophie's. I was hotter'n a pistol!"

"Jeez, Karen, don't be foolish." She didn't appreciate lectures from me, but the subject was too important to keep my mouth shut. "Ron's a good husband. Why would you want to do that?"

She put her elbows on the table, rested her chin on her hands, and made a pout-face. "I'm sick of being alone." The pout changed to batting eyelashes. "Besides, he thinks I'm sexy."

"You *are* sexy! Just like I always said you'd be someday, but you're *married*. Why not just have fun with him? Don't sleep with him." I waited while our waitress refilled our coffee, and then lowered my voice. "And I don't mean prick-tease the poor guy to death either."

"What's going on with you and lover boy?"

"We did it again—twice!"

"Well, well. Things are picking up the beat."

I leaned toward her. "Seriously, there's something strange about him. He's hot and cold. Sometimes very loving…but he keeps me at arm's length. Here it is Friday, I haven't seen him since he crawled out of my bed Monday evening. You think I'm being too easy?"

She slapped the vinyl seat, laughed loudly. "Hell no! You didn't screw him 'til the third date! Isn't that the rule?"

"God, Karen. Keep it down. There's that Florence thing. It worries me."

"Forget it. Suzanne, you worry too much."

After breakfast, we spent two hours at my house, then parted company in the early afternoon, with my final advice about sleeping with Joe.

Later that night at work, the Milligan sisters were at it again. They seemed to be angry about Lindy's son Paul, who was having some kind of problem and planned to come and live with them. From things they said, I got the impression that Paul was a serious thorn in Marge's side—an unpleasant reminder of her younger sister's affair with her husband.

"Paul always comes running home when he's in trouble." Marge got louder. "Why the hell don't you make him stand on his own two feet?"

"He's my only child. If you had kids, you'd understand."

As I passed back and forth in front of them, I strained my ears to hear parts of their argument. My curiosity about these two consumed me as I put together bits and pieces.

"…couldn't have kids."

"If you'd stuck with men, things might…"

Marge looked upset and they were yelling at each other. As I went to their end of the bar to try to quiet them, Lindy said, "Well, why don't you just go on back to Rachel?" They turned away from each other, and then Lindy said to me, "My son Paulie moving in with us. When he gets settled in you can teach him to tend bar."

"How old is he?"

"Twenty-five this September."

"Where's he live?"

"Lane County's jail!" Marge blurted. Lindy glared at her, and I immediately had something that needed doing at the other end of the bar.

It was Saturday night and still no sign of Mark. The way he stayed away for days at a time irritated me, made me feel cheap. In my mind, sleeping with someone meant you should stay in touch. I tried to convince myself that his was a more worldly approach, but the feeling of being used kept creeping into my head.

Around midnight he appeared. "Hi, pretty lady, how are you?"

I didn't want to, but I smiled. "Just peachy, thanks."

I got his drink, then spoke to him when I could as I rushed back and forth. When I refilled his drink, he steepled his hands under his chin and begged. "Please, have breakfast with a starving man."

Just like that. All he has to do is turn up and turn on the charm.

"You'll have to wait while I close up. We're so busy tonight, it'll take me half an hour."

When closing time came, he put up the chairs for the sweeper and carried beer cases for me while I restocked.

Over breakfast, he talked about the space program, Brezhnev and Francis Gary Powers—and I felt stupid. I had no television, only music on the radio and the town's weekly newspaper. All I could do was listen and nod my head. At times I hated my small-town upbringing. If I didn't escape the White Water and Barkerville I'd never get the education I needed to improve myself and become independent.

Later, when we were parked at my door, he put his arm across my shoulders and drew me to him. "Are you all right?"

"No, Mark, I'm really tired. I have a killer headache." I wanted to be alone to think about my life—about what I wanted to do with it.

"I'm sorry." He massaged my neck and shoulders while leaning over to kiss my forehead. "I can fix that. May I come in and give you a massage?"

I hesitated, looked away. I'd made up my mind at the restaurant not to invite him in.

"It'll be good," he whispered. "That's all I'll do, I swear."

I felt drained and depressed. Saturday nights were hard work, and all the stewing going on in my head had exhausted me. *Now is the time to be strong, Suzanne.*

"No, I'm serious. I have to get some rest."

"Have it your way," he said, and just sat there.

"Well, good night. Thanks for breakfast."

I went into the house feeling unsure about whether I'd made him angry, but proud that I'd stuck to my plan.

CHAPTER 15

▼

In the morning, I awoke to sun on my face and sounds in the kitchen. I sniffed. Was that coffee? Bacon? It took me a minute wake up and my first thought was that Karen was there. I put on my robe, shuffled into the kitchen and was shocked to find Mark at the sink.

"Good morning." He lowered his head to search my eyes. "Are you better this morning?"

"I'm okay." I leaned my head against the cupboard as he poured coffee, then took my cup and went to stare out the front window. It was awkward waking up to him in my house, let alone cooking in my dumpy kitchen. He had to have brought in groceries. My refrigerator was empty except for coffee, pickle relish and a few dried-up leftovers from the bar.

He spoke over his shoulder from the kitchen. "I've only got half an hour. I wanted to fix this before I leave." In a minute he brought two plates of bacon and eggs to the TV trays that served as my dining table. "Your breakfast is served, my dear lady."

He ate quickly, in silence. Then he rose, left his dirty plate, and pecked me goodbye.

While I washed the dishes, I thought over what had troubled me last night. How could Mark act so lovable at times, then so distant at others? I didn't want to become too attached to him. I already knew there was no future in it. It didn't fit my growing desire for independence, and besides, there were things about him I definitely didn't like.

Karen walked in before I finished cleaning the kitchen. "I came earlier, but Mark's car was out front." She grinned slyly. "Did he sleep over?"

"No way. I sent him home last night."

"Likely story! What about *our* breakfast?"

"Don't worry. I'll drink coffee while you eat."

She sat on the bed while I dressed. "How's it going with the new owners?"

"They drink a lot…and fight a lot. Lindy's son's coming to live with them. I'm supposed to teach him to tend bar. Isn't that just ducky."

When we got to the coffee shop, Karen hugged herself and gushed about Joe. "Suzanny, he's just gooder'n gum!"

Once again, I said my piece about her being married.

She went right on talking. "He's taking me out to Sophie's tonight. Why don't you and Mark come?"

"Joe is Jimmy's friend. Wouldn't it be a little weird?"

"They're not bosom buddies or anything. Jimmy's only known him a couple months…at work."

"Sounds like fun, but I have no control over Mark. I might not see him again until next week. He never asks me out ahead of time. He just shows up. I don't know what to think about that, Karen. What would you do?"

"I know damn well I wouldn't hang around waiting for him for no week. He doesn't own you, Suzanne. You can just go with us. Piss on him."

"Let's wait until it's time and I'll see."

When Karen dropped me off an hour later, she said they'd stop by around eight and I should be ready to go.

"I want to look this Joe over anyway, even if I don't go."

The next two hours I cleaned, and then lugged my laundry down the street. Not having a car made it a real struggle. I felt like poor white trash walking down Main Street with my laundry in a pillowcase. Thanks to Mr. Wilke, it wouldn't be long before I could afford my car.

Later that evening, about seven, I sat on the steps reading when Mark drove up. "Hi, beautiful lady! What you reading?"

"Nothing much, just some wicked reincarnation stuff."

He frowned, took the book from my hand and walked into the house. "Want to go get a steak?"

"Sure." I motioned to the couch. "Have a seat while I change."

"About this morning…hope I didn't overstep my bounds."

"No harm done, Mark. It was nice waking up to frying bacon."

I put on a purple and red peasant dress, slipped on red high-heels, then braided my hair into pigtails and tied them with red ribbons.

He whistled when I came from the bedroom. "Take it from an artist…you're a knock-out in those colors." He stood and faced me, then touched my pigtails and pulled my blouse up to cover my shoulders.

Ignoring his gesture, I twirled and flared my skirt. "I'm hoping we might go to Sophie's after dinner."

He bowed and opened the door in a grand gesture. "Your slightest wish is my command."

Without mentioning Karen's plans to stop by, I taped a folded note to my door telling her I'd see her there.

He held his arm out, guided me down the steps and to the passenger side of his car. His grandiose gestures were sometimes embarrassing and seemed out of place in Barkerville, but maybe they were appropriate where he came from.

At dinner, we talked about growing up and school days, topics where I could hold my own. Driving the twelve miles to Sophie's with the top down and the radio playing, I leaned back and closed my eyes. The cool breeze flowed over me, and I imagined myself in a cream-colored Jaguar, zipping down Big Sur toward my home on the beach at Santa Barbara. Just as I pictured my white stucco house with its cool tile floors and lush Spanish courtyard, we slid to a stop in front of Sophie's.

Karen, slender and radiant in her tight black sheath, stood at the jukebox showing off her long, perfect legs. She motioned toward a table. "Sit over there with us."

The handsome dude at the table had to be Joe. When he stood to greet us, his turquoise eyes, rimmed with thick black lashes, lit up like we were long lost friends. He offered his hand to Mark, and I looked him over thoroughly. Tall and slim in new jeans, shiny tan cowboy boots and a crimson shirt that showed off his head of curly black hair. No wonder Karen was gaga over him.

Sophie hurried to our table, straight for Mark. "Why, honey, I knew you'd have to come back and get some more of Sophie's lovin'." She plopped down on Mark's lap and put her arm around him. "What you kids drinkin'?"

Mark gave her a squeeze, and then lifted her up. "Bring us a Bud and a Rainier."

When the music wasn't playing, the four of us talked—mostly about the glories of Oregon. Both men were newcomers to my birth state. When the music played, we danced. It turned out, happily for me, that Mark was an excellent dancer. I loved to dance. I started as a baby, when I went to dances with my family and slept on a pile of coats on the dance hall's bench.

When Karen and I visited the ladies' room, she squealed and ran her hands over her body. "I think I'll do it tonight…if I get up the nerve. I've never slept with anyone but Ron. What do you think of him?"

"You know what I think…but you'll do what you want. He's a damn handsome cowboy." I put my hands on her shoulders and looked into her pleading-for-my-approval eyes, then pulled her to me for a hug. "Honey, for God's sake don't get pregnant, whatever you do."

We returned to the table to find Sophie on Mark's lap again, his arms wrapped around her big butt. "Sophie, that's my seat." Laughing, I pulled her up, then sat in her place. I could smell her trademark White Shoulders on his shirt. I sniffed his chest. "You're her tomcat now! She's marked you."

An older man at the bar, who had spoken to Mark when we came in, sent over four beers. He touched his brow with one finger when Mark looked over to thank him. Near closing time, the same man caught Mark's eye and motioned for him to come to the bar. When Mark came back, he said to Joe, "Lefty's in a bad way. His ride took off. I said I'd take him home. He's a real mess and I don't want Suzanne to have to ride with him. Would you and Karen mind taking her home?"

"Not at all," Joe said.

Mark sat down, put his arm around me and whispered, "Sorry. I'm getting him something to eat before I take him home. He lives halfway to Springfield. Guess that kills our date. But I'll be over tomorrow. Okay?" He kissed me on the ear. "Thanks."

We stayed until Sophie's closed, then Joe drove us back to my house. He and Karen got out with the six-pack they'd bought at Sophie's and followed me up the steps. I was tired and not particularly pleased to have them come in, but figured I could just go to bed and leave them to their own devices. When the three of us crowded through the door, I spotted it first, then stumbled backward into Karen. Deep in the shadows, Jimmy sat on the couch with a rifle across his lap.

His voice was flat. "Howdy."

"Well, howdy to you, too," Karen said. She spun around and shoved Joe back out the door. "We'll see you two later."

CHAPTER 16

▼

"Karen, wait…" My voice wavered and died in my throat. I heard their car door slam.

"You don't need Karen." He sounded sleepy, like we'd just awakened him. At that moment, I didn't sense any danger, but still stood in the doorway, ready to bolt.

"Come on. Sit by me." He patted the couch beside him—the side where the rifle pointed.

Instead, I sat on the chair on his other side.

"Where's your boyfriend?" He sounded casual, like a friend passing the time of day.

My stomach turned over. "You mean Mark?"

He bellowed, his whiskey breath hot on my face. "You know fucking-A well who I mean! Don't try to hand me that crap."

While fear surged through my body, I did my best to keep it out of my voice. "He's gone home."

I hid my shaking hands in the folds of my dress and clenched my knees together, afraid he'd see them quiver in the sliver of light that fell across my skirt.

Sounding drunk for sure, he pronounced each word slowly and deliberately. "When Chief Pretty Boy comes through that door, I'm going to blow his head off." The room was too dark to make out his expression. "I'll teach him to sneak around with my wife. You two don't fool me…Karen bringing you home doesn't fool me either."

"He's not coming here."

Quite sure he wouldn't return, but still straining my ears for the sound of a car, I sat listening to Jimmy's heavy breathing. He constantly clicked the bolt on his Winchester 30'06. My mind scurried, planning my defense. With the barrel of the rifle pointed away, I'd have a moment to act if he blew up. Pretending to look straight ahead, I watched from the corner of my eye for any move.

My sight adjusted to the dark corners of the room and I spotted a weapon, my heavy glass ashtray—big as a dinner plate. In time, my shaking subsided enough for me to reach for a cigarette from the table. When he moved toward me, I spun my head around to look at him.

He chuckled, and reached over to light my cigarette. "I'm not going to shoot *you.*"

From habit, I touched his hand to bring the flame closer, managed not to recoil from him while I held the touch and drew on the cigarette. I picked up the ashtray, situated it in my right hand, ready to strike if he moved to point the rifle my direction.

Silent time passed as we chain-smoked in the shadows. My thoughts replayed our life together, and the fear slowly drained out of me.

Finally, he talked a little, sounded less angry. "Babe, you know I've loved you since sixth grade. Why'd you want to leave me over one mistake?"

I kept my voice soft and sympathetic. "Jimmy, I know. Can we talk about this tomorrow? I'm real tired."

"You know I love you, don't you?"

"Yes."

He laughed softly. "Remember that time in ninth grade…we sneaked off to the coast? Your dad wanted to kill me."

I reminded him of other good times we had together, although I could easily have counted as many bad ones. But not while he held a rifle in his hands.

While the hours passed, he sobered from whatever passion had brought him to my cabin.

Dawn extinguished the yard light then filled the shadows in the room. With the daylight, I decided I'd had enough. If I waited too long, Mark might come and start it all up again.

I stood and faced him. "If you're going to shoot me, take your best shot, 'cause I'm leaving."

He rose and pointed the rifle at the floor, then jacked the action several times. He laughed sheepishly. "The gun wasn't even loaded."

"You bastard!" I tried to sound angry. All our reminiscing had softened me. "If you ever point a gun at me again, it had better be loaded." I stepped close, inches from his face. "I'll take it away from you and wrap it around your neck!" I'd lapsed into feeling like we were kids playing a silly game.

"You're so cute. You should stand up to me more often." Putting his hand to the back of my neck in the familiar way, he pulled me to his chest and kissed the top of my head. "Suzanne, Suzanne, Suzanne, what are we going to do about us? Let's go get some breakfast."

I must be crazy. He scares hell out of me. Now I'm agreeing to eat breakfast with him?

When we walked into the diner, Karen and Joe were just leaving.

Joe pointed his trigger finger at Jimmy. "Well, if it ain't Billy the Kid!"

"Well, if it ain't the dirty little cowards that left me with Billy the Kid."

Karen laughed and threw her arm around me. "We knew he was harmless."

"Just how in hell did you know that?"

They all hooted.

I made a face at them. "You three are about as funny as life in prison."

Karen and Joe joined us at a table and saved me from the serious conversation Jimmy wanted us to have.

Karen slapped the table and heehawed. "That big-eyed look on your face. Him sitting there with the gun. You didn't know whether to shit or go blind."

The jokes and laughter felt good, normal, like the old days. But I knew that nothing had changed. The long night was only another act in the drama, which left us no closer to resolution. I saw the pattern. When Jimmy was between women, he loved me.

When he drove me home that crystal summer morning, he tried to talk to me. "Babe, we're so good together, we've got to try to work this out."

"Listen to you. You never even use my name. You treat me like one of your babes." Defeat, disgust and lack of sleep were all in my voice. "I'm just too tired to talk about it, Jimmy. Besides, you've only got thirty minutes to get to work."

He reached for me as I started to get out of his car, but I kept going.

"Good night, babe," he said.

Mark awoke me with a cup of coffee about four hours later. "I've been here about an hour. You've sure been sleeping hard." He sat on the side of the bed and stroked my hair.

Still groggy, I said, "I didn't get to sleep until seven." I didn't want to tell him what happened. I was sure that it wouldn't happen again. "Jimmy was here when I got home. He wanted to talk."

"Did you talk for *five* hours?"

Sarcasm? *Just what I need.* I ignored it. "We had a lot to talk about...got nowhere."

"Good." His voice sweetened. "I've been thinking about you a lot lately." He stroked my shoulder. "I'm going to be leaving my friend's house."

My stomach gave a flip. "You're going away?" I sat up in bed, took a drink of coffee, and couldn't look at him.

"That depends." He tilted my chin, looked into my face. "I've been thinking I'd like to move in here with you."

That was a shot from left field. My mind went bonkers. *Am I ready for this? Do I care for him or not? He treats me good, but sometimes he's strange. I love being on my own. He's so sexy. Oh, God, another decision. I'm not ready to be a grown up.*

I looked away. My thoughts were muddled, searching for reasons to say yes but only finding reasons to say no.

"Look, if this is too big a step for you...you're young, inexperienced." He stepped away from the bed. "Guess I just misread your feelings."

"It's not that." My words rushed. "I'm still married. What if Jimmy caused trouble? I'm scared he'd—"

"You think I can't handle him?"

"I'm sure you could." He'd never understand the love I still felt for Jimmy. I didn't want to be his wife, but I still cared deeply for his welfare.

Why did the decision have to come up so soon? How could I look him in the face and say no—after I slept with him? To rationalize that, I had to care about him. If not, I hated what that said about me.

Don't do it, Suzanne. You don't even know him.

"Well, what do you say? I need an answer." He pulled my face around to his again.

Lowering my eyes, I nodded.

He pulled me to him, squeezed me hard. "My stuff's in the car. I'll get it."

I sat there in bed, feeling very young and scared. People lived together all the time, but it wasn't something I'd ever imagined doing. I'd barely had a chance to live alone.

Mark carried his clothes in on hangers and hung them next to mine. "I'm going out to Scott's and get the rest of my stuff. I'll probably be a couple of hours. Why don't you get some more sleep? You've got bags under your eyes."

After he left, I jumped into the shower and washed some of the cobwebs from my brain—enough to make me regret my decision. I felt like I'd put myself in a corner again, like I did with Mr. Wilke. But, unlike Mr. Wilke, he made me feel good. Sometimes.

When I'd dressed, I violated my phone rule and walked across the street to the booth to call Karen. Maybe Paisley wouldn't listen on that phone the way he did the one in the bar. When I told her, she exploded.

"Whaaaat? Are you crazy? Why did you do that? You hardly know him. We can't go anywhere. Damn it, Suzanny!"

She didn't make me feel any better. "We'll still do lots of things. Maybe not go out and raise hell...you're all tangled up with Joe anyway." I was embarrassed and didn't want to talk about Mark anymore. "What happened after you dropped me off last night? You two didn't spend a whole three hours eating breakfast."

"We went down to the swimming hole...necked for two hours."

"And?"

"Then we got in the back seat...for another hour."

"I knew you'd do that. That's why you went off and left me with Jimmy."

She laughed. "We were going to borrow your couch, but it was occupied."

"He's a little long-legged for back seats, isn't he?"

"We managed just fine, thank you."

"This doesn't mean you have to throw away your marriage. Now that your horns are trimmed, think about it seriously. Believe me, where I am isn't much fun sometimes."

"Sure! I'll think about it. See you Sunday, if not sooner."

I hung up the phone and went into the bar.

"Marie, I need a pick-me-up. Will you fix me an Irish coffee? Where's Lindy and Marge?"

"Lindy went to get her son. Marge went to some kind of city council meeting. The mayor called and asked them to come. She figured they wanted to welcome them to town."

The liquor spread through my body, perked me up a little, and I sat humming to the jukebox.

Before I'd finished my coffee, Marge came through the front door. Red faced and wild eyed. "Those sons-a-bitches can't tell me what to do! They can go screw themselves!"

"What happened?" Marie, the day-shift bartender, said.

"Give me a drink!" She sputtered and pounded the bar. "That fat friggin' cop was there. They want me to fire you." She looked straight at me.

"What?" My voice came out in a croak. "What for?"

"Remember? That pot-gutted bastard...said he came in here last week and asked if you'd served Timmy John. Well, he put in his report that you'd served him for over an hour...he was visibly drunk."

"I don't believe this. I told him—But he wasn't drunk anyway. That's a god-damn lie. Why would he do that to me?"

Tears stung my eyes and I blinked frantically. I thought he liked me. When I started driving in high school, I'd always park beside his car in my old pink and blue Willys and we'd talk. He'd said he was proud to see I edited the school paper and he'd seen me sing at concerts. My cheeks burned. It hurt me deeply to think that Sid would lie about me.

"He said these construction people coming in here for the dam are a rough bunch. You're too young to handle them. I've seen a lot of girls work. I happen to like the way you handle drunks. So, fuck him...and the horse he rode in on! What the hell does he know?"

"Timmy John's mother probably called up and bitched. You know how it is in this town," Marie said. "She's probably related to Sid."

"Yep, it's politics. Seen it in every town I been in...but the only one who says you go is me. Or Lindy. Or the Oregon Liquor Control Commission. So don't worry. We just won't be calling the damn cops. If we have a problem, we'll handle it ourselves."

Everyone talked about Barkerville's politics for the next hour, while I had another Irish coffee and calmed down enough to realize that Mark would probably be back.

When I got home, he'd moved in. His easel stood in a corner of my cramped living room and several paintings leaned against the wall. Two cardboard boxes sat at the end of the couch.

What no luggage?

He spoke without looking up from the book he was reading. "Where have you been?"

"Over at the bar. I'm really pissed. That goddamn Sid Delaney lied about me in his police report. The city told Marge to fire me."

He whirled around, his angry eyes flashed. "Don't damn The Lord in front of me. I don't like His name used that way." As quickly as it came, the anger was replaced by a smile as he reached toward me. "What's this all about anyway?"

I felt like he'd slapped my face. "I'm sorry." *Sorry? Why do I always say that?* "It's a long story. They think I'm too young to handle drunks. Marge told them to go to hell." I bit off the word "hell" and waited for a reaction. *I've been cussing a long time, mister.*

"She's not going to fire you, is she?"

"Not now anyway. But maybe they'll make her."

"Come here." He patted his knees. I sat on his lap and he put his arms around me, gently pressed my head down on his shoulder. "You look beat. Just relax. It wouldn't be the end of the world if you lost that job anyway." He rocked me slightly and stroked my hair.

The two drinks I'd had, my lack of sleep, and the all-night ruckus took their toll. I soon felt myself drifting off.

He carried me to the bedroom. "You need a nap. I have to go to work soon anyway. I'll be back by midnight."

At that moment, my dog-tired, battered brain didn't care about anything—the job, Jimmy, or Mark. I fell across the bed and hugged my pillow.

When I awoke in the dark, disoriented, I thought it must be near morning. I could see the clock radio read eleven, but for a moment I couldn't make sense of it. Finally, shaking off my deep sleep, I remembered—Mark would be coming in an hour, sleeping in my bed. How strange. *Things are happening too fast.*

After another shower, I thought about what to wear to bed. Usually an old tee shirt or nothing served just fine. Karen had given me a black, shorty negligee when Jimmy and I married, but after the first month, in the interest of comfort, I quit wearing it. I found it in the bottom drawer, put it on and stood in front of the mirror. It was almost too sheer for comfort, but my hair covered my breasts.

I prepared the bedroom for Mark—draped the lamp in a silk scarf to dim the light, tuned the radio to soft music. I perfumed myself, then posed with my hair spread across the pillow and my upper body out of the covers. Just as I relaxed, I heard his car.

I called out as he came through the front door, "Mark, please lock the door. The key's on the coffee table."

When he entered the bedroom, he stopped and smiled. "Isn't this something to come home to. It smells heavenly. You must be an angel."

His eyes never left me. He unbuttoned his shirt, dropped it to the floor, slowly rubbed one hand across his chest while he unbuckled his belt, and then dropped his pants to the floor. Our eyes stayed locked as he bent to step out of them and shuck off his underwear. The muscles of his hairless chest rippled in the lamp-light, pulled my gaze to his hardened nipples, then downward to his part that was just coming alive.

He lifted the covers and slid into bed, then his hand shot under my nightie and drew me to him. Hard. After no more foreplay than a deep sucking kiss, he mounted and plunged into my body. Thrusting and thrusting. One hand under my hips held me to him, the other tangled in my hair and pulled my head back-ward. Squeezing my breasts against his chest, his mouth never left mine, his tongue thrusting and thrusting. It was over quickly. He rolled to the side and gasped. "Woman, you are something!"

I couldn't speak. Disappointed, but blaming myself for setting the scene for his arousal, I tried to keep down the lump in my throat.

He reached over and shut off the radio and the light. "Good night, angel."

Good God. Is that any way to treat an angel?

CHAPTER 17

▼

Not much past daylight, I lay staring at the wall, thinking about last night's fornicating. *Sure can't call it lovemaking.* I felt the bed heave, and then heard the rustle
and tinkle of Mark's belt buckle as he pulled on his pants. When he sat back
down to put on his shoes, I rolled over and looked at his back.

"I have early business today." He leaned across the bed and his goodbye kiss
missed my mouth. "I'll see you later."

Sick of thinking about last night, I curled into a ball, pulled Mark's pillow
over my head and counted backwards until I went back to sleep.

At eleven, when I awoke and went to the White Water for breakfast, Lindy
and a pale young man with hair like straw came into the café where I sat at the
counter.

"Suzanne, I want you to meet my son, Paulie."

He shot her a dirty look.

She smiled at him and stroked his shoulder. "Paul, I mean."

"Hello, Paul." I held out my hand and received a limp handshake. "I hear
you're going to be a bartender."

He pulled down the corners of his mouth in what I guessed he considered a
smile, and then studied his fingernails. "Only if I have to." He pulled at saggy
skin under his receding chin. His whiney nasal voice left me cold. "Aunt Marge
thinks I should work for my keep."

He and Lindy went to sit at a nearby table. I watched them while I ate.

Lindy talked to her son in a quiet, loving voice, but Paul wasn't having it. He
stared at the floor somewhere beyond her, wore a pout-face and slumped in his
chair. She had never mentioned Paul being in jail, so I hadn't repeated Marge's

remark to anyone. From his sullen look, I could imagine the jail was glad to be rid of him.

After I'd eaten, I took my coffee into the bar and Lindy and Paul soon followed.

"That thing about the cops is the shits," Lindy said. "Why'd they do that? Construction workers can't be any worse than loggers."

"Mrs. Mallory had to blame somebody for her little darling staying out. She'd never guess it was because of her."

"Guess we'll see soon enough. They say some of the tunnel workers will be getting to town this week," Marie said.

As we talked, Paul clipped and cleaned his fingernails. Occasionally he brushed dust off the bar, but never once looked at any of us. I wondered if he put on that bored act all the time.

Before long, Bruce Beene, a local logger, came in and sat next to Lindy. He'd spent a lot of time in the bar since she arrived. Although he had a wife and children, he also had a reputation as the town's Romeo. Lindy, becoming quite giddy when he showed up, seemed to share the interest.

About twelve, I went back home and sat on the cool concrete step, reading until the sun drove me inside. The weather had turned hot for mid-June, and my little cracker-box cabin had no shade trees. By four, it was boiling, so I returned to the bar to keep cool until time to begin work.

Lindy and Bruce, the logger, sat at a table with their heads together. Paul kept popping in and out, scowling at his mother.

At five minutes after five, my friend, Greg came in. "Hi, love. This is no place to spend your time off, what you doin' in here?"

"Why not? It's the coolest place in town."

"You're telling me. I've been out all day tramping the brush with clients. Now I got to go take my girlfriend swimming. I'd rather be here drinking beer…with you."

Greg worked for our town's oldest real estate office and had moved to Barkerville two years earlier, in 1960. Our friendship started on my second nightshift—a slow, rainy winter evening. He'd watched me work, and we'd talked over his endless girlfriend problem—as if I were any authority on matters of the heart. His girlfriend was still in high school and from what he said, seemed to be a handful. As time went on, he didn't help matters by spending more evenings in the bar talking to me.

Some nights we had great fun together—making up new drinks, imitating customers, and gathering new jokes. He wanted to learn my job so he could pick up extra money on weekends. Lindy and Marge had said they seldom hired men bartenders, except of course Paul—if you wanted to call him a man. Greg's personality, unlike Paul's dead fish one, was perfect for the job, and the bosses had both come to like him.

Greg took hold of my sleeve and tugged it. "How come you're not off doing something with Mark? I thought you guys were an item."

"I guess we really are an item now. He just moved in with me."

"Boo! I hate that." He made a sad-face. "I was just getting up the courage to ask you out."

"You're full of baloney! You just made that up." I was flattered. "What about marrying Becky...settling down, making all those babies?"

"We need to practice first." He laughed loud, flipping his cigarette ashes in his familiar Groucho Marx imitation. "I'm not getting married any time soon. If she doesn't stop..." His voice trailed off on a note of seriousness. He chugged his beer, then gave a little wave. "Catch you later, love."

Yum, he's cute. Forget it, Suzanne. You just got yourself a live-in.

When I went home to change for work, Mark was unloading groceries from his car. "Hi. I got us a couple of rib steaks...some groceries. What you been doing all day?"

Besides the steaks, he had potatoes, lettuce, salad dressing, bread and milk. It looked like one meal to me. If we were going to be cooking at home, which I rarely did, he'd have to do better than that.

My bosses provided me with dinner on days I worked, so I only ate one other meal a day. I definitely couldn't feed two people on my pay—or wouldn't. I was determined to put away at least $25 each payday toward buying a car, and I was still paying old bills. I needed my tips for my weekly expenses. Counting Mr. Wilke's money, I now had $525 under the mattress with the jewelry.

"Let me do the cooking." He kissed me on top of the head. "You sit on the porch where it's cooler."

Arms wrapped around me, he walked me backward out of the kitchen. The faint odor of perfume, mixed with sweat, jolted me as my nose bumped his shirt. I raised my face, maybe to question him. He kissed me before I had time to open my mouth. His alcohol breath was no surprise. He'd seemed high when he came in.

As I changed for work, listening to him sing a barroom ditty in the kitchen, I wondered where he spent his days—and his nights. It didn't seem like any of my business before—maybe it still wasn't. Anytime I wanted, Karen would gladly take me to Springfield to check on him, but I'd be too embarrassed to ask her.

He brought our trays to the couch where we ate side-by-side. "I'll be getting in very late. I have this gig in Springfield."

I didn't comment. I was hit hard with the realization that most of my thoughts about my new roommate were negative. What was I thinking?

While I washed the dishes, he showered, and then shaved while talking with me through the open door. "You never said what you did today."

Neither did you, Mark.

I told him about meeting Paul, and what was brewing between Lindy and Bruce. He came out of the bedroom looking so handsome a flush ran through my body. The late afternoon sun through the kitchen window sparkled off his wet hair. His lime-green Hawaiian shirt, which he left half unbuttoned, complimented his muscular brown arms. Aftershave filled the room. When he kissed me his tongue was minty, his face silky smooth.

He held me so tightly, my back cracked. "Uhmm. Sometimes I just want to squeeze you to death." I felt his arousal pressing my stomach. He loosened his hold and said, "Better get going before I get in trouble."

"Me, too." Already late, I dashed out the door with him.

When I walked in, Marie was eager to go home. "Lindy's getting pretty drunk," she whispered to me as she was leaving. "I hope you don't have to cut her off. Bruce is holding his own. Maybe he'll get her out of here soon."

Handling Lindy was a type of problem that plagued many a bartender— bosses who had too much to drink. On the one hand our jobs were at stake, on the other, our license to work.

Marge and her nephew, Paul, sat near the end of the bar. They pointedly ignored each other, but watched Bruce and Lindy who were in their own private world of love—or lust. Eventually Bruce came to the bar for two more drinks. Marge frowned at him and spoke with authority. "You better lighten up, Bruce. Lindy's getting a snoot full."

He ducked his head apologetically. "Soon as we finish this one, I'm taking her out for supper."

Paul sniped at him as he turned away with the drinks. "Bet you're taking her for more than supper."

"Paul, you need to…" Marge started loud, and then lowered her voice, "treat your mother with some respect." She motioned me in close. "Suzanne, did I see that young man in the red car moving into your house yesterday?"

I nodded, my face turning hot.

"Are you really that serious?" Her eyes, soft with concern, held mine.

I couldn't take it and looked down at my hands. "Uhm, I don't know…I guess." As soon as I could, I walked away to talk to someone down the bar.

After work, when I got home Mark wasn't there. Since the negligee had affected him the way it did, and because I was aggravated about the perfume I'd smelled on his shirt, I decided to sleep in my old tee shirt—with the light out. I heard his car at four o'clock and kept my breathing sounds long and smooth, pretending to be asleep as I always had with Jimmy. He quietly undressed and slid into bed. I could smell his liquor breath as he settled down with his head toward me. I moaned a little, as if sound asleep and turned away.

CHAPTER 18

▼

All week things stayed the same. The heat scorched the air. Mark went off, God knows where. I pretended sleep when he came in late, then lay awake wondering what kind of crazy relationship I was in. Nights at work were busy. Jimmy came in twice with Alice, so I worried less about him bothering me.

When several strangers trickled into the bar late in the week, I wondered if they were construction workers. They didn't look scary, just seemed like ordinary people.

To escape the miserable heat, Mark and I drove to the coast again Sunday. First we stopped at the shack in Florence, and then drove up the beach to Lincoln City, where he took his briefcase upstairs into an apartment building. As we drove those many miles along the foggy coastline, we didn't step foot on the sand.

On Monday morning, the usual end to the streak of hot days arrived. The sky clouded and a breeze flowed cool and fresh through the bedroom window.

"I'm going up to Washington for a few days," Mark announced while we lay in bed.

"When?"

"Today. I'll probably be back by Thursday or Friday."

It irritated me that he hadn't mentioned anything sooner, but we seemed to be winging it most of the time, so why should anything surprise me? When he reached for me, I let him kiss me, and then pulled away. I wasn't ready for another of his quickies.

"I've got to get to the Laundromat before it gets muggy." I quickly dressed and started pulling the sheets off the bed.

He went to his box beside the couch and took out an armload of clothes. "Here's mine." Without thinking I reached out and took them. He smiled and patted me on the butt.

I jerked away, "Don't ever do that to me."

He shrugged.

I said nothing more, but seethed as I sorted his dirty underwear and shirts. The way I was raised, a woman's purpose in life was to serve her man, and although so far I seemed to be following my mother's lead, I wanted to be different.

After he left, I stared out the window, feeling frustrated and used. Was he making a fool of me? Was I just a roof over his head, his laundress and occasional sex partner? I knew the answer, but refused to give it the light of day. Instead, I dumped his dirty laundry back in his box.

When my clothes were loaded into two washers, I called Karen. "How about going out to Sophie's tonight? Have dinner somewhere first?"

"I'd love it. What about your roomy?"

"He's out of town for a few days. Pick me up about six? This laundry will take me a couple hours."

"Sure, I'll be there. Let's dress up. I'll wear my new sun dress." She clicked her tongue. "Short and sexy."

When I finished the wash, I waxed the floors of my tiny house, still working off my anger and frustration. By four, when I'd finished a long shower, I started to get excited. Sophie's was always a lift. I chose my white spaghetti-strap sheath because I loved the double takes I got from men when their eyes dropped from my face to my bare shoulders and suntanned cleavage. Since Karen wouldn't be along for over an hour, I went next door to the bar to keep my make-up from melting.

Right on schedule, my buddy Greg came through the door. He gave a low wolf-whistle as he sat beside me. His blue eyes snapped. "Look here, boys and girls, she's letting her hair down!" He grabbed my wet hair and lifted it to his face. "I came in here to get cooled off. Look what she does to me!"

I laughed and slapped him on the shoulder. "You are *such* a flirt! No wonder Becky's mad at you half the time."

He lit two cigarettes and gave me one. "Here. I want to see those lips wrapped around this. That little pucker makes me crazy!"

"You nut!" I dragged on the cigarette, puckered and blew a smoke ring his way.

He grabbed his chest. "Oh, no! It's my heart!" When he'd settled down to drink his Hamms, he spoke seriously. "What *are* you doing all dolled up? All by your lonesome on your night off? Where's the boyfriend?"

"He's out of town. I'm having a wee problem with him."

His eyes flashed concern. "Already. What's he done?"

I could be frank with Greg. We'd spent many slow nights in honest, soul bearing conversations about his relationship with Becky and my failed marriage.

"It isn't that he's done anything…really. Letting him move in with me wasn't the smartest choice I ever made. He's kind of strange."

"Why not tell him to skedaddle?"

"That would be so hard. You know what a wimp I am. I should have said no at the beginning. Sometimes he's really neat and romantic…something I've never had. Sometimes he's shitty. I'm so confused."

"Boy! Do I know about that. I'm confused most of the time. Right now, I've got to drink up and go. I'm already in the doghouse. Take care, love."

Karen showed up at the bar's back door about five-thirty. While we ate dinner, we talked about Mark's behavior and about the perfume on his clothes.

"No telling what he does when he's not with you." She leaned across the table and half-whispered. "Hell, he could have a wife and six kids for all you know."

"God, don't say that. I wouldn't go out with a married man in a million years. He wouldn't be moving in if he was married, or even if he had a steady girlfriend, would he?"

Karen stopped cutting her steak and gave me a sad look. "How could you tell, he's never there?"

"He's so good to me sometimes. He cooked dinner. Even gave me a great massage." Hearing myself say things that sounded so lame made me blush. I had no defense.

She raised her voice, stabbed at the air with her steak knife. "Damn it! Suz, that's no big deal. You deserve way more than that. When are you going to figure out you're a prize. You deserve the best."

"So you've told me. Maybe…one of these days."

On the drive to Sophie's, I asked Karen what was happening with Joe.

"Seen him a couple times. Last weekend and Saturday night. We went to a place in Springfield and danced all night. The people who own Kelly's market came in. They'll probably tell Ron's dad, then he'll call Ron." She looked down, twisting her wedding ring. "I don't give a shit."

"You do too, Karen. Are you sure this is what you want?"

"You bet. I want fun. Not being tied down. I have never had any fun."

"I know how you feel. I haven't either. But…"

The rest of the twelve miles to Sophie's she talked about serving her childhood as an ugly duckling.

I assured her, as I had for years, that she was a swan who had absolutely matured into full plumage.

When we walked in, Sophie announced our arrival by shouting, as always. "Looky here, fellas, it's my dancin' girls!" A dozen strangers filled her bar and they all turned, then catcalled and clapped. "Meet Karen and Suzanne, a couple of my favorite gals."

Two men stood to give us their seats. Karen and I looked at each other, shrugged and took them.

"Girls, these here fellows just got off their first day up at the tunnel. They're staying next door in those cabins. We're gonna be seein' a lot of them for the next year. So be nice."

"We're always nice." Karen looked down the bar. "Who's buying the beer?"

"I am." A handsome young one raised his hand. "Give these haybags whatever they want."

Hands on hips, Sophie stamped her foot and spoke loud enough for all to hear. "Now, just a damn minute, bub!"

Karen joined in. "Who the hell you calling a haybag?"

The kid who said it threw up his hands. "Whoa! Hold your horses!"

"There's nothing wrong with that," someone chimed in. "A haybag's just somethin' warm to lay on."

Sophie clapped and laughed. "Well. Guess that makes me a haybag, don't it girls?"

Karen made a face. "I'm still not sure I like that."

"Aw, come on, no one means any harm, it's sweet-talk. It's what we call our girlfriends. And our wives…when they're not mad at us."

Everyone laughed.

As usual, Karen zeroed in on the good-looking one. "Okay, so I'll let you buy me a Bud."

The man on my left reached out for a handshake. "Hello. I'm Sid. These men are part of the site prep crew. They just like to sound like miners. The real hard-core stiffs won't start work for a couple of weeks…but they'll be drifting in soon."

"I think they already are. There have been a lot of strange faces in town this week."

Sophie brought our beers. "Suzanne tends bar in town, fellows. She's going to be takin' care of you 'til the tunnel's done."

Hoots from the men felt good.

Karen talked loud and drank fast, gaining most of the men's attention. As usual, I drank slowly and watched quietly. My style was subtle—but plenty effective.

Sid, who looked about forty, didn't join in the noise either. "Your little town's going to change a lot in the time it takes to build this diversion tunnel, and then the dam." He leaned back and looked at me. "You lived here all your life?"

I nodded.

"You've probably never seen men who drink like tunnel stiffs then. They're like gypsies, roaming from job to job, wherever there's a tunnel being drilled. Few of them stay out the contract. Just come and go, always looking for the 'big job' they can get rich on."

"Is this considered a big job?"

He laughed. "That's a mythical job. One in a perfect place, pays a lot and lasts forever. What those guys do is dirty, noisy, dangerous work…and they love it. It takes a certain kind of man to be a tunnel stiff—to stick with that body-busting life. Someone who just doesn't give a damn."

"Then you're not a tunnel stiff?" Saying the new word felt strange.

"Not me. I never enter that portal. Once the job's underway, I'll be gone. I'm just a trouble-shooter for the contractor."

"How many men, do you think?"

"Oh, there'll be a couple hundred, at least. When they get going they'll be working three shifts—on both ends. Plus all the guys coming and going. You're going to be one busy gal. Hope your boss has more bartenders lined up."

"They probably don't all drink, but that's still a lot."

"They damn near all drink, honey. They're taking home four hundred bucks a week. Half of them got nobody to go home to." He stood and picked up his change. "Since I do have somebody to go home to, I'd better get going. I'll be seeing you."

"Why'd you let that one get away, sweetie?" Sophie asked. "He looked mighty fine."

"Well darn, Sophie, guess I can't have 'em all."

The beer kept coming, as it always did when Karen and I were out drinking. It seemed there were lots of men who thought a woman could be had for the price of a drink. For that reason, I preferred to buy my own, but they'd say, "What's the matter, you too good to drink on me?"

We danced a lot, sang barroom songs, heard some wild stories. Karen, in her favorite element, had guys all around. She could be as wacky as Sophie. Between the two of them, they kept the troops entertained.

Near midnight, I felt cool fingers on the back of my neck and "Hi, love," whispered in my ear. I spun around to find Greg standing behind me with a silly grin on his face.

"What in the world are you doing up here?"

"I went to the bar looking for you. The way you seemed this afternoon, I figured you'd be there. They told me you'd gone stepping."

"Why were you looking for me?"

"I just had to get another look at that white dress."

"Oh, come on…real reason. It's a weeknight. You should be in bed."

"Swear to God. Couldn't get it out of my mind."

"Bet you had a fight with Becky and wanted somebody to feel sorry for you."

"True story…so's the part about the dress."

Since the seats on both sides of me were occupied, I picked up my beers and moved to a table. "Here you can help me drink these. Now what happened with Becky?"

"Oh, she's just acting her age, I guess. She's so jealous."

I laughed. "Why wouldn't she be? You're terrible."

We talked about Mark and Becky for a while, and then someone played the jukebox—Patsy Cline's "Crazy."

He stood and held out his arms. "Dance with me."

Although we'd never touched before, it felt perfect to go into his arms. We danced close, singing the words into each other's ear. His aftershave was subtle and sweet as I rested my chin on his shoulder.

When the song finished, he held me at arm's length, caressed me with those baby blues. "How come we've never done this before?"

"Guess we just never thought of it." I was being flip, denying the fact that it added a new dimension to our friendship.

At my insistence, Greg finally went home around one o'clock. I hated to see him go.

Karen and I stayed until closing time. She handed me the keys and we followed two carloads of construction workers to the all-night greasy spoon.

When Karen got her fake ID, she found the attention she'd been looking for. How could she turn back? She'd bloomed into a creature with power—power to lead men, many men, around by their noses. *Not exactly noses.* Her life would probably never be the same.

When I'd eaten, I wanted to get to bed, but Karen was having too much fun. There was talk of going on to someone's trailer. "I'm going to walk home," I whispered in her ear.

She gave me a little finger wave, and yelled, "Party pooper," as I walked out the door.

CHAPTER 19

▼

The following afternoon, I timed it to be in the bar at 5:05, when Greg usually came in. He walked through the door with a big smile and settled beside me. Marie reached for his usual.

He raised his unruly eyebrows. "You look rested."

"You don't. You look like something the cow stepped in. Did you forget to shave this morning?"

"Didn't have time." He laughed, rubbing his long fingers over his face. "Had a nap in my chair at lunch though."

"So, what else is new? You been burning the candle at both ends ever since I've known you."

He rolled his eyes skyward. "I'll be burning my bridges if I don't go home and get cleaned up. I'm expected promptly at 5:30. She's shortening my leash." He drained his beer, then saluted me. "Bye, love."

Late in the week, Bruce and Lindy did their all-day drinking thing again—openly playing kissy-face. I knew Bruce's wife when I saw her, but she'd never been in the bar with him. As I watched him playing with Lindy, I couldn't help being disgusted. He and Jimmy and all the other chippy-chasers I saw in the bar sickened me.

At about thirty-five, Bruce was twelve years younger than Lindy. Slim built, with sandy hair. Some might call him handsome. To me he looked like a bantam rooster dressed up like Clark Gable. He wore pleated trousers, Italian loafers, and white shirts with cuffs turned under, bartender-style, and usually topped with a suede bomber jacket. Always tanned, with never a five o'clock shadow. His perfect teeth sparkled with touches of gold. He certainly stood out in the crowd of jeans-clad loggers—in a *slick* kind of way. He looked more like a car salesman than a logger. But Bruce knew how to romance a woman—how to make her feel like a lady and act like a tramp.

While I sat drinking coffee before work, Marge came in with an older woman. "Suzanne, I want you to meet my dearest friend, Rachel. She's spending a week or two with us."

"Hello, Rachel." I wondered if Rachel was the woman Lindy said Marge should go back to.

Marge touched her arm, steering her to the end stools. "Rachel lives up in John Day. She's a cattle rancher."

I could believe that, judging by her neatly pressed overalls, red plaid shirt and lace-up boots. What the well-dressed rancher wore in John Day?

Rachel was a big woman—not so much fat, as big boned. Her dark hair, with almost no gray, was pulled back severely in a single long braid. Compared to Marge, she was a handsome woman.

"I had to come down here to see Margie's bar." She looked lovingly at Marge, and grabbed her hand, maybe like sisters.

I listened while Rachel talked about friends they had in common. I hadn't seen Marge so animated—at least not when she was sober. Her eyes sparkled and her usual paper-white complexion had become rosy-cheeked. I wondered why she'd left John Day when she obviously enjoyed the woman so much. They reminisced, and Rachel, in her soft-spoken way, used the term "Margie" over and over—like she loved the soft sound of it. She expressed her great fondness for Marge's sister Lindy, and even the brat, Paul.

As days passed, I noticed Rachel drank very little, and wondered about her having such a dear friend who drank so much. However, after Rachel arrived, Marge spent less time in the bar. Instead, just Paul was underfoot at night. He stood in my way when he was behind the bar, but mostly sat on the other side— watching and drinking. Learning the new job, he said.

Maybe he's leaving the women alone together? Could they be lesbians? Just because a woman dresses like a man doesn't make her a lezzie. Since I'd never known a lesbian, I didn't know what to expect—besides, Marge had been married.

Paul put in several shifts with the day bartender, and then Thursday night he decided he was ready for the night shift. "I'll just take care of the bar and you can stand by." It sounded a little like an order and made me wonder if I'd be taking orders from the twit.

I moved to the other side of the bar with a cigarette and cup of coffee.

Tunnel stiffs were drifting into town, and for parts of my days, I'd been sitting around the bar looking them over, listening to their stories, and having a few laughs with some of them. After they'd checked out the job-site, they had nothing to do all day but hang out in the bar.

Two men called Catfish and Haywire, brothers-in-law, were the first, then came more with names like Swede, Blackie and Gringo. Each time another man came through the door, it was like old home week. The guys all knew each other, but often hadn't seen one another for a year or two. They'd hug and backslap down the line. What they liked best was drinking and swapping tales. Tales of where they'd been, what they'd done, stiffs they'd seen.

"Hey, Catfish, got some walkin' 'round money?" someone asked.

"Sure here's a twenty. Where you comin' in from?"

"Oh, man! I been coast to coast on a piece of toast. Hit that subway job in New York City, got laid off and damn near starved. Thought I'd never get out of there. Don't think I seen you since we worked together for old Shotgun up in Idaho on that dam job. Remember that?"

Job talk went on in big and little groups all day.

"I seen Myers up in Washington, he was on the bum. Gave him fifty. He lit out with a set of matched Oly cases. Said he'd be hittin' this job when it got goin' good."

Paul, with his bush of blond hair and effeminate way of moving—like a young girl, as he flitted about picking up glasses from tables—had been called haybag twice on the day shift. By accident, I thought, but he didn't agree that it was a mistake. I was afraid he didn't have the maturity to realize he needed to walk softly.

The second time I heard it, I chimed in with a big smile and a wink, and a hope for the best. "Hey, where you guys been? You can't tell the boys from the girls? The girls in this town have bumps on the front."

In the first few days, I'd decided my strategy—I would make friends with as many as I could. I'd laugh at their jokes, be properly awed by their stories and I'd gain their respect.

Poor Paul just didn't stand a chance against these men's men after some of them heard his mother call him Paulie.

"Hey, Paulie, how about a Grave Digger?" someone said.

He scowled, and in a voice coarse and bitchy, answered, "What the hell's a Grave Digger?"

Why couldn't he just ask them how to make it? Because the tunnel stiffs traveled all over the world, they often called for exotic drinks—more than likely to show off, as well as to fluster bartenders.

About eleven, Gringo said, "line 'em up from the front door to the shitter!" Some stiffs made a circle in the air, like swinging a lariat, others used the shitter line. They seemed to love outdoing each other buying drinks.

Buffaloed by the big order, Paul said, "Get back here and help me."

The frown between his eyes stayed there while I mixed and he delivered. I liked it when they ordered rounds for the house because it usually meant a nice tip and gave *me* a chance to show off. Luckily, I'd become a faster bartender than the rest and had a knack for remembering what everyone in the house drank. By the time Paul started toward me with orders for a table, I'd have them half made.

After everyone was served, Paul collected Gringo's money—and kept the five-dollar tip. For that, I sat back down on the other side of the bar and took pleasure in watching him struggle the rest of the night.

"I'm waiting cocktails this weekend," he said. "We're getting pretty busy and that's something I know how to do."

"Great." I was relieved not to have to stumble over him behind the bar.

I went home thinking Mark would be there. He wasn't.

Friday and Saturday came and went. I was very busy and frustrated as Paul and I ironed out the wrinkles and tried to work together. Lindy and Bruce sneaked out of town somewhere and Marge stayed home with her friend.

Where the hell's Mark?

CHAPTER 20

▼

Sunday morning, as soon as I'd dressed, I rushed to the phone to call Karen. "Let's go somewhere. Damned if I'll spend my day off hanging around a hot house waiting for Mark. He's two days late."

"Sure. Be there in a jiff. Where do you want to go?"

"First, breakfast. We'll decide later. Bring your bathing suit."

While we waited for our food I complained about Mark.

Karen gave me one of her wise-woman looks, with the brows knitted. "It sounds like you made a mistake letting him move in."

"I'm sure of it! It happened so fast. He seemed so handsome and worldly...guess I lost my mind." I studied my fingernails to avoid those eyes. "I not sure how I feel about him. When he's out of sight, I feel like this, but...sometimes it's nice."

"Hey!" She grabbed my fingers. "Sounds like strictly sex. Just don't try to make anything more out of it. You don't have to love the guy!"

How'd she get so damn smart?

I kept my mouth shut while the waitress set down our sweet rolls and orange juice. "You could be right. It's hard to admit I've made another damn mistake." I buttered my roll and cut it into squares. "I'm trying to improve my life, not screw it up."

"Speaking of loving the guy, what was up with you and Greg at Sophie's? You were both looking kinda dreamy-eyed."

"I'm not sure." I popped a square into my mouth and licked my fingers. "I *do* know I'm really wanting more of him."

Karen smiled at me over her orange juice. "Good."

By the time we finished breakfast, we'd decided to spend the afternoon at the swimming hole. When we arrived, a large group of tunnel stiffs had nearly taken over the beach. They'd built a pool with rocks at the edge of the river and filled it with bottles of beer.

Wolf whistles and catcalls came from the crowd. "Wahoo! Look who's here!"

Catfish smoothed his blanket. "Suzanne. Here's a nice spot, come on."

Karen and I smiled and said hello, but walked past them to the edge of the beach and spread our blanket. We flopped down on our stomachs where we could watch them, and stayed there talking until the heat drove us to the river.

I could feel all eyes when we hurried across the hot sand, plunged in and swam across the river. Men hollered and waved as we stood on the gravel bar on the other side, then whistled and hooted while we swam back and came out.

"How about a cold one?" Someone held up a six-pack. "Just came from the store. Icy cold Budweiser."

Karen strode to their area. "You bet!" She took the beer and plopped on the nearest blanket. They left me little choice—sit down or be accused of being anti-social. I chose to sit.

We drank one beer, then another, while listening to the tall tales the men told each other—sidesplitting and heartbreaking tales. We laughed a lot and learned a lot about their way of life. All their stories centered around jobs and bars, but between the lines, the troubles caused by too much drinking—and their fear.

"I'm gonna do as I damn please every day of my life…who knows when she'll come down on my head," one miner said in a boastful tone.

"Yeah, old Frank Barlow thought he'd live forever. Got out of a couple scrapes. Thought he was through with trouble…'til that rock fell out.

"He never felt a thing."

As the afternoon passed and the sun burned down, everyone got drunker. Their noisy hell-raising brought disgusted looks from the locals who watched their children swim, and curious stares from the teenage girls baking their bodies on the beach.

I got my usual headache—from beer on a hot day—and my skin was frying, so I moved back from the beach to the shade of an oak tree. A couple of the more sensible guys joined me and we sat together watching the crazies on the sand. Men threw each other in the water, dunked, rubbed faces in the sand. I watched Karen pour wine in the mouth of a scrawny, sunburned guy lying beside her. The crimson stream spilled into his ear and onto the blanket.

As I gazed at the river, I spotted a man halfway across that seemed to be struggling and shouting. Suddenly, he went under, and then bobbed up waving his arms. No one seemed to notice. For a second, I thought he was playing a joke. When he went down the second time, I turned to the men sitting beside me. "That man's in trouble!"

I ran through the deep sand toward the beach, pointing, while watching the spot for him to come up. By the time I reached the water's edge, there was still no sign of him. The two men who'd been sitting with me followed, but they'd never spotted him.

"Hey! Someone's drowning!" I yelled as loud as I could and started into the water. "Over here! Quick!"

Several locals were on their feet scanning the water. A few of the stiffs heard me and started toward me. Others were making too much noise.

"Help! Help!" I screamed louder, wading deeper into the water. I realized if someone didn't do something fast the man would die. Several men dove in. Heads came up, looking around for direction and I kept yelling. "There, right there!"

What seemed like minutes passed. People lined the water's edge, shouting orders.

"He's got him," a man named Barney shouted after coming up for air, then dove down again to help.

They pulled a big man in a maroon bathing suit to the shore. Four men lifted his limp body to the sand.

Barney yelled, "Get back, give me room," and went to work on him. "Come on, Spitz. Come on, breathe you son-of-a bitch," he repeated over and over as he pumped his chest and gave him mouth to mouth.

Someone sped off to get an ambulance. People were running in circles, ditching the beer. I stood on the sidelines and helplessly wrung my hands. Beside me, a small man with a big mustache hopped from foot to foot in the hot sand, eyes closed, hands together, his mouth moved in prayer.

Come on, damn it, breathe. Breathe.

Finally, Barney spit to the side and wiped his mouth on his arm. "He's coming around!"

I heard choking, and then saw water, followed by vomit, gush from the guy on the ground as they rolled him to his side. One man pounded his back while another brought water from the river in a beer bottle. They poured the water over his neck and face, flushed away the vomit.

"Jesus Christ, Spitz, what you trying to do, kill yourself?" The man with the mustache, teary eyed, helped him sit up. "You told me you can't swim a lick."

When he'd stopped gagging and spitting, he looked around. "Man, I just wanted to dive off that board…see what it felt like. Thought I could make it back." He took the beer someone handed him, swished out his mouth, spit, then took a big glug. "Good shit."

"You fool, you're just damn lucky this little gal was paying attention. You'd be fish food. This bunch of drunks wouldn't have missed you 'til Monday morning."

Spitz sat with his legs apart, his head bowed, looking down at his feet. Maybe he was thinking about how foolish it would be if a man who lived the dangerous life of a tunnel stiff died because he got drunk and jumped in a river.

The spirit had gone out of the party and the men began to gather their blankets and hidden beer bottles. After that scare, Karen had sobered enough to let me drive. We changed out of our swimsuits at my house, doctored our sunburns and went to the White Water Grill for dinner.

Some of the men from the beach ended up there too, and the one called Spitz insisted on buying our dinner. We accepted. He brought us double shots from the bar, then he and the man who'd prayed for him sat down at our table while we ate. Karen tossed her shot down and pushed her empty glass toward me. If my bosses came in and saw her drinking, I'd be in trouble.

Just as we finished our T-bones, Mark walked around the corner from the bar side. His smile turned sour when he took in the scene. "Hello, ladies, I hope I'm not interrupting anything." The way he said "ladies" left no doubt about his disgust at seeing me sitting with Karen and the two strangers.

Karen ignored it. "Suzanne just saved this stiff's life." She giggled, waving her hands toward the men. "I'd introduce you but I don't know their names."

Something about Karen's gestures, and how guilty I must look, struck me funny. I giggled, too.

"I'll be in the other room when you're done acting foolish." He turned and walked away, his back poker-stiff.

When he left, we burst out laughing. "That's Suzanne's boyfriend!"

"Used to be," Spitz said.

I worried about Karen getting home in her state, but she made it clear that she had no intention of going home—and furthermore since she couldn't drink at the White Water, she announced to her new friends that she was heading for Sophie's. They were too.

When I walked into the other room, Mark sat hunched over a highball. I could see the anger in his posture. I slid onto the stool next to him. "When did you get back?"

"About noon." He spoke to the mirror behind the bar. "Looks like you've been at the river all day." He jerked his head toward the cafe. "What was that?"

The day's alcohol had worn off, leaving me with a headache—sunburned and vulnerable. "I was sitting on the beach watching these tunnel stiffs, when one went under. Nobody saw him and—"

"Tunnel *stiffs*?" His face looked like he'd bitten a lemon. "What kind of word is that?"

"It's just what they call themselves."

"Why would you want to have dinner with total strangers? Just because Karen acts like a tramp, you run with her…you'll be just like her."

I was on the verge of tears, but mostly angry tears. "We weren't really having dinner with them. They came in and sat with us."

"Really," he said, more a statement than a question.

"Running with Karen won't change who I am. Besides, she's my best friend. I love her, and I need to look out for her."

He put his hand on my shoulder, abruptly changing his tone. "I just thought all the way back how you'd be there waiting." He stroked my back. "I hoped I'd get to wake you up this morning."

When Paul came over, I ordered a drink—not ready to go home for kiss-and-make-up. When it arrived, I paid for it myself. His judgment of Karen angered me, because he knew nothing about her. Everything seemed black and white with him. *Aren't you the one who's been out tomcatting for a week, Mark?*

As I looked up from my drink, I locked eyes with Greg who sat at the far end of the bar. He winked as he ran the tip of his tongue across his lips like a kid licking ice cream. That secret gesture affected me in a new and special way. I smiled at the warm, sexual feelings it conveyed, then quickly lowered my eyes as Mark turned to me.

He thought my smile was for him and pressed his cheek to mine. "I missed you this week, I'm glad to be back."

It embarrassed me to have Greg watch me pretend. "Let's go home."

As we walked home, Mark's arm around me, I tried to let go of the anger. "How was your trip?" I hoped he'd open up about where he'd been.

"Fine." He shook me in a playful way. "What did you do all week?"

"I worked mostly."

He had never answered my questions about his whereabouts.

"What did you do Sunday?" He looked into my eyes, waiting for my answer.

In that split second, I decided to lie. "Just hung around. Went to the bar to cool off." Then, to skip over Sunday night, I said, "Today we spent the day at the river."

"I can see that. Your sunburn is terrible." He touched my shoulder as we walked into my hot house. "I'll put something on your poor back."

My bra straps burned like sandpaper on my shoulders, so I stripped off my tank top and bra, and covered myself with my silk scarf.

He pulled me toward the bedroom. "Do you have ice?"

I nodded, sat on the edge of the bed while he brought ice cubes in a bowl. The burn wasn't bad enough for all the attention, but he was obviously trying to make up for his earlier remarks.

I gasped and writhed as he rubbed ice across the top of my shoulders. Goose-bumps ran down my arms. I'd never heard of rubbing ice on sunburn, but maybe that's the way they did it in California. As the melting ice ran down my lower back I squirmed and thrust out my chest. He ran his other hand under my scarf and brushed my hardened nipples.

"Ahh. That turned you on."

I didn't answer. Still angry, I was far from turned on, but didn't want to go into why. I was too miserable and tired to go through an end-the-relationship scene. Even if I hadn't been angry, I certainly wasn't interested in sex.

I tried to be nice and hide my feelings. "Mark, please, just let me get some sleep. I'm beat."

Gentle, and careful of my sunburn, he dried me, then turned back my bed.

"These cool sheets will help."

CHAPTER 21

▼

At sunrise—the time I loved most in summer—I awoke to the light on my face and Mark's head next to my pillow. I slipped out of bed, put on a robe and sat on the front porch. The morning's cool air settled over my body as I watched the pigeons on the roof of the bar and listened to the early morning sounds. A couple of dogs barked at each other on the other side of town, someone ran a saw and hammered nails, and next door, a television played the early morning news. The smell of frying bacon reached my nose through the still air.

Sitting on the step, enjoying a perfect morning, I found it hard to concentrate on the uncertainties of my life—I felt too good.

Mark made noises in the kitchen, then the shower. Soon the smell of coffee brought me back to earth. Still, I sat in the sun.

He came out the door with two cups and my cigarettes. "Good morning, Suzanne. How's your burn?"

I smiled my best smile. "Lots better, thanks."

He sat beside me on the step and I talked about the barking dogs, pigeons, and everything else I could think of to keep the conversation away from Karen, tunnel stiffs and the White Water.

In about an hour, he announced he was leaving and wouldn't be back until after work. "Will you get me a carton of cigarettes from the bar?"

"Sure." Marge let me buy mine by the carton, wholesale from her suppliers.

That evening at work, I overheard Bruce-the-slick talking to Lindy. "I've wanted a divorce for a long time." He squeezed her to him. "Now I have a reason. It won't be long, she's gone to Reno."

I didn't hear Lindy's answer, but her face told me she felt good about it.

"We just got back from San Francisco," he bragged. When I set down their fresh drinks, he pushed five dollars toward me and motioned for me to keep the change. "I bought her dinner at the Top of the Mark."

She stroked his cheek. "Dinner by candlelight."

Bruce Beene knew well how to impress a woman—but I doubted his intentions.

Just then Marge and Rachel came in, laughing at something Rachel said. She had a dry sense of humor and a deep booming laugh that I looked forward to. I could tell Marge enjoyed it too. Rachel came across quite reserved and serious, which made that laugh all the more a pleasant surprise. They sat down several stools away from Bruce and Lindy.

Marge spoke loud enough that other customers turned to stare. "Well, did you two finally come up for air?" She looked agitated, and I noticed Rachel's hand close over hers.

"The kid is having a good time, Margie," Rachel said quietly.

The two couples pointedly ignored each other from then on. The rift that had developed between them worried me. I didn't want anything to disrupt my job.

Lindy and Bruce left early and I wondered where they'd bed down. With Bruce's wife gone to Reno, that wasn't hard to figure.

As soon as Marge and Rachel went home, Paul came in and sat on the corner stool. He ordered a Grand Marnier, but didn't offer to pay for it. I never knew whether to ask him to pay, write it down somewhere—although we never ran bar tabs—or just let it slide. It was expensive and he drank a lot.

About midnight, Greg came in, as he often did after his dates. "Hi, love," he said to me, as he hopped on the stool next to Paul, then nodded politely in his direction. For once, Paul's pouty face cracked into a smile—almost a flirtatious smile.

Oh my gosh, what's up here? He's not…limpwristed, as they say?

Greg must have been a gorgeous boy five years earlier, before he fell asleep at the wheel. It was barely dawn on the first day of his eighteenth year. He'd spent two months in a hospital while they put his body back together and reconstructed his face. The scars were only fine lines, but his lumpy cheeks, the flatness of his nose and its funny bend, told me he'd been hurt. I loved his one-side dimple beside his still-perfect mouth and his deeply cleft chin. His happy, black-flecked eyes distracted most from his damaged features.

Those eyes cast a different light when he talked to me. "Did you have a problem with lover-boy last night? He looked like he'd just stepped in a cow pie with his fancy loafers."

"No problem. Thanks."

"By the way, that's a honey of a tan."

Paul looked back and forth at us, obviously wondering about our relationship.

Greg, who knew I had no love lost for Paul, played with him. "When are we going dancing again, Suzanne?"

I looked at him blankly and winked the eye Paul couldn't see.

You stinker, you're going to get us both in trouble. He'd blab in a minute if he thought he could score something against me.

Greg only stayed for one drink, touched his finger to his lips and left.

Paul drank hard all evening, and by two-thirty he was plastered and loud. "Shit, I gotta stay here drinkin' all night so's Aunt Marge and Rachel can be alone. Mom's screwin' Bruce, Aunt Marge's screwin' Rachel and I'm the one gettin' screwed."

I didn't say anything because I couldn't say what I thought.

After I closed, I helped him off his stool and out the back door.

All that week, incidents kept repeating themselves with the family, as I'd come to think of Marge, Rachel, Lindy, and even Paul. About all that changed was more tunnel stiffs drifting in. They made my nights interesting but sometimes challenging.

Early Friday evening, some men from the tunnel dropped in to kill time and swap stories.

"Wait'll Two-Fingered Shooter gets here," said the guy drinking the Black Russian. "You never seen nobody like him."

I was getting used to their strange nicknames and enjoyed the stories behind them. "How'd they come up with *that* name?"

"Well, I'll tell you one thing, Suzanne, he damn sure earned that handle."

"He first got the name Shooter in prison," Haywire broke in. "Blew his brother-in-law's brains out when he was only twenty. Shot the bastard in the backa the head with a twelve gauge." He studied me for a reaction.

"How come?" I acted as though I heard stories like theirs every day.

It seemed this Shooter's beloved little sister, Polly, married a savage rounder who worked her over shortly after their honeymoon. Fortunately, Shooter picked that day to visit. When he opened the front door, he saw his brother-in-law throw Polly across the room. He grabbed the shotgun, which stood by their front door, and blasted the man.

The foursome at the bar went on and on about him as I mixed drinks at the well. Each one had a story, probably exaggerated for my benefit. As I listened, I worried. How was I going to handle their wild man when he got to town?

"He did twenty at Folsom," said the beer drinker. "Then he went to work for Haywire here. That was down in Feather River country, wasn't it, Haywire?"

Haywire nodded and signaled for another round. "Over ten years ago. Hadn't been on the job two months when he tangled with that muckin' machine. That sucker tore his first two fingers off and—"

"You should've seen him," the guy with the Black Russian cut in. "With his left hand...whips off his belt, gets it around that arm before anyone even knows what happened."

"Never let out a peep," Haywire said, "just walked out the portal to the first-aid shack. Shit, his fingers came out with the muck. Looked like hunks a' hamburger."

Someone said Shooter was finishing up a job in northern California. They'd heard he'd be along in a couple of weeks.

Because of the incredible noise of their work, most tunnel workers were hard of hearing, which made for loud talk. Four loggers who sat at the bar overheard the story and made snide remarks. When I heard them, I rushed to turn up the jukebox.

"Boy, these must be tough sons-a-bitches," one logger said.

"Ooooh! They're scarin' hell outa me," another said in falsetto, waving his hands in front of his chest.

I went to their end of the bar to distract them if I could. "You guys aren't going to cause me problems, are you? How about letting me buy you a drink?"

"Sure you can buy us a drink. You trying to protect your precious jackhammer-jockeys from the big bad loggers?"

"Come on, Ted, that's silly." I laughed, tried to tease him out of it. "They're not bothering you guys."

"The hell! Them bastards just being here bothers me." He crossed his hands over his heart. "You women are all twitterpated." He swept his arm around the room. "You like all these pukes calling you haybags."

"Shit, Ted, that's bull. It's just a word."

While I left to get their drinks, I tried to think of something clever to say to diffuse their jealousy, but when I returned they were debating the merits of

McCullough versus Homelite chain saws, the tunnel stiffs forgotten for the moment.

"Enjoy." I put down their drinks and my two bits worth about the chain saws. "My dad always used a Mall."

"No shit? Granddad has one of those. Can't get no parts now though."

I stayed away from the tunnel stiffs as much as I could, favoring the loggers—until Greg came in. I'd missed seeing him on Thursday. He always gave me such a lift.

"I'll have a beer, Suzanne. Hated not seeing you last night."

I got his beer, but barely had time for a smile. The next thing I knew, he'd gone.

The tiring, busy night finally ended with nothing more than petty squabbles, at least no more problems with the loggers. The miners were used to the jealousy they stirred up in each new town, so usually kept to themselves and tried to keep the peace with the locals.

Mark continued to come home long after I did every night. It was just as well. We spent less and less time together in the mornings because he usually left before I woke up. I wondered where he might be catching up on his sleep.

Saturday he woke me early. "Would you like to ride to Florence with me?"

"I'm just too tired." I yawned and rubbed my eyes to keep from looking at him. "We were so busy last night. There's lots of construction workers. Tonight will be even worse."

The truth was, I didn't want to make any more trips to Florence. Something Karen said last time we talked made me wonder if his trips had something to do with drugs. I associated drugs with New York City or Chicago and found it hard to even imagine that I could be involved with someone in little Barkerville who'd push—or even take—drugs.

As soon as he left, I got up and went to call Karen. She picked me up in thirty minutes, and we went to breakfast.

"What you been doing, kid?" We hadn't talked all week. "Did you go to Sophie's Monday night?"

"Sure."

"Did those guys from the river go?"

"Yeah, they were there, but I didn't stay with them. I spent the night talking to this hand, Billy Boy."

I laughed. "Talking to a hand?"

"Stiff. He's a sweet young thing that's nuts about slot machines. We played all night. He staked me a ten spot and I won twenty-five bucks…he lost over fifty."

"Did you give him back the stake?"

"Hell no. He gave it to me."

"Girl, you're one of a kind! Did this Billy Boy have loving on his mind?"

"Nope, just gambling and drinking. He bought me a steak afterwards. He's kind of sad. Grew up in an orphanage. He's all fucked up—like me. Stutters. Got a nerve problem…blinks his eyes real fast sometimes. All the guys look out for him."

When we'd finished our breakfast, we drove to the river and sat on the sand under the oaks and talked.

"What happened with you and Mark the other night? Was he as pissed as he looked?"

"He didn't have too much to say. At first he was snotty, but he was too horny to stay nasty. Didn't do him any good though." I laughed, but it wasn't funny. "He wanted me to go to the coast with him this morning. I begged off."

"I think you ought to get rid of him. He's trouble. Besides, you're missing a lot of fun with all these hunks in town.

"I don't know. I'd probably just get in another mess if I got out of this one. Speaking of messes, what's going on with Jimmy? You seeing anything of him?"

"I saw him at Mom and Dad's this week for Mom's birthday. Alice and her kids were with him, but he sure as shit didn't look happy. He got me alone and asked if you were getting serious about Mark."

"You said?"

"Said I didn't know. Let him stew. Are you divorcing him?"

"I'm in no hurry."

Three stiffs I knew showed up at the river around noon with their wives—or girlfriends. They had small children, picnic baskets and sand toys. It pleased me to see some of them had families. I showed no recognition—nor did they.

A few days before, I'd learned a valuable lesson. One of the men, a flirt I'd gotten to know by name, came in with a woman I could only describe as a brassy broad—brassy looking and brassy talking. My first mistake was to smile and say, "Hello, Stuart." I'd smiled at her first, as I made it a practice to do, but that didn't help.

She grabbed his arm, her long fingernails digging in. "How do you know this little twitchit?"

"Well, honey, I was in here the other day, before you got to town. That's all."

I stood there, flushing, waiting for their order.

"See that face. You bastard, that tells me all I need to know. Give us a couple double Martinis, then get the hell outa my sight."

As I hurried away, I heard her unload on him. They drank their doubles, then left. It sounded like they were having a hell of a fight as they went outside. Actually, it sounded like they loved a good fight. Never again would I call a man by name in front of a strange woman. Another of life's little lesson I had to learn the hard way.

Karen took me home from the river early that afternoon. She had plans to spend the night at Sophie's working behind the bar. Sophie's business had exploded and she didn't care that Karen wasn't licensed. Sophie knew Karen would keep the boys coming back.

When I walked into work at six o'clock, a half-hour early, I started into the dining room for coffee. Before I got there, I heard Paul and Lindy arguing. Lindy's paramour, Bruce, sat with them. She looked half-sloshed, eyes red, lipstick gone. Paul wasn't far behind. Their table held the remains of dinner, several empty highball glasses and an ashtray full of butts.

"Jeezus, Mom, how can you think of marrying this guy. You've only known him a month," Paul said.

"It's none of your damn business, mister," Lindy said.

"Why don't you just shack up like you usually do?"

"Watch how you talk to your mother, young man," Bruce said.

"Up yours, Bruce! Why don't you just butt out?"

Fortunately, there were no paying customers in the dining room—there never were. The only people who ever ate there were drunks, employees, late night truck drivers or an occasional tourist who didn't know any better. The Liquor Commission required food receipts to equal a percentage of liquor sales so owners often pumped up food records, at the same time shaving bar receipts.

I got out quickly and took my coffee to the bar. Marge and Rachel were also drinking coffee, looking toward the noise coming from the dining room.

"Paul's being a snot. He's spoiled and wants Lindy to himself." Marge seemed sober, but a bit riled. "He'll have to get over that when they get married."

Rachel patted her shoulder. "When she marries Bruce, she won't be needing you so much either, Margie."

Marge and Rachel?

When I began my shift, the Saturday night crowd had already started to kick up its heels. The regulars, plus a dozen tunnel stiffs, kept me hopping—and the stiffs drank much faster. I wondered if Paul would be in shape to wait cocktails for me at nine. He flounced out the back door a few minutes later.

By eight o'clock, couples began to drift in. I barely kept up. The fancy, blended drinks that young women called for took three times as long to mix as highballs.

Finally Paul came back.

"I'm sure glad to see you. I'm getting swamped."

"Well, I don't go on 'til nine." He plopped himself on a barstool. "Gimme some aspirin. I got a bitch of a headache."

I slammed the aspirin box in front of him as I went by. Damned if I would stop and make him a drink. Any decent bartender would have jumped in and helped me catch up.

He came behind the bar and mixed his own—a Bloody Mary.

By the time the clock struck nine, I was rolling and nearly caught up—and fuming. Paul's hangover made him fuzzyheaded, so as the evening wore on he drove me crazy with mistakes he tried to blame on me. I had no time to argue.

Mark came in around eleven. He sat at the bar, next to the mixer station where he could talk to me as I worked.

Marge and Rachel went home. Everything started to smooth out until about one o'clock when Stuart and his haybag came in. After the crap she gave me before, I hated to see them. I plastered on a smile and walked up to her. "Good evening. What would you like?"

"I'd like a different fucking bartender!"

Oh, brother, I needed to call her on her language. *It's so noisy, maybe no one heard.* "I'm afraid I'm it." I never so much as glanced at her precious man. "Would you like Martinis?

She glared and snapped, "Make them doubles."

While I mixed their drinks, I told their story to Mark.

A few minutes later Greg came in and sat next to Mark. "Hi!" He left off the "love."

"Hi! Beer or toddy?"

"I need a little toddy for the body tonight. Make it 151 Rum and Coke."

I poured heavy and pushed it toward him. "This rum'll knock you on your keester."

As I worked, Mark and Greg talked and joked with Paul as he came up for drink orders. I noticed my least-favorite customers' drinks were nearly empty, so reluctantly, I went back to see if they wanted a refill.

"No more." She waved her arms for me to leave. As I hurried away, I heard her say, "Now tip that fuckin' cunt and I'll knock her on her ass." As they left, she gave me a chilling look over her shoulder.

The bar clock showed 2:45 by the time we cleared the last drinks. Bar clocks always ran fifteen minutes fast—to absolutely get all drinks cleared by 2:30. Mark and Greg handed me their empties, and then Greg picked up ashtrays and straightened tables as he sometimes did when he stayed late.

After I shoved the last customer out the door and locked it, I offered the two of them drinks. Paul mixed, then we sat down to catch our breath before restocking. We talked about the crowd, tunnel workers, how much we'd made in tips.

Suddenly, I remembered Stuart and his bitch. "Did you see that couple that sat down at the far end of the bar—the woman with all the hair and the gold lamé jump suit?"

"I saw her and smelled her." Paul made a face. "She was drenched in Evening of Paris."

Greg said, "I noticed they got kind of loud when they left."

"I hope to hell I never see her again," I said, getting excited. "When I went down there to see if they wanted a refill, she said, 'Tip that fuckin' cunt and I'll knock her on her ass.'"

Paul laughed.

Greg said, "Hope he didn't tip you."

Like a black thundercloud, Mark rained on me. He spit and sputtered his indignation. "How could you say...*that*...in front of my friends? You embarrass me."

"I didn't say it. I was only repeating what she said."

"There's no excuse for language like that." He swept up his change and stormed out the back door—slamming it behind him.

"Jeezus, what kind of boyfriend you got there?" Paul said.

Tears of embarrassment burned my eyes and my cheeks flamed. Greg came and stood behind me, folded his arms around me. "Don't worry, love, he just made an ass of himself, not you." He kissed me lightly on the temple.

"He's just so damn weird—I never know what's going on."

"He didn't sound too pure when we were talking before," Greg said. "He sounded like any other guy to me."

"Yeah, if he's so friggin' pure, what's he doin' in a bar in the first place," Paul said. "He's shacked up, ain't he?"

"I don't get it. He thinks Sophie's the cat's meow. You know how she talks."

We continued discussing Mark as we finished stocking beer. Paul thought I should go right home and throw him out. Greg didn't offer an opinion.

I didn't know what I'd do when I got home. But, finally, I had to go.

CHAPTER 22

▼

Mark's car sat in front, but the house was dark and the front door stood open. When I warily stepped inside, the streetlight's silver beam stretched across the floor and spotlighted his black loafers. He slouched on the couch, well hidden in the shadows. When he drew on his cigarette, I could see the angry set of his jaw. I didn't know what to say. I knew I would cry, no matter what—and I'd be humiliated. My grandfather, father and husband had called me "crybaby" all my life—shamed me for my tears, even when they rose from anger or frustration.

I went to my bedroom, undressed in the dark.

"Suzanne, come back here."

Damn. I might as well get this over with. I put on my robe and went to stand before him.

"What I don't understand is how a beautiful woman like you can have such a filthy mouth."

"I don't have a filthy mouth." My voice barely came out past the lump that rose in my throat.

"You don't call what you said tonight filthy?"

"I was just telling you—"

He held up his hand. "Stop! Don't repeat it. There's no excuse—"

"Damn it, Mark, don't talk to me..." Angry sobs cracked my voice. "like a child."

"I'm sorry, Suzanne, but I like to think I'm spending my time with a lady."

I pushed away his hand and shouted, "If you don't think so, then why are you here?"

No answer.

I stalked into the bathroom and slammed the door. Fighting to rein in my emotions, I sat on the toilet dabbing my eyes. Echoes of his words played through my mind. Wasn't I a lady? I thought of myself as a lady, but maybe he was right. Being here with him wasn't too ladylike. *Stop it, Suzanne. You're every bit as good as he is.* When I regained control, I came out.

He lay in bed in the dark.

I finished undressing and slid in, keeping as much space as possible between us.

Sometime, just after the rising sun sent bright stripes up the wall, I slept.

After noon when I awoke, Mark had gone. I jumped up to see if his stuff was gone. No such luck. I'd hoped all trace of him would be gone and the worst would be behind me.

As usual, when things were bad, I called Karen. "Come get me. Let's go somewhere. Mark's being a shit."

"What'd he do?"

"It's just something stupid. I'll tell you when you get here. I don't want the whole town to know."

When she roared up in a cloud of dust, I dashed out to meet her with a beach blanket, small suitcase with two changes of clothes, and my stash from under the mattress. "Let's get out of town. I don't have to work 'til Tuesday night. Where can we go?"

"How 'bout Portland? My friend Sandy's between boyfriends, she'll put us up a couple nights."

"Let's boogie. Mark might be back any minute."

We stopped at Karen's to get her clothes. We were in high spirits as we drove out of town—a couple of kids running off to the big city.

"What did the asshole do this time?"

"He flipped out because I said fuckin' cunt. I was just repeating somebody."

"You're kidding. He sure has delicate ears for a criminal."

"I don't think he's pushing drugs, but he's sure a hypocrite. I thought it was so neat to have the handsome stranger on the hook. Looks like he's got me hooked now."

An hour later, we stopped at a bar in Salem for burgers and a beer. The crowd was in the middle of a pool tournament. We ate and stayed to watch. Karen, for a change, remained on her stool.

"You're pretty quiet all of a sudden. What's going on?"

"Ron and I talked last night. He asked a lot of questions about what I've been doing. I think he knows something."

"Have you made a decision?"

"Suzanne, I'm having fun for the first time in my life." She stared into her glass of beer. "I don't know if I ever loved Ron. Maybe I just wanted somebody to care about me."

"That's probably true, Karen, but it's not so bad. Up to now you've been a good wife to Ron. You kept your part of the bargain. Until you slept with Joe."

"So, what do I do now?" She looked at me with brimming eyes. It wasn't often Karen shed tears.

"You have to do the right thing. Otherwise, you'll hate yourself."

"I don't think I can tell him." At that, she raised her chin and wiped her eyes, tossing her head in that don't-give-a-shit gesture I knew too well. "Bring me a shot of Tequila." She squared her shoulders. "With salt and lime."

The sad little girl was gone in a flash, replaced by the tough cookie most people recognized as Karen Daugherty.

When the men at the bar saw her lick salt from her hand, down the Tequila, then chomp the lime, I could read their minds—here's a gal who knows how to party. Their eyes lit up and their attention left the pool game.

Predictably, it came right on schedule, from the man on Karen's right. "Can I buy you girls a drink?"

"Sure." She smiled big. "We're running away from home. Can't fly on one wing, you know." Realizing where she was headed, I declined. "You're not going to be a party pooper, are you, Suz?"

"Yeah, don't be a party pooper," somebody echoed.

"I'm not." I raised my half-full beer glass. "I'll have one next time."

Satisfied, he bought Karen's and snugged in close to her. He took away her lighter after she put a Camel to her mouth and made a big deal of lighting it.

I sat on her left, pretending great interest in the pool tournament on the other side of the horseshoe bar. The bartender, one of those old guys who's been at it for thirty years, looked at us like he'd seen a million—he probably had. His watery eyes, perpetually squinting in the dark, smoky room, watched us—ready to pour those Tequilas he knew the men would buy. His yellowed fingers rested on the bottle. Karen wouldn't disappoint anyone—except me.

While she tossed down the shots, she also tossed out pieces of information. "We're going up to Portland to have a good time. Suzanny's mad at her lover-boy."

By then, guys were standing around her, falling all over themselves to buy her drinks. I figured she must have been the best prospect they'd seen in their dinky bar in weeks—maybe months.

The guy sitting on my left kept nudging me. He smelled like a horse blanket and his nasty breath blasted me in the face each time he spoke. To get away from the smells, I turned my body toward Karen. He pestered me about buying me a drink. I kept saying no.

Finally he tapped me on the shoulder. "Oh, I get it, you're one of them." He spoke loudly to the person seated next to him. "These two are queers. They're just in here moochin' drinks. See, the short haired one's her..." He curled his lip, showing his rotten, black teeth as he drawled the word, "boyfriend."

It wasn't the first time the label had been hung on us though I never understood why. I wanted to tell him that I'd like a real man to buy me a drink, not some smelly asshole like him, but I didn't have the guts. Besides, if I did, Karen would hear and the fight would be on. Instead, I sat with my imitation smile, hoping we'd soon be on our way.

A fellow sitting across from me with his back turned, watching the pool play, heard the loud mouth and turned to look. When he saw my smile, he smiled back—with warmth and sympathy. Since Karen was so engrossed with her little playmates, I decided to get away from Mr. Horseblanket and show him how he rated. I picked up my beer and walked around to the opposite side of the bar.

"Mind if I sit? I won't bite you, but that character's bothering me."

"I noticed that. Where you ladies from?"

"Barkerville. On our way to Portland for a couple days—I hope."

About then, Karen, noticed I'd moved. "What the hell? You don't want to sit with us?" She slurred her words and waved her hand at the fellow next to me. "These guys are doin' Portland with us. You goin'?"

"Nah, I'm working tonight."

The shots of Tequila were catching up with her fast and it showed in her high-stepping walk to the ladies room.

"Excuse me," I said, and followed her. "Karen, let's get out of here."

In the stall, she groaned. "Oh, Suz. Shit!" She coughed and gagged. Vomiting sounds echoed off the walls and its sour odor filled the room. "Shit, I'm sick."

"Well, of course you're sick, who wouldn't be, drinking like that."

She blew her nose. "Let's go home."

"Okay, but what are you going to tell these guys you've been leading on?"

"Piss on 'em!" She washed her face, straightened her back and marched out of the ladies room with her head high. She swept up her Camels and purse, tipped the bartender and said, "See you around."

"Wait a minute...you can't leave just like that," the clod sitting closest to her said. He stood and grabbed her arm.

She slapped his hand away. "The hell I can't!"

I'd moved to the other side of the bar to gather my stuff.

"I hope you're driving," the bartender said.

I'd picked Karen's keys up from the bar before I moved. "I am."

As we started out the door, I heard the two men say, "Chicken shit broad. Told you they was queers."

Karen didn't argue when I climbed behind the wheel and headed south. During the drive home she cried about her marriage, whined about her headache, and finally slept the last thirty miles. My thoughts bounced like pinballs during those miles. I could do nothing about Karen's marital situation, but advise and protect her like always. It wasn't my job to judge her. Even though I was disappointed at the change of plans, I didn't blame Karen. She was who she was, and I loved her.

We arrived at her house just after dark. Holding her head, she staggered into the house. "I'm going to bed. Make yourself at home." She unbuttoned her blouse, groaning as she made a beeline for her bedroom.

"Can I take your car for awhile?"

"Sure. See you in the morning." Hanging onto the doorframe, she peeled off her jeans. The poor kid looked like a hundred miles of gravel road—eyes bloodshot, lipstick gone and hair cocked up on the side. "Don't do anything I wouldn't do, Suzanny."

"Not a chance!"

First, I drove down the back street behind my house to see if Mark's car was there. No lights showed so I circled the White Water and looked over the cars. No sign of him.

Sitting on the side street wondering what to do next, I thought about my mess. My concerns were not how to save the relationship, but how to end it. I'd taken the coward's way out as usual, hoping that my leaving town would cause him to move out. I could lecture myself all night about behaving like a grown-up, but what it boiled down to was I simply didn't have the nerve to stand face to face and tell him to leave.

Rather than go back to Karen's, I drove out to Sophie's. When I got there, I was surprised to see Mark's car. I parked around back, got out and looked in the side window. He sat with his back to me at a table with two men, strangers, whose faces looked pinched and grim as they leaned close and talked. Mark took something from one and dropped it in the pocket of his sport jacket.

I watched Sophie bring them a tray of drinks and hurry away, and then a nearby couple rose and headed for the door. I didn't want to be seen lurking around the side of the building, so I dashed to the car.

On the drive back to Barkerville, I decided to stop at the bar for something to eat. I figured I'd have time before Mark could drink up and leave Sophie's. Paul was behind the bar, and although the crowd was fairly heavy, many of his customers were sober men drinking Cokes and coffee before graveyard shift. A few day-shifters who'd already had their quota, sat with an empty bar in front of them—eighty-sixed by Paul.

Marge and Rachel sat drinking coffee.

"Hello, ladies. How's things tonight?" I said.

"We're excellent. Please, join us," Rachel said. "Paulie, I'd like to buy Suzanne a drink."

"Thank you. I'll just have a Bud. I'm getting something to eat." As we chatted, I remembered the cigarettes Mark had asked me to get. Why I cared, I didn't know, but he couldn't fault me for forgetting. I said to Marge, "I'd like to buy a carton of Pall Malls if you can spare one."

"Don't you smoke Salem? You buying cigarettes for that drifter that's sponging off you?"

Stunned by her remark, I nearly lost my voice. "Yes…he asked me to."

"Does he pay his share of the rent?"

"But, I have to pay rent anyway." Heat rose in my face.

"Does he buy the groceries?"

"Sometimes." How lame that sounded.

"Honey, in my opinion, he's using you. I'm not going to let him use me too. He can buy his own damn cigarettes at the grocery store." She patted my hand.

"You've got a good head on your shoulders, girl," Rachel said. "Don't let men use you." She smiled at Marge. "Though I mostly prefer the company of women, there are some very good men that—"

Marge interrupted. "Mark Bradley's not one of them."

"Your friend Greg's a good man," Rachel said. "He has eyes for you, you know."

I stuck out my lower lip and made a face. "But he has a steady girlfriend."

After I'd eaten my fish and chips, I started to worry that Mark might show up, so I said goodnight and left.

Driving through the night to Karen's, I got a little kick out of imagining Marks's dismay when I didn't come home all night.

CHAPTER 23

▼

Of course, Karen was sick the next morning, so we lounged around her house until afternoon when she felt well enough to go to the river. The beach was crowded with tunnel stiffs with lots of beer, and, as usual, we helped them drink it. Karen apologized for ruining our trip to Portland. I told her about driving out to Sophie's, and the mysterious men Mark sat with.

As the afternoon wore on, we made a plan. I would sneak Mark's keys from his pocket, then look in his briefcase. It seemed foolproof when we were half full of beer. He took long showers and the plan called for getting the keys, looking in the trunk, then getting them back before he finished.

By evening, when she drove me home, we were melodramatic lunatics.

Karen cheered. "Yeehaw! Your last great challenge as the mistress of the dark stranger."

"A challenge I take in the interest of truth and justice!"

A stupid plan. But bravado carried me through the moment of seeing him again.

He sat in the living room reading a book. I lugged in my armload of beach stuff and the suitcase, trying not to show I was tipsy. He jumped up, took the bag and ice chest.

"Where have you two been?"

"At the river."

His eyebrows rose. "All night?"

The beer in me wanted to say yes, but in the interest of peace and my secret mission, I didn't. "I stayed at Karen's last night. She was sick."

"About what I said to you the other night." He put his arms around me and nuzzled my neck from behind as I stood by the bed unpacking. "I shouldn't have come on so strong." I stiffened at his touch, but he went on, "I want to save you from the influence of people like Karen. You're too good for them."

"I don't want to talk about it, Mark. It's my night off. I'd like to have some fun. Do you want to take me somewhere?"

"Sure. Let's have dinner and some drinks."

"I'll shower first, it takes longer to fix my hair." I pulled away, went into the bathroom and closed the door. I quickly showered, then came out in my robe with my hair wrapped in a towel. "Your turn, I left the water on."

He stretched his pants across the bed, went into the bathroom and left the door open. Speaking from the shower, he said, "I saw Greg at Sophie's last night. He asked about you."

"He what?" I pretended I hadn't heard.

"He asked about you."

"Oh. What were you doing at Sophie's?" Because he kept talking to me from the shower, I could see my plan wouldn't work. I answered while I rifled through his jacket pockets. Nothing.

"I went out there thinking you might be there."

"Did she have a crowd?" I grabbed his wallet. It bulged with money. His driver's license and social security card gave me a shock. Both documents listed him as Donald Lightfoot. I was still staring at them when the water shut off. All thumbs, I closed the wallet and tried to jam it back in his pocket. It finally fell in just as he stepped out of the bathroom. I gave the pants a pat, and giggled. "Sorry, I sat on your britches."

"Get dressed, lady, I'm starving."

While I quickly dressed and put my hair in a ponytail, I stole glances at him, wondered who the hell he was.

We saw Jimmy at the Steak House, apparently waiting for Alice to get off work. He looked like he'd lost weight, and I felt a familiar twist in my stomach. We said hello, walked past and sat in the next booth where I faced toward Jimmy. He stared at me while we ordered dinner. I had trouble keeping my eyes off him. I hated him thinking I cared about Mark. Before we were served, Alice came from the kitchen with her purse and tapped Jimmy on the shoulder. They walked out the door, arm in arm. He glanced back with a sad looking smile on his face.

When our steaks came, Mark said, "How about some wine?"

"Sure. Burgundy?"

He ordered a bottle and drank three glasses while we ate.

I'd started to sober, and to hatch another plan to get into that briefcase. "Let's go to the White Water for awhile."

"Okay, but I'd rather go out to Sophie's."

"Fine."

During the two hours we stayed at Sophie's, I sipped one beer while he drank several. Around midnight I insisted we go to the White Water so I could put my plan into motion.

When we walked into the bar, the "family" all stared at us. No doubt, Paul had told them about the episode after we'd closed Saturday night. Lindy and Bruce sat alone at a table and Marge and Rachel held their usual end-of-the-bar seats.

I led Mark to a table near the jukebox and playfully pushed him into a chair. "I'll get our drinks. What'll you have?"

He opened his wallet and handed me a five. "Vodka tonic, with lime."

The jukebox covered me when I said to Paul, "I'm getting even with him for Saturday night. Put doubles in his and make mine plain orange juice. I want him blotto by closing time."

"With pleasure. I'm surprised to see you with the jerk."

We played the jukebox, and I kept him occupied for the final two hours. Drinking my virgin Screwdrivers fast, I set the pace. Near closing time, Mark began showing the results of the doubles—slurring words and putting his hands on me. I led him on, although it embarrassed me to have the few customers see me. Marge and Rachel had gone home and I didn't care what Paul thought.

Finally, Paul called, "Drink 'em up time."

"Let's go home, Mark."

"Saddle up, Suzanne."

Where the hell did that come from? The real Mark?

We went out the back door hip to hip. Mark staggered against me and I laughed and carried on as we lurched along, making lewd remarks about what we'd do to each other when we got home. I was sure he wouldn't be able to do much.

I led Mark straight to the bedroom, unbuttoned his shirt as we went. He flopped down on the bed and closed his eyes.

"Come on Mark, you'll wrinkle your pants." I giggled as I undid his belt and tugged on his pants. He pulled me down on him and kissed me hard. "Hold it, let me get my clothes off...it's too damn hot in here."

He rolled around enough to help me pull off his pants. I stepped into the living room and hung them over the back of the couch.

"Shit, the bed's spinning!" He spread his arms like wings, flailing the air. "Get on here...help me hold it down."

I pulled up my dress and straddled him, stroked his chest. "Is this what you want?" I crooned, and my untied hair smothered his face. He murmured as I rubbed myself on him. Soon his murmurs stopped and his breathing took on the rhythm I was waiting for. I sat up, tossed my hair back and looked at him. His relaxed jaw and slack mouth confirmed he'd gone to sleep.

I sat astride him, feeling the regular rise and fall of his chest. I decided that, if he awoke, I'd be ready to continue the seduction. However long it took.

After a couple minutes, deliberately making a lot of movement of the bed, I dismounted him. He didn't stir. I stood in the doorway between the bed and the couch, watched him and the clock. When he'd snored for five minutes, I slowly reached into his pants' pocket for the keys. Cautiously, I removed them without a sound, then slipped outside and left the door open.

The car stood fully illuminated by the yard light. My heart pounding, barely breathing, throat nearly closed with fear, I put the key in the lock. The trunk hinge squawked like a screech owl when I raised it. Frozen, I stood listening, searching my mind for a lie I could tell to explain. None came. If he caught me, I'd just have to face whatever resulted. I sensed he'd hurt me, but I couldn't turn back. I had to know what he was up to.

The edge of the briefcase showed under some odds and ends of painting stuff and his beach blanket. Before I moved anything, I memorized how they were arranged, and then carefully slipped the briefcase out. My hand shook as I fumbled with its latch. Locked.

Damn! Why did I ever start this?

My sensible mind told me to shut the trunk and forget it, but after taking such chances, I couldn't. There were more keys on his ring so I reached up and took them from the lock—a small key and the two for the car. My fingers felt like clumsy stubs trying to fit the tiny key in the lock. In the shadow of the trunk lid, I could barely see the keyhole. While I fumbled, a nearby dog barked. Startled, I nearly dropped the briefcase. Another dog answered him. I stood still and prayed for them to stop.

Calm down, Suzanne, calm down.

Finally, as my heart pounded and my terror grew nearly beyond control, the latch snapped open. When I lifted the lid, a glint of metal caught my eye. A shiny, snub-nosed revolver lay on top of some papers. I gasped. Loud. As loud to my ears as a scream in that silent night. I stood perfectly still, looked toward the house.

My God. He might kill me.

My knees quivered as I listened.

Terrifying thoughts shouted inside my head. I imagined him leaping off the porch like a wild dog and knocking me to the ground. No way in hell could I lie my way out of the situation.

I forced myself to continue, bent down, and looked closely at the papers under the gun. My eyes saw them, but my brain didn't believe. I touched them, felt the familiar texture. Bundles of money. Twenty-dollar bills. Layers two inches deep, completely filled the bottom of the briefcase.

I'd seen enough.

Quietly snapping the briefcase shut, I once again fought my shaking fingers, trying to fit the small key into its lock. Somehow they slipped from my sweaty grip and landed somewhere on the trunk's floor. The night's stillness amplified the clatter to the magnitude of thunder. My hand grabbed at the sound, but found no keys.

Calm down, calm down.

Nearly gasping from holding my breath, I concentrated for a second on breathing—slowly sucking in the night air as I carefully moved my hand around in the black bottom of the trunk. In what seemed like minutes, but was only a couple of deep breaths, my fingers found the keys. Carefully, my left hand still steadying the briefcase on the trunk's rim, I positioned the smallest key in my fingers before picking them up. They tinkled softly in my shaking hand, but I hit the lock at my first jab and it turned.

Thank God.

After tucking the keys inside my bra, I used both hands to place the briefcase exactly where I'd found it.

I knew I had to make one more sound—to latch the trunk. My heart rattled my rib cage as I prepared myself. There was nothing to do but slam it—gently, but hard enough to latch on the first try. I slammed it down, and then raced on tiptoes into the shadows next to the house. The sound it made echoed in my ears and stirred the dogs again.

I leaned against the house, forced my breathing to slow and I listened.

Calm down, calm down.

Fear gripped my chest. I pictured him standing inside, ready for me. I waited. I reasoned with myself. If he'd seen me, he'd have charged out. I waited. My heart slowed enough for me to hear the dead silence of the night. I waited.

Finally, I came out of the shadows, gathered my courage and hurried up the concrete steps, into the house. Inside, I stopped and listened. I could hear Mark's steady breathing as he slept. I slipped the keys back in his pocket, and then grabbed a pack of cigarettes and went out on the porch.

As I smoked and thought, my shaking soon stopped but adrenaline in my bloodstream kept my mind racing. I thought about what I'd seen. First, about the gun. What a shock to find that Donald Lightfoot, whoever he was, carried a concealed weapon. And the money—there had to be thousands in there. Was he buying something or selling something? Was all that money his? I wished I could talk to Karen. Instead, when my cigarette was finished, I had to get into bed with a stranger.

CHAPTER 24

▼

When morning came, Mark seemed chagrined and complained of being hung over. "I'm sorry I let you down last night."

He nibbled my neck as I poured our coffee. His touch sent chills up the back of my arms.

"I think we both had too much to drink." I moved away and dressed quickly, before he could get any ideas. "I've got to see Lindy and Marge this morning, about the schedule."

"Too bad. I hoped we'd have some time together. I have to go up north for a few days."

"When?"

"In a couple of hours."

Thank God. "I'm sorry, but I need to be at the bar."

He pulled me to him, ran his hand under my shirt, felt me up and kissed me sloppily. The old feelings were gone. Completely. Disgust was all I felt.

When I walked in the bar's open back door, Lindy and Marge sat hunched over their cups of coffee. Marie polished the mirrors on the back-bar. No one heard me.

"Lindy, I won't put up with this shit. We're short at least twenty dollars a night."

My breathing stopped. Me? I wanted to back out of the room—but couldn't.

"Maybe you're wrong, Marge. You're always so quick to blame him for everything."

"He's drinking all the Grand Marnier, too. That's the second bottle since he got here. No one else drinks that stuff."

I exhaled, long and silent. My first thought had been Paul, but I'd jumped to the conclusion he'd managed to put the blame on me. I said hello to everyone and walked through to the dining room and ordered breakfast. In a few minutes, I heard loud voices and went to the doorway.

"I've had all the bullshit I can take, Lindy. You can buy out my half of this operation. I'm going home with Rachel."

"Marge, damn it, why do you take your hate out on Paulie?"

"'Cause he's a spoiled brat. I never should've left John Day."

"Okay, if that's the way you want it, I'll get a lawyer to do the paperwork. I'll give you back your half."

I went on slowly eating my breakfast, taking as long as possible. Thoughts of Marge leaving gave me rocks in my stomach, and my food tasted like nothing I'd ever eaten before. Lindy was so much under the influence of Bruce that things were bound to change around the White Water.

Later, when I carried my coffee into the bar, Marge was gone. I sat down by Lindy. "Sorry you're having a bad day."

"It's all right. With Bruce and me getting married, it's better this way. Marge doesn't approve of him either."

"When are you getting married?"

"As soon as his divorce is final. His wife's in Reno. Probably two weeks."

"That's great." I didn't believe the words I said.

I called Karen from the bar. "Can you come and see me? I carried out our plan last night."

"Oh, God. You didn't!"

"Just come get me. I'll tell you all about it."

"Five minutes."

"I'll be home…unless his car's there. If it is, I'll be in the restaurant."

When I hung up the phone and looked out the back door, Mark was gone.

Karen burst into the house wide-eyed. "What'd you do?"

"First, I got the wallet. He's no Mark Bradley, he's somebody named Donald Lightfoot."

"No! Shit, then he is a crook."

"I got him drunk…passed out. Looked in his briefcase. He had a gun and a pile of money."

"I can't believe you did that! Jeez, Suzanne, maybe he's a bank robber."

"Judas priest! I never thought of that."

"He could be dangerous. You've got to get rid of him. He could get you in big trouble."

"As soon as he gets back, I'll tell him to leave. I'm scared shitless, but I got myself into this…I'll get myself out. It is my house."

Karen stayed until time for me to go to work, telling me about the good times she'd been having at Sophie's nearly every night. "Billy-Boy's nuts about me. Have you met him yet?"

"Yeah, he came in the other night and played the slot machine for awhile. He's a fiend on that thing. Must have spent fifty bucks. Played Wolverton Mountain…over and over and over."

"Sophie doesn't have it yet. He just sings it out there."

"Lucky Sophie. He's got a cute southern accent. You aren't sleeping with him, I hope."

She shook her head. "Doesn't seem to want to. Plenty others do. 'Course now they think I'm Billy-Boy's girl so they steer clear."

"I'm sure you'll find a way to let them know different."

Though most of the tunnel workers I'd seen so far were too rough and ready for my taste, I envied the fun Karen was having.

"Sophie's having a barbecue two weeks from Sunday. It'll be a dilly. You coming?" Karen said, as she was leaving.

"Probably."

I dressed and went to the bar at five. I hadn't seen Greg since Saturday night and I felt sure he'd been looking for me at Sophie's on Sunday. Five after five, like a burst of fresh air, he bounced through the door. I recognized his way of slapping the door even before I looked up. He moved toward the bar like a dancer—graceful, fluid movements on the balls of his feet.

We made eye contact. "Hello, love. Where you been? I missed you."

"Karen and I went to Salem Sunday. She was on her ass before dark."

"Saturday night? I was worried."

"Nothing happened."

"How did you like his little fit?"

"You can imagine. It's over. Just a matter of time. Soon."

"Good." He gave my hand a quick squeeze. "Got to go. I'll be back later. We can talk."

He touched his finger to my lips, and I kissed it.

Later, after I went to work, I overheard two tunnel stiffs. "Two-Fingered Shooter blew in today. Said he'd be downtown tonight."

"I'll be glad to see the old cuss. Haven't seen him since last fall."

I felt less nervous about Shooter since I'd gotten to know some of the other hands—and made friends of the best of them.

Not ten minutes later, two strangers came in.

"Shooter! How the hell are you?" someone yelled.

"I'm a mean son-of-a-bitch and thirsty as a camel. Set 'em up from the front door to the shitter! Me first."

"What'll you have?"

"Scotch and soda, honey. Double Johnny Walker Red. Keep 'em comin'."

All evening I studied him. Two-Fingered Shooter had the face of a fighter, no neck, cauliflower ears and a nose that went every which way. Short and stocky, powerful like a little rhino. From the stories about him, I guessed his age to be just the other side of fifty, but with the wear and tear on his face it was hard to tell.

When he spoke, his thick, scarred lips got in the way. He'd lisp and spray droplets of spit in all directions. The more he drank, the more he spit. It wasn't long before the twinkle in his sky blue eyes gave him away as a pussycat—at least where I was concerned.

Near midnight, Greg came back. "Got your little honey tucked in?"

"Yes, ma'am." He saluted and clicked his heels. "At your service."

I wanted to spill out my story to him but being so busy with Shooter's welcome-home party, all I could do was give him hints while I mixed drinks.

"You figured out how to get him out?"

"Not exactly, but I'll do it."

Each time I returned to my station, we exchanged a few words.

"Anything new with him?"

"Yes." I shook my hand like I'd touched a stove. "Hot, hot stuff."

He leaned close. "Gimmee."

"Uh uh. Can't talk about it here."

"Yow! Woman, you make me crazy. A hint?"

I looked around, and then pointed my index finger, thumb up.

His eyes widened. "No! We've got to talk, love."

"Not tonight, I'm too busy. You've got to get some sleep. Let's meet somewhere at lunch-time tomorrow."

"Where? The river? I'll be killed and fed to the dogs if I'm caught with you."

"No car, remember? Come in here…the cafe. Nobody goes in there."

"Okay, but I won't sleep a wink tonight."

"I know you won't, if you don't go home and get to bed. You have a heavy date tomorrow." I laughed. "A nooner."

"You're the boss." He finished his beer, and then put his finger to his lips in that gesture I loved. "'Til noon, pretty lady."

The last hours of the night flew by in a blur of Johnny Walkers and rounds for the house. The weeknight crowds were getting to be too much for me. Night shift at the tunnel ended at midnight, then the men showered and changed at the job. By one o'clock, they were ready for that last hour and a half of hard drinking. After three, I finally crawled into my bed. Alone.

At eleven the next morning, I looked in my closet for something special to wear for my date with Greg. After trying on a couple outfits, I settled on a bright yellow sundress that showed off my tan. I wanted to look stunning—but not like I planned to. My hair, still damp from my shower, hung loose and wavy against the yellow.

A few minutes to twelve, I walked in the back door. Bruce, who stood behind the bar, whistled. "Well, who's this little ray of sunshine?"

Lindy gave him a strange look. "You're pretty in that color, Suzanne."

I felt my cheeks flush. I hadn't intended to attract so much attention. "You our new bartender, Bruce?" He seemed to be moving right in.

"I figured I'd better learn something about this before we get married." He ran his hand over his wavy hair and pushed up his turned-under sleeves. To me, every move he made showed his ego. "Paul will have to start working week nights with you. I'll fill in on your nights off."

It sounded like Lindy had handed him the reins of her business. I didn't trust him—once a cheater, always a cheater. I headed for the dining room.

Just as I sat down, Greg slipped through the door. "Oh, baby." He sighed, stopped in his tracks. "Stand up. Let me see." He motioned with his graceful hands for me to turn.

I stood and whirled, flipping my hair behind my back. He made me feel *so* special.

"You are such a knock-out woman." His eyes were soft and true.

I didn't think of myself as beautiful, and I loved it when he said it, because I believed him. "Thank you."

"You ordered yet?"

"No, I'm having eggs."

He spoke to the cook, ordering for both of us, then sat close to me in the corner where no one walking by could see him through the window. "Now, give. What's this about a gun?"

Starting with Saturday night, I told him everything up to looking in the briefcase.

"God, Suzanne, what if he'd caught you?"

"I was scared stiff. You'll never guess what else."

"Drugs?"

"Money. Huge piles of twenty-dollar bills. There were twelve or fourteen stacks, two inches high. Filled the whole thing. I figured, looking at the bills in the cash register, there was over fifty thousand."

"Christ, what's he doing?"

"Karen thinks he might be a bank robber. I don't know. He's gone out of town again. He must take money to that house in Florence."

"Suzanne, there's no telling what this is all about. I'm scared for you. How are you going to get rid of him? What if we called the cops?"

"We can't do that. First of all, you know this town's cop. He'd probably have me in jail. Remember how he lied about me back in April. Second, they'd probably let him loose and he'd kill me."

"You have a plan to get rid of him?"

"Nothing…maybe pick a fight, order him out."

"That won't be too hard. Just say the c-word a couple times." He laughed. "Sorry. Not a laughing matter, huh? For God's sake, be careful. I'll loan you my Colt .45 just in case."

"No, thanks, I don't think I could shoot anybody."

"Okay, but if you need any help call me."

"I have no phone, but I'm close enough to the bar. I'll be very careful from here on. As soon as he gets back, it's over."

After we ate, he looked at his watch. Time was up. "I'll be around as much as I can. Take care, love." He kissed my forehead and slipped out the door. I sat a few minutes longer, thinking about Greg. I never got enough of that guy—never enough of him calling me love, never enough of that sweet smile on his sexy mouth, and never, never enough of those deep-blue, loving eyes.

My warm mood changed like a summer storm when I thought about what I'd have to do when Mark got back.

CHAPTER 25

▼

The week passed quickly. Each night I expected Mark to be there when I got home, and each night I was thankful he wasn't, but the strain of being prepared weighed on me.

Greg came in twice a night, lighting up the place for a few minutes. Friday night he talked to Lindy about letting him do some bartending on weekends. She liked the idea. She said young female bartenders had better skills for handling drunks, but "Greg's charm and wit will be an asset."

Saturday night he came in at nine, full of enthusiasm.

"What's this?" a tunnel stiff asked. "We want pretty haybags to mix our drinks."

"Well, what about these poor women? Don't you think they like someone pretty to take care of *them*?" He leaned close and spoke in a stage whisper. "Besides, I have a heavier pouring hand than these girls, or the boss's kid."

We had fun behind the bar, even though the crowd got out of control for a few minutes.

Two red-haired brothers, husky timber fallers who'd grown up in Barkerville, started it. After downing enough beer for two Paul Bunyons, I heard them making ugly remarks about the construction workers.

I kept my eye on them, and after awhile the younger brother swaggered toward the bar. "Excuse me," he said, and elbowed his way between two men standing mere inches apart. "You damn boomers don't own this place, you know."

"Oh? Do you?" the miner said.

"Damn site more'n you do!" With his jaw stuck out, he came close enough to kiss the cheek of the miner on his right. "Move it! Your kind aren't wanted around here."

Here comes trouble.

The miner picked up his beer, saluted with it, then stepped back as if to give up his spot. Just as I breathed a sigh of relief, he came from somewhere with a left hook and dumped the kid on his butt. Still holding the beer, he took a long pull, set it down and reached to help the kid up.

I saw the older brother across the room. His face matched his hair.

"Take it outside!" I yelled as I came around the end of the bar. Greg grabbed my arm and pulled me aside just as five miners surrounded the downed logger, lifted him by his arms and legs, and rushed him out the open back door.

The guy who'd swung the punch followed. "Okay little fellow, let's finish this right. You people, step back."

Just then the brother burst through the crowd like a big red bull. "You sucker-punched him, you bastard!"

"You wanta fight his battles, Red, come on out."

Fists flew and they went down, rolling in the gravel. The younger one who'd started the row allowed himself to be held back by the miners, while he yelled encouragement to his brother.

I couldn't see how the fight ended because all my customers rushed to the back door. But, I could tell by the cheers that the miners were winning.

In minutes, when the dirty, bloody men filed back into the room, Bruce and Lindy showed up and took charge, informing all three parties they were cut off for the night. Bruce and the fighting brothers went way back, but Bruce's soon-to-be ownership required him to put friendship aside.

The more civilized loggers and townspeople sat staring at the wild and woolly newcomers while I listened to them grumble.

"It used to be nice down here on a Saturday night—before this friggin' dam."

"These guys are plumb crazy."

I couldn't see anything too crazy about thumping someone who got in your face like he had. And, I'd watched fights among the local loggers since I was knee high to that grasshopper.

Up and down the bar, the opinions varied.

"You see that son-of-a-bitch, he was big as a Buick coming through that crowd," one of the miners said.

"Old Lefty surprised the hell out of that kid. He'll know not to push him next time."

After we closed, Paul, Greg and I sat talking about the big changes. We were excited by the huge increase in business and tips, fascinated by the personalities, and a little scared of handling trouble. When we finished our after-shift drinks, we got busy on our restock and clean up. Greg caught my hand when we were in the back room. "He hasn't come back yet, has he?"

"Not unless he came tonight."

"Want to have something to eat after we're done?"

"I *really* do, but I'd rather clean up this thing with Mark first. You coming by for the sing-along tomorrow afternoon?"

"Are you?"

"Plan to. Marge is leaving Monday. It's kind of a going-away thing for her."

"I'll try to make it."

"You better spend some time with your girlfriend. How's she like you working weekends?"

"Not for diddley. She's jealous of you."

"Why?"

"'Cause I spend time here. She's got her spies."

When we'd finished our work, I said, "Better watch your Ps and Qs, Greg. One of these days I'll take you up on your offer, then you'll be a dead duck."

"Only the good die young, love. I'll see you tomorrow.

He went out the front door, Paul and I went out the back. Mark's car wasn't there, thank goodness. After the hard night I'd had, I didn't want to deal with him.

Sunday morning, Karen woke me at eleven. "Let's go get some sun."

"Okay, fix me some toast while I dress. I don't have a lot of time. There's a going-away party for Marge at two. She's leaving with her girlfriend, Rachel."

"Whoa! Tell me more."

I told her the whole story on the way to the river.

Luckily, we had the beach to ourselves, so we unhooked our tops and lay on our stomachs on the blanket. Soon we were both asleep.

When the cold water hit, Karen yelled, "Eeee yiiii!" followed by, "Son of a bitch!"

We both reared up and our unhooked tops stayed on the blanket.

Our tormentors, six roaring drunk tunnel stiffs, whistled, clapped and cheered.

Karen's friend Billy-Boy, with a paper cup in his hand, bent double laughing. "Oh man, I didn't m-mean to s-scare you out of your suit."

I flopped back on the blanket, but Karen, undaunted by her bare chest, caught him with a flying tackle that took him backwards into the river—clothes, shoes and all. They wrestled in the water for a few minutes, dunking each other until Billy-Boy yelled, "Uncle! Uncle! My w-w-watch. My w-w-wallet. Haybag, I give up."

Karen stood shoulder deep in the water while he struggled up the bank, his pants drooping low with the weight of the water. I managed to put my top on while everyone watched Karen, but looked away as Billy-Boy started to peel off his dripping clothes. A sneak glance revealed he wore swim trunks.

"Next time, better strip off before you start on that gal."

"Hey Karen, come on out," someone yelled.

They chanted. "Come out! Come out!"

A few local families, who'd arrived while we napped, took in the show—some smiling, some not.

"Come out! Come out!"

Karen walked toward us, her small, firm breasts coming out of the water, her eyes directly on Billy. She stepped onto the beach with her head high. "Who's buying the beer? You owe me one, Billy."

Embarrassed, I threw her a towel. She threw it back. "Damn it, Karen, you want to get arrested?"

"Oh, all right, party pooper." She picked up her top, then turned her back to the crowd to put it on.

When she turned back, Billy handed her a beer. "Woman, you are a hell of a sp-sport."

She reveled in the attention and when I reminded her I had to go, she told me to take her car and she'd catch a ride.

I went home, showered and put on my white embroidered dress. My skin had a pink glow from two hours in the noonday sun—a look I liked. Instead of a ponytail, I put my hair in a braid down the back, tied with a white satin ribbon that trailed to the bottom of my dress. I remembered how Greg liked the white dress the night we'd danced.

When I went to the bar, the party had been underway awhile. On a table, a decorated cake was inscribed "Grace and Rachel." Marie was behind the bar. Grace, Rachel, Lindy, Bruce, Paul and Greg sat at pulled-together tables with a handful of friends.

"Here's our Suzanne," Lindy said. "We started without you."

"Bring her a double," Marge said. "She's got catching up to do."

I looked over at Greg seated between Paul and Lindy. He licked his lower lip in his secret way, then puckered a quick little air-kiss.

I pulled a chair from another table and squeezed in between Bruce and Rachel. "I'll have a Blackberry Brandy, and make it just a single."

Everyone seemed high, except Greg, Rachel and me. Paul kept slapping Greg on the back, grabbing the back of his neck and his bicep. Greg raised his eyebrows and rolled his eyes at me a couple of times. We drank hard, told war-stories about the bar, and laughed ourselves hoarse for two hours.

Bruce lit up a Corona and Paul said it smelled good and he wanted one. Lindy too. I went to the bar for a box, passed it around the table, and we all lit up. Greg did his Groucho Marx routine and Paul and I tried to imitate him.

I didn't see Mark come in the back door, but I saw Greg's expression change. His eyes widened, trying to tell me something, as he looked over my shoulder. Before I could understand, Mark jerked the cigar from my mouth, grabbed me by the arm with his other hand and lifted me from my seat.

Startled, I twisted away. "What the hell do you—?"

"Come on!" He grabbed me again and pulled me toward the door.

"No!"

Bruce jumped up. "Get your damn hands off her!"

Paul and Greg were on their feet.

He released my arm, but grabbed my wrist. "It's now or never, Suzanne."

When he said that, I realized "now" was what I wanted, and glanced at Greg. "All right, I'm coming." I wanted to take the scene away from all these people, and I'd had just enough Blackberry Brandy to make me brave.

CHAPTER 26

▼

He half-dragged me along. "There's no hope for you. Is that all you want out of life, to make a fool of yourself? You're disgusting. Smoking that cigar, like a street tramp."

"Goddamn you! Stop calling me a tramp. You're the goddamn tramp."

He hauled me up the steps into the cabin. Just inside, he grabbed my braid with one hand and my chin with the other. He bared his teeth just inches from my face in a frightening grimace and jerked my hair with each word. "I told you not to say that." He sprayed me with spit and his liquor breath.

The realization that he'd been drinking sent fingers of fear up the back of my neck. But, I pressed on. I had to finish what I'd started.

I shouted, "Let go of my hair!"

With an angry grunt, he shoved me and I fell on the couch.

I jumped up, grabbed a box of his belongings and headed for the open door. "I want you the hell out of my house. Now!" Before he could react, I threw it off the front porch.

"You little bitch nobody. Who do you think you are?"

"I'm the one who pays the goddamn rent." As I reached for his other box, he grabbed my hair again, pulled me backward toward him, forcing me to squat. "Let go of me you hair-pulling bastard!"

I heard the click of his switchblade just as I saw its glint out of the corner of my eye. I froze. The cold blade touched the back of my neck. My knees quivered. I tried not to move.

"I thought you had some class, Suzanne. I thought I'd take you out of this one-horse town and make a lady out of you. But no. You'd rather be like that whore, Karen. Now you'll be even more like her." His voice was low and cold. "You won't attract another man with that swishy hair of yours."

I heard and felt the blade slice upward through the braid at the back of my neck. As he sawed through it, he pushed me forward with his knee. I screamed like a cougar as I fell to my knees and scrambled away from him.

He threw the braid at me.

Fury blinded me to the danger of the knife, to the fact that he stood between the door and me. I grabbed one of his pictures leaning against the wall and threw it. Next, my hand fell on my heavy glass ashtray. I raised it over my head and hurled it a hard as I could. It hit him a glancing blow to the knee and rattled across the room.

"You rotten Christian bastard!" I yelled, looking around for something else to throw.

He crouched with his arms out, bouncing from one foot to the other, the blade shining. "Maybe you need another lesson, you whore. Maybe I should—"

I saw Greg through the window as he sprinted past, then burst through the doorway.

"You should grab what's yours and get the hell out of here." He stood behind Mark, holding his .45 with two hands.

Mark whirled to face him.

"Drop the knife!" Greg stepped into the room. "Now!"

Mark stared at him for a minute. Greg's eyes were steady, black with hate. "I own the Marksman's medal. Better think twice, asshole."

Mark broke the stare and dropped the knife on the coffee table.

Greg motioned toward the bedroom. "Suzanne, get back."

Mark, eyes on Greg, edged toward his pictures. He gathered them and put them on the front seat of the car.

I pulled his clothes from the hangers and tossed them out the door. When I pitched his last box off the porch, I shouted. "That's all of it, you goddamn hypocrite."

Mark's eyes were slits. "We'll see."

Greg lowered his pistol to his side and stood watching from the porch.

Mark slammed the trunk lid, climbed in the car and turned to look at me. Never had I seen him so ugly—eyes bulging, the cords standing out in his neck. He opened his mouth to say something, but clamped his jaw.

Greg bounced down the stairs and slammed Mark's car door. "You should keep driving right out of this town." He leaned closer. "If I see or hear of you around here again, I'm talking to the law. They'll be real interested in you."

Mark fired his engine and spun away, gravel flying.

Greg took my arm and led me back into the house.

Anger turned to tears as I pushed hair out of my eyes. "Look at me!"

He put down his gun and took me in his arms and patted my head while I cried on his shoulder. "God, Suzanne, if I'd come sooner. I got my weapon from my car when he took you out. Then I heard you scream." He sat me down on the couch and wiped my tears with his fingers.

He held my face. "You're just as beautiful as always."

"Look! My hair's six inches long here." I pulled at the front. "An inch back here."

"Where's your scissors? I'll fix it." He raised his pinky finger, smiled that wondrous smile. "You didn't know I was a hairdresser, did you?"

I had to smile, too. "All I have is cuticle scissors."

"Perfect! Teensy scissors…joss right for zee leetle peexie cuts."

As I brought them, I glanced in the mirror and laughed. "I look like the scarecrow in the Wizard of Oz."

He seated me on the coffee table, wrapped a towel around my shoulders and began snipping. For fifteen minutes, he hummed and clowned, while hair rained on the floor.

"Voila!" He led me to the dresser mirror.

I loved it. A perfect cut with tendrils around my face and ears. I looked older, even sophisticated.

Greg stood behind me, smiling into my eyes. Serious. "You could get to be a habit, woman." He kissed the back of my bare neck. "Let's get out of here before I get in trouble. They'll all be worried about you." He stepped to the bed and tucked the gun under my pillow. "I'll get my weapon later."

We walked in the back door together and the group cheered.

Rachel reached out her hand. "Looks like Greg rescued our girl."

Paul slapped his forehead. "Jeezus, what'd you do to your hair?"

"Greg gave me a haircut. Like it?"

"I love it." Lindy looked from one of us to the other.

"I don't," Bruce said.

Paul patted his straw-patch hair. "What's so hot about long hair?"

"What became of Tarzan?" Marge asked.

"Ask Greg."

"He's gone." He dusted his hand together. "Now, Paul, where's our see-gars?"

Paul got us new cigars and drinks, and then we toasted Grace and Rachel. In a little while, Greg whispered to me. "Got to go, love. I had a date at five."

"Oh no! I'm sorry."

"You didn't do it, I did."

"Thank you for being there."

He gave me a squeeze. "My pleasure."

I sat watching everyone, thinking about their lives, Lindy and Bruce would be married soon. Marge would probably be happier out of the bar business, enjoying her later years with Rachel. They each had someone—for better or worse. I thought about Jimmy. I still loved him, but I knew in my heart we'd never be together again as husband and wife. My feelings for him weren't gone, but had changed.

The party ended with everyone but Paul moving into the dining room for dinner. Lindy insisted I join them. Although my stomach still had that kicked-in feeling from the scene with Mark, I went along for the company. Instead of eating, I drank. I felt sorry for myself because I'd screwed things up.

Everyone talked at once—loud like drunks talk. I sat in the corner getting sadder by the minute. Crying jags were nothing new to me—the usual result when I drank too much.

Rachel noticed when the tears began to drip off my chin. "Why, Suzanne, whatever is causing those tears?" Although I hadn't seen her have more than one highball, she spoke carefully, like many do when they're inebriated.

"It's nothing." I sniffled and wiped my chin.

"It's that bastard, Mark!" Marge's face was red, with beads of sweat on her upper lip. "What'd he do to you?"

Before these intoxicated people worked up too much passion on my behalf, I wanted out of there. "Everything's going to be just fine." My tears had stopped. "I just want to go home. Goodbye Marge…Rachel." I went on, speaking carefully, "I'm happy to have known both of you."

"We'll be down here to see you again," Rachel said.

I hugged them both, stumbling over their feet in the process then lurched out through the kitchen so none of the customers would see me red-eyed and drunk. Outside, I let my tears pour as I made my way to my house.

Inside, in the dark with my forehead pressed to the window, my drunkenness magnified everything I'd been feeling earlier. I cried for the shame of allowing myself to be used, falling too quickly for Mark's line. I cried to be eighteen again, filled with dreams, instead of divorced at twenty-one. And I cried because my only two friends, Greg and Karen were off with others, while I wallowed alone in self-pity. I wailed.

I threw myself across my bed and wailed some more. Sleep came as I sobbed into my wet pillow, without a thought of Mark and my unlocked door.

CHAPTER 27

▼

I awoke early next morning, still in my white dress, lying crosswise on the bed, both my feet numb from hanging over the edge. I groaned and dragged myself into the bathroom. My stomach felt like it was filled with fuzzy caterpillars. I drank two glasses of water, but still couldn't quench the thirst.

When I looked in the mirror, a shorthaired, puffy-eyed stranger looked back at me. Remembering, I groaned again. I'd put myself in serious danger with Mark. What a fool I'd been to take him on like that, and probably a bigger fool to get drunk and pass out alone. He could have waltzed right in and slit my throat. I shook my head at myself in the mirror, took off my dress and stepped into the shower.

When I came out of the bathroom, I saw my braid and the rest of my hair scattered over the floor. Mark's knife lay on the coffee table. Staring at it, I wondered what Mark would have done to me if Greg hadn't come—probably something far more permanent than a haircut. I shivered to think of the way he'd looked.

I got the pistol and put it under the mattress with my treasures, and the knife on a shelf in the kitchen, then dressed. When I started across the street to call Karen, I remembered driving her car home from the beach. She must have picked it up while I was at the party.

"He's gone," I said on the phone.

"Great! Hard?"

"You'll never guess."

"I know you won't talk on the phone, so I won't ask. I have to take Mom to town to pick up her car, want to come?"

"No thanks, I wouldn't be comfortable. I still have a night off, let's go to Sophie's this evening and celebrate my liberation."

"Sure. See you soon as we get back. We'll have dinner. My treat."

Back home, the first thing I saw was the picture Mark had painted on my wall. Although I loved the likeness, I couldn't have it reminding me every day of the mistake I'd made. I opened the leftover paint and covered it. My first coat left a ghostly image. I could have left it as the "Ghost of a Foolish Lady," but I intended to put on a second coat later.

In the afternoon, I sat on my porch and watched slow moving thunderclouds rolling down from the north toward Barkerville and the Three Sisters. I loved a summer storm—how it cooled the dry, hot air and washed everything clean.

While I sat waiting for the rain, I remembered what Mark had said about taking me out of my one-horse town. He was right about that. What future did I have in my little town? Somewhere inside, I knew Barkerville would never fulfill my real dreams—not my dreams as the daughter of the hard-up logger, or my dreams as the handsome musician's wife. My fulfillment had depended on someone else. I knew, to realize my own dreams, I would have to leave Barkerville. But that would take time.

Finally, the rain came. Big splashing drops. I stepped inside and stood at the window and watched the lightning and the wind whip the trees.

In fifteen minutes it ended. The blacktop steamed, and the air smelled like cedar as I walked to the bar at five o'clock.

I spoke to Paul, who sat at the end of the bar. "Wasn't that wonderful?"

"What's wonderful about it? I hate thunder."

"What's going on today?"

"Aunt Marge and Rachel left about noon." He made a face. "Bruce is moving in."

Marie had a happy crowd, excited by the storm. The jukebox blasted "Itsy Bitsy, Teeny Weenie, Yellow, Polka Dot Bikini."

Paul jerked his head toward it. "Jeezus, I'm sick of that dumb song."

Greg burst through the door on schedule, his eyes searched the crowd and smiled when he found me. The barstools were filled, so he stood between Paul and me and ordered a beer. "Wasn't that storm awesome?"

Paul chipped in. "You two are sickening! I suppose you like this muggy air."

I spoke quietly to Greg. "Are you in the dog-house?"

He grimaced. "Big time."

"She'll get over it. How could she stay mad at a charmer like you?"

"She's had practice." He laughed and turned my face toward him. "How are you today?"

"Other than a little hung over, I'm fine—thanks very much to you."

Starting at my eyebrow, he ran his finger down my cheekbone and touched the corner of my lips. "Look at those red eyes."

"Just a crying jag. I drank too much."

We talked awhile as Greg sipped his beer. I liked the feel of his body where we touched hips. He liked it too, and kept bumping me gently.

"I don't know whether to go make peace with Becky or just forget it." He held his head. "Sometimes I don't feel like trying this hard."

I secretly hoped he'd forget it. "You better go see her, Greg, then you'll know how you feel."

"You're probably right. I guess I don't want to leave it like it is. We were both pretty mad. We said a lot of things. You're not working tonight, are you?"

"No, Paul's working. Karen and I are going out to Sophie's for a while. Karen's got a bunch of playmates out there."

"Sure wish I could go. But, I'm dead. We fought 'til three last night. I've got to get some sleep. I've got this big prospect at work. I can't handle him half awake."

"I wish you could, too. But you better take care of your job."

"You're right. I'll go see Becky now, then get to bed. Be careful, love, that Karen's a maniac."

I stared into his tired eyes and slowly licked my lower lip. "If I want to be bad, I'll wait for you."

"Ooh, you make leaving hard, woman." He gave my hip another bump, brushed my ear with his lips, and then strode out the door.

I finished my coffee and went home.

After trying on my three outfits, I decided on the purple and red peasant dress. I wanted to look pretty and have some fun. As I put on my make-up, Karen came in.

I looked at her in the mirror. "You sure look sexy. New outfit?"

"Just got it in Eugene. Well, what's the story?" She flopped backwards on the bed. Then, it finally sunk in. She shrieked and jumped up. "Suzanne, your hair!"

I tugged at my bangs. "*This* is the story."

She touched my hair. "Who? What?"

"Mark cut off my hair…he'd have cut me too, if Greg hadn't shown up."

"Shit! What happened?"

I told her all the details while I finished getting ready.

"Think he'll come back?"

"No. I think he'll steer clear. He doesn't want trouble. Mark will find another stupid woman…probably already has one on the string."

Karen bought our seafood dinners at the Steak House before we drove up river to Sophie's. On the way she promised to let me drive home, then gave me the keys when we got there.

Even though it was Monday night, Sophie's tiny bar was packed. "There's my girls!" Sophie yelled at the guys at the bar. "Some of you fellas give these little gals a seat."

"Karen, here's a seat right here, honey." A stiff patted his knee.

"Your heart couldn't take it, Digger!"

"I'll buy you a beer anyway. Give 'em a beer, Sophie."

Half the men at the bar stood and offered their seats. We chose the two stools exactly in the middle of the action. The giant man whose seat I'd taken stood close by my elbow, and I could feel his eyes on me. After a few minutes, he patted his heart. "Sophie, I'm in love. This filly has captured my heart."

"Aw, Tex, you're just horny."

"No, no. This is love. I'm takin' this little thing back home to Texas with me."

I laughed at him, so did everyone else.

He put his hand under my chin and tipped my face up. "You don't believe that, do you?"

"No, I sure don't." He made me nervous standing too close, touching me.

Sophie came down the bar in front of us. "Suzanne, ignore him! You haven't met my new fella yet, have you?" She put her arm around a narrow shouldered, scruffy kid sitting at the end of the bar. "This is Chester."

Sitting down, Chester looked to be about my height. His straight, dishwater-blonde hair fell in his eyes like Dennis the Menace. He had a scraggly patch of dirty brown mustache. His pale, thin face looked younger than he could possibly be—and be bellied up to her bar. He grinned my way, proud as a fifty-pound peacock.

"This boy's got what it takes to keep old Sophie happy, and he knows how to use it." She rubbed her face on his pimply cheek.

Karen and I looked at each other. "God, where'd she dig him up?" I whispered.

There was never a dull moment when drinking at Sophie's. I shook her for the music and lost.

"Here, let me get that." The Texan reached in his pocket. "I'll help you pick 'em."

We went to the jukebox and he dropped in four quarters. It took awhile for us to pick twenty songs. At first, he stood behind me, reaching around both sides of me to make selections. I ducked out of the circle of his arms and stood to the side. I didn't want him to get ideas.

I'd never been as close to such a big man. He must have been six foot-six or more. My head only came to the top of the pockets on his western shirt. His huge silver belt buckle came up to my chest. His smile was nice enough, with even white teeth behind thin lips—everything was just so big.

"How about this dance?"

I took his huge hand and went into his arms, holding back as I always did when dancing with strangers. He put his right hand high on my back, pressing my breasts into his stomach. I couldn't avoid that part of us touching. His height gave me nowhere to put my face except turned to his armpit, or buried in his chest—I simply didn't fit him.

Just before the song ended, he wrapped his other arm around me, his hand low on my waist and pulled me closer. I could feel something besides his belt buckle on my midriff.

I pushed him away. "I don't like dancing this close."

He continued harping on his father's ranch in Texas. "Daddy wants me to find a woman and settle down. You're it."

"You're crazy!"

Karen, busy with her fan club, chimed in a couple of times, "She's not interested, Tex. She just got rid of two men. Why would she want another anchor tied to her ass?"

"She's never had a Texan." He grinned, looking like he expected me to respond. "Let's play the slot machine, I'll stake it, we'll split what we win."

"Okay." I loved playing but couldn't afford it, and his offer seemed harmless enough. We took our beers to the table by the machine. After an hour, we'd run our wins up to four hundred nickels. Billy Boy came in, and he and Karen sat at our table.

Karen came and stood at my elbow. "You two going to hog that game all night?"

"I'll play you the next pull double or nothing." Tex ran his hand up my back. "You win, you get it all. You lose, I get it all."

I ignored his double meaning. "Sure. I'll bet. It's not my money."

I pulled the handle and three monkeys came up. Sophie cashed us out at forty-five dollars. He folded the bills and stuffed them down the front of my dress.

We'd lost our seats at the bar, so we stayed at the table next to the machine with Billy and Karen. I hated having the other men think I was with him. I wanted to dance with someone my size.

We learned Tex worked as a truck driver on the construction crew, not in the tunnel, so Billy didn't know him and didn't seem to like him either.

Before closing time, Karen had several men besides Billy Boy sitting at our table and she'd plopped herself on one guy's lap. She whispered to me, loud enough for all, "Sandy here wants me to go for a moonlight dip. You take the car, I'll pick it up on my way home."

Just before closing time I slipped through the crowd and out the door. I didn't want to deal with Tex, I just wanted to go home and sleep.

CHAPTER 28

▼

The next evening at five, I went to the bar planning to see Greg, then eat before I started my shift. He hadn't shown by five-thirty, so I asked Lindy to send him into the dining room when he got there. As I ate, I listened for his familiar slap on the front door. Maybe he'd worked overtime.

After dinner, I sat at the bar with my coffee, waiting for six-thirty. Five minutes before time to start work, Tex walked through the door smiling like a gorilla eating fleas, carrying a spectacular bouquet of red roses.

"You sneaked out on me last night, but I got you now." With a flourish, he presented them to me. In bold print, a card pinned to a leaf, read "To My Fiancée."

I was speechless and my face turned crimson. What could I say to a crazy man?

Lindy looked puzzled. "Who's this?"

"I'm gonna marry this little peach blossom." He draped his arm around my shoulder. "And take her to my daddy's ranch in San An-tone."

I shrugged off his arm.

Lindy stared.

"Let's call Daddy right now, honey." He stepped to the pay phone on the wall close by, and pulled a handful of change from his tight jeans' pocket.

"No way! You're loony." I felt like he was poking fun at me, or trying to make a fool of me for some reason. His come-on had to be some kind of a joke—but I couldn't figure out the punch line. Maybe he'd made a bet or took a dare?

"Okay, Sweetheart, if you're not ready...I've got time. You'll be nuts about my daddy."

"Jesus Christ." I overheard Paul as I got up to go behind the bar. "She'd be nuts all right. Nuts to fall for that line of crap."

I found a vase under the bar and put the roses in water. They added a classy touch to the backbar, and their scent filled the air as I passed back and forth.

Tex stayed around awhile, charmed Lindy and Paul with his Texas drawl sweet-talk. Before long, they were laughing and joking with him like old friends.

I stayed busy, avoided Tex and watched for Greg. I wanted to see him, but didn't want him to see the goofy drink-of-water's performance. Finally, at around ten, Tex left.

Lindy popped the question the minute the door closed behind him. "Where the hell did you find him?"

"At Sophie's last night. Weird, isn't he?"

Paul chimed in. "Sounds pretty damn good to me."

"You can have him, Paul. He's missing some cards in his deck."

"The man's in love." Lindy must have been overcome by his Texas charm.

"And what a hunk," Paul said. "Bet he's hung like a horse. Every girl's dream."

I slapped at him with a bar towel. "Good God, Paul, where'd you get that idea?"

The night ended without Greg coming in. I felt empty inside as I went home at three. Seeing him every day was even more important to me than I realized.

The next evening, I repeated my pattern of going in at five in hopes of seeing Greg. But no luck. About six, Tex marched in, beaming, with a box of candy.

"You're too sweet already, Peaches, but I gotta fatten you up some. My daddy likes women with meat on their bones—and so do I. With a thousand acres to ride, you'll need some padding on your cute little bottom."

"I don't ride. Horses hate me and I hate them."

"We got two hundred beauties running in the hill country. We'll find you one."

I walked away to get his drink, but he just kept talking, only louder.

"You'll have Cookie to take care of everything. You'll just look beautiful and take care of Daddy and me."

Take care of Daddy. What the hell does that mean?

I brought his drink back and tried to be as convincing as possible. "I'm not going anywhere with you, Tex, so just forget it." I didn't want to hurt his feelings if he meant what he said—but how could he?

When he finally left, Paul started in on me. "Jeez, Suzanne, this guy's serious. It sounds like he's rich."

"Then what's he doing driving trucks out here in Oregon?"

"He said he'd fought with his dad 'cause he wouldn't marry someone daddy picked for him."

"I'll bet!"

"He could be your ticket out of here." He looked at the box of candy I'd put on the back-bar. "If a chance like that came along for me, I'd be out of here tonight."

Maybe he would. We'd begun to wonder about Paul. *Maybe even with a guy like Tex.*

Another night without Greg came to an end. I finally realized he'd made a promise to Becky. Probably the right thing for him to do, but it made me sick to think I might not see him again in the same old way.

The next night, like a faithful goose, I went back to the bar at five—no gander. Six o'clock came and went and as I started work, I said to Lindy, "Looks like the long, tall Texan's given up."

"I doubt it, he seemed pretty determined. I'll bet he shows."

"I hope not. I don't know what to do with him."

"Maybe you should give him a chance—just because he came on so strong doesn't mean he's a bad guy."

"I'll think about it." I definitely wasn't interested and my intuition kept shouting, *beware!*

Jimmy came in about seven-thirty and sat by my station. He stared at me while I served some people at the other end of the bar. As I came toward him, I realized it was the first time he'd seen me since Mark went away.

"The haircut's great." He gave me one of his tender, I-just-love-you-so-much looks. "Makes you look older."

I laughed. "Thanks. Just what every woman wants to hear. How you been?"

"Okay, I guess." After I'd gotten his beer, he asked if we could talk for a minute. "I've been offered a millwright job down in Medford. Think I'll take it. Pays lots more, so I'll be able to take care of our bills."

The thought of him being so far away made my stomach flip-flop for a moment. "That sounds like a good chance for you to get out of here."

"Why don't you come with me? We could make a new start."

Unable to meet his eyes, I scrubbed the bar in front of him. "I don't think so, Jimmy. There's too much water under the bridge."

He leaned toward me and whispered, "Are you going to divorce me, Suzanny?"

I wavered, momentarily feeling sorry for him, then, brought my eyes back to his. "I can't afford that, Jimmy. I guess if you want one, you'll have to get it."

He half-smiled. "Well, I don't want one."

Feeling the familiar sting in my eyes, I moved away to another customer.

He chugged his beer, then slapped the bar in front of me on his way out the door. "Bye, babe. See ya."

A little before nine o'clock, Tex came through the door, hiding his face behind a giant bouquet of yellow roses—singing "The Yellow Rose of Texas" at the top of his lungs. I wanted to drop through the floor. Some customers clapped and cheered, others looked puzzled.

"Sorry I'm late, sweetheart. Had to go all the way to Eugene for yellow ones."

He handed them across the bar and I just dropped them on the backbar. "Everybody, this sweet little thing's gonna marry me. She don't believe it yet, but she is."

I motioned for Paul to come behind the bar, then retreated to the back room where I took ice from the machine and held it on my burning cheeks.

He yelled through the doorway. "Don't hide from me, honey, I'll come back there and kiss you."

Lordy! I had to go back out there to shut him up. "Shhh! Tex, I'm too busy to talk to you now. Please go away."

"Only if you promise to give me a chance."

"Sure, sure. I'll give you a chance." Anything to shut him up. I couldn't concentrate with everything going on. My customers had started to grumble.

He sat down by Lindy and talked for about an hour, then left.

The same show went on Friday night. I knew by the box it was lingerie and so did the men at the bar. They hooted and hollered.

I shoved it back across the bar. "No, Tex. You've gone too far. Take it back!"

He held it to his chest. "Did I do wrong?"

"I'm not taking it. That's all. Don't make a scene."

"I'll make it up to you next time," he said, as he walked out the door.

In one way, I appreciated the distraction from missing Greg. I knew he wouldn't be back.

Saturday morning, Karen and I drove to Eugene to buy new outfits for Sophie's barbecue on Sunday. Karen talked about her sex life, and I filled her in on the week's episodes with Tex.

"Shit, he sounds pretty serious. He's good looking and clean? Why don't you screw him and see if you like it."

"No way. I'm not interested. One-night-stands are not as easy for me as for you."

That evening, from the time I started work we were swamped.

"Where's Greg?" Lindy had come behind the bar to help. "I thought he wanted to work weekends."

"I think his girlfriend put her foot down."

"I thought you were his girlfriend."

"No, no. Just close friends. He's got a nice little girlfriend."

"Oh, brother! You could've fooled me."

Bruce stayed behind the bar and Paul took the floor. He kept me busy at the well and Bruce took care of the hold checks and the bar. Seemed like the tunnel stiffs were buying rounds for the house every half-hour or so. That should have made the locals happy, but it didn't.

After closing, the four of us sat in the light of the backbar unwinding with our drinks.

Lindy brought it up first. "Wonder what happened to Tex tonight?"

"He probably got lucky out at Sophie's, I hope."

Paul fanned his face. "I'd like to get lucky with him."

"Paulie!" Lindy put her hand over Paul's mouth.

"Well, shit, she don't want him. I'd just as well have him."

"Suzanne knows what she's doing." Bruce put his face close to Paul's and spoke through his teeth. "You keep that fucking queer talk to yourself if you want to stay around here more than the next five minutes."

After I went home, I thought some about Tex. How long would he keep up with the chase? I wanted no part of another man for any reason, and I wished he would quit bothering me. The two entanglements I'd had in the time since leaving Jimmy had brought me nothing but trouble.

CHAPTER 29

▼

It was Sunday, and Karen and I had volunteered to help with Sophie's party. As I stood in front of the mirror, waiting for Karen, I admired my tan against my white shorts and halter-top, twisted the tendrils around my face into their half curls. The girl in the ponytail was gone—in her place, a woman whose new look I liked.

Karen bounced through the door, wearing a blue sundress, backless, and the exact color of her eyes.

"God, that's sexy. You'll drive the little boys wild."

She wiggled her hips.

When we rang the bell at Sophie's house, she yelled, "Come on in...whoever you are."

I nearly choked when we walked into the kitchen. She stood at the sink in full make-up, barelegged, in gold, spiked-heeled sandals, and decked-out in dangling rhinestone earrings that hung to her shoulders. What popped my eyes was her hot-pink, thigh-length negligee with ostrich feathers floating around the bottom.

Karen's mouth gaped, and she clapped. "Damn, Sophie, you'll steal the show. Didn't do me any good to buy this new playsuit."

"There'll be plenty to go 'round, honey. I've invited all my boys from the tunnel."

I was speechless, but I couldn't take my eyes off her either. The sixty-year old spectacle in her nightgown was certainly not the attractive Sophie I loved. As the feathers fluttered, I could see hanging folds of flesh on the inside of her thighs. Her large breasts shone through the pink nylon, hanging low and swinging as she hurried back and forth from the kitchen to the patio. My wild friend was doing her thing.

Sophie's ranch-style home on the edge of town was a party house. Her dim living room spelled sex with a capital S. Dark colors, lighted candles, deep carpet and animal print cushions invited adventure.

Double French doors opened from the kitchen onto a large flagstone patio. On its east side stood a sparkling aqua-tiled swimming pool, on the west, a massive wooden deck suspended over the McKenzie River, with stairs leading down to its sloping bank. All around the deck, benches padded with colorful cushions. Half a dozen wooden tubs overflowed with fuchsias and dahlias.

Stereo speakers that hung from the eaves already blared cowboy love songs across the river. The huge river-rock barbecue pit was ready to touch off. Sophie handed Karen a stack of yellow place mats for the four umbrella-covered tables on the deck.

"Suzanne, honey, take this ice…fill that tub for the pop and beer."

While we rushed around under Sophie's direction, I wondered if she really intended to wear that outfit for the party.

By two o'clock, Sophie had the sheen of perspiration on her forehead and bosom. "Whew! That's it, girls, we're ready for 'em."

Karen opened a beer as we stood admiring our handiwork. Sophie had all the tools of the perfect hostess. She hadn't missed a trick—all for a bunch of drunks.

She went into the house—to change her clothes I hoped—while Karen and I stood at the deck's rail waving at some boaters floating by. I heard the distant sound of the doorbell, then loud laughter.

Sophie ushered two couples out toward us. She'd put on a crisp, organdy apron—ruffled, with a bib. It helped to cover her, until she turned her back. The apron's strings pulled the nylon close to her dimpled butt, which was bare except for a G-string and the fluttering ties.

I heard doors slam and went to see. Two carloads of stiffs had arrived, including Billy Boy, Sandy, Digger and two others whose names I didn't know.

They all talked at once.

"We the first ones here?"

"Where's our sweetheart, Sophie?"

"Hey, Karen!"

Just then, Sophie danced in from the back. A chorus of wolf whistles nearly broke my eardrums.

"Lookit you, gal!"

"Hot damn, I knew this'd be a hell of a party."

She kissed each one loudly on the mouth, leaving greasy red marks, then grabbed the arms of two and paraded them through the kitchen to the back. "Just bring that hooch on back here. Put that beer in the ice bucket."

Karen met them in the doorway and gave Billy and Sandy each a kiss. Watching her hug Billy, I thought of what she'd just told me about her moonlight swim with Sandy. *Guess they don't mind sharing her.*

People kept coming and more and more booze bottles lined up on the card tables we'd set for a bar. Never comfortable at parties, I'd volunteered to play bartender, and planned to pace myself. My hangover from last Monday stayed fresh in my mind and I knew, missing Greg the way I did, I'd be susceptible to another crying jag.

Karen lit the charcoal and every once in awhile Sophie bent to check it, producing howls from everyone who happened to be behind her.

"Where's Chester, Sophie?"

"Oh, he'll be along presently. He's takin' a nap." She gave a sly wink. "I worked him over pretty good this mornin'." She two-stepped from group to group. "Come on you all, get up and dance. You're wastin' good music." Then she slipped into the house.

People mingled, cutting up, singing along with the music, a few dancing. I mixed drinks as fast as I could. There must have been forty people by then.

Suddenly, in the middle of "Your Cheating Heart," the music stopped. Everyone looked toward the house. Sophie and Chester came out through the French doors with their clasped hands held high like children dancing around a May Pole. Sophie had taken off her apron, fully revealing her costume. Chester, smiling proudly, wore one identical—same hot pink, same feathers on the bottom, same G-string beneath.

The crowd roared, clapped and whistled, and then the music interrupted—the "Missouri Waltz." Chester and Sophie swept around the patio, ballroom style. Chester dipped and twirled her, bent her backward over his arm. I watched the crowd. Everyone appeared to enjoy the show. Feeling the redness creep up my neck, I wondered if I was the only one embarrassed.

When the song ended, everyone stomped and cheered.

"What a hell of an ice-breaker," I heard someone say.

The next piece, the "Johnson Rag," got a couple more dancers on their feet and sent Chester and Sophie into orbit. Their jitterbug was flawless. I feared Chester would break his G-string as he swung Sophie between his legs and over his shoulder—she might break more than that.

After that dance, Sophie came panting for a drink. "Wow, I'm havin' a royal ball. Better wet my whistle and get to cookin' some chicken."

Karen, who was draped across Sandy and Billy, said, "Let me do it."

Sophie motioned her to stay put. "I'll put it on, honey. You can just get your cute little butt over here shortly and watch it for me."

The group, getting bigger all the time, kept me busy mixing drinks and opening beer. I enjoyed myself watching people acting silly, but I wished Greg had shown.

CHAPTER 30

▼

About five o'clock, the food was served and the drinking slowed. The hard drinkers didn't bother to eat, but everyone else filled their plates with chicken or burgers, salads, and desserts.

I left my post and took my plate to the far rail of the deck. Across the river at the edge of the woods, a deer picked her way along the bank. I blocked the sounds of the party, remembering my last time with Greg. I longed to talk to him, dance with him.

Suddenly someone's arms encircled me. My heart flipped. For half a second, I thought my wish had come true.

"Hope you didn't think I forgot you, Peach Blossom," Tex whispered into my ear. "I been to town shoppin' for this." He held a gift-wrapped box about the size of a book in front of my face.

I pushed him and the box away. "Damn, Tex, stop buying me things!" I looked around to see if anyone saw him. "You embarrass me."

"Come on, take it." His gaze followed mine around the deck. "I'll behave, Scout's honor. Open it now. Please."

Afraid he'd call everyone over, I held it low and popped off the lid. Inside, wrapped in tissue, a lemon-yellow bikini.

"Go put it on and we'll dip in the pool."

"There is no way I'd wear this in broad daylight!"

"Okay. You can wear it when we get to the ranch. Our pool makes Sophie's look like a puddle."

God, will this guy ever shut up about Texas?

"I'm not going to Texas, I told you." I closed the box and handed it back to him. "You're wasting your money. And your time."

"Where's our bartender?" Billy Boy yelled.

I excused myself, glad to get away.

Tex followed me to the table full of booze. "I'll have a Black Velvet." Still holding the box, he plopped on the bench behind my table. His long legs stretched out so I had to lean against him to reach beer in the tub. After a few minutes, I noticed him put the box under the bench, behind his feet.

I'd been sticking to Coke, but I'd need booze to put up with Mister Texas. Maybe I'd have to tell him off to end it. I knew the bikini was not forgotten.

I filled several guys' empty glasses, then sat beside Tex on the bench and tried to make everyday conversation. I did not want to hear about his big daddy, his big ranch, or even his big state. "What do you do out at the dam?"

"I drive a Uke. Just movin' dirt from place to place. The dam won't start 'til the diversion tunnel's done. I'll be outa here before then."

"Is this your first job on a dam?"

"Nah, I worked on a couple down in California."

My liar-alarm went off. I turned to watch him answer. "Didn't you tell Lindy and Paul you just came out west because you had a fight with your father?"

"That was before." Just as he looked away, I imagined a sinister flash in his green eyes. What was going on? He'd probably lied about everything.

Before I could ask more, Lindy and Bruce showed up and sat beside us. "Hi, kids. You the bartender?"

I pointed to the table. "Help yourself."

Bruce fixed drinks for the four of us, while Lindy wandered over and filled a plate. "We could hear Sophie's party all the way downtown."

"Have you seen her new boyfriend, Chester?" I asked.

"Real young, isn't he?"

"Really, really young." I gestured toward the pool. "Looks like they're over there. You've got to see this."

"We'll drift over pretty soon," Lindy said, raising her plate. "We've got some catching up to do."

I could see the top of Sophie's platinum head and Karen's, surrounded by tunnel stiffs. I focused for a minute and listened to the splashing and squealing.

"I dare you!" a man said.

"Take it off! Take it off!" someone else yelled.

That had to be for Karen and Sophie. Other guests scattered around the deck and patio picked up on the excitement and began to look that way. Soon the entire crowd moved toward the pool, clapping and chanting to the beat of the music. "Take it off! Take it off!"

Tex ambled over, followed by Bruce and Lindy. Because the crowd was already five deep around the pool, I knew I'd never be able to see anything so I stayed put, drinking my first highball.

More splashing. More male voices hollering.

Soon Tex sauntered back. "Karen's in her skivvies. Sophie and Chester are in…" He made a sour face. "…their nightclothes?" He plopped down beside me, touched my hip with his. "The guys are peelin' off…jumpin' in after them. You people shore are crazy around here."

Lindy came back, shaking her head. "Sophie's boyfriend's sure an ugly bugger."

Tex pointed his chin toward me and spoke to Bruce who slid in next to him. "Doesn't she look plumb sexy in white?"

Bruce probably agrees with that. Anything in skirts looks plumb sexy to him.

He pulled the box from under the bench. "I bought her this little yellow bathin' suit, and I want her to model it for me."

Bruce wiggled his eyebrows in approval and looked at me. "Well?"

Tex opened the box and held up the bottom of the suit—no bigger than his hand.

Lindy picked up the top and held it out toward me. "That's adorable, Suzanne. You're built just right." She whispered in my ear, "Isn't he sweet?"

I didn't answer.

Of course the suit was adorable, but taking something like that from him meant a lot more than candy and flowers. Besides, I truly would never, ever wear something so revealing in public, and where I lived there was no such thing as tanning in my back yard—mine was a street.

"What do you say?" Tex pulled a beggar's face, glancing back and forth between Bruce and Lindy.

"Maybe, when it gets darker."

Tex had me in a corner with my bosses.

Without alcohol to give me courage, I knew I couldn't wear the suit in front of Tex—or anyone else. As usual when I needed courage, I poured myself a stiff drink.

The sun, low in the west, dressed up the river in the soft syrupy light of a summer evening. In another half-hour it would drop below the Coast Range.

The audience at the pool settled back down in their seats, clearing the way for me to see what Karen and Sophie were up to. Men flopped around in their wet underwear, and less. An occasional butt came out of the water as its owner dove for God-knows-what. Karen pranced, splashed and squealed—every few minutes coming to the edge of the pool to suck on her beer. Her firm little breasts, unlike Sophie's, barely bounced as she cavorted.

"You're killing me!" Voices rang out from the pool. "It's too crowded in here!"

Chester climbed out first, his feathers dripping, his G-string transparent. "Last one in the river's a rotten egg!"

He dragged Sophie up the pool ladder. Bare bodies pulled themselves out all around the edge. Like lemmings, they followed Chester and Sophie across the deck, down the stairs, across the lawn and into the river.

The river water, much colder than the pool, had a sobering effect on some, including Sophie. She let out a scream and backed out. "Suzanne, throw us down some towels. They're in the pool-house."

Tex trotted back with a stack and, one by one sailed them off the deck.

Sophie, and three other couples wrapped in the gigantic towels and sat on the grassy slope like a row of colorful toadstools.

As we lingered on the deck, watching the craziness, Lindy said, "I don't know if I can take that cold either."

Bruce pushed her toward the steps. "Sure you can." Then he started on me. "Get your suit on Suzanne, or we'll just throw you in like that."

"Okay, okay. Just give me time."

I took a towel from Tex and headed for Sophie's bedroom. I locked the door and quickly changed. It was skimpy on top and didn't match my tan lines at all, but otherwise looked sensational. I felt sexy and daring—there in the bathroom mirror with a couple double shots in me—but not daring enough to walk out before wrapping in the towel.

Tex waited for me at the top of the stairs. Lindy and Bruce had gone down to the water and were edging in. Tex wore the kind of swim trunks I'd only seen in movies on foreign beaches.

He caught my glance at his bulging front. "Pretty nice, huh?"

My cheeks flamed.

His big frame didn't have an ounce of fat and his arms and thighs were thick and muscular.

He reached for my towel. "No fair! You've got to take that off."

I held up my hand. "Now just wait!"

I ducked under his arm and scurried down the stairs, across the lawn and dropped the towel before I dove in. The icy water took my breath away, and the dive pushed my top down to my waist. Struggling to get it up and get back to shallow water, I took on some water. Tex came from behind, in water too deep for me to stand, and lifted me by the waist. I coughed and sputtered.

"Put me down!"

He moved me toward shore and stood me on the bottom.

"Let me see the suit."

I backed into shallow water. With the light nearly gone, my untanned parts blended with the bikini. I didn't look as bare as I felt.

Karen came by. "Cute tan, girl! Come play tag."

"Speak for yourself!" I said. Her bare chest had tan lines that looked exactly like a bikini, except for dark circles in the middle of each breast.

I wanted to join the fun, but to act with wild abandon was not easy for me. If I had just the right amount to drink I could sometimes let my hair down, but whenever I did that, I hated being out of control. So, instead, I stood aside watching, neck deep to keep warm.

Soon deep darkness came, except for reflection of the lights high on the patio. I could barely see Tex's head a few feet out from me. He moved closer and held out his arms.

He coaxed me. "Come on out here, I'll hold you up."

I shook my head.

"I promised I'd be good. Haven't I?"

He had.

Moving toward him, I reached out and took his fingertips, but kept my distance.

Quick as a boa constrictor, he encircled me and wrenched my right arm behind my back. His big mouth covered mine and his tongue rammed deep into my throat.

I gagged, tried to pull away, but had no leverage in the deep water. Holding pressure on my bent arm, he pressed me to his chest. I twisted away from his lips. He sucked my ear into his huge mouth, biting down on my earlobe.

"Don't fight me, Suzanne," he whispered. "You'll only hurt yourself."

"Damn you! Let me go, you crazy son-of-a-bitch," I hissed. With both arms pinned, I squirmed and twisted with all my strength. Like the boa, his grip tightened.

Clamping my legs between his, he pulled us both beneath the water. When I thought my lungs would burst, we surfaced. Though choking, I bit him hard on the shoulder.

He grabbed my skull, like a football, and his white teeth shone in the dark. An inch from my face, he breathed stale alcohol into my nostrils. "I told you, bitch." He squeezed my skull for emphasis. "Don't fight me!"

In the next moment, his hand left my head and slithered down between my legs. He pulled my suit aside, plunged his fingers into me. Gasping in indignation, I clawed at him with my free hand. His fingers snatched my wrist with a crushing grip that forced my hand open and onto his hard, bare penis. I arched my back, tried to pull away, thumping my knees like pile drivers into his thighs.

He jerked my arm higher behind my back. "Don't fight me!"

My mind went crazy for a way out—without letting anyone know I'd been fool enough to let this happen. *Everyone will blame me for putting on this suit.*

"You been cute long enough, girl. Now it's time to pay up," he growled, while he used my hand to guide his penis. Jabbing and bruising.

I had almost no breath to speak. "If you don't…let me go…I'll scream."

"No, you won't. I know your type. Besides, if you do, you'll get a lung-full of water." Evil with menace, he whispered, "I'll just hold you under 'til you can't scream."

Fear exploded in my mind. "Why? Why are you doing this to me?"

"Because I can! Because you deserve it, you tight-ass priss." He threw back his head and laughed. "You think you're too good for the stiffs. I made a bet…I'd get in your pants in a week."

A dozen possibilities battered my brain as he thrust at me. If I continued to fight, would he really hold me under? Here in the dark, who would know? Was anyone paying attention to us? Loud, drunk, and chasing each other up and down the river, would anyone hear? I glanced over my shoulder. No one sat on the bank. How long would it be before anyone missed me?

I thought of my experience with old Mr. Wilke. *I can get through this, too.*

"Go ahead, you low-life bastard," I said through clenched teeth, and then spread my legs, went limp and sent my mind away. I hoped my giving in would take the fun out of it for him. That he'd be shamed enough to stay away from me. *What makes you think a monster like this can be shamed?*

He quickly finished and pushed me away. He adjusted his suit as he strode out of the river and up to the deck where he grabbed his clothes and disappeared into the house.

I stood in the shoulder-deep water, tears of humiliation streaming. Tears turned to rage, which coursed through me like a river of lava. An image of him putting on his shirt, admiring himself in Sophie's mirror flashed in my mind. I wanted to run into the house, grab Sophie's butcher knife and cut his guts out.

Karen swam up behind me. "Hey. You having fun, Suzanny?" She put her hand on my shoulder. "I'm getting pretty damn cold. How 'bout you?"

My lips were so numb I could barely speak. "I'm f-f-freezing, Karen. Take me home?" I couldn't tell her what had happened—not tonight anyway. *She'd cut his frigging guts out all right.* Maybe I'd never tell her.

We got out of the water, wrapped in towels and went up to the deck. I picked up a whiskey bottle and took a couple of swigs, then decided to take the bottle with me. *I'm as bad as they are, always reaching for the bottle.*

Karen picked up her sundress from beside the pool and we went into the bathroom to dress. Most of the lovers were gone home and Sophie slept on her bed. Karen didn't notice when I slipped the bikini in Sophie's wastebasket.

Swimming had sobered Karen. "I'm bushed, I'm going home, too," she said, as she dropped me at my house.

Inside my house, my back against the door, I crumbled to the floor. Clutching the whiskey bottle, I fought the nausea that washed over me as my thoughts pulled back to the river. My body ached. My teeth chattered. I was frozen to the depths of my soul. *Why me?* My mind was too numb to answer.

After a long while, I lifted my head and took a swallow of whiskey. Its burn sobered me enough to rise and undress. Two more swallows as I prepared to step into the hot shower and scrub the shame from my body.

I'd rather jump off the McKenzie River Bridge than let my mind return to the assault, but I had to know why. "Because you deserve it," he'd said. He'd called me a tight-ass priss. What did that mean? I thought back over my actions since I met Tex, looking for my blame. All I'd ever done was play the slot machine with him at Sophie's, dance with him once. What made him so angry with me? All along I'd tried to tell him no without hurting his feelings.

I'd had bad vibes from the start. Why didn't I listen to my gut feelings? Why did I let people push me to act against my better judgment? Drained, I forced my mind to stop replaying that scene in the river.

As the hot water flowed over me, washing away the tears, I felt so tired—dead tired and disgusted with low-life people. *I've got to get out of this insane place. Somewhere where people are civilized.*

CHAPTER 31

▼

"Suzanne, you here?"

Waking to a vague memory of Lindy's voice calling me, I realized her knock had barely penetrated my sleep.

"Come in!" I called and scrambled out of bed. When my feet hit the floor, I winced in pain from the attack by Tex. I pulled on my robe, smoothed my hair and opened the door. "I didn't hear you."

She stood in the doorway, her eyes bright, cheeks flushed. "Bruce's a free man today. We're leaving early tomorrow for Las Vegas. Can you come over so we can talk to you?"

"Sure, I'll dress and be there in a minute."

Bruce poured me a cup of coffee when I got there. "Let's go sit over there where we've got some privacy."

The three of us carried our cups to a table.

Lindy leaned in and spoke softly. "Suzanne, we'll be gone until next Monday. We're going up to the Grand Canyon for our honeymoon. I want you to be the straw boss while we're gone. Can you do that?"

"I guess so. What does that mean, exactly?"

"You'll be in charge."

"What about Paul?"

"Paul's too headstrong."

"He drinks too damn much!" Bruce's voice carried and a frown from Lindy lowered it. "We know we can depend on you to take care of everything. We'll give you an extra dollar an hour."

"You know how to do the liquor orders and bank deposits," Lindy said.

Concerned, but secretly pleased, I had to ask. "How's Paul going to react to this?"

Bruce looked straight at Lindy as he spoke. "We've told him how it's going to be. If he doesn't like it, he can move on."

I glanced at her to see what effect he had on her. She nodded. "Would Greg work with you on the weekend?"

"I don't think I dare ask." My face flushed at the thought. "Could you go by his work and ask him, Bruce."

"Okay. If he won't come in, we'll try to get someone else."

My stomach grew queasy at the thought of Greg working. I missed him even more after what happened last night. It seemed like he'd be the one I could talk to about it. He'd comfort me and tell me it wasn't my fault.

After our meeting ended, I called Karen. "You up and at 'em?"

Her voice crackled with sleep. "Sure. For hours. What you doing today?"

"I feel like baking at the beach. You interested?"

"Sounds good to me. You buying the beer?"

"No. See you in a few?"

Lindy called me back when I started out the door. "I hear Karen's been tending bar up at Sophie's. Does she have her server's license?"

"No, she's got fake ID. Don't worry though, she won't try to drink in here."

"I know I don't have to worry about you, Suzanne. I just wondered about using her in here. We're getting too darn busy for you and Paul at night."

"She'll be twenty-one a week from Sunday."

"That won't help us now, but as soon as she's legal, let's get her in here and let you train her."

"Great."

By the time I got home and put on my bathing suit, Karen pulled up. The afternoon sun turned my house into a dry kiln that baked me. I piled into her car with an armload of towels and a beach blanket. "God, get me to the river, quick. I'm dying."

"Me, too!" Karen said. I'm sweating out all that booze I drank yesterday."

We found a spot away from the other swimmers and spread our blanket. No tunnel stiffs in sight.

I dove in the icy water, stayed long enough to chill down, then got out and flopped on the hot blanket. Its heat felt especially comforting, like backing up to the fireplace on a stormy night.

"Where's that new yellow bikini, Suz? You looked like a million—the little bit I saw of you.

"It's in the garbage."

"What? If you don't like it, I'll take it."

"You don't want it."

"The hell! What's with you?"

"He raped me last night, Karen."

"Who? Tex?" She rolled over to look at me. "My God, Suz." Her eyes narrowed. "I don't believe it. When? At Sophie's?"

"In the water."

"How…with all those people around? Why didn't you yell?"

"Jesus, Karen, he held me in the deep water." *Does she blame me?* "I couldn't touch bottom. He nearly broke my arm." I showed her the handprints just above my wrists. "He twisted it behind my back. Said he'd drown me…the bastard meant it." The words spilled out, sounding like excuses even to my ears. I pointed to my inner thighs where he'd bruised me. "Look at these."

"Christ, why'd the son-of-a-bitch do that?" She stroked my arm. "He probably could have had you in another week or two."

"He said I deserved it." Reliving his low opinion of me brought angry tears to my eyes, and doubts choked my throat.

"Bullshit! I might deserve it sometime, but Suzanny you've never done anything to deserve that. He's just a fuckin' screwball."

"I knew there was something wrong about the way he treated me, but everyone kept telling me to give him a chance." I wiped my eyes on the edge of the towel. "It's over now. I don't think he'll come back around me."

"He might. Maybe you should tell the cops."

"You know how that would go. Sid would throw me to the wolves. 'Raped in a crowd of people, huh?' I can't tell anyone. It's not worth it. It's over now."

"It ain't over 'til it's over," Karen said, getting up for another dip in the river.

Later, when the day cooled a little, we picked up and went back to my place. I told Karen about Lindy wanting her to tend bar.

"I'd love it. We could work nights together. Just two weeks, I'll be there."

"You'll have to start out on day shift." I told her about being in charge while they were gone. "Don't you love it? What a kick in the pants to *Paulie*. Just what he deserves."

Karen stood at the door, ready to leave. "You want to go out to Sophie's with me tonight?"

"I might run into Tex. Besides, I told Lindy I'd be back in tonight."

"Okay. See you later. Keep your chin up."

Paul, behind the bar, hardly looked at me when I came in the back door. Lindy and Bruce weren't there, so I went straight to the cafe for a burger. My confidence level had slipped drastically after what Tex said. My old shyness was back. Everyone seemed to look at me when I walked through.

While I ate dinner, I heard Bruce come in the back door and speak loudly to someone. Congratulating voices spoke back. Then Lindy laughed. When I finished and went back in, she motioned me over to the bar. "Sit here, Suzanne. Here's a rough list of the liquor you'll need, but take a look at the call liquor before you go. There's extra cash over at the house—you know where. Keep an eye on the hold-checks—don't let anyone get in too deep."

"She'll be fine," Bruce said. "She's got a good head on her shoulders."

"And I don't?" Paul spoke from halfway down the bar.

"Paul, we've been all over this. Let it alone," Bruce said. "Suzanne, I talked to Greg. He'll come in Friday and Saturday night at nine. He was reluctant, said he'd promised his girlfriend. But, I twisted his arm." He winked at me. "It didn't take much."

"We'll give you an extra day off when we get back," Lindy said. "Here's the keys to our trailer and the Olds. Feel free to drive it wherever you want."

Finally, after a few more instructions, Bruce and Lindy said good night. "We have packing to do, we're leaving early in the morning. If I think of anything, I'll leave you a note on the backbar."

"Have a good time, and don't worry."

After they left, I finished my Coke and went home. I didn't want to talk to Paul until he cooled down.

Going into my house in the dark, I suddenly felt scared. Mark and Tex hadn't been far from my mind all day, but when I stepped through the door they'd taken front and center. I flipped on the lights, went quickly to the kitchen and picked up Mark's open knife from the shelf. Holding it high, I turned on the bedroom light and looked behind the bed—and under it—then into the tiny bathroom, pulling aside the shower curtain.

I looked silly marching around my tiny house with a raised knife, but I felt much better after checking it out and locking the door.

I turned off all the lights and stood at the window smoking a cigarette. I liked being in the dark, unseen, looking out at the world. It looked safer from behind the locked door.

When I was ready for bed, I remembered Greg's .45 under the mattress, checked to see it was loaded and left it on the nightstand. I'd been handling guns since my early teens and I had no doubt that I could shoot Tex if he came through that locked door. But I knew that my imagination worked overtime, so I soon forced myself to think of the future instead of the past.

Tuesday morning early, I remembered my new duties and hurried to work. Quiet as possible, I unlocked the door to Lindy's mobile, stepped in and took the cash boxes from the table where Paul had left them.

It seemed strange opening the back door to the bar so early, but I wanted lots of time to get organized before we opened at eleven. The stale smoke filled my nostrils as I stepped into the semi-darkness. I left the back door open, letting in light and fresh air.

After I started a pot of coffee in the kitchen, I looked on the backbar for a note—nothing. The hold-check box held mostly money, meaning all but a few had picked up their checks Monday. I made a mental note of those who hadn't. I counted the money and checks—it balanced at $1000. Before I started on Monday night's receipts, I got myself a cup of coffee.

First, I counted all the money in the cash box, compared the total with the cash register reading from the night shift, and then I took out a bank of $200 to start the day. Carefully noting a discrepancy of $22, I made a deposit slip and a list of change I needed from the bank for the jukebox and slot machine.

It was illegal to pay off cash on the slot machine and it scared me every time I had to do it—especially with strangers in the house. I'd heard stories of bartenders being hauled off to jail in handcuffs. The Liquor Control Commission regularly sent around spies to catch us paying off, so if a suspicious stranger started to play, I always said, "These machines are strictly for entertainment. We don't pay off, you know."

A typical answer was "Then why would I want to play it?"

Taking care of the bar's business felt good to me. I'd taken all the available commercial courses in high school and enjoyed figures and paperwork. I also felt proud to be trusted with all their money, as well as their very livelihood. For a few minutes, I daydreamed about what it would be like to own a business. Was it such an impossible dream?

The outside door to the dining room creaked open and the morning cook stuck his head around the corner. "Good morning, Suzanne, I didn't expect to see you here. Where's Lindy?"

I told him their news. The kitchen was not my responsibility. A couple had leased it for $1 a month after the Milligan sisters took over. They hadn't wanted the hassle, but needed it to be open.

"So, you're taking care of things? I'm surprised they didn't leave Paul in charge. Bruce's not too crazy about him from what I hear."

"I don't know. Will you fix me some eggs when you get the grill hot?"

"Sure, honey. It won't be long. I see you made the coffee. Thanks."

Back in the bar, I strolled around and checked every detail with a new eye. I opened the cold box doors, took inventory, then went into the back room and looked at the beer stock. Actually, the delivery drivers took care of our supply, but I was really getting into my new role.

"Here's your breakfast, hon." Along with my breakfast, the cook brought the coffeepot and refilled my cup.

While I ate, Marie came in the back door. "Good morning, Suzanne. I hear you're my new boss." She smiled pleasantly.

"Well, sort of, but I doubt you need a boss, Marie."

She went about her work, filled the ice bin, put out clean ashtrays, turned on the machines, wet fresh bar towels, and checked the stock.

"Looks like Paul was pretty busy last night. He almost ran out of sour mix. I better mix up a batch before I open. It's not so slow in the mornings anymore since the tunnel started."

I took notice of what Marie was telling me—Paul hadn't done his side work. "I'm going to the bank, then I'll be home. If you need me, just send someone out back to holler at me."

Getting into Lindy's new Oldsmobile hardtop gave me a thrill, but scared me at the same time. It was the sportiest car I'd ever driven, and it fit me like it had been custom-built around my fanny. I felt like Mrs. Vanderbilt as I drove to the bank.

After I made the deposit, I drove through town and past where Greg worked. I could see his shiny '50 Ford parked in front and the back of his head bent over his desk. My stomach gave the same flip-flop it used to give for Jimmy when I was in the eighth grade. As I turned around in the parking lot, he stood and glanced toward the street. It embarrassed me to be caught acting like a lovesick high-school girl, so I sped off hoping he hadn't noticed me.

I parked Lindy's car back in her carport and took the cash box into her house. Paul sat at the table in a kimono with a cigarette dangling from his lips. His eyes were bloodshot and watery.

"Good morning, Paul. Hope I didn't wake you when I came in earlier."

"You didn't."

"Well, I'll see you later. You're off tonight aren't you?"

"Yes."

"Enjoy your day off then. Bye."

"Suzanne, you don't have to kiss my ass. It's not your fault Bruce doesn't like me. I'll probably see you tonight."

I went back to my house and sat on the porch reading until the sun drove me inside. I'd started a novel about a girl who grew up poor in a small town in Idaho. Desperate to be a doctor, she worked her way through college with no help from anyone. She'd washed dishes, scrubbed floors, waited tables and even tended bar in a tavern…and met some real characters on her way. I found a lot of myself in the story, and I couldn't put it down.

When I'd finished the last page, I sat thinking. Why couldn't I do something like that? She had no one else to rely on, but she got stronger and more confident every year—from her good and bad experiences. *I have a good start on the bad ones.*

I glanced at the clock. No more time for daydreaming, I had to be at work in twenty minutes.

The bar was filled with after-work drinkers and Marie was happy to see me. "Boy, the natives are restless." She pointed toward the tables. "Couple guys been asking about you."

"What?"

"Just wanted to know where you are. If you're all right. If you're working tonight."

"Who were they?"

"Tunnel stiffs. Two-Fingered Shooter over there. Don't know who the other one is."

Shooter's hands drew pictures in the air as he told some story to the men on each side of him. I'd find out later what was on his mind.

Paul sat at the bar, dressed up, drinking his usual Grand Marnier. He looked like he'd been sitting there awhile. I handed him a couple quarters. "Why don't you play the music for me. We need some noise in here." The house found it paid to keep the jukebox primed. People drank faster and stayed happier when the music played. I watched him walk across the room and he seemed sober enough.

Getting into the swing of things as Marie finished her side work, I talked to three timber fallers sitting at the far end of the bar in their dust-covered, "stagged-off" Levis. Their red suspenders, worn over once-white tee shirts, all had identical canvas pads sewn on the right shoulder for carrying the saws. They'd traded their caulk boots for Romeo slippers before coming into the bar. To a stranger, they'd look pretty silly sitting there in their high-water pants, bare feet in shiny slippers. To me, they looked like home.

"Seems you guys been here awhile." I gathered up their empty bottles.

"Yep. They got us on hoot owl with this heat. We left town this morning at three…knocked off at noon. Been right here ever since."

The cute one grabbed at my hand. "Where you been all my life?"

"Just got here. I'll be here the rest of the night. You guys need anything?"

"Oh, baby. That's a loaded question." He stroked my fingers. "Holding this will do me for the moment."

I laughed, patted his arm and pulled loose. "Sorry, boys, there's about forty other people in here that want my services, too."

I felt for all three of their wives, seeing how much time and money they spent in the bar—and how much flirting they did, although I'd never seen any of them go any further.

In a couple of hours, the crowd thinned out, and I had a breather before the swing shift crowd would arrive. I stood at the end of the bar smoking a cigarette, when Shooter got up and came down beside me. He turned his back on the nearest person and motioned me in close.

"Tex had a real bad accident yesterday morning." He spoke so low I could barely hear him. "Darned if he didn't bust his nose and a few ribs. Three of the guys went with me up to McKenzie Bridge to help him pack…so's he could leave town. Had a scrawny little wife and four kids livin' up there in a shack. You won't see him around these parts again."

I stared at him. "Shooter, I…"

"No need to say nothing. Only four of us knows about it and we ain't talking." He patted me on the shoulder. "You're a sweet gal and you didn't deserve that. Guy like him gives us all a bad name. We'll never speak of it again, honey." He gave me a little squeeze and walked back to his seat.

I couldn't keep the smile off my face as I thought about Tex getting his and the way those men had looked after me.

Nosy Paul saw the interchange. "What was that all about?"

"Nothing. Just had a joke to tell me. You're sure dressed up…that pretty yellow sweater, your hair slicked down. You got a hot date tonight?"

"Well no. Not like a date." He looked over my left shoulder as he stumbled on. "One of the guys from the tunnel office. We're uh…going into Springfield. Do some bowling." He sounded half-sheepish, but defensive at the same time. His white skin had blotched red. "I need friends too, you know."

Paul kept tossing down Grand Marniers and watching the door. He sat twisting and re-twisting a cocktail napkin into a roll, then ironing it out with his fingers. When ten o'clock rolled around, I glanced at Paul when an older man in a business suit walked in and scanned the room with wary eyes. Paul's face crinkled into a faltering wistful smile that touched my heart.

The poor little misfit.

The man went to the opposite end of the bar, ordered a straight shot, downed it and walked back out the door. Paul looked around as he drained his glass. I avoided his eyes so as not to embarrass him, but he came to where I stood and said he guessed he'd been stood up, so he was going to go for a walk. I felt real pity for Paul at that moment, even though he drove me crazy with his mama's boy crap most of the time. It must have been terrible to be stuck where he was.

When closing time finally rolled around, I stashed the money in the appropriate place, and then dragged myself home by three-fifteen—happily replaying what Shooter told me. I'd sleep better knowing Tex was history.

CHAPTER 32

▼

My second day in charge started the same as Tuesday, except Paul was due to come in instead of Marie. I knew he'd be a bitch after the kind of night he probably had. No telling when, or where, or if he got to bed.

When he hadn't shown by ten-thirty when his shift started, I began doing his prep work. Eleven o'clock, our official opening time, rolled around and no Paul. Before I unlocked the front door, I ran out back and knocked to see if he was up.

"Jeezus! All right. I'm coming!"

When he came into the bar, he made himself a Bloody Mary before he opened the front door. Allowing him to drink behind the bar wasn't smart, but maybe it would pick him up a little. I sure wasn't going to call him on it in the mood he was in. He might just walk out and leave me trying to roll the ball uphill.

Several stiffs from graveyard, including Shooter, were waiting as he opened the door, which gave him a little flurry right away. He sure wasn't Mister Congeniality, but did manage to get everyone served.

After thirty minutes, Mad Max came in, sat at the open end of the bar and ordered a shot of Black Velvet, beer back. Max had been one of the first stiffs in town and, although I tried, I hadn't been able to warm him up—nor had any of the other bartenders.

Mad Max seemed like a good handle for him, although I never heard where he got it. Over six feet tall, well built, with a dark complexion. He was a handsome man, except for the deep purple acne craters on his cheeks and the scowl on his heavy brow. His brooding eyes were as black as his hair. I'd seen him smile only once—at a straggly dog that came trotting through the bar. That smile changed his eyes and showed his big white teeth. He'd seemed almost approachable.

That morning he looked rumpled, unshaven, his hair stood on end and his shirttail was out. His bloodshot eyes looked like he was coming off an all-night drunk.

Paul was flip, as usual. "Jeezus, you look like you been rode hard and put away wet."

When I heard that, I looked up from the liquor list I'd been working on at the table. *Paul, why do you have to lip off? You know Max is mad at you for cutting him off Friday. Just once, use your head.*

"What the hell's it to you, Blondie? How I look's none of your damn business." He finished off the shot.

He snapped back, loud and brassy. "Well, well. Ain't we touchy this morning."

"I'll show you fucking touchy." He crashed his beer bottle down, jumped up and knocked over his stool. He whirled around the end of the bar—within feet of Paul—and raised his fist. "I'm in no mood to take shit off a pissant like you."

"Watch your language, bucko," Paul shot back. "You know we don't allow that kind of talk in here." Hands on hips, he stood his ground.

I looked around at the other people in the room. Most were our daily regulars—old men making their morning rounds, plus three tunnel stiffs at the bar, including Two-Fingered Shooter. Max had everyone's attention.

While he took another step forward, I rushed over. There was a law in the barrooms—no one steps behind the bar without a license. He'd just taken that step.

"Whoa, hold on Max." I moved past the upset stool, to his side, and gingerly touched his arm as I spoke. "He's only trying to be friendly."

He jerked away from my hand. "Get the hell—" His face close, his sour breath blasted me. "I'm sick of this bullshit."

Without thinking, I did what needed doing. I put both hands on his shoulders and pulled him back from behind the bar. "Damn it Max! Hold it right there." At that moment, I realized what a mistake I'd made, cornering him between us. I quickly backed off, but kept my voice strong. "You just can't be back there. They'll shut us down."

Shooter was already on his feet. He slammed his beefy two-fingered hand down on the bar like a sledgehammer, pounding each word he spoke. "Max! Straighten up! Now!"

Max shouted back. "Are you gonna make me?" Then he lowered his head and took one step away from Paul.

Shooter sat back down, and barely loud enough to hear, he said, "If I have to."

Silence filled the room. My fingernails dug into my palms as I waited for Max's next move.

He reached for his beer, took a long chug and glowered at Paul.

Don't say a word, Paul. Just clam up for a change.

Max stood there with one foot resting on the overturned stool and drained his beer, then picked up his empty shot glass and looked into it. I knew Paul would never serve him another one in his mood. I held my breath, hoping he wouldn't ask. Seconds passed as he pulled at his ear and stared into the glass. Suddenly, he slammed it down on the bar, kicked the barstool out of his way and headed for the door.

"To hell with all of you." He walked straight out the front door into the sunny morning.

With a sigh of relief, I went back to my business, at peace with the quiet hum of normal conversations. The old-timers took up their daily yarns where they'd left off—with some new material to talk about.

Paul bought Shooter and his friends a drink and stood leaning over the bar, buttering up to them. *Sure, Paul, you can laugh now—somebody else has finished what you started.*

By the time I began my shift, Paul's mood had improved. He had a drink and filled me in on who was who, and which men were close to their limit. New miners drifted into town every day making our job harder and harder.

About seven-thirty, two middle-aged men came in. Strangers no one seemed to know. They sat at a table and ordered beers. Both were dressed in new plaid shirts, with new suspenders holding up new jeans, over black leather dress shoes.

"What do you think of those two?" I asked Paul who sat drinking his third after-work drink. "I don't think they're for real."

"Hadn't noticed." He laughed. "But now that you mention it, they don't look too real."

"I'm betting they're liquor inspectors."

"Billy Boy's been playing the machine for a couple hours. He's built up at least twenty dollars," he said. "Been drinking hard, too. Looks like you got a problem, toots."

"Cutting him off's no problem, but we sure can't pay him."

The strangers sat near the machine and watched Billy, talking to him as he played. Positive they were trouble, I needed to keep everyone cooled down. I put two quarters in the jukebox and played ten slow songs.

In a few minutes, the phone rang. It was Jay, the bartender at an old tavern down toward Springfield. "There's a couple inspectors out tonight. Keep an eye out." He laughed. "They're supposed to look like loggers."

"They're here. They didn't write you up, did they?"

"Nope. No problem here."

"Jay, thanks for calling." Leaving the receiver dangling, I walked halfway over to Billy. "That call's for you, Billy."

He looked puzzled and walked to the phone, which was out of range of the plaid-shirts.

"There's no call, Billy. Those guys you been talking to are liquor inspectors, and I can't pay you off while they're here."

"That's okay, I'll just wait 'til they leave."

"But, I have to quit serving you, too."

"Okay, Suzanne." Blinking as always, he studied me, like he didn't quite understand—but agreed nevertheless.

"Go on back and play as long as you want, but no more beer and no pay off. I'll give you twenty bucks tomorrow."

"Okay, Suzanne." Billy Boy did all he could to please us bartenders. Like everyone that knew him, including some locals, I'd become very fond of him.

As the inspectors nursed their beers, the tension in the room mounted. Paul had blabbed to the guy sitting next to him, and the word soon spread through the crowd. I heard extra-loud remarks up and down the bar.

"…dime-store loggers…"

"Who do they think they're foolin'?"

"…damn liquor dicks."

Knowing that the city fathers had made their views of me known to the Liquor Commission, I felt sure they had come to see how I handled the crowd. I went from person to person. "Be nice, please. No swearing, no singing. You'll get me in trouble." Singing and swearing were considered prima facie evidence of drunkenness in 1962.

Finally after a miserable hour, I looked up and they were gone.

Paul snickered. "They leave you a tip?"

"Hell no! They just took five years off my life."

"Well, I'm going home now, kiddo. The fun's over. You're on your own."

Handling the crowd, plus the tension, wore me out and when I finally got home at three, I slept like a fat bear.

Thursday morning, I put everything in Marie's dependable hands. Karen and I planned a trip to Eugene to look at cars, so I got in Lindy's Olds and drove to her house.

"Well, well, look at you. Miss Rich Bitch. You look like you belong in that car. Let's take it instead of Old Yellow. We'll impress the shit out'a somebody."

I thought for two seconds about what Lindy had said. "Okay, but no bars." We flew down the highway, windows down, singing cowboy songs. "I brought my money. I'm going to open an account in Eugene."

"Why Eugene? Why not Barkerville?"

"You know how gossipy it is. I don't want anyone guessing about where I got seven hundred dollars. Got the jewelry, too. Thought I'd get a jeweler to tell me what it's worth."

"Oh boy! You going to sell it and buy a car?"

"Don't know yet. I'm just looking."

Eager to find out about the jewelry, I made our first stop the T. Martin and Sons, Jewelers.

"I have these two things my grandmother just gave me. Can you tell me about what they're worth?"

The man seemed eager to see a customer, dropped his newspaper and hurried to the counter. "Of course, it will just be an estimate. I would need time to do an appraisal."

"An estimate is fine."

He looked closely at the two of us, then put on his loupe and started with the pendant. "This is a very fine stone—nearly flawless. You say your grandmother gave it to you? Do you know where she acquired the stone?"

"No. Why?"

"It's an unusual European cut. Hmm. The setting's fourteen-karat." He looked over his glasses at me again, then at Karen who slouched on his counter, a cigarette dangling from her lips. "Did you wish to sell it?"

"No, I just wanted to know what it's worth."

He went on, as if he didn't hear my answer. "I wouldn't be able to buy a thing like this without documentation of its ownership." He picked up the antique ring box. "Very nice," he murmured to himself as he opened it. His eyes widened when he saw the ring. "This ruby is exquisite. My, my. Extraordinary." He seemed to be talking to the ring—almost crooning.

"Are those diamonds on the sides?" I asked, the picture of innocence.

"Oh yes, I'd say four carats in all. Fine diamonds, too, and platinum setting. Your grandmother must be very fond of you." He looked up for the first time since he opened the ring box. His eyes bored into me. "Did your grandmother pass on?"

"Yes." It was the first answer that popped into my head.

"Were these appraised for her estate?" He had the ring on his index finger and I could still feel his stare as I dropped my eyes to the ring.

Karen stepped up beside me. "Damn it! Are you going to tell her...or cross-examine her?"

He looked at her with his nose raised, as though he smelled something worse than cigarette smoke. Staring straight at her, he reached in his vest pocket and took out a business card. With his gold fountain pen, he wrote "pendant" and "ring," then looked again for a few seconds. He quickly wrote two numbers—with an angry dash behind each, and then handed the card and jewelry to me.

I put it in my purse without looking. "Thank you very much." I turned for the door.

"Yes, fuck you very much." Karen followed me.

We burst out laughing as soon as we were past his window. When we got in the car, I glanced in the rear-view mirror. He stood on the sidewalk outside his shop, writing on something.

"Damn, he's taking our license number," I said.

"The ass-hole probably thinks we killed somebody for this stuff."

As I drove away, I handed her the card. "How much?"

"Jeezus, Suz, twelve thousand dollars."

"What! You're kidding!"

"Five on the necklace and seven on the ring. No shit."

"He probably just did that to jerk us around." Still, I dared to hope.

"God, Suzanny, you could buy six cars with that—or even a house."

"I could do a lot with it—but I don't believe it. I'm going to rent a lock-box at the bank and put them in it, just in case."

After we finished my business at First National, we drove to the used car lots out on Highway 99. The money I had would buy me a decent used car, but after looking for an hour, I didn't see anything I liked. Driving Lindy's Olds spoiled me.

We stopped for lunch at a popular drive-in near the college—a place to see and be seen.

"Nice car," said the guy parked on Karen's side.

"She just got it. Her daddy bought it for her graduation present."

"Nice daddy," he said.

Karen flirted while I dreamed. Dreamed what it would be like to go to college—or to own a business—or to own a red Olds.

When we got back to Barkerville, I dropped Karen off, and then checked at the White Water to see if Marie needed anything before I went home to get ready for work.

My shift, busy and fast-paced, passed quickly—putting me closer to the time when I'd see Greg again. I went to sleep that night thinking of his sweet ways.

The August night hadn't cooled my house at all. When I woke up in the morning at ten, it was unbearable. I dressed quickly and took refuge in the cool bar. After taking care of all the errands that morning, I stayed inside until five-thirty, then went home, took a cold shower and put on my white dress—just for Greg. I was sweating before I could put on my make-up and get back to the bar.

Time crawled as I watched the clock—waiting for nine when he'd be there.

At seven thirty, Paul came in and made himself a drink. "Jeezus, you're having a bitch of a time. Guess I'd better start early."

"Thanks, Paul, I'd appreciate it. Looks like it's going to be a night from hell."

He took over the tables, and I stood at the well mixing drinks nearly non-stop except to take care of the orders at the bar. When I finally turned to look at the clock behind me, it read 8:50. My heart hammered and my cheeks flushed. I trembled like a teeny-bopper as I poured drinks. My eyes constantly darted toward the door.

Above all the noise I heard him slap the door and looked up as he came through it. His little concentration frown disappeared when our eyes locked. A bolt of love passed between us before he lowered his eyes.

He greeted everyone he knew.

"Where you been, boy? We've missed you around here."

"Hey there's Greg…"

"Good to see you, Greg."

"Hi, Suzanne," he said, quietly, as he went to work. Shaping up the bar, catching up the glasses, breaking empties—he was strictly business with me but laughed and joked with all the customers.

My heart broke. My eyes filled. I went to the back room and sat on a beer case, blinking away tears. I couldn't give in to my feelings and lose my concentration. *Think of something else, keep going.*

About eleven, Paul took a break and I took over the floor. One of the tunnel stiffs at a table of eight had his underage, pregnant wife with him. A scrawny little

Mexican, she looked about fifteen. Paul told me he'd been slipping her drinks. "She don't speak English, but I told him if he did it again, he's out of here."

As I bent over a nearby table cleaning ashtrays, I glanced their way. She had a beer to her lips.

"You'll have to leave, Henry. Paul warned you about that."

"Like hell!"

"Come on, don't give me trouble. You know I can't serve her."

"You didn't serve her." He was loud and angry.

"Come on, Henry, don't give her a bad time," his friends said. "We can go out to Sophie's."

They all stood to leave, but as they went out the door, I saw a bottle in Henry's hand. "You can't take that outside." I went after him.

He stopped on the sidewalk and, holding the bottle by the neck, tipped it up. I grabbed it below his hand and pulled it away from his mouth. He jerked it upward while I hung on.

"Give me the damn beer!" I shouted in my biggest voice.

We struggled, but when his wife came out of nowhere and grabbed me by my hair, I lost my grip.

"Here's your fuckin' beer," he yelled, spraying it in my face. He raised the bottle above my head. I spun loose from his wife and raised my hands just as he crashed it down on the sidewalk. Glass and beer splattered my legs. They both cussed me out in Spanish, and then jumped in the car with the others.

Shaken, I gathered the broken glass and went inside—behind the bar where I felt safe. In the back room, I used a clean bar towel to clean my face and legs.

Greg came in and lit a cigarette. His fingers shook as he handed it to me. "You could get killed, pulling a stunt like that."

"I don't know why I followed him outside. It was real dumb."

Greg took the broom out to clean the porch, then got back to work.

When closing time finally came, I said, "What'll you have, Greg?"

"Nothing for me. I've got a deadline."

He wouldn't look at me as he finished his side-work. Then he grabbed his cigarettes and rushed out the door.

"What the hell's happened to our Greg?" Paul said. "He's like a whipped puppy."

"Girlfriend problems." I downed my blackberry brandy.

"I thought he was pretty hung up on you. What happened?"

"He had to make a choice."

Paul and I sat drinking, giving life hell for nearly an hour. I went home feeling deeply sad. I'd lost my best buddy. Full of brandy, I cried myself to sleep.

CHAPTER 33

▼

Saturday morning, hot, still air made the town seem as if it could burst into flames. At the foot of the Cascades, August often brought several days of endless, oppressive heat and nights when sleep was impossible.

When I went in to work, the air conditioning in the bar gave me goose bumps, but I'd appreciate it later. We'd poured lots of booze and written lots of hold checks, so I went to work taking careful inventory, assuming we'd be just as busy come evening. The hold-check box appeared to be $50 short and I rechecked it. No matter how hard I tried to change it, only $950 total in cash and checks.

A count of the register was no help. It came up $50 short, too. I counted and recounted the cash box. No question—we were $100 short. I felt sick. Shortages like that may have happened before, but it was upsetting when I was responsible.

I sat staring at the numbers when Marie arrived at ten-thirty. "It's going to be a scorcher. Glad I'm in here. Weatherman said we might get a thunderstorm this afternoon."

"If we get rain, maybe it'll cool off."

Marie shook her head as she wet the bar towels. "If we don't, we'll have forest fires up the ying yang."

After going to the Green Front, as everyone called the state-owned liquor store, to pick up the day's supply, I drove down to Karen's. She was still in bed.

"Hey, sleepyhead. Just because your house is in the shade, doesn't mean you get to sleep all day. Get up and suffer with the rest of us."

"My head hurts, bring me some aspirin."

I called out from her medicine cabinet. "You get drunk last night?"

"Think so. Don't remember it all. My car here?"

"Yes, Karen, your car's here, I'm sorry to say." I handed her the pills and a glass of water. "You've got to quit that. You'll kill somebody."

"Maybe me." She groaned, and then tossed down the aspirin.

"Want to go to the river? My house's too hot. I don't want to spend all day in the bar."

She groaned and fluffed her pillow. "Just let me sleep awhile. I'll pick you up."

"Sure. I'll be in the bar."

When I got back, Marie had a crowd—refugees from the heat. The men off Friday night's graveyard shift got their start at Sophie's then came down river for the hard liquor. Her tavern opened at eight, a smart move—something Lindy planned on too, but not until she had more bartenders.

Several stiffs looked like they'd been at it all night—Billy and Catfish included. Billy stood by the poker machine with a glass of buttermilk in his hand. He looked wasted, rather than drunk. His blood-shot eyes blinked, he scratched his scroungy two-day beard, and asked about Karen.

"Just came from her house. She's asleep."

"She pooped out on us this mornin'. Just cain't cut it." Even as hung over as he was, his grin was adorable. "Ya know I'm crazy about that woman, don't ya?"

"I gathered that, Billy. By the way, I'll get your twenty bucks from the other night."

"Nah. I'd a played 'em all off anyway. Never mind."

I went to the kitchen and ordered a burger, then sat at the counter to eat. From there, I could see the end of the bar nearest the back door. Mollie and Mel sat arguing, loud enough for me to hear. Mel, one of the first tunnel stiffs in town, was about five foot six and Mollie was a big woman, maybe six foot. Many times she'd come in during the day, sporting black eyes and bruises. Then, when he got off work she'd be all lovey-dovey. At first, it puzzled me that she could be like that with a man who beat her.

But, late one hot night, after closing, I sat on my front porch listening to them yelling from their second-floor apartment across the street. Their voices echoed off the brick buildings that lined mainstreet like cougars up a rock canyon.

"Moll...eee, now don't...make me hit you. Moll...eee, ouch! Damn! Put down that knife!"

"Go ahead, hit me, you pissy little shrimp."

Bang. Crash.

"Moll...eee, honey. Stop! That hurts."

Bang. Crash.

"Put it down, Mollie! Don't make me hit you."

Finally, the argument ended in the sound of fists on flesh, grunting and cursing.

That was the last time I listened to Molly's sad tales. She disgusted me.

As I sat eating, they got louder and louder. Marie stood before them and glanced toward me. I gave her the finger-across-the-throat signal. They could take their sick little game somewhere else.

About then, Karen opened the back door, squinted into the darkness, then left. I tossed down money for my lunch, went out the dining room door, and caught up with her on my porch.

"You're early."

"Couldn't go back to sleep."

"Billy's in there. Asked about you. Were you with him last night?"

"Yeah. I saw him, but I don't want to talk to him right now. Let's go. I'm roasting."

"Just a sec' and I'll put on my suit."

I changed and got my blanket, baby oil, and towel while she waited in the car.

The riverbank swarmed with people and the water churned with kids.

I knew Karen wasn't ready for the noise, and neither was I. "This looks like a mistake. Let's dip, then walk up-river."

We stayed in the water a few minutes, then gathered our stuff and hotfooted it up the dirt trail that ran beside the river. The first patch of sand we came to, we spread our blanket in a partly shady spot and plopped down in our wet swimsuits. Music came from upriver, beyond a patch of willows.

Knowing we had close-by neighbors, I kept my voice low. "What'd you guys do last night? Billy and the rest looked like hell."

"We closed up Sophie's, then went to this stiff's house. He invited us for fried cabbage."

I chuckled. "Fried cabbage?"

"Yeah. He fried a couple pounds of bacon in this giant pan, then chopped up two heads of cabbage in the hot bacon grease. Damn good, too."

"Pretty weird, inviting people home at two in the morning for fried cabbage. Fried eggs, maybe, but that's a new one."

"While he cooked, the rest of us played strip poker."

"No! Were you the only girl?"

"Me, two other gals, and six guys."

"Did you strip?"

"Hell no. I won. Two guys were down to underwear. Nobody started out with much. It was too damn hot. The game didn't last long. After we ate, I lost track…'til you woke me this morning."

We both raised our heads at the sound of a man's laughter and a woman's voice. The voice was vaguely familiar. We looked at each other with question marks on our faces.

The man's wheedling voice said, "Come on, Sweetums." Although their radio played, we could make out most of their words. "…like it when you get on top, Sweetums."

The woman giggled. "What if somebody comes?"

"Nobody comes down here but us. Hee hee."

Karen and I smiled at each other, ears straining.

"Oh, Punky, you're so…I can hardly…you."

"God, Karen, I know that voice," I whispered. "It's Mrs. Peterson, the gym teacher."

"Damned if it isn't. Who's Punky?"

"Ooooh, Punky, oooooh."

Karen rolled to her hands and knees. "Let's have a look."

He sounded like a pig grunting. "Uh, uh, uh, uh."

We heard sweaty flesh smacking sweaty flesh and crept in closer at the base of the willow clump that separated us from the fornicating couple. Our bodies shook with silenced laughter as we listened to their slapping and moaning.

Crawling on my stomach deeper into the bushes, my face nearly in the dirt, I saw bare legs—then *her*, astride his gigantic white belly. The big-boobed, Mrs. Peterson bounced on him like a bareback rider—her huge sweaty breasts spanking his watermelon belly.

I glanced at Karen, who, trying to stifle her giggles let out air between her fingers. I knew if we made eye contact, we'd crack up and be caught before we got to see who Punky was.

"Ooh, ooh, ooh, ooh." She crooned, in rhythm with her slaps. "I'm com…ing. Punk…ee…ee…ee."

Then with a loud bray, Mrs. Peterson reared back, thrusting her breasts skyward.

That was too much. We looked at each other and let go at the same time. Laughter spewed past our hands.

I grabbed Karen, put my finger to my lips and backed out of that thicket like a hound dog from a skunk's hole.

We scooped up our blanket, and sprinted all the way back down the path with sand flying.

Karen gasped for breath. "Who the hell was he?"

"Couldn't tell…him talking that high baby-talk." I shook out the blanket and spread it under an oak. "Let's just sit here. They'll come down the trail."

We blended with the crowd, and tittered about what we'd seen, while we watched for them.

In ten minutes or so, I saw Mrs. Peterson in an inner tube. "Look who's floating downstream."

Karen glanced at her, then back to the trail. "Clever. He'll come down here any minute."

Mrs. Peterson climbed out of the water and spoke to several families on the beach. I warned Karen not to get caught staring and fought hard to keep my own face straight.

Karen elbowed me. "Look!"

"I'll be damned."

"The old bastard is more than just a liar, Suzanne. He also likes dickin' other people's wives. Some Christian."

I rolled onto my stomach and put my face into the blanket, not trusting myself to look at him. "Be careful, here he comes."

"He's looking all around," she said quietly. "His face is red as a beet. He's wiping sweat off his neck."

"Is he coming this way?" I whispered.

She kicked my foot.

"Hi, Sid. Sure a hot one, isn't it? Too bad you can't get out of that damn uniform. See you got your radio. Been having lunch by the river?"

Careful Karen, don't get cute. Old Punky's still the Chief of Police.

"Yeah." He cleared his throat and spit. "You see some kids run down this way?"

"Couple of boys came tearing down the trail. Rode off on their bikes. Don't know who they were."

Karen kicked me again. "He's gone."

As we drove back to my house, I said, "Let's not tell anyone what we saw, okay? Maybe next time he decides to lie about me, I can put a bug in his ear."

"Sure. It won't be much use to us if word gets around."

"Old Punky and Sweetums! God, it felt good to have that laugh. I've been so down."

"'Bout Tex?"

"Partly, but mostly about Greg. I really got attached to him, now he'll hardly look at me. I guess he decided to be straight arrow with his girlfriend. We never did anything wrong, but we were getting close."

"Well, forget him then, there's lotsa fish in the sea."

"I guess. I'm not much interested in fishing anyway." I got out of her car in front of my house. "Tonight's going to be a lulu. You working at Sophie's?"

"Yeah. See you later."

I thought about Greg as I dressed in one of my sexiest work outfits, a purple peasant blouse and white hip-huggers. If he liked being pussy-whipped, I'd just see if I could make him as miserable as I was.

By nine o'clock, as Greg bounced through the door, every seat in the house was filled. Paul and I were behind in picking up glasses, with less than a dozen clean ones left. He saw the problem and went directly to the sink, sizing up the crowd while he washed. Our hands kept touching as we worked so close.

He spoke without looking at me. "Hell of a crowd, huh?"

"Been like this since seven."

"Soon as I catch up this side-work, I'll give you a break."

Between drink orders, I went out on the floor to gather glasses and speak to some people I knew. Several local couples sat at two pulled-together tables. One fellow I hadn't seen since we graduated caught my hand as I went by.

He stood and pulled me into a hug. "Suzanne, you're looking so good. I hear you and Jimmy split the sheets."

"It's true." I looked toward Greg, who glanced away.

"You dating anyone?"

"Not really." I poured on the body language, knowing Greg was watching. "Hey, nice seeing you. I've go to get busy, but I'll have a break pretty soon."

Later, when Greg relieved me, I took a drink and went back to their table where I laughed and showed off for fifteen minutes.

Throughout the evening, while I flirted with several men as much as I dared, I felt Greg's eyes on me. Passing each other constantly in the confined space behind the bar, we bumped several times. Those touches were like chocolates—I wanted more.

While I worked, my mind spun out questions. Why was I so obsessed with Greg? Because of the way he looked at me? Because I knew him to be gentle and kind? Or because I couldn't have him?

When closing time drew near, it struck me that I wouldn't be seeing him again. I fought off the familiar tight throat and stinging eyes while I shooed off the customers. Paul went to work cleaning the tables and Greg restocked beer, as I jumped in to wash glasses.

Oh God, I can't let him go without a word.

When he went into the back room, I followed him and spoke quickly before losing my nerve. I grabbed his arm, turned him toward me, and blurted it out. "Greg, tell me you don't care about me." The surprised look on his face changed instantly as those blue eyes searched my face.

"Oh…Suzanny, love…I can't tell you that."

His arms hung limp at his side. The pain in his voice and the sadness on his lips brought back my tears. I took my hand from his arm and stumbled backward. His image swam before my eyes.

"Why, Greg? Why did you let me love you, damn you. You knew she'd win. Damn you!" I whispered through trembling lips. I hit his limp arms. "Damn you! Talk to me, Greg."

His eyes glistened as he continued to stand with his shoulders slumped, his lips moving as if to speak, but uttered no words. Seeing his tears, I reached out to him—to hold him.

He came into my arms with a groan. His voice cracked. "I love you, too." We clung to each other for a few seconds, rocking. Calmer, he said, "This was the hardest thing I've ever done. She's so young…so heartbroken. I gave in, just like now." He nuzzled my face, whispered in my ear. "I miss you so much. What am I going to do?"

"Kiss me. Please, I've waited so long." I covered his lips with mine. Our first kiss. A gentle, trembling kiss that nearly dropped me to my knees.

Behind me, Paul spoke. "Well, well. What do we have here? Lovebirds?"

We jumped apart like kids caught smooching on the school ground. Greg turned back to what he was doing, and I went out to the sink to finish the glasses. When he came by me with a case of beer, I felt his stare burn the back of my head and I glanced over my shoulder.

He flashed me his famous smile, tinged with sadness. "Fix me a drink, will you, Suzanne?"

"151?" *Why offer him that stuff? It'll knock him silly.*

"Good idea," he said, but sounded less than enthused.

I finished two Brandy Alexander's in the time it took him to drink his rum, and we broke all records on the clean up.

Greg started around the bar with his car keys and cigarettes when Paul said, "Sit down and have a drink with us, Greg. To hell with Becky's stupid deadline. She won't know the diff."

He hesitated a moment, threw up his hands in surrender and climbed on a barstool next to him. "You know what we like, love."

I made him another 151—a stiff one—and refilled Paul's and mine.

"You better keep your eye on her, Greg," Paul teased. "This Texan's been trying to get her to marry him."

From where I stood taking cash from the register, I shot him an angry sideways look. *Damn blabbermouth! What's he trying to prove?* Greg lowered the unlit cigarette he had half way to his mouth. I quickly returned to counting the money, but watched him in the backbar mirror, waiting for a reaction.

"Is that so?" he said, slowly fitting the cigarette back in its pack. "Well, she'd be a prize to any man."

Paul wouldn't let it go. "Tex looks like a hell of a prize to me," he said.

Abruptly, Greg tipped his glass, drained it, and stood. He was halfway to the front door before he said, "See you fine people," without a backward glance.

His ramrod back and jerky movements, so unlike my graceful sweetheart, looked like pain to me. "Take care of yourself," I said as he unlocked the door and let himself out.

He nodded, but didn't look back.

CHAPTER 34

▼

Blinking back tears, I finished my drink and handed Paul the money. "It's counted. Please put it away for me. I'll see you in the morning."

Numb, eyes blurred, I stumbled home. I didn't turn on the lights, just moved around my cabin by the light of my mercury vapor moon.

I undressed, put on my silk kimono, sat in the shadows and looked out my open door. A cool breeze ruffled the silk. I lit a cigarette and reviewed my life. The crush I had on Greg would pass in time, I told myself. Things always looked their worst at three o'clock in the morning.

I heard a car, moving slowly over the graveled street behind my house. When it stopped, I got up to look out my open kitchen window. The darkness was too deep to see more than black shapes. I heard the click of a car door as it was quietly shut, then footsteps in the gravel.

Terror clutched me. Adrenaline spurted through my body. There wasn't time to find the key and lock the front door. On tiptoes, I dashed to my bedroom. I fumbled to tighten the belt on my wrap and momentarily thought of trying to pull on my jeans. No time.

The chrome barrel of Greg's loaded Colt caught my eye in the dim light. I grabbed it from my nightstand and drew deep into the shadows.

I couldn't see the front door, but knew I'd see him when he stepped into the shaft of light shining through the bedroom's doorway. Both Tex and Mark were in my mind. I stood there with the gun gripped tightly, as I'd been taught by Jimmy—in both hands, one cradling the other. I had no doubt I could use it on either of them if they cornered me.

Over the boom of my heart, I could hear more gravel crunch as the footsteps came around the front of the house. Then came the scuffing sound of him climbing the concrete steps. I took a slow, calming breath to prepare myself. *Come on bastard. I'm ready.*

A whisper. "Suzanne?"

I strained to recognize the voice. Mark or Tex? Or Jimmy? I held my breath. Footsteps crossed the living room.

He spoke just above a whisper. "It's me."

Oh, God. Who is me?

"It's me, Greg."

"Sweet Jesus!" I stepped out with the gun lowered. "You scared me half to death."

"I'm sorry, love." He took the gun from me, set it on the nightstand, and then took me in his arms. "I'm so sorry."

Relief unraveled me. "I thought it was Tex...or Mark."

He pulled me closer. "What?"

Knees weak, I dropped to the bed, pulling him with me. Shaking and crying, I babbled. "I'd shoot the bastards...without blinking an eye!"

Holding me to his chest, he rocked me, wiped my tears and stroked my head. "What did you mean, Tex? Isn't he the guy Paul said...about marrying you?"

I raised my head, spat out my secret. "That was bullshit! The pervert raped me!"

"Oh, Suz." He gasped. "God damn him! I'll kill the bastard!"

"He's gone." I told him about Shooter.

He breathed a deep, sad sigh. "Oh, Suzanne." Holding me away, he looked at me in the half-light. "Are you all right? Did he hurt you? Where did this happen? Here?"

"Sophie's party."

"Damn! Why didn't I go? I wanted to go...be there with you. Why didn't I? This is so lousy."

He gently pushed me down on the bed, then stretched out beside me and stroked the hair from my wet face. "Love, tell me what happened."

Alternately swearing and crying, I stumbled through the whole story, starting at Sophie's bar when I first met Tex. When I told him what Two-Fingered Shooter had done, he said, "Good. Good. Going to the cops wouldn't work. I just wish he'd killed him."

As I talked, he fingered the ties on my kimono. Then, untying them with one hand, he leaned and kissed the cleft at the base of my neck. "I've wanted you so long. I want to make love to you. Could we?"

I didn't answer, just reached for his shirt. As I unbuttoned it, our lips met for the second time—that time not so gentle and tentative—and we passionately explored each other's mouths. The taste of rum still lingered in his. I was grateful for the rum. Without it, I knew he'd never have given in to coming to me.

"I tried to go home…the thought of someone else having you scared me."

I went to close and lock the front door. He lay naked when I returned, the upper half of his body visible in the pale light. He held out his arms to me. I dropped the robe and lowered myself into them.

We both moaned with the long-awaited touch of our bodies. We pressed and kissed, rubbed every part of our bodies together, writhing on the bed. Our legs entwined, his toes massaged the top of my foot as he kissed my neck, while I fondled his muscular butt and hairy thighs.

I rolled to my back and opened my legs.

"No, no, too soon. This has to last." His mouth moaned its way down to my breast. "Yum. You are so sexy." He murmured as he nibbled my aching nipples. His hands were everywhere, doing things that made me crazy.

"Oh. Oh. Don't stop."

He fluttered from place to place with skills I never dreamed of. He teased. "Do you want me, Suzanne?"

"Oh, yes." I ached. I begged. "Please, now."

"Yes, now." He covered my eager body, pressing deep, but ever so gently. "I love you." The words were a sigh of pleasure as we lay still to savor our first moment. "Is it all right?" he whispered as he kissed my ear.

"Yes, everything is all right. Please." I raised my hips to his.

We never spoke again. The bedroom filled with the animal sounds of two people making love.

Both far beyond satisfied, we rolled apart. He lit two cigarettes, then lingered on my lips with the back of his fingers as he put one in my mouth.

"Where do we go from here, Greg?"

"I don't know. I know I can't give you up."

"You can have me any way you want, you know."

He ran his soft fingers across my cheek. "I've got to leave now, love. It'll be light soon."

After he'd dressed, he bent for one more kiss then let himself out. When I heard his car start, I felt a wave of love for him. At the same time, I knew that it could only be a late night affair. At that moment, it seemed like enough.

Sunday morning, I awoke with a start and remembered it wasn't my day off as Sunday usually was. I had to open the bar at eleven and the clock read ten-thirty. I threw on clothes, brushed my teeth and hair, and dashed to Lindy's to get the money. Flying from place to place, I got all the opening chores done—lights and beer signs turn on, chairs lowered from the table-tops, ashtrays distributed, clean bar towels dampened, mix and condiments out of cold box, etc. I put the money in the cash register, and then went to the kitchen for coffee.

At exactly eleven, I opened the door to find two carloads of Saturday night refugees pulled up in front waiting.

"Suzanne, we're dying. We need a nurse, honey." Digger raised his hand, made the round-for-everyone circle, and then he asked for a hold-check to pay for it. By the time I'd served their drinks and written his hold check, more stiffs drifted in. It looked as if I might have quite a day on my hands.

Even though I'd had little sleep, I felt great and had no trouble keeping up with my crowd.

"Your sidekick got us drunk last night out at Sophie's. Then we all went swimmin'," someone said.

"I think her and Billy Boy got married," another one said.

The stiffs called sleeping together getting married. From what Karen had told me about her relationship with Billy, I'd be surprised if that happened.

My shift sped by, with little time to think about Greg, and when Paul came in at six-thirty I finished the bookkeeping from the morning. To my horror, we were missing another $55.45. That made me short $175 for the week.

I sat at a table in the dining room where it was quiet and counted and recounted. The figure I'd written down when I gave the money to Paul the night before didn't agree with the total of what remained in the bag plus the $200 bank I'd started the day with. The till was sometimes off $5 one way or the other, especially since we'd gotten so busy, but this was no error.

It had to be Paul. It looked to me like he's simply lifted another $50. I remembered the snippet of conversation I'd heard between Lindy and Marge about him stealing. Would he deliberately sabotage me—just because they'd left me in charge instead of him? *He can't be stupid enough to think I won't miss it.* Counting it a hundred times wouldn't change the facts. Nor would my agonizing over it.

There was no mistake in my calculations. I put the excess cash in a new safe place in Lindy's mobile—a place that Paul would never look.

When I'd finished, I called Karen. "What you doing, girl? I hear you and Billy got married last night."

"Sorta."

"Why don't you come see me for awhile and we'll swap stories. I'll buy you a beer."

"Well, well, did you fall in love last night, too?" she said.

"Sorta."

She laughed. "I'll be there in a few. I haven't dressed yet."

After I walked to the store for a six-pack, I turned on my new fan. Sitting on the porch with it blowing on my back, eyes closed, I replayed my night with Greg. When Karen drove up in a cloud of dust, it drew me back to the present with a jolt.

"You look like warmed-over doo-doo, Karen. What have you been up to?" I got each of us a beer, set them on the coffee table, and turned the fan around. "Come on in here. I don't need to have Sid nail me for furnishing alcohol to a minor."

"Last night was a bitch. We were so damn busy." She guzzled the cold beer from the can. "Then after we closed, a bunch of us went to the river and drank a lot of cheap wine. Billy took care of me, so he stopped drinking when I started getting smashed. It's a good thing. I blacked out somewhere along the way."

"Jeez, Karen, you need to be careful when you do that."

"Anyway, I woke up about daylight at home. Billy was in bed with me. I was still drunk, and horny as a two-peckered Billy goat. He had on boxers so I just ran my hand up the leg and started ticklin'." She laughed so hard she choked on her beer. "He started getting hard before he woke up."

"God, Karen! You're awful!"

"Christ, you should have seen him when he woke up, buck-naked woman with her hand up his skivvies, and him with a hard on. He sits straight up, blinking like he does, stuttering. 'W-w-what! What you doing to me?' I told him, 'just lay there and take it like a man.'"

We both cracked up, rolled around on the couch. "Then what? Did he co-operate?"

"Not at first. He just went limp. But, you know me. That was a challenge. It took me damn near an hour, but I fucked him. I bet that's his first piece in years."

"Poor guy."

"He did okay after he got started. Then he says, 'Karen, you're sh-sh-sure a good sport.'"

We nearly peed our pants on that one.

"He couldn't get out of there fast enough. Called Digger to come and get him, then paced the floor 'til he got there."

I went to the refrigerator for two more beers while Karen loudly continued with the lurid details. I cringed and hoped the neighbors weren't home.

"Now, let's hear your story. I'm damn sure it won't top mine."

"I'm damn sure it will...on the Richter scale. Greg came calling at three this morning."

"Whoa! I thought he was giving you up."

"He was, but I was just too irresistible." I chuckled. "I teased the crap out of him all night Saturday, then Paul told him Tex wanted to marry me. That, and two shots of 151 did the job."

We talked about the details some and about Greg's other woman. I told her about the money shortage and she told me not to worry. "Bruce and Lindy know how honest you are."

After Karen left, I returned to the bar and gave Paul a break before I went to bed.

Monday morning I went in early to take stock of the liquor and do the banking before I had to open at eleven. Lindy and Bruce would get back sometime during the day and I wanted everything to be as perfect as possible.

There was no crowd waiting, but I kept busy the first hour with the redemption of hold checks and the stiffs that drifted in every day, using the White Water Bar as their meeting place.

At noon, as I polished a glassware shelf, I heard a familiar slap on the door and looked in the mirror to see Greg coming toward the end of the bar.

"Can I get a ham sandwich in here? I didn't pack a lunch today." His eyes were bright with mischief. "I'll take a brew, too." He sat on the end barstool.

My only customers were stiffs and a couple local old-timers—no one who'd know Becky. I went to the kitchen to order his sandwich, dragging my hand across his butt both going and coming.

I stood next to him, leaning my elbows on the end of the bar. Hidden from everyone's view, I wound my leg around his as I lit a cigarette.

He kept his public face straight as he whispered through his smile. "I'd rather eat you for lunch." He took my cigarette from the ashtray, pulled a drag, smacked his lips.

After his sandwich came from the kitchen, he picked up a half. With each bite, he rolled his sexy eyes as if eating something far finer than food. The tip of his tongue flicked at the corners of his lips. After the last bite he slid his mayonnaise-covered finger fully into his mouth, half closed his eyes and made a quiet sucking sound. "Yummm."

Oblivious to my customers, I watched and felt it down deep.

He picked up the second half, touched it to his lips then held it out to me. "Want some?"

"You know I do."

His eyes crinkled into laughter and we both broke up. "Aren't we a pair to draw to!"

Greg looked past me at the clock. "Damn. Got to go. Can I see you later, sexy?"

"I'll be ready."

That thirty-minute lunch gave me a warm glow for the rest of the day.

CHAPTER 35

▼

"Look who's here!" someone said when Bruce and Lindy came dragging in the back door about five o'clock.

"It's the newly-weds. Give them a drink, Suzanne."

They spoke in unison. "The usual."

"We're pooped," Lindy said. "Soon as we have this, we're turning in. Everything okay?"

"Fine." *I'll tell her about Paul tomorrow.* "We had a visit from a couple undercover guys…didn't say anything. Just made life miserable for an hour."

"Bet you're ready for a day off. Busy weekend?"

"Thank goodness Greg was here. It was a madhouse."

More of the newlyweds' friends came by, so they moved to a table, and told everyone about their honeymoon at the Grand Canyon.

Paul came in the front door with Digger O'Dell, Billy's friend from Wyoming. They'd gotten chummy in the last couple of days. "Do I get a before-work drink, Suzanne?" He hadn't noticed his mother and Bruce at the table. I poured him Grand Marnier and gestured toward them with my eyes. He made a face. "I saw them."

When he came behind the bar at six-thirty, I mixed myself a Collins and went to the table where Bruce and Lindy still sat talking. "Lindy, all the banking's done except today's and the liquor's okay. I'm going to Eugene early in the morning. I'll talk to you when I get back."

"Thanks for taking care of things, Suzanne."

I stayed, downing two more drinks someone bought, and then strolled home. A hint of autumn in the air-cooled the evening as I sat on my porch looking east toward the mountains. The last rays of the sun lighting a jet trail in the sky set me dreaming of far away places. Would I ever fly on a jet plane? Go somewhere like Hawaii or New York City? I'd only been in three states so far—barely into Nevada when I got married, and crossing California to get there.

Listening to the tunnel stiffs' stories of exotic places made me envious, and hungry for more than Barkerville. For a few minutes, I gave my dreams free rein and imagined myself as a stewardess on that airplane, taking care of passengers on a Portland to New York flight, serving coffee to handsome travelers. One of the men, an actor, asks me to dinner in New York. I decline because I have a date with the pilot.

Smiling at my foolishness, I brought myself back to earth. Remembering Greg's promise, I went into the house.

I got my negligee from the bottom drawer and stepped into the shower. When I finished, I stood in front of the mirror and looked at myself in black lace. Déjà vu. The night I waited for Mark in the same lace. *But this is Greg. He's different.* I arranged myself in bed, the lamp shaded with the same perfumed silk scarf. The lamp's heat filled the room with White Shoulders, soft music played on the radio. Soon I slept.

"Suzanne." The whisper penetrated my sleep and my eyes popped open.

Greg, already naked, pulled back the sheet and slid in beside me. The clock read twelve. We held each other and kissed for the longest time, trying to get enough of each other's lips and bodies touching head to toe. Slipping off my negligee, I straddled him, stroked his chest, felt his pounding heart. He held my breasts, raised his head to kiss them.

When he began to writhe, I whispered in his ear, "Lay still, Greg."

I did all the things he did to me our first night—until he groaned and thrust and begged. "Please, love…oh, please."

I mounted him, teasing at first, then deadly serious in my rhythm. When his back arched and he was nearly ready, I withdrew and lay panting beside him.

"You brown-eyed vixen!" He laughed softly while rolling onto me to begin again.

When we'd both come, we held each other so tightly we could barely breath, murmuring each other's names. Soon I felt Greg relax into sleep. The clock read three.

I gently shook him. "You've got to go. You'll be dead on your feet tomorrow."

"Uh huh." He nuzzled his face in my chest, purring. "I'm already dead. In heaven."

"Get serious." I laughed and pushed him toward the edge of the bed.

After he'd gone and the familiar rumble of his car faded from the night, I lay thinking. Thoughts I didn't want to think. Was he with Becky before? Did he utter the same love sounds to her somewhere on a blanket at ten o'clock? Finally, near dawn, I let it go.

In the morning, Karen came at nine. "Thought we were getting an early start. How come you're still in bed?"

I jumped up, heading for the bathroom. "Sorry. I'll hurry."

"Whoa, what's this? Nightgown on the floor? Company last night?"

I rolled my eyes toward the bedroom. "Greg was here for three hours."

"Holy shit, three hours! That boy must be somethin' else."

"That he *is.*"

I dressed quickly and got my lock-box key. "Let's get going. I can't wait to look at cars."

On the way to Eugene, Karen told me about her latest sexual adventures. I lectured her, as usual, and we laughed a lot, as always when we were together. I felt free and independent to be buying my own car at last.

"Stop at the bank first."

"You going to sell the jewelry?"

"I'll try selling the pendant."

When I came out with it, I put it on and dropped it inside my blouse. "Stop at that little jewelry store on Fifth. Park around the corner." I'd dressed to fit the part I planned to play. "You stay in the car, okay? I don't think I can pull this off with you there."

"Sure, I'll be here." She tapped the accelerator. "With the engine running!"

As I walked toward the jewelry store, I prepared myself, mentally rehearsed my part and rubbed my eyes to make them red and watery. Inside, I walked directly to the man behind the counter and spoke in a sad, halting voice. "Maybe...you can help me." I pulled the pendant from inside my simple white cotton blouse, slipped it off over my head, and handed it to him.

"This is my mother's. My father gave it to her when they were married. He's gone now. She's very sick and this is all we have left." I blinked a lot and sniffled, lowering my head as if to hide tears. "She sent me to sell it so she can have her operation."

He looked down at the diamond, then looked at it with his glass. "It's a fine piece. What did you expect to get from it?"

"Mother was told last year it's worth five thousand dollars. She'll need even more than that."

He studied the pendant and then studied me. "I'm just not in a position to buy it from you, but if you'll go see Detrick over at the pawn shop on the highway, maybe he'll help you. I'll call and tell him you're coming." He picked up the phone and while he dialed, he said, "Don't let him cheat you. It's worth as least that much. Hello, Detrick? I'm sending over a little gal who has a fine pendant I think you'd like for your collection...yeah, the stone's a knockout...great setting. She's on her way." He hung up and handed back the pendant. "Honey, just go over to Highway 99. Valley Pawn."

"Thank you so much for your help. When mother's better, she'll be in to thank you, too."

Outside, as I walked to the car, I couldn't keep the satisfied smile off my face. "Jeez, Karen, he said it's worth what that other jeweler told us. We've got to see this guy at a pawn shop."

"God, I can't believe this. Old man Wilke gives you a five thousand-dollar necklace for lettin' him feel you up. That's fuckin' fantastic."

We found the pawnshop easily and again I went in alone. Same act as before.

"Are you Mr. Detrick?" I fished out the necklace and held it toward him. Detrick reminded me of a younger Mr. Wilke. White and clammy-looking. He took the pendant in his fat, soft fingers and used his loupe to look at it.

"What's the story on this?"

His beady eyes probed mine, but I held their gaze, repeating and embellishing my story.

"I'll give you two thousand."

Still holding his rat-like stare, I held out my hand. "I'm sorry. I know it's worth more than five thousand. I'll just have to take it up to Portland. We need the money."

"Just a minute." He stood looking at it. "Come back in half an hour. I'll call the cops...check it out. If there's no stolen jewelry reported I'll have five thousand for you. No more."

I took the necklace and put it back on. Inside my blouse, the diamond rested safely between my breasts. "I accept your offer. I assure you, it's not stolen."

Back with Karen, I was ecstatic. "Let's go car shopping! He's going to check with the cops, then he'll give me five *thousand* dollars!"

"Hot damn! You're getting a new car? You could buy a hell of a car for five grand."

"I've been thinking about that. I'd like a new one, for sure, but the money could do a lot more for me than just buy a car. Think I'll use the seven hundred I have saved and maybe five hundred more."

We walked through four used-car lots before I saw it.

"It's cherry," Karen said. "Look at those leather seats. It's got every gadget they make."

I ran my finger down the tail fins, getting excited.

A rumpled salesman ambled across the lot. "This Caddy catch your eye, did it? She's only got thirty thousand. This DeVille two-door hard-top's the classiest car on the road, in my book." He opened the door, leaning to look inside. "Leather seats. Real soft. This baby's owner loved her...took care of her. She spent all her time under cover. See how new her paint looks. Blue fades, but she's been waxed all her life."

I'd heard enough. "I'd like to take a test drive."

Karen got in the front seat and he got in the back. I adjusted the power seat. Everything fit my small frame perfectly. As we pulled onto the highway, the eight cylinders snapped our heads back. I loved her. The price painted on the window beside the big fifty-six was fourteen ninety-five.

Back at the lot, inside the cubicle where the salesmen start wearing customers down, I said, "I have twelve hundred dollars cash in my pocket, not a cent more. My friend and I are going for lunch. When we get back, have it thrashed out with your sales manager. I don't want to go through any back and forth crap, okay?"

The salesman looked from me to Karen, who sat smoking, drumming her fingers. She had on cut-off jeans and a sleeveless blouse, while I wore my prim, starched middy blouse over a pleated skirt. Twelve hundred seemed like a big hunk of money to me, I expected to call the shots when I spent it.

"Yes, Miss McTavish, I'll do my best." He opened the door for us.

As soon as we were out of sight, Karen exploded. "No back and forth crap...yes ma'am, Miss McTavish. I love it! You're starting to toughen up. I love it!"

"Feels good to me, too. It's been over a half-hour, let's get back to the pawn shop."

A thin vein of fear ran down my arms from my stomach, but I squared my shoulders going in. "Well, Mr. Detrick, have you decided?"

"Sure have. Everything's okay. I have your cash."

I took off the pendant and handed it to him. Although I had no attachment to it, I noticed how warm it was from where it lay. The warmth took me back for a second, to that last night with sad old Mr. Wilke. He probably thought I'd keep it forever. But I couldn't afford the luxury of owning it.

Mr. Detrick counted out the cash, put the stack of bills in an envelope and handed it to me. "You better go straight to the bank."

I stuffed the envelope in my purse and said, with all sincerity, "Thank you, Mr. Detrick. My mother thanks you, too."

Outside, I showed Karen the cash. "Holy shit! You're rich!"

"Let's get back and see if I've bought a car."

We pulled up by the sales room and Mr. Enthusiasm came bounding out to meet us, a lot more interested than he'd been at first. "Congratulations, girls. You've just bought yourself a fine Cadillac. Come inside and we'll take care of the paperwork. The shop guys are gassing her up."

He seated us at his desk then left the room. Feeling like Mrs. Vanderbilt, I pulled out twelve one hundred-dollar bills and spread them in a fan on the table. When he came back, he did a double take at the sight of the money.

"When you said cash, you meant it, didn't you?" His eyes kept going to the money, like maybe he thought it was counterfeit. "Sign here and I'll give you a receipt and your temporary registration. They've got it ready for you out front. Thanks for the business, Miss McTavish."

He walked outside with us and opened the car door for me.

"Karen, I have to go by the bank before we head back. Want to meet for a beer?"

"Nah. I've got to stay straight today. Ron's calling tonight. I'm going to tell him I want a divorce."

"Oh no. Why didn't you say something? You want to talk about it?"

"No. That's why I didn't mention it. I was afraid you'd talk me out of it."

"You're nearly twenty-one. You can make your own decisions. You already know my opinion, so what else is there to say? I know you'll be kind to him."

Karen walked to her car, looked over her shoulder and gave me a thumbs-up.

As I drove off the lot with my windows down, tuning my new radio, I couldn't have been happier—unless it was going into the bank and depositing forty-five hundred dollars.

The teller said, "What'd you do, rob a bank?"

"No. I just sold my house." That was all the explaining I did.

Driving upriver, singing at the top of my lungs, I felt different. The day had changed me. My hand on the wheel of my own car, its free and clear bill of sale in my purse, was heady stuff. I felt proud of the way I'd handled the jeweler, the pawnbroker and the car salesman.

Driving through my hometown in my new Cadillac felt great. When I parked in front of my house, I got out and sat on the top step, just staring at my baby blue beauty.

Thank you, Mr. Wilke. From the bottom of my heart.

When I started to open my door, I found a business card tucked in above the doorknob. It read: Phillip Mason, Special Agent, Federal Bureau of Investigation. *The FBI?* Fear shot through my body. My hand shook as I turned the card over. On the back, a carefully printed message, "Please call my office to establish an appointment."

Oh, God. Now what?

I went into the house and sat on the couch, holding my stomach, reading the card over and over.

CHAPTER 36

▼

Federal Bureau of Investigation. FBI. I could think of nothing else.

Tex's beating? Is it the jewelry? No, it's too soon. I didn't steal it. He gave to me.

After I'd smoked a cigarette and told myself to settle down, I took the card and went to the bar.

As soon as I walked in, Lindy said, "Did those suits find you?"

"No, I had this on my door."

She looked at it. "What could they want with you?"

"I can't imagine. Can I go out and use your phone to call them?"

"Sure, honey. Don't look so scared. You haven't done anything wrong. It's probably nothing."

I went into her mobile and dialed the number. "May I speak with Mr. Mason, please?"

"Special Agent Mason is in the field. May I take your message?"

"This is Suzanne McTavish. He wanted an appointment to speak with me. I'll be home from nine to noon tomorrow. I don't have a phone. Thank you."

Back in the bar, Lindy asked if I'd found out what it was. "No, damn it, he wasn't there. Maybe tomorrow. Lindy, I need to talk to you. Can we go in the dining room?"

She picked up her drink and followed me, a quizzical look on her face. We sat across from each other at a table.

"You've probably discovered the shortage by now."

Her eyebrows shot up. "No. I haven't looked at the books. How much?"

"All together, $175." Looking her straight in the eye, I said, "I can't explain it."

I told her how part was missing from the hold-check box and the other over three different days. Dread filled me as I rummaged my brain for how to tell her I suspected Paul.

"One night it counted one way, but in the morning…"

"It's Paulie." She lowered her face and rubbed her temples. "I don't know what to do about him…he's like that. We got him out of jail…made restitution for him."

I sat staring at a pattern on the table, embarrassed to see Lindy near tears.

"If Bruce finds out, he'll throw him out. I've warned him. He has nowhere else to go." She raised her head, blinking her reddened eyes and squared her shoulders the way I'd seen her do when fighting with Marge. "I'll talk to him again. Don't say anything."

"I won't."

When we started back into the bar, she put her arm around my shoulder. "Thanks for being so dependable, Suzanne."

The FBI development took all the fun out of my new car so I just climbed on a barstool and had a beer. There were lots of customers, and watching their antics soon took my mind off it.

Next thing I knew, it was after five and Greg bounced in, sweaty and sweet. "Wow, Suzy Q, what's that big blue hunk of metal parked in front of your house?"

"That's Cassy, my new love. Isn't she something?"

"That's yours? No wonder you're grinnin' like a beaver in an aspen grove." His voice went low and sexy. "You takin' me for a ride tonight?"

I whispered, close to his ear, "Sure, I'll give you a ride anytime."

"I love it when you talk dirty!"

We played kneesies under the bar, asking for trouble. No telling who might report us to Becky. Everyone was related in Barkerville.

He chugged his beer, blew me a kiss and said, "Later."

Around six, I decided to go see how Karen had made out with her phone call. I felt so free having my own car. She came out of her house when I drove up.

"How was it?"

"Awful. Shit, Suzanny, he cried. I felt like a complete ass-hole. He blames himself because he's not here." Her eyes were dry, but she looked like she'd been crying too.

"Want to go for a ride? Let's run out to Sophie's for a couple hours. We can't stay longer though, Greg's coming later."

"I'll change and be right out."

On the way to Sophie's, I told her about the FBI wanting to talk to me.

"Could it be about Mark?"

"I don't know what else it could be."

"Mrs. Wilke's jewelry?"

"No, they only go after kidnappers and bank robbers and stuff across state lines. I think."

"Maybe Tex. Maybe he raped other women."

"God, I never thought of that. He probably did. Maybe I *should* have turned him in. I'm just not going to worry. I haven't done anything wrong."

Sophie's had a crowd, as always. "Howdy, gals. What you two luscious things doin' out all alone?"

"We're trying out my new car, Sophie."

"Well, let's see it." She came around the bar and dragged me out the front door. "Whoo-ee, she's a beauty!" She looked over her shoulder and spoke quietly, "I came out here to talk to you about Karen's birthday. We're havin' a surprise blowout for her Sunday afternoon. Can you bring her about two?"

"I'm sure I can. Want me to bring anything?"

"Just your smile, honey."

We stayed a couple of hours. Karen got sadder instead of happier and was ready to go home.

"You think I did the right thing, Suzanny?"

"What else could you do? You can't stay married and live the way you want to live. That would be worse than what Jimmy did to me."

"You're right. But, I feel so shitty. My mom's having a hemorrhoid."

"She'll get over it." I pulled into her driveway. "Go get some sleep. You'll feel better in the morning."

Back home, I prepared for Greg's visit. I heard his car about eleven and met him at the door. We stood inside leaning against the closed door, kissing and holding each other for a while. Then he took my hand and led me to the bed.

After we'd undressed each other, he said, "Remember what you promised to do to me?"

I did remember. And I did it.

I awoke with a start and looked around. The light in the room told me it was nearly morning. "Greg, wake up, it's daylight."

"Oh, crap!" He jumped up, threw on his clothes, and then bent to kiss me. "Later, love."

I went to the kitchen window and watched as he hurried to his car, looking both ways. It wasn't six o'clock yet but already plenty of light to be seen sneaking out of someone's bedroom. I went back to bed and crawled between the still-warm sheets that smelled faintly of him.

Sleeping soundly, I thought I heard a knock. I glanced at the clock and lay listening, trying to decide if it was a dream. Another knock.

"Mrs. McTavish, are you in there?" A loud male voice came from outside. *Oh, damn it! Nine o'clock. It's the FBI.*

"Just a minute. I'll be right there."

I didn't want to talk to the FBI in my flimsy silk robe, so I scrambled into clothes. Barefoot, finger combing my hair, I dashed to the door. Two men in charcoal-gray suits with blue and red ties stood on the porch and showed me their badges and identification.

"I'm Special Agent Mason. This is Special Agent Austin. May we come in?"

Not trusting my voice, I motioned them. My insides churned as much as my hands shook. Mason, the red-faced, older man appeared stern, with deep frown lines between his eyes. Austin, the baby-faced one, filled out his suit nicely and had beautiful hands—with no ring on his third finger. His smile was almost reassuring.

I was ashamed of how I looked, how my house looked and what they must think of me, as they unbuttoned their jackets and sat on the rumpled couch.

"We're looking for this man." Mason took a large photograph from a file folder. "We have information that he's been living with you."

"That's Mark." My voice came out too high and I cleared my throat. "He lived here for a short time, but he's been gone about a month."

"His name is Gunther Hafer," agent Austin said.

"But, I saw his driver's license and social security card. They said Donald Lightfoot. He's an Indian, isn't he? Gunther sounds like a German."

They looked at each other. "Donald Lightfoot is a man who appears to be missing. Tell us what you know about Hafer."

I told them about the house in Florence, about my growing suspicions, his frequent absences, and the men he met at Sophie's. Then I told them about sneaking into his trunk—about the money and the gun. They both took notes as I talked.

When I told them about him cutting my hair and Greg running him off, Austin said, "You are very lucky your friend showed up. This guy is extremely dangerous. He's quirky about women."

"What did he do?"

"He's wanted for smuggling, dealing in black market gold. Flight to avoid prosecution," Austin said. "California wants him for aggravated assault on two women. Cut one's face."

Mason gave him a dirty look.

My stomach felt like I'd just swallowed a rock. The image of him crouching low, coming at me with the knife flashed in my mind. "I have his switchblade. Do you want it?"

"We certainly do." He reached into his briefcase and pulled out a plastic bag. "Show me where it is." I pointed to the kitchen shelf where it lay.

"We've checked you out. We feel you have no involvement in Hafer's activities, but you may be called upon to testify to certain facts," Mason said.

"I've written up what you've told us. Please, read this and sign if it is accurate," Austin said.

The two men were all business, and as I read, their eyes surveyed my tiny little house. "You didn't say anything about him painting," I said.

"We already had that information. He painted that?" Mason motioned toward the faint image still showing on my wall.

"Yes. I need to give it another coat."

I signed their statement, and then they stood to leave, buttoning their jackets in unison. "When we catch up with him…we'll be in touch if we need your testimony," Mason said.

"We probably won't need you, so don't be worried," Austin said, shaking my hand, smiling in a friendly way for the first time. I noticed his soft hand and smelled the fresh gum he'd just sneaked into his mouth. "If you should see anything of him or think of something else, call me." He handed me his card.

"I hope I never see or hear of him again." I stood on my porch as they climbed into their big black sedan.

When they'd gone, I finished dressing and went straight to Karen's and told her all about it.

"Damn, Suzanny, the bastard could have really hurt you."

"I'm so glad it's over. I think I learned a valuable lesson. I need to listen to my intuition. It was working with Mark and Tex both—but I didn't listen. Maybe there's a lesson here for you, too, kid."

"I'll be fine. You don't need to worry about me."

"Only four more days, you'll be ready for your new job."

"I feel like I'm already twenty-one, going on thirty. But, I'm excited about working with you."

"Lindy's got your application ready to go next Monday. In less than a week, you'll be back there behind the bar."

I stayed at Karen's playing Monopoly until late afternoon then went home to get ready for work.

That night, Greg came knocking at three o'clock. I told him about the FBI as we lay in bed smoking after we'd made love. "Thank God, I was here that night. You don't know how precious you are to me."

The rest of that week, leading up to the Labor Day, went the same as the week before it—busy and hectic. I didn't see Greg Thursday night. When he came in to work at nine on Friday, he looked very tired. His double life was starting to show on his face and his sparkling eyes were dulled, with dark circles under them.

"Greg, you've got to get some rest, you look terrible."

"You're telling me. Had a long night with Becky last night—about me working tonight. I'll sleep tomorrow."

The night passed in a blur. Labor Day had always been a busy time of local festivities, plus there were about a hundred tunnel stiffs added to the crowd. At two-thirty, we all collapsed on bar stools with drinks, staring at the mess we had to clean up.

Greg put his head down on his arms. "Wake me about noon, okay?"

"Drink that 151, it'll put some starch in your drawers," Paul said.

We each had another round before we tackled our clean up at three. Two shots of 151 put Greg in a silly mood, but didn't overcome his tiredness, as he hauled out case after case of beer to restock.

As I followed him into the back room, Paul yelled, "No hanky panky back there."

Greg yelled back. "I couldn't hanky panky if my life depended on it."

I took him in my arms for a moment. "Not tonight, okay? Go home and rest. Tomorrow night will be even worse." I kissed him and went back to work. By three-thirty, we all dragged out the White Water's door.

My spirits lifted momentarily as I walked past my car, sitting there with the artificial light turning her blue paint to violet. Cassy's chrome sparkled as I took one last look out the window before I fell into bed.

Every muscle in my body ached as I lay staring at the ceiling, too wired to sleep. I didn't want to think about Mark for another minute, so I pushed him from my mind and thought about Greg. He was getting static from Becky. I couldn't blame her. I felt the same gut grinding when I knew she was with him.

CHAPTER 37

▼

Saturday started cloudy and cool. Perfect sleeping weather. I stayed in bed until noon, and then walked to City Park to look at the booths set up by local civic organizations for the Timber Carnival. I'd agreed to do a one-hour stint in a dunk-tank at two o'clock with Lindy and Paul to benefit the high school Booster Club.

I watched the schoolgirls, lips blue from the cold, struggling up the ladder, only to be knocked down again by a screaming, laughing bunch of teen-age boys. They were having a great time, but it didn't look like my idea of fun. I went back to the White Water and had a beer.

"You ready for this?" Lindy asked. "We should be able to make some real money during that hour."

"I just walked over there. Looks damn cold. How about jeans and a T-shirt instead of a bathing suit?"

"Sure. Sounds good to me."

I had two more beers while Lindy and Paul fortified with hard stuff. Everyone in the house knew where we were going, and when we walked out a crowd followed us to the park. Our entourage drew a huge crowd. They spent the entire hour throwing balls to unseat us. Unseat us they did. Time after time. By the end of the hour, I was hoarse from yelling and choking, my hands were cut from the chicken wire enclosing us and *my* lips were also blue.

Our mob followed as we dripped our way back to the White Water. The ones who hadn't gone cheered when we got back and they bought us drinks.

I just wanted a hot shower. Then a nap.

By five o'clock, I felt renewed and ready to face the worst Saturday night of the year. Bruce and Lindy would help until seven, and then they'd leave to work in a booth at the carnival. Paul would start with me at six-thirty and then Greg at nine.

When I went behind the bar everything seemed to be under control. Paul, cheerful for a change, jumped in and took care of the tables, while I served the bar and mixed drinks for him.

Soon after we started, a dark, Amazon of a woman about thirty-five blew into town. "She's fresh out of Tehachapi women's prison," a stiff at the bar told me. She was glad-handing a few of the stiffs, and as she got to the end of the bar one of her friends proudly introduced her to me. She wore a beehive hairdo, far more make-up than anyone in Barkerville, long red fingernails, and Shalimar hung around her like fog. Her huge breasts nearly burst her low-cut pink satin blouse that was tucked into a tight pair of shiny red pants. She took a step back, looked me up and down, then drawled, "I think I *like* you, Babydoll."

Stunned, I mumbled a response and busied myself behind the bar. *Does that mean what I think it means?*

The Amazon left the bar and joined a hard-drinking group of her friends at a large table.

At about eight-thirty, I took a break, walked outside for some fresh air and sat on the step of Lindy's porch smoking a cigarette, listening to the noise from inside. Paul stuck his head out the back door and yelled. "Your new friend's on a rampage!" His voice sounded high pitched, scared. "One of her buddies said he'll slit my fucking throat if I try to cut them off."

I remembered her earlier remark as I rushed back inside and hoped it meant she wouldn't give *me* trouble. I had no doubt the woman could be trouble with a capital T.

Damn, Paul, how come it's my problem? Why do you have to be such a wimp?

When I walked through the door, the scene shocked me—I hadn't been gone five minutes. Seven men at the table with the Amazon, one by one, took turns holding out their glasses and bottles, and letting them crash to the floor.

"Oops! My drink slipped."

"Oh, no, there went another one."

Broken glass surrounded their table. The smell of spilled beer mixed with the cigarette smoke. Booze and ice made puddles among the shards. The customers sitting at the bar, mostly men, were turned backwards on their stools watching the drama. A brawl between the locals and the stiffs would likely start if I didn't handle the problem quickly and quietly. What I didn't need was some logger coming to my rescue.

Paul, coward that he was, ducked behind the bar.

I had no idea what to do.

With a smile plastered on my face and my heart thumping, I walked to their table and pulled up a chair as if nothing was happening—as if I didn't see the mess on the floor. I made eye contact with Chuck, the most powerful man in the group, then with the Amazon. In a helpful, friendly tone I said, "What's the problem here?"

Several talked at once in loud angry voices, "Hell, we ain't drunk, we're just havin' a good time."

"That queer little prick said he's gonna eighty-six us."

The Amazon's hands were on her hips and blood was in her eye. "He'll play hell! I'll stomp his ass 'til it's a mud puddle."

I looked at her, keeping my voice low, but strong, "I'll be the one to decide if anyone gets cut off. But we can't have you guys breaking our glasses."

Look who's talking tough, she scares the crap out of me, too.

"Good for you, Babydoll." She gave me a big false-eyelashes wink. "Come in to the loo, I wanta talk."

With wobbly knees, I followed her into the ladies' room. In closing the door behind us, I brushed against one of her breasts.

"That felt real special, honey."

Oh, damn. Now what. I pretended not to hear as I moved as far away from her as possible in the tiny alcove. With my cheeks afire, I forced myself to look at her.

"What's that little blonde prick to you?" Her eyes bored into mine.

"You mean Paul?"

"That one behind the bar."

"Paul's the owner's son. He's really nothing to me."

"Then you won't mind if I have a piece of him, will you?"

"Do what?" I stammered, looking down at the floor. "I don't want a fight—"

"No, baby, I ain't gonna hurt him. I just like to scare 'em." She moved toward me, laughed softly and pinned me to the wall. "You really are a baby, aren't you?" Those giant breasts nearly rested on my shoulders. I stood on my tiptoes, barely breathing as she whispered in my ear.

"I want *you*, lovey...you're such a baby. Uh huh, I could pet you all night."

Pressed to the wall, I stood on my toes, rigid, shaking my head from side to side.

"That's my little sweet." She flicked my ear with her tongue.

I tried to hide the shudder that ran through me. Panic, fear and anger clogged my throat. Memories of Tex's attack flooded my mind. "Please, *don't*," I croaked, and twisted away.

Why does all the shit happen to me?

Self-pity tears filled my eyes, spilled down my cheeks and splashed on her chest. She drew back instantly, cupped my face in her hands and forced me to look at her. Through my blurry tears, she looked genuinely concerned.

"Don't cry. I wouldn't hurt *you*. I really dig white-skinned little boys like that one behind the bar." She stepped into the stall, grabbed toilet paper and dabbed at my eye make-up. "Girl, you're a mess! We can't let you go out there looking like that. Let's put some cold water on those red cheeks." She wet towels and held them to my face, clucking all the while. "I didn't mean to upset you."

She led me by a light touch on my arm as we left the ladies room. I was relieved to see the men had calmed down and the bar was quiet.

Chuck stood up and held a chair for the Amazon. "Sorry," he said to me and nodded at the floor. "You guys help her clean us this mess."

A couple men began picking up glass as I went to get the broom. My knees were still shaky, but my fear was gone, and with no more need to defend me, the loggers turned back to the their drinks.

When I went back behind the bar, Paul took a break and headed for the men's room. As he passed their table, the Amazon rose from her chair, winked at me and followed him around the corner toward the cafe. After ten minutes, when Paul's break ended, he came back to the bar with blotched cheeks and a proud smirk on his face.

Maybe I've been wrong about him.

Greg glided in a few minutes later, looking refreshed—a welcome sight. I'd gotten behind while I took care of Paul's problem and hadn't quite recovered from the encounter with the Amazon.

"What's going on? This place smells boozy. You look upset."

"It's over now. We just had a little problem. Notice the Amazon at that table and the wet floor. I'll explain later."

He skillfully took care of everyone I'd neglected, made them happy again. We had no time to talk as he rushed from customer to customer and I mixed drinks as fast as I could pour.

The night stretched on endlessly. My back ached, my feet hurt and I was starving. Finally Greg got us some fries from the kitchen and we ate as we could.

Men stood three-deep at the bar and all around the walls, giving the available seats to the women. The band played so loud, I was hoarse from shouting to be heard. Cigarette smoke burned my eyes. Our ventilation system couldn't keep up with the throng. The dance floor was a dark sea of people, flowing back and forth between sets, with Paul snaking his way through the waves. The noisy voices and pounding drums gave me a headache.

"Are we having fun yet?" Greg shouted over the crowd as two-thirty approached.

"Last call!" I repeated it up and down the bar. "Ten minutes."

A dozen or more people pressed to the bar for one last drink.

"Drink up! Two minutes."

All three of us circulated, picking up empties.

"Drink up!"

"Times up!"

"Good night, damn it!"

In a crowd of such size, there were always some that didn't want to give up their drinks. We'd stand, waiting while they chugged the last of it—or argue with them over it. Most knew the routine and the urgency of the clock and quit at the first call.

When Greg ushered out the last reveler, I lit us both a long-awaited cigarette and made drinks for the three of us.

"Jeezus, am I glad that's over. Good thing Labor Day only comes once a year." Paul, trying a coy look that didn't work, then wheedled, "What's chances of you two lovebirds doing my clean-up tonight. I'm meeting someone…for breakfast."

"Sure, Paul, but you'll owe me three, okay?"

"You drive a damn hard bargain." He drained his Grand Marnier and grabbed his cigarettes. "See you tomorrow."

"Not me! I'm the lucky dog that's off tomorrow."

Greg locked the door behind him. "Wonder who he's meeting?"

As we finished our drinks and started a second one, I told him about the episode with the Amazon, laughing at myself, and my reaction.

"What a gas! I'd like to have seen your face."

"It wasn't very funny at the time." I got up. "Let's get this joint cleaned."

With the last energy I could muster, I quickly put everything in order behind the bar as Greg restocked, then we both did Paul's work, wiping the tables and putting up the chairs.

"That's it. Let's get the hell out of this smelly hole."

Greg held me. "My car's in front. I need to move it out back."

"We're both so tired, why don't you just go home."

"Sure?"

"Yes. I'm beat."

We stood holding each other, teetering in our exhaustion. After one long, sweet kiss, I pushed him toward the front door.

"Good night, Greg."

I locked the door behind him, picked up the money, and let myself out the back door just as I heard his hot rod roaring east. After I put the money in Lindy's mobile, I slogged home.

The sight of Cassy's shining chrome made me smile inside. I gave her a pat as I passed, then one last look back as I climbed the steps.

I felt old and tired and used as I stood in the shower and the hot water soothed my aching muscles. Thoughts of Becky kept bugging me. I'd convinced myself in the beginning that my affair with Greg didn't count as cheating because he and Becky weren't married. What I knew in my heart was that the two of us were cheating her just like Jimmy and the Bimbo cheated me.

I wanted it to be different, but it wasn't.

Damn it, leave it alone. Think about Karen's birthday tomorrow.

CHAPTER 38

▼

Sunday, I got up earlier than usual to corral Karen for the day and called her from the Laundromat at nine. "Happy Birthday. I've got a surprise. I'm taking you to Eugene for breakfast." I told her to put on something fancy. "We'll pretend we're rich. See you in half an hour, okay?"

"Sounds great. I'll be ready."

I dressed in my green sheath, three-inch pumps, and I even put on make-up. Happy with what I saw in the mirror, I grabbed my purse and hurried out to Cassy.

Karen, with her deep tan, looked stunning in a swishy white dress and high-heeled sandals. Riding down the sun-flecked highway, we talked about how complicated life had become in our little town. We pulled up to the Westland Hotel, famous for its champagne brunch, and handed Cassy over to the parking attendant.

Karen's eyes widened. "This place must cost a fortune."

"Told you, we're playing rich bitches."

When we were seated and served our coffee, we looked around. Crystal chandeliers twinkled. Peach colored drapes and burgundy linens contrasted with the chairs covered in moss-green tapestry. Delicious, mouth-watering scents poured forth from the pyramids of pastries and mountains of exotic fruits on the long buffet table. It started and ended with life-size swans sculpted from ice.

Most of the men wore suits, and the women wore what I called church clothes. Many seemed to know each other, visiting quietly as they passed to and from the buffet.

I tried to act at home, didn't mention being uncomfortable, and by the way Karen sat with her hands in her lap, I assumed she was too. The thought crossed my mind that maybe the Westland wasn't such a welcome present for her after all. In spite of feeling self-conscious, I loved being in such an elegant setting.

After watching a few minutes to see how everyone else went about it, I stood. "Well, shall we?"

"I'm ready."

"Did you ever see such food?" I whispered, while daintily loading bites of fruit and a pork chop. "Look at those desserts. Is that cherry cobbler?"

Appearing totally at home, if she wasn't, Karen loaded her plate high.

A hatchet-faced woman with manicured nails and piled-up white hair stared over her glasses at Karen's plate. She spoke aloud to the scrawny wimp that hovered at her elbow. "I suppose she'll ask for a doggie bag."

Karen looked her straight in the eye. "Hell yes!"

She gasped and clutched at her pearls like she thought Karen might snatch them from her neck. Karen's skirt flared as she turned her back on the woman and glided toward our table like a top-notch model. We both stared for a few delicious minutes at Mrs. Hatchet Face as she returned to her party and proceeded to point us out to all her tablemates. The waiter interrupted the fun to check our identification before he poured our champagne.

I toasted Karen. "Happy Birthday, little sister. May life bring you everything you ever want...and *no more.*"

"I feel so grown up, Suzanny. This is the nicest place I've ever been. Thank you for thinking of it."

We took our time, eating and drinking and feeling grand. Then we drove slowly back up the river. It was nearly one when we got back to Barkerville and stopped at the White Water.

"Who are these fancy ladies?" Lindy said.

"This is your newest customer. Karen turned twenty-one today."

"Her first drink's on the house," Bruce said.

The crowd got in on the act and sang the Birthday Song. Lindy spoke to her about working and told her to bring in her birth certificate Monday so they could send for her license.

At one-thirty, I interrupted. "We can't drink it all in one place, Karen. Let's go out to Sophie's pretty soon." I'd promised Sophie two o'clock, so I herded her to the door.

We arrived just two minutes late.

"Looks like Billy Boy's here," Karen said as we piled out of the car. When she opened the door, it was like peering into a dark cave. "What the hell?" She jumped back, stumbling into me.

"Surprise!" The packed house roared, and the lights flickered on.

Karen gasped and grabbed her chest. "Jesus Christ!"

Two men picked her up and set her on the bar as everyone sang. A huge cake, full of candles, filled the little room with chocolate perfume. Arranged on a table beside it stood a money tree covered with tens and twenties.

I stayed back and watched, remembering my twenty-first birthday party—the day it all started. It seemed so long ago, and I felt so much older. All that had happened to me in that five months had forced me to grow up. Watching people acting crazy was beginning to look very different to me. I stood at the fork in the road. Increasingly, I felt impatient with the constant partying and drinking. Some of my customers at the White Water were starting to disgust me.

As I watched Karen, I worried about her. *She loves this mess.* Maybe in six months, she'd start to tire of it—but I doubted it. My mood made it hard to laugh and carry on like everyone else, but I didn't want to be a drag at Karen's party, so as always, I looked happy.

By dark, I was eager to leave. "Karen will you want to go any time soon?"

"You poopin' out on me? Go on home if you want. I'll get someone to take me home later." She gave me a hug and kissed me on the cheek. "Thanks for being my big sister, Suzanny."

"Okay. Have a good time, honey. Be careful."

Driving home in the dark, wind in my hair and the radio playing, I felt great confidence in myself. With Mr. Wilke's gifts, I was no longer tied to the White Water. I could do anything—go anywhere.

When I got home, intoxicated by my thoughts, I changed to my robe, took out the University of Oregon catalog I'd sent for, and lay on my stomach on the bed. As I thumbed through the listings my visions wandered. I imagined myself becoming a doctor, a lawyer who defends rape victims, or a banker, or an accountant, or a writer. Everything sounded exciting. With my forty-five hundred dollars and the ruby ring, I could easily escape all the madness that surrounded me. What about leaving Karen? Who would take care of her?

Just then, I heard Greg's car outside. *What about leaving Greg?* When he came through the door, I spoke to him. "I'm in here...dreaming."

Coming through the doorway, he looked so boyish in the downcast light of the bed lamp. He kicked off his shoes and dropped to his stomach beside me.

"What's this, love?" He put his cheek to mine and nodded at the catalog. "You're going to school?"

"Maybe so. I want to make something of myself, Greg. Tending bar at the White Water is not good enough."

He rolled to his back to look into my face. "Would you drive every day?"

"I don't think so. If I go there, I'll live in Eugene so I can work."

"You're scaring me."

I went into his arms, my face resting on his chest. "It scares me too."

"Then why?"

"This is not the life I want. I've got to get out of the White Water. Barkerville."

We lay together, silent for a long time—each deep in thought.

"What if we got married?" He said it softly, with little conviction.

The words hit me like a shot of bourbon on an empty stomach—the last thing I expected. "What about Becky? Your engagement?" I raised my head and gazed at him.

He stared at the ceiling. "I don't know, love." Unshed tears choked him. "I just know I don't want to lose you."

Anger, born of frustration, brought bitterness to my voice. "You don't know? What does that mean? See, that's the problem. You love me when you're with me. Her when you're not."

I knew in my heart that the problem wasn't Becky. I knew she would lose if I fought for him, but would I fight for him? I wasn't prepared to talk about it. A part of me wanted to say yes, yes, we'll marry. We'll have those bouncing babies we've talked about. We'll buy a little house and you'll be a successful broker and I'll wipe snotty noses—and my dreams will wither. *No!*

Still staring at the ceiling, he reached out for my hand and squeezed it, then brought it to his lips. Those beautiful, sensuous lips moved across the back of my hand, and then kissed the inside of my wrist. My heart broke into little pieces. He pulled me closer, kissing my neck. "Do you want to make love to me?"

"Not tonight, Greg. Will you...do you want to hold me?"

"More than anything." Emotions clogged his throat. "More than anything, love. I've missed you so much since Wednesday."

With my cheek pressed to his chest, I heard his thundering heart. Several minutes passed without words, then his heartbeat slowed and his muscles relaxed.

Soon his breathing told me he was asleep. His double life kept him in high gear with little time to unwind and rest. I gently disentangled from his arms and watched him for a while. Thoughts of life with Greg washed over me like incoming waves, only to be drawn away by the strong currents of my desire for a career. I could no more deny that pull than the tides could the moon's. Finally, my mind numb, I turned off the light and pulled a blanket over us.

The sound of a siren woke us at dawn. We clung to each other, both moaning softly then letting go. Our time together was over.

"Think about what I asked you, Suzanne. I love you." He straightened his clothes, combed his hair and hurried out into the first light.

I went to the kitchen to start coffee. While it perked, I showered and dressed, then took a cup and the catalog to the front porch to watch day come to Barkerville. I was filled with a strange excitement. A feeling of urgency gripped me when I realized a decision had to be made. Thumbing through the catalog, my thoughts soared with new possibilities. It was too late for the fall term, but maybe design school in Portland. Or would I decide to accept Greg's proposal?

The sound of a car roaring down Main Street broke the pre-sunrise stillness, pulled me from my thoughts. It sounded like Greg's Ford, coming fast. When he let off the gas and rolled into sight, I was shocked. I moved down the steps toward his car as he slammed to a stop and jumped out.

"Come quick." He grabbed my arm and pulled me toward the car.

The look on his face made my heart nearly stop. "What, Greg? What is it?" I knew it was something terrible but I couldn't fathom what.

"Karen." He was breathless and words gushed from his mouth. "I came around...on my way home. I couldn't tell what kind of car it was at first. When I saw it was yellow, I ran up there."

"Karen?" I jumped in the driver's side and slid across. "God damn it, Greg! What?"

He jammed gears and threw gravel as he turned around and started east. "She's wrapped her Lincoln around a tree."

"Greg. Is she...?" I screamed over the roar of his car, "Tell me!"

"Suzanne, calm down," he yelled. "You have to be calm. They're working to get her out."

"How bad is it, Greg?" Sobs tore at my throat. "How bad, damn it?"

"I couldn't tell, but she's cussing a blue streak. When she saw me, she said, 'Get Suzanne.' Billy Boy's with her."

"Oh, no."

We rounded a corner and slid to a stop behind the ambulance. Greg grabbed me in his arms, held me tight as I struggled to get out. "Love, calm yourself." He rocked me for a moment, speaking quietly into my ear. "You need to tell her...calm her...everything's going to be all right."

"Okay, okay," I whispered into his shoulder.

"It looks worse than it is, Suzanne. Are you ready?"

"Okay, okay." In my head I kept repeating *okay, okay, everything's okay*.

He pulled back and looked at me, wiped tears from my cheeks then helped me out of the car. My knees went weak as he led me past the ambulance. I braced myself for the sight of the car. Still it knocked the breath out of me to see it nearly vertical in the deep ditch, its entire front crushed against a big oak. The smell of oil and rusty water ripped from the radiator sickened me.

Several men worked with their arms through the windows as Greg guided me down the embankment and toward the far side of the car.

"Let me out of this *mother*." Karen's voice was high-pitched and her speech slurred.

The car must have rolled before it hit the tree. Its top was crushed downward and the passenger side door was unrecognizable as such.

I found a place out of the men's way where I could look inside, then steeled myself. Karen's legs, jammed in the tiny space between the seat and steering column had to be crushed. Her dress, dirty and in disarray, no longer covered her thighs. I reached across and pulled it down and tucked it between her legs. From my position, I saw the IV in her hand, but I couldn't see her face.

The men, using jacks to move the car, grunted and swore softly as they went about struggling to remove the door.

I moved back up the embankment to the back seat window, trying again to see her face. From there I saw Billy as a medic worked on him. Behind Karen's seat, upside down with his head crammed in the corner, he looked gray as winter sky. I watched him for a minute, staring at a little bubble of bloody saliva in the corner of his mouth. The bubble inflated with each breath.

"Oh God. Please don't die Billy." I repeated the prayer in my mind—*don't let them die, God, don't let them die*.

Greg, who'd been holding onto my arm all along, led me to the other side of the car. "Come around here where you can talk to Karen. Billy's out of it for now."

The medic stepped back. "Talk to her through here."

I wasn't prepared for how she looked. The left side of her face was a purple mass with an oozing cut over her swollen-shut eye and probably broken nose. Her good eye stared at me like a doe I once saw tangled in a fence. One side of her mouth and chin were torn and swollen, blood and puke soaked her dress front and one shoulder. The alcohol-vomit smells coupled with how she looked nearly brought me to my knees. I stumbled back, gasping in fresh morning air, and then put my head in again.

"Karen, how are you, honey?"

"Not worth…a shit." She spoke slowly, her voice weak.

"They'll have you to the hospital soon, honey. Hang in there."

"Suz, I'm so sleepy. Didn't get no damn sleep last night." When she talked, blood and saliva trickled from her split lips.

"Don't talk, sweetie. Just rest. I'll be here."

Her good eye closed and I moved back for more fresh air. The medic stepped back into his spot and Greg pulled me up to the edge of the road and held me in his arms.

The adrenaline rush I'd experienced at the beginning left me weak and shaking. "I have to sit down."

We sat close together on the ditch bank. "You said you drove her out to Sophie's? Somebody must have taken her home to get her car," Greg said.

"Not a one of those damn fools had sense enough to keep her from driving. I shouldn't have left. Damn me. I shouldn't have left."

"Don't beat on yourself. You know Karen. They said they'd have them out in a few minutes. Shall I drive you to the hospital?"

"You've got clients, you have to get to work. Just take me home and I'll drive myself. Soon as they're out." My mind was finally clearing—steadying, instead of bouncing all over. "Will you call her mother when you get home?"

"Is there anything else I can do?"

Chief Delaney, who'd been directing traffic past the wrecker and ambulance, walked up to where we sat. "Your buddy's got herself a peck of trouble this morning, Suzanne. That boy with her is pretty bad off."

His "peck of trouble" remark at such a time infuriated me. "Just what do you mean, Sid?"

"You know she's drunk as a skunk."

"How do you know that?"

"Just smell the car!" He straightened to attention, adjusted his glasses and peered at me. "What I mean, missy, is, if he dies, she's up for manslaughter."

"What makes you so sure she was driving? I sure as hell can't tell by looking." I shocked myself talking to Sid that way, but I'd lost all respect for him when he lied about me, then that day at the beach. Greg nudged me with his leg; probably afraid I'd make things worse by going head to head with Sid.

"Well, the way I see it, she *was*. That's what matters."

"What do you mean, the way *you* see it?" I stood up and took a deep breath, looking him straight in his little pig eyes. "I wonder how your *wife* will see it when she hears about Snookums? Or your pastor hears?"

Knowing dawned on his face. He seemed to shrink before my stare. "What?"

Before he could say anything more, someone rushed up. "They got 'em out."

Two men carried Billy toward the first ambulance. I ran to its back door, watched as they loaded him. He moaned, still very gray, eyes closed, not moving. Someone closed the doors and slapped the back fender. When they drove away, the first deep notes of the siren's scream sent chills up my spine as it cut the quiet air. *Please, God, don't let him die.* I prayed as hard as I ever had in my life.

By that time, another ambulance had arrived from Eugene and they were bringing Karen up the embankment toward it. Her head was cradled in a neck brace, her hands strapped to her sides, and splints immobilized her crushed legs. Ragged, bloodstained folds of her skirt hung over the side of the gurney.

"Suzanne. Where the hell are you?" She whimpered through swollen lips, most of the fight gone out of her.

I rushed to the side where she could see me with her good eye. Tears rolled down both sides of her face, bringing instant tears from me.

"What *you* crying for?" she whispered, a smile crinkling half her face.

"Don't laugh honey, you'll hurt your face."

"I already did, Suz." She tried to chuckle at her joke, but went into a coughing spasm that brought a bellow of pain.

"Let's get going," the attendant said.

I stepped back while they loaded her.

Greg steered me back toward the car, his gentle touch a great comfort. "She'll be all right, love. She's young and a real fighter."

In front of my house, Greg pulled me to his chest and gently stroked my back for a few minutes. The tender way he held me and the silence was the comfort I needed. Before I got out of the car, he took my hands and pressed them to his lips. "Don't drive too fast, love. Promise? You won't be able to see her for a while anyway. Remember, I love you."

CHAPTER 39

▼

On the drive to Eugene, I thought about my part in Karen's tragedy. Maybe I shouldn't have left her at Sophie's. But what could I have done? Although I often felt like Karen's mother, she was very much her own person. I loved that about her. All I ever hoped to do was set a good example, be there when she needed me. But I hadn't been there. My thoughts raced to all the what-ifs but I knew all my lectures about drunk driving had never helped her. Maybe in the end, her painful experience would bring a change.

At the hospital, a male nurse stepped in front of me as I pushed open the swinging doors marked emergency. "You need something?"

I'd decided on the ride in to present myself as her sister, so the lie came easy. "My sister...Karen Daugherty. They brought her in the ambulance from Barkerville."

His brusque manner changed. "Don't worry. She's with the best doctor in town and the orthopedic surgeon's on his way."

"What about Billy?" I stretched on tiptoes to look past him.

"They took him up to surgery. It will be at least a couple hours. Is he family?"

"He has no family." My throat ached for Billy when that realization struck me.

"You need to go down to admissions and answer some questions about them." He motioned to a group of overstuffed chairs in an alcove. "Then you can wait out there. You'll find coffee and pop down in the lobby. What's your name? I'll tell them you're here."

"Suzanne McTavish."

On wobbly legs, my mouth dry as desert dirt, I passed by the waiting room. Following the arrows that said admissions, I set forth down the long hall. The hospital smells, unidentifiable, but filled with foreboding, made me queasy.

At the front desk, a young woman looked up as I pawed through my purse for change. "You Miss McTavish?"

I nodded and put a quarter in the pop machine. I wasn't sure I could speak until I drank something. I pulled out the 7-Up, and said, "This might settle my stomach."

Just then Karen's parents burst through the door, disheveled and puffy-eyed. I took her mother in my arms and whispered, "She's going to be all right. She's just banged up…the doctor's with her. I told them I'm her sister."

"I knew something like this would happen." She stiffened and pulled away. "You damn fool kids. She's got so wild. Why couldn't she just stay home at night?"

"Where is she, Sis?" her father said. He'd always called me Sis. It was his gentle loving way. "Come on Mamma, settle down."

"We can't see her yet. There's a place to wait down by the emergency room. Just follow this hall. I'll be there in a few minutes."

Karen's father supported his wife as they walked down the corridor. I turned to the girl at the desk and gave her the information about Karen. Full name, birth date, Ron's name, and that she was a military dependent. That was the first time I'd thought of him. He'd been out of the country for so much of their married life he seemed like a distant relative.

"I don't know how to contact her husband."

"We'll call the Red Cross. They'll get a message to him, wherever he is."

"Good. Then you'll take care of that?"

"Yes, as soon as I hear from Emergency. When she's stabilized. You'll be in the emergency waiting room?"

"Yes."

I put down the emptied bottle and poured myself a cup of coffee, then started back toward the other end of the hospital. Waiting with Karen's parents would not be pleasant. Especially her mother, who thought I was a fool for leaving her precious Jimmy. And she'd never been one to mince her words.

As I rounded the last corner, I heard a sound that chilled my soul. A man's voice keening, "No, no, no, God, no." Hot coffee sloshed on my hand, as I stopped mid-step to listen. The sound went on like the yowl of an injured animal. All the blood drained from my head as I realized what I was hearing. I grabbed for the wall as my knees folded, and I crashed to the floor.

Some pungent, breath-stealing smell assaulted my nose. I twisted my head to escape its bite.

"You better now?" asked the white-clad lady kneeled beside me with a small capsule in her hand.

When my head cleared, I remembered the sound that sent me to the floor, and I struggled to get up. "I've got to go…that waiting room. Karen."

"Let me help you, dear." I could tell by her tone, she *knew*.

"She's okay, isn't she?" She wasn't okay and I knew it, but I wanted to hold on to the hope for a few more seconds.

The nurse picked up my coffee cup, and tried to support me as I staggered the last twenty feet to the waiting room doorway, then she gently pushed me into the first chair. The scene before me told it again, as surely as the wail I'd heard. Karen's mother sat on the arm of a chair, staring out the window, hands raised to her face. Her shaking shoulders revealed her silent sobs.

Her father's wail had stopped, but with his eyes squeezed shut, his tear-bathed, pain-wracked face still screamed without sound. The sight of him wrenched a gasp from my throat and his eyes popped open. "Oh, God. She's gone, Sis." He moaned and wrung his hands. "Our Karen is gone."

"She can't be! She was fine." My throat clenched so I could barely whisper. "She just had broken legs." I thought my chest would explode with grief as I reached out for him. "What happened? How?"

He stroked my cheek as I kneeled at his feet. "She…her head."

I turned to the nurse who'd helped me in the hall and begged. "Please. How can she be dead? I saw her."

"I'll get the doctor," she said, edging from the room.

Karen's mother turned from the window. Her mouth twisted as she spat the words. "If *you* hadn't started working at that goddamn White Water, this wouldn't have happened."

"Me? What are you saying?" Her words hit me like a kick in the stomach.

"She always looked up to you. Wanted to be just like you." Her wild eyes narrowed and her voice rose. "Then you leave poor Jimmy and start running around. Course she'd do just like you."

"Come on mamma, settle down. Sis, she's just out of her head with the grief."

She pushed him away. "Then she has to leave Ron. Just like you." She shook her fist at me. "Damn you."

"Damn me? Are you crazy? You made her all that she was." Rage I'd bottled up for all the years exploded in my head. I didn't want to stop, but clamped shut my jaw and forced myself to look away. *Damn you. You took them to bars when they were little kids. You exploited Jimmy, and never had a moment for Karen.* My anger vanished when her face crumpled. She loved her daughter, and made mistakes just like the rest of us. Mistakes she'd probably have to live with for a long time.

I looked into the pain-filled eyes of Karen's father, who'd reached out again to his sobbing wife. "I'm sorry. I shouldn't have said those things."

"It's okay, Sis. You're right. Karen always got the short end of the stick."

When I returned to Barkerville, I drove to the river, the place where we'd spent so many hours. Sitting on the deserted beach, I remembered Karen throwing Billy in, listened to her laughter echo in my head. I felt her spirit with me. When we were younger, we had lounged here on quieter days. One day, on the very spot where I sat, we'd talked about life after death. Many times we joked about coming back to haunt each other. From that vantage point, death had seemed a million miles away.

Tears poured from my heart as I spoke to the sky. "Karen, I love you, little sister. I'm so sorry I didn't stay with you last night. I promise you, I'll see you again along the way."

Head bowed, I closed my eyes. I wanted to feel close for a little longer, then to say goodbye. Soothed by the sound of the river and the gentle breeze on my tear-soaked face, the hideous stone in my chest finally slipped away. Acceptance took its place. I knew then that I could go on without guilt for her wasted life. Her short life taught me that loving someone was not enough, that I could never change anyone but myself.

At 5:05 Greg found me where I lay on my bed. He kneeled beside me and touched my forehead. His sad voice deep and gentle, he said, "I heard. They say it was a blood clot in her brain. How are you doing, love?"

Speaking took too much effort. I reached out my arms and he held me as more tears rolled from my swollen eyes. He went to the bathroom and returned with a wet cloth, which he held to my face. "Shall I stay here with you?"

"No, Greg. I want you to go home to Becky. Forever. I've thought about last night. It wouldn't be fair to you...marriage is not what I want."

"But, Suzanne, you're upset. You'll feel—"

"Greg, please. I knew it last night. I just couldn't say it."

He buried his face in the bedspread and I stroked the back of his head. The two of us, lost in misery, stayed that way until dark. Finally when he roused himself, he stood for a minute looking down at me in the moonlight. Then, he took my face in his hands and kissed me gently. "Good bye, my brown-eyed love."

Emotionally spent, unable to speak, I squeezed his fingertips. Then he was gone.

On Thursday, a little before two o'clock, I sat beside Jimmy at the graveside in one of the chairs provided for the family. Ron, in dress uniform, sat on my other side. Karen's mother and father were out of my line-of-sight on the opposite side of Jimmy.

All around the flower-draped coffin stood Karen's friends and lovers. Billy Boy was unable to attend, but was off the critical list. Two dozen tunnel stiffs, some turned out in dark suits, stood murmuring to each other as we waited for the service to begin. Sandy stood apart with his head bowed.

Sophie, in dark glasses, her face crimson and puffy from crying, leaned on Chester. Bruce and Lindy nodded and gave me sad half-smiles as they moved into the circle. Beside them was Paul with the same sour look he'd worn the first time I saw him.

When the preacher stepped up to the head of the grave my stomach contracted and a sob worked its way up to my throat. With clenched fists, stabbing my fingernails into flesh, I stared at a white chrysanthemum on the coffin blanket and closed my mind to his words. Jimmy reached over, unclenched my fist and intertwined our fingers. With my other hand, I squeezed Ron's and he squeezed back. The pain of hearing someone who didn't even know her talk about her life was unbearable. As I continued to stare at the flower, I forced myself to leave the past and think of the future. I had said goodbye to Karen at the river, but her strength and her spirit were with me.

Lindy and Bruce had found someone to replace me all that week, so after the funeral I planned to tell them I wouldn't be back to the White Water—ever.

Wednesday Jimmy had begged me to return to Medford with him. I told him I'd always love him and be his friend, but I was going forward with our divorce.

Jimmy jarred me from my peaceful state. "Service is over, Suzanne."

When I stood, turning away from the cold resting-place of Karen's body, I saw Greg standing next to a nearby tree. The look of pain on his face stabbed at my heart, and my arms ached to go to him. To tell him I'd made a mistake—I'd marry him if he'd have me.

Just then Jimmy squeezed the back of my neck. That familiar touch reminded me of my big mistake. The mistake I'd made in thinking love would change a man who had a roving eye. Hadn't I repeatedly seen that same pitiful look in Jimmy's eyes each time he came back after cheating on me? And still I'd married him. As I remembered, I stared back at Greg and shook my head.

He nodded, touched his finger to his lips then turned and walked away.

CHAPTER 40

▼

Silhouettes of jagged peaks against a pink-tinged, silver sky, tugged my heart that last morning while I packed my car. It was a familiar sight I'd surely miss and would never forget. At least, until I finished college and moved on, Barkerville would be just down the road. And it would always be my hometown.

I knew that as time dulled the ache, what Greg and I shared would become one of those whispers from the past that lovers remember all their lifetime.

Karen would be with me forever.

THE END

978-0-595-37235-5
0-595-37235-X

Printed in the United States
40458LVS00006B/67-96

9 780595 372355